Scandalous Whispers

Watch for
Castonbury Park: Ladies of Disrepute,
coming soon!

CAROLE MORTIMER
and HELEN DICKSON

Scandalous
Whispers

HARLEQUIN®
entertain, enrich, inspire™

Recycling programs for this product may not exist in your area.

ISBN-13: 978-0-373-77793-8

CASTONBURY PARK: SCANDALOUS WHISPERS

Copyright © 2012 by Harlequin Books S.A.

The publisher acknowledges the copyright holders of the individual works as follows:

THE WICKED LORD MONTAGUE
Copyright © 2012 by Carole Mortimer

THE HOUSEMAID'S SCANDALOUS SECRET
Copyright © 2012 by Helen Dickson

Contents

The *Wicked* Lord Montague

CAROLE MORTIMER

One

··

Castonbury Park, Derbyshire, April 1816

'His Grace seems much better today, Lily, thank you for asking,' Mrs Stratton, the widowed housekeeper at Castonbury Park, assured Lily warmly as she led the way through to her private parlour situated at the back of the grand mansion house that had long been the seat of the Dukes of Rothermere. 'His Grace's valet informed me only this morning that the advent of a late spring appears to be having an advantageous effect upon the duke's spirits.' She glanced approvingly at the sun shining in through the window.

Lily wondered if it was the advent of spring which had succeeded in reviving the grief-stricken Duke of Rothermere, or the possible return of Lord Giles Montague. His homecoming was in response to the letter Lily's father said the duke had written to his son four days ago, in which he had demanded that Giles Montague return home and take up his duties as his heir. Sadly, Lord James Montague, previously the eldest son and heir of the Montague family, had died in Spain during the campaign against Napoleon. It had been a devastating blow to the long-widowed Duke of Rothermere, further exacerbated ten months ago by the death of Lord Edward, the duke's youngest son.

Being the daughter of the local vicar, and an adopted daughter at that, had put Lily in the unique position of making friends both above and below stairs at Castonbury Park, and she was friends with the two daughters of the household, Lady Phaedra and Lady Kate. But it was the late Lord Edward Montague who had been her dearest and most beloved friend. The two of them had been of an age where they had played together about the estate as children, and remained good friends as they had grown too old to play and had instead turned their attention to dancing together at the local assemblies.

Indeed, their friendship had been of such warmth and duration that Lily had been deeply shocked when Edward had succeeded in persuading his father into buying him a commission in the army a year ago, so that he might join his brother Giles in his regiment. She couldn't bear that Edward had died in that last bloody battle at Waterloo, his life coming to an abrupt end at the point of a French bayonet in only his nineteenth year.

Edward's life.

Not Giles, the brother who was eight years older than Edward, and who had been the inspiration for Edward's desire to gain a commission in the army.

'Thank you, Agnes.' Mrs Stratton nodded approval as the maid brought in the tray of tea things.

Lily waited until she had departed before continuing the conversation. 'I have always thought this room to have a particularly lovely view of the gardens.'

'Why, thank you, Lily.' Mrs Stratton's already ample chest puffed out with pleasure as she poured their tea. 'His Grace has always been very generous in regard to the comfort of his servants.'

'I am sure his kindness is only commensurate with the care and devotion all of you have shown towards him and his family for so many years.' Lily sat forward slightly so that she might take her cup of tea from the older woman.

It was now four long days since Mr Seagrove, Lily's adoptive father, and vicar of the parish of Castonbury—and a particular friend of His Grace—had returned from dining at Castonbury Park to confide in Lily concerning the letter the duke had written to his son Giles in London, where that haughty gentleman had chosen to reside since resigning his commission in the army nine months ago.

It was a confidence which Lily had listened to with horror as she recalled the last occasion on which she and Giles Montague had spoken!

Having lived in a state of turmoil these past four days at the mere thought of Giles Montague's return, Lily had been unable to contain her restless anxiety another moment longer. She decided to walk the mile to Castonbury Park in order to pay a visit to the kindly Mrs Stratton, in the hope that the duke's housekeeper may have further news concerning the heir's return.

Presenting Mrs Stratton with a jar of Mrs Jeffries's legendary gooseberry jam on her arrival—everyone in the parish knew that the gooseberries in Mr Seagrove's garden were far superior to any other in the district—had gone a long way towards paving the way to an invitation from Mrs Stratton for Lily to join her in her parlour for afternoon tea.

Not that Mrs Stratton was one for gossip. Her loyalty to

the Montague family was beyond reproach. Nevertheless, Lily hoped there would be some way in which she might steer the conversation in the direction in which she wished it would go. 'It must be somewhat lonely here for His Grace since most of the family travelled down to London for the Season?' she prompted lightly.

'Perhaps.' The housekeeper frowned a little.

Lily sipped her tea. 'Did none of them think to stay behind and keep His Grace company?'

'I believe Mrs Landes-Fraser had intended on doing so, but Lady Kate was called away on other business, and her aunt decided it prudent to accompany her.'

Lily smiled affectionately as she guessed that the eldest of the two Montague sisters, having pooh-poohed the idea of attending the London Season, was no doubt now off on another of her crusades to help the underprivileged and needy, and that her maternal aunt, Mrs Wilhelmina Landes-Fraser, had accompanied her in order to ensure she did not stray too far from the bounds of propriety.

Mrs Stratton offered Lily one of the meringues made by the duke's French chef. 'Besides which, I believe His Grace is more...settled in his manner when he is not troubled by the rush and bustle of the younger members of the family hurrying here, there and everywhere.'

Lily bit back her frustration with this unhelpful reply as she carefully helped herself to one of the delicacies. 'Perhaps there will soon be news of Lord Giles returning...?'

'None that I am aware of.' The older woman looked puzzled. 'I must say that I do not completely...understand his continued absence, given the circumstances.'

'No,' Lily prompted softly.

Indeed, she had never understood Edward's excess of affection for his brother Giles. He was a gentleman whom Lily had never found particular reason to like in the past, but for over a year now, she was ashamed to admit, she had detested him almost to the point of hatred!

Mrs Stratton gave a slightly exasperated shake of her grey head. 'And he was such an endearing scamp as a child too. I find it hard to believe—' She broke off distractedly, not one to give, or condone, any criticism of a single member of the Montague family to whom she had long devoted her time and emotions, the more so since her own son did not visit as often as she might have wished.

Lily had discovered this past year that she was not so generous of nature in regard to Lord Giles Montague. Indeed, she found it hard even to begin to imagine him as anything other than the disdainful and arrogant gentleman who, the last time they had spoken together, had so wilfully and deliberately insulted both her and the possible lowly origins of her forebears. The mere thought of his ever being 'an endearing scamp,' even as a child, seemed positively ludicrous to her!

The eight years' difference in their ages had meant that Lord Giles had already been away at boarding school by the time Lily was old enough to be allowed to play further afield than the vicarage garden, and he had not always returned home in the holidays either, often choosing to spend those times staying at the home of a friend. The occasions when he had come home for the holidays he had scornfully declined to spend any of his time with children he considered should still be in the nursery, and upon reflection, Lily had come to believe that he had only suffered Edward's company because of the young boy's obvious hero-worship of his older brother.

A hero-worship Lily firmly believed to have succeeded in bringing about Edward's early demise.

The fact that Mrs Stratton had obviously received no instructions in regard to airing Lord Giles Montague's rooms for his imminent arrival did, however, seem to be a confirmation of his continued absence. It enabled Lily to relax for the first time in days as she devoured the delicious meringue with gusto. She had always been naturally slender, and besides, this news of Lord Giles—or lack of it!—was surely reason enough for celebration on her part.

She did feel a slight pang of guilt on behalf of the Duke of Rothermere, but ultimately believed that he, and everyone else at Castonbury Park, and the surrounding village, were far better off without the oppressive presence of Lord Giles Montague and his conceited arrogance.

Lily felt happier than she had for days as she walked back to the vicarage. She had removed and was swinging her bonnet in her gloved hand, allowing the sun to warm her ebony curls as she strolled through the dappled glade, which she invariably used as a shortcut onto the road leading back to the village.

Spring was indeed here; the sun was shining, the wildflowers were in bloom, the birds were singing in the branches of trees unfurling their leaves after the long winter. Indeed, it was the sort of pleasant early evening when one was assured of God's existence and it felt good just to be alive and in His—

'Well, well, well, if it is not Miss Seagrove once again trespassing on the Rothermere estate!'

The sun disappeared behind a cloud, the wildflowers lost their lustre and the birds ceased singing as they instead took flight from the treetops at the sound of a human voice. At the same time, the colour drained from Lily's cheeks and her heart began pounding loudly in her chest, her shoulders having stiffened defensively in instant recognition of that hatefully mocking voice. A voice which undoubtedly belonged to none other than the utterly despicable Lord Giles Montague!

'I do not remember you as being this…accommodatingly silent during the last occasion on which we spoke together, Miss Seagrove. Can it be that "the cat has finally got your tongue"?'

Lily drew in one, two, three steadying breaths, as she prepared to turn and face her nemesis; all of her earlier feelings of well-being had flown away with the birds in the face of the shocking reality that Giles Montague was returned to Castonbury Park, after all.

In the end it was the impatient snorting of that gentleman's horse which caused Lily to turn sharply, only to come face to face with the huge, glistening black and wild-eyed animal as it seemed to look down the long length of its nose at her with the same scornful disdain as its rider.

Lily took an involuntary step back before chancing a glance up at the owner of that horse, her breath catching in her throat as the late-afternoon sun shone behind the imposing and wide-shouldered figure of Lord Giles Montague, and succeeding in casting his face into shadow beneath the brim of his tall hat.

Not that Lily needed to see that arrogantly mocking face clearly to know what he looked like; each and every one of those dark and saturnine features was etched into her memory! Cold grey eyes beneath heavy brows, a long and aristocratic nose, hard and chiselled cheeks, the wide slash of his mouth invariably thinned with scorn or disdain, the strength of his jaw tilted at a haughty angle.

She moistened her lips before choosing to answer his initial challenge rather than the second. 'It is impossible to do anything other than walk in the grounds of Castonbury Park when one has been visiting at the house, my lord.'

'Indeed?' he drawled in a bored tone, holding his skittish mount in check without apparent effort. 'And whom, might one ask, can you have been "visiting" at Castonbury Park, when most of my family are away or in London at present?'

Lily's cheeks flushed at the derision in his tone. 'I came to deliver some of last year's jam to Mrs Stratton from our own cook,' she revealed reluctantly.

'Ah.' He nodded that arrogant head, a contemptuous smile curving his lips, no doubt at the knowledge that Lily had been visiting below stairs rather than above.

Now that she could see Lord Giles's face better Lily realised that there was, after all, something slightly different about him than the last time she had seen him. 'You appear to have a smudge of dirt upon your jaw, my lord,' she told him with a feeling of inner satisfaction at his appearing less than his usual pristine self.

He made no effort to raise a hand to remove the mark. 'I believe, if you were to look a little closer, you would find that it is a bruise, and not dirt,' he dismissed in a bored voice.

Lily's brows rose. 'You have taken a tumble from your horse?' It seemed an even more unlikely explanation than the dirt, as Edward had told her years ago that the duke had placed all of his sons up on a horse before they could even walk, and Lord Giles's years in the army would only have honed his already excellent horsemanship.

'Not that it is any of your business, but I chanced to walk into a fist several days ago,' he drawled in cool dismissal. 'Mr Seagrove is well, I trust?'

Lily would much rather have heard more about the 'fist' he had 'chanced to walk into' than discuss her adoptive father's health, which had never been anything but robust. 'My father

is very well, thank you, my lord,' she assured huskily, still staring curiously at the bruise upon his jaw. 'How did you—?'

'Please pass along my respects to him when next you see
him.' Lord Giles nodded distantly.

Obviously the subject of that 'fist' was not for further discussion, which only increased Lily's curiosity as to who would
have dared lay a fist upon the aristocratic jaw of Lord Giles
Montague. Whoever he might have been, Lily knew a desire
to shake the gentleman by that very same hand! 'Certainly,
my lord.' Her tone was dry at the obvious omission of any of
those respects being paid towards her; Giles Montague had
not so much as raised his tall hat in her presence, let alone offered her polite words of greeting!

Because, as they were both only too well aware, there could
be no politeness between the two of them after the frankness
of their last conversation together. Not now. Or in the future.
Lily disliked Giles Montague with a passion she could neither
hide nor disguise, and he made no effort to hide the contempt
with which he regarded her and her questionable forebears.

'You have come home to visit with your father, my lord?'
She offered a challenge of her own.

Those grey eyes narrowed. 'So it would appear.'

Lily raised dark brows at his challenging tone. 'And I am
sure His Grace will be gratified to know you at last feel able
to spare him time, from what I am sure has been your…busy
life in London, these past months.'

Giles's expression remained unchanged at this less than subtle rebuke. A rebuke which told him all too clearly that Miss
Lily Seagrove had heard something at least of his rakish behaviour in London these past nine months. 'If I had known
you were counting the days of my absence perhaps I would
have returned sooner…?'

Colour brightened the ivory of her cheeks even as those moss-green eyes sparkled with temper at his obvious derision. 'The only reason I would ever count the days of your absence, my lord, would be with the intention of thanking God for them!'

Giles looked down at her from between narrowed lids. As a young child Lily Seagrove had been as wild and untamed as might have been expected, given her ancestry. Her long curly black hair had seemed always to be in a loose tangle about her thin and narrow shoulders, smears of mud and berries invariably about her ruby-red mouth, her tiny hands suffering that same fate and her dresses usually having a rip or two about them where she had been crawling through the undergrowth with his brother Edward on one of their adventures.

Quite when that untamed child had become the composed and confident young lady Giles had met just over a year ago he was unsure, only knowing that he had returned home to find that his brother Edward was completely—and quite unsuitably—infatuated with the beautiful young woman Lily Seagrove had become.

The beautiful young woman she undoubtedly still was....

Her hair was just as black and abundant as it had ever been, but without her bonnet it was visibly tamed into becoming curls at her crown, with several of those shorter curls left to frame the delicate beauty of her face which boasted smooth, ivory skin, moss-green eyes surrounded by thick dark lashes, a tiny upturned nose, high cheekbones and full and sensual lips above her pointed and very determined chin.

She wore a dark brown velvet pelisse over a cream and fashionably high-waisted gown; her tall body was slender, the swell of her breasts covered by a wisp of delicate cream lace, matching lace gloves upon her hands, and tiny boots of brown leather upon her feet, the latter obviously out of deference to her walk about the countryside rather than fashion.

Yes, that wild and seemingly untameable child had grown into this beautiful and alluring woman of composure and grace. But, nevertheless, she was still one who had been, and always would be, a foundling of questionable ancestry and who was, and would ever remain, socially inferior to each and every member of the Montague family. It was an indisputable fact she still resented having heard from Giles's own lips a year ago, if the anger that now burned so brightly in Miss Lily Seagrove's moss-green eyes was any indication!

He gave a haughty inclination of his head. 'I am sure your prayers this evening will not be quite so full of gratitude on the subject.'

'I might always pray for your visit to be of short duration instead, my lord,' she returned with false sweetness.

Giles permitted himself a hard and humourless smile. 'I am sure that we both might pray for it to be so!'

She blinked up at him. 'You do not intend your visit to Castonbury Park to be of long duration…?'

In truth, Giles had no idea how long he would be able to endure being in the home where he would be reminded, on a daily basis, of all that the Montague family had lost—namely Jamie and Edward, the eldest and the youngest sons.

He quirked mocking brows. 'No doubt it would please you if that were to be the case?'

'As you made so clear to me on the last occasion we spoke, my lord, it is not for someone as lowly as I to be pleased or displeased by any of the actions of a member of a family as superior to myself as the Montagues!' Those moss-green eyes met his gaze with unflinching challenge.

She really was quite remarkably beautiful, Giles noted admiringly, as she stood there so tall and proud, with her cheeks flushed and those green eyes glittering angrily. In fact, Miss Lily Seagrove was far more beautiful than any of the numerous women Giles had known so intimately in London these past nine months.

It was a thought totally out of keeping with the strained nature of their acquaintance. 'Even you must acknowledge it really would not have done, Lily…?' Giles quirked a dark brow.

Her eyes widened incredulously. 'You would dare to talk of that again now, when Edward has been dead these past ten months, and so lost to all of us for ever?'

No, Giles would prefer never to have to speak of anything ever again which forced him to acknowledge that his brother Edward was dead. Indeed, he had spent the past nine months avoiding returning to Castonbury Park in an attempt to do just that. Without any success, of course, but there was not a fashionable man, or willing woman, in London who could not confirm how vigorously he had attempted to achieve that oblivion, in the company of the former, in the beds of the latter.

How ironic that the first person Giles should meet upon returning to Castonbury should be the one woman guaranteed to remind him of the losses he had been trying so hard to avoid!

His mouth twisted bitterly. 'No doubt ten months has been more than long enough for you to have recovered sufficiently from your hopes regarding Edward, and to have some other unsuspecting—and, for your sake, I hope wealthy!—young man ensnared by your charms?'

Lily drew her breath in sharply, so deeply wounded by Giles Montague's dismissive scorn of the affection she had felt for Edward that for several minutes she felt completely unable to speak. She almost—almost!—pitied Giles Montague for his lack of understanding.

No—she did pity him, knowing that a man as arrogant and insensitive as Giles Montague could never appreciate or attempt to understand the love she and Edward had felt for each other, or how their friendship had been of such depth and duration that Lily had come to regard Edward as the brother she had never had, as well as being her dearest friend in all the world.

A year ago the haughty and disdainful Lord Giles Montague had been blind to the nature of that affection, and chosen instead to believe that as she was only the adopted daughter of the local vicar—her real parentage unknown—then she must necessarily be out to ensnare his rich and titled youngest brother into matrimony. It must have been a match he considered so unsuitable he had felt no qualms in arranging to talk to Lily without Edward's knowledge, so that he might inform her of such. It had been a conversation that had so stunned Lily by its forthright audacity she was ashamed to say she had felt no hesitation in returning that frankness in regard to her own less than flattering opinion of Giles Montague.

She raised her chin now. 'I will continue to love Edward until the day I die,' she stated softly and evenly, too heavy of heart to feel the least satisfaction when she saw the way Giles Montague's eyes widened upon hearing her declaration. 'Now, if you will excuse me, my lord, I believe it is past time I returned to the vicarage.' She continued to hold that guarded and icy grey gaze as she sketched the slightest of curtseys before turning on her booted heels and walking away.

Her head was held high as she refused, even for propriety's sake, to resume wearing her bonnet. Giles Montague already believed her to be socially inferior to him, so why should she care if her actions now confirmed that belief.

Except Lily did care what people thought of her. She had always cared. Not for her own sake, but for the sake of the kindly Mr and Mrs Seagrove.

Lily had only been eight years old, and had not understood, when one of the children from the village had first taunted her and called her 'Gypsy.' She had questioned Mrs Seagrove as to its meaning as soon as she had returned to the vicarage. That dear lady had taken Lily gently in her arms and explained that it was merely another name for the Romany families who stayed at the Castonbury estate during the spring and at harvest time.

Again, having rarely bothered to waste time looking at herself in a mirror, Lily had not understood why one of the village children should have chosen to taunt her with such name. Until Mrs Seagrove had stroked Lily's long and curling black hair and explained that she was not the true child of Mr and Mrs Seagrove, but had in fact been left, as a baby of only a few weeks, on the doorstep of the vicarage eight years previously; of how she and Mr Seagrove suspected that Lily's real mother had perhaps been one of the young and unmarried Gypsy girls who travelled the roads of England with their tribe.

Gypsy.

Lord Giles Montague had made it obvious a year ago that he was both totally aware of such a heritage, and disapproving of its being connected with his noble family.

Two

Giles had put aside the encounter in the glade with the beautiful Miss Lily Seagrove by the time he handed over the reins of his horse to one of the grooms at Castonbury Park. His thoughts were now on the signs of neglect, both to the outside of the house itself and other parts of the estate, which he had noted as he rode down the hillside and along the side of the lake.

Several tiles were missing from the roof at the back of the house, the stonework at the front was also in need of attention and there were weeds growing in several places about the foundations. The gardens that surrounded the house seemed to be well tended, but Giles had noted that several trees had toppled over in the woods at the back of the house, and the lake was also in need of clearing of the debris that had accumulated from the past winter. And they were only the things that Giles had noted at first glance; there were sure to be others he had not had the chance to see as yet.

They would no doubt confirm that things here were as dire as his sister Phaedra had warned they were. Something which did not please Giles at all, if it meant he would have to prolong his stay here…

Lumsden—the butler who had been with the Montague family for more years than Giles could remember—opened the front door as he reached the top step. 'Master Giles!' His mouth gaped open in surprise. 'I mean, Lord Giles,' he corrected as he obviously recovered his usual calm equilibrium. 'We had not been told to expect you.'

'I did not send word of my coming,' Giles assured as he strode past the older man and into the house.

It was almost ten months since Giles had last stepped through this doorway, on the occasion of Edward's funeral, and whilst the inside of the house was as clean and neat as it had ever been—Mrs Stratton, Giles knew, would allow nothing less from her household staff!—there was nevertheless an air of emptiness about it, of a house that no longer felt like a home.

An emptiness that Giles had expected—and so determinedly avoided these past nine months.

His mouth tightened as he turned back to hand the butler his hat and riding crop before shrugging off his outer coat. 'My father is in his rooms in the east wing?'

'Yes, my lord.' Lumsden's seriousness of tone somehow managed to convey so much more than was said in those three words. 'I will go and enquire of Smithins if he considers His Grace well enough to receive you—'

'No need, Lumsden,' Giles dismissed airily. 'I am sure I will be able to judge that for myself once I have seen my father.'

'But—'

'What is it, Lumsden?' He frowned his irritation with this further delay, anxious now to see his father for himself, so that he might best decide what needed to be done here in order that he might leave again as soon as was possible.

The butler looked uncomfortable. 'Smithins has issued orders that no one is allowed to see His Grace without his permission.'

Giles raised autocratic brows. 'Am I to understand that my father's valet now says who is and is not to visit him?' He conveyed his incredulity in his tone.

'I believe that sums up the situation very well, my lord, yes.' The butler looked even more uncomfortable.

'We shall see about that!' Giles assured determinedly. 'If you could organise a decanter of brandy brought into us, Lumsden, I would be most obliged?'

The elderly man straightened with renewed purpose. 'Certainly, my lord.'

Giles turned with that same sense of purpose, his expression grim as he strode through to his father's suite of rooms in the east wing of the house, more than ready to do battle with the man who was employed to be his father's valet and not his jailer!

'His Grace will be overjoyed, I am sure.' Mr Seagrove beamed approvingly, having just been informed by Lily that Lord Giles Montague was returned to Castonbury Park, after all.

There was no answering pleasure in Lily's face as she sat across the dinner table from her father in the small family dining room at the vicarage. 'No doubt,' she dismissed uninterestedly. 'Would you care for more potatoes, Father?' She held up the dish temptingly in the hopes of changing the conversation from the subject of the hateful Giles Montague, knowing full well that the creamy vegetable was one of her father's weaknesses.

'Thank you, Lily.' He nodded distractedly as she spooned the potatoes onto this plate before replacing the bowl on the table, a worried frown marring his usually smooth brow. 'I trust you and Lord Giles had a pleasant conversation together?'

She gave that earlier conversation some thought. 'I believe I can say that I succeeded in being as polite to Lord Giles as he was to me,' she finally replied carefully.

'That is good.' The vicar nodded, apparently unaware of the true meaning of Lily's reply. 'However, I think it best if we both call at the Park tomorrow morning to pay our formal respects.'

Lily felt her heart sink. 'Oh, must I come too? I have several calls to make in the morning, Father. Mrs Jenkins and her new baby, and the youngest Hurst boy's leg is in need of—'

'Yes, yes, I appreciate that you are very busy about the parish, Lily.' Mr Seagrove beamed his approval of the care and attention she had given to his parishioners since the death of his wife five years ago. 'But His Grace is my patron, after all, and it would seem rude if we did not both call upon his heir.'

Lily could appreciate the logic of her father's argument; Mr Seagrove's tenure in Castonbury, although of long duration, was nevertheless still dependent upon the Duke of Rothermere's goodwill. She just wished she did not have to see Lord Giles Montague again quite so soon. She had no wish to see that unpleasant man ever again, if truth be told! Though Lily knew it would never do for her father to suspect such a thing, which meant Lily had no choice but to accept she was to accompany her father to the Park tomorrow morning and make polite conversation with Lord Giles Montague.

'It is good to see you again, Mr Seagrove.' Lord Giles smiled with genuine warmth as he strode forcefully into the elegant salon where they waited.

Lily was momentarily taken aback by the change wrought

on that haughty gentleman's countenance when he smiled down at her father as the two men greeted each other; those grey eyes had softened to the warmth of a dove's wing, laughter lines grooved into those hard and chiselled cheeks, his teeth appearing very white and even between the relaxed line of sculpted lips. Even the bruising on his jaw could not succeed in detracting from his pleasant demeanour.

Indeed, for those few brief moments Giles Montague looked almost…rakishly handsome, Lily realised in surprise. A rakish handsomeness, his sister Phaedra had confided to Lily, he had reputedly taken full advantage of these past months in London!

'And Miss Seagrove.' Lord Giles turned to bow, the genuine warmth of the smile he had given her father fading to be replaced by one of mocking humour. 'I had not expected to see you again quite so soon.'

'My lord.' She met that gaze coolly as she curtseyed, her best peach-coloured bonnet covering the darkness of her curls today, a perfect match for the high-waisted gown she usually wore to church on a Sunday, her cream lace gloves upon her hands.

Mr Seagrove had been born the fourth son of a country squire, and so possessed a small private income to go with the stipend he received yearly from the Duke of Rothermere, but even so Lily possessed only half a dozen gowns, gowns she made for herself after acquiring the material from an establishment in the village. Unfortunately only three of the gowns Lily owned were fashionable enough, and of a quality, to wear out in company; including the gown Lily had been wearing yesterday, Giles Montague had already seen two of those gowns.

Which was a very strange thought for her to have—was it

not?—when she had absolutely no interest in Giles Montague's opinion, either of her personally, or the gowns she wore…?

No one likes to appear wanting in front of another, she told herself firmly as she answered, 'My father, once told of your return, was of course anxious to call and pay his respects.'

Giles gave a knowing grimace as he easily discerned Lily's own lack of enthusiasm at seeing him again. He fully appreciated the reasons for her antagonism after the frankness of their conversation a year ago. It was a conversation Giles had had serious reason to regret since Edward's death; a marriage between his youngest brother and this particular young lady would still be most unsuitable. But Giles would far rather Edward had enjoyed even a few months with the woman he had declared himself to be deeply in love with, than for his brother to have died without knowing the joy of a union he so desired.

Surely Lily's words yesterday, regarding her intention of loving his brother until she died, implied her heart still yearned for the young man she had loved and lost…?

'Would you care for tea, Miss Seagrove?' Giles's voice was gentler than he usually managed when in this particular young woman's company.

'I—'

'That would be most acceptable, my lord.' Mr Seagrove warmly accepted in place of what Giles was convinced would have been Lily's refusal. 'His Grace is no doubt pleased at your return?' Mr Seagrove looked across at him pleasantly.

Giles frowned darkly. As Lumsden had warned, Smithins had stood like a guard at the door of the Duke of Rothermere's rooms the day before, his initial surprise at finding Giles walking through that doorway unannounced lasting only seconds before he informed Giles that his father was resting and not to be disturbed.

It had taken every effort on Giles's part to hold on to his temper and not bodily lift the insufferable little man out of his way. Instead he had icily informed Smithins what he would do to him if he did not step aside. The valet may be a bumptious little upstart, but he was not a stupid bumptious little upstart, and so had had the foresight to step aside immediately.

Not having seen his father for nine months, Giles had been shocked, deeply so, at his first sight of his father seated in a chair by the window, a blanket across his knees as evidence that, despite the warmer weather, his almost skeletal frame was prone to feel the cold. The duke's grief at the death of his two sons appeared to have aged him twenty years in just one, his hair having turned grey, his eyes having sunk into the thin pallor of his face whilst deep lines marked his unsmiling mouth.

His dull eyes had brightened slightly at the sight of his son, and his spirits had rallied for a short time too, but Giles could see his father's strength failing him after they had spoken together for ten minutes, and so he had made his excuses and gone to refresh himself after his journey.

'I believe so, yes,' Giles replied to Mr Seagrove; his visit to his father's rooms before breakfast this morning had led to the discovery that the Duke of Rothermere had completely forgotten his son's arrival the day before, thereby making it impossible for Giles to ascertain whether his presence back at Castonbury Park was having a positive effect upon his father or not.

The guilt Giles now felt at having neglected his father by remaining from home these past nine months was not something he intended to discuss with anyone, even the kindly Reverend Reginald Seagrove. Certainly Giles did not intend to reveal his feelings of inadequacy in front of the quietly attentive Lily Seagrove. Indeed, she was a young lady who saw far too many faults in him already than was comfortable!

'Perhaps now that you are home you will be able to see to the necessary repairs about the estate, my lord?' It was almost as if that young lady knew of at least some of Giles's thoughts as she smiled sweetly.

'Perhaps,' he dismissed stiffly.

She gave a gracious inclination of her head. 'I am sure His Grace would be most gratified. Not to mention the tenants of the estate.'

Giles's mouth tightened as Lily Seagrove's comment hit home. It was a way of pointing out his own shortcomings, he was sure. Shortcomings which Giles needed no reminding of when he had only to see the frailty of his father's health, and the neglect about the estate, to become all too aware of them himself.

'Shall I pour, my lord?' she prompted lightly as Lumsden returned with the tea tray and placed it on the low table in front of her before departing.

'Please.' Giles gave a terse inclination of his head. He suffered more than a little inner restlessness as he felt the chains of responsibility for Castonbury Park tighten even more painfully about his throat. Chains which Lily Seagrove no doubt prayed might choke him!

'Perhaps now that you are home, I might broach the subject of this year's well-dressing, and the possibility of the celebrations afterwards returning to Castonbury Park?' Mr Seagrove prompted hopefully. The Duke of Rothermere, having been in a turmoil of emotions the previous year, had requested that the garden party after the well-dressing take place on the village green rather than in the grounds of the estate as was the custom.

Although, as everyone knew, 'garden party' did not quite describe the celebrations that took place after the villagers had attended the church service and seen the three adorned wells in the village blessed. Much food was eaten, many barrels of beer consumed, with several stalls for bartering vegetables and livestock, and there was a Gypsy fortune-teller in a garishly adorned tent, and of course there would be music and dancing as the day turned to evening.

Giles was slow to turn his attention back to the older man, so intently was he watching Lily's slender, gloved hands as they deftly managed the tilting of the teapot. Good heavens, sitting there so primly, her movements gracefully elegant, it was almost possible to imagine that Lily might, after all, have made Edward a passably suitable wife!

Almost.

For one only had to look at that black and curling hair, the ivory-white of her complexion, those lively green eyes and her full and berry-red lips to be reminded that Lily Seagrove's true parentage was of much more exotic stock than the homely Mr and Mrs Seagrove.

No, as Giles had said only yesterday, it simply would not have done. Lily Seagrove was the type of young lady that gentlemen like the Montagues took to mistress, not to wife. An opinion, if Giles remembered correctly—and he had no doubts that he did!—to which his brother Edward had taken great exception a year ago. And which, when Giles had made those same remarks to Lily Seagrove, had resulted in her landing a resounding slap upon his cheek!

Giles's mouth tightened at that memory even as he turned his attention back to Mr Seagrove. 'What exactly would that entail?'

'Oh, there is nothing for you to do personally except give

your permission, my lord,' that cheerful gentleman assured him eagerly. 'Lily and Mrs Stratton usually work together on the organisation of the celebrations.' He beamed brightly.

'Indeed?' Giles's gaze was unreadable as Lily Seagrove stood up to hand him his cup of tea.

Lily kept her lashes lowered demurely as she avoided all contact with Giles's long and elegant fingers as she handed over the cup of tea into which she had placed four helpings of sugar, despite having no idea whether or not that gentleman even liked sugar in his tea. Perhaps he would understand that she believed his demeanour could do with sweetening also.

She had felt a slight uplift in her spirits as she saw Giles Montague's discomfort at mention of the neglect currently obvious about the estate, only to have her heart sink upon hearing her father put forward the idea of the celebrations after the well-dressing once again taking place at Castonbury Park. She knew that if Giles Montague were to agree, it would necessitate her spending far more time here than she would ever have wished, now that he was back in residence.

Lily moved across the room with her father's tea. 'I am sure it is not necessary to bother either His Grace or Lord Montague with something so trivial, Father,' she dismissed evenly. 'The venue of the village green proved perfectly adequate for our purposes last year.'

'But, my dear, the garden party after the well-dressing ceremony has, by tradition, always been held at Castonbury Park—'

'Mrs Stratton informed me only yesterday that His Grace is far more comfortable when he does not have too much rush and bustle about him.' Lily could literally feel Giles Montague's gaze upon her as she resumed her seat on the chaise before taking up her own cup of tea.

'I had not thought of that…' Mr Seagrove murmured regretfully.

Lily felt a pang of guilt as she saw her father's disappointment. 'I am sure that everyone enjoyed themselves just as much last year as they have any of the years previously,' she encouraged gently.

'Yes, but—'

'Perhaps I might be allowed to offer an opinion…?' Giles Montague interjected softly.

Lily's gloved fingers tightened about the delicate handle on her teacup as she heard the deceptive mildness of his tone, to such a degree that she had to force herself to relax her grip for fear she might actually disengage the handle completely from the cup. She drew in two deep and calming breaths before turning to look at Giles Montague with polite but distant enquiry.

He was seated comfortably in an armchair, the pale blue of the material a perfect foil for the heavy darkness of his fashionably styled hair. He wore a black superfine over a pale blue waistcoat and snowy white linen, buff-coloured pantaloons tailored to long and powerful legs and black Hessians moulding the length of his calves. He looked, in fact, the epitome of the fashionable dandy about Town.

Not that Lily had ever been to Town, Mr and Mrs Seagrove never having found reason to travel so far as London. But she had often been privileged to see copies of the magazines Lady Phaedra, the younger of the two Montague sisters, had sent over, and the fashionable gentlemen depicted in the sketches inside those magazines had all looked much as Giles Montague did today.

She gave a dismissive shake of her head, as much for her own benefit as anyone else's. She simply refused to see Giles

Montague as anything other than the cold and unpleasant man
he had always been to her, but especially so this past year. 'I
trust the tea is to your liking, my lord?' she prompted as she
saw the involuntary wince he gave after taking a sip of the
hot and highly sweetened brew.

Narrowed grey eyes met her more innocent gaze. 'Perfectly,
thank you,' he murmured as he rested the cup back on its sau-
cer before carefully placing both on the table.

Lily's cheeks warmed guiltily as she realised he was not
going to expose her pettiness to her father. 'I believe you were
about to offer us your opinion concerning the well-dressing
celebrations, my lord?' she prompted huskily.

Giles, the taste of that unpleasantly syrupy tea still coating
the roof of his mouth, did not believe that Miss Lily Seagrove
would care to hear his 'opinion' of *her* at this particular moment! Instead he gave her a smile that did little more than bare
his teeth in challenge, and was rewarded by a deepening of the
blush colouring those ivory cheeks. 'I have very fond memories of the celebrations being held here when I was a boy.'

'Of course you must.' The vicar eagerly took up the conversation. 'I recall Mrs Seagrove telling me of how, before you
were old enough to go to Town for the Season with the rest
of the family, you and your brothers would help to put out
the tables and chairs and hang up the bunting.'

Giles and his brothers… Of which there was now only one.
And Harry, in his role as diplomat, currently resided in Town
when not out of the country on other business.

If anyone had asked Giles if he really wanted the garden
party to be held at Castonbury Park this year, his honest answer would have been no. But having now seen his father,
witnessed the way in which his grief had caused him to become withdrawn, not just from his family but from the estate

and village as well, and the way in which that estate had been allowed to fall into a state of gentile decay, Giles was of the opinion, no matter what his personal feelings on the matter, that the return of the annual celebrations in the grounds of Castonbury Park was exactly what was needed to bring about a return of confidence in the Montague family's interest in both the tenants and the village.

An interest which, it was becoming all too frustratingly apparent, Giles himself would have to facilitate!

As the second son, he'd had very little reason to pay heed to the running of the estate, or the other duties of the Dukes of Rothermere, and had left such matters to his father and Jamie after he had joined the army twelve years ago. Unfortunately Jamie's death, and his father's failing health, now necessitated—as Lily Seagrove had all too sweetly taken pleasure in pointing out—that Giles's disinterest in such matters could not continue.

Fortunately for Giles, his years as an officer in the army had given him an insight into the nature of people—although he thought the villagers of Castonbury would not in the least appreciate being compared to the rough and ready soldiers who had served under him for eleven years, many of them having chosen to serve only as an alternative to prison or worse!— and as such he knew that the quickest and easiest way to win a man or woman's confidence was to show an interest in them and their comfort.

In the case of the villagers, Giles had no doubts that the return of the annual celebrations to the grounds of Castonbury Park would be the perfect way of showing that interest.

'Indeed we did,' Giles answered Mr Seagrove ruefully. 'And I will be only too happy to offer assistance this year. Under

Miss Seagrove's direction, of course…?' He raised a dark and challengingly brow as he turned to look across the room at her.

Lily, having lapsed into what she now realised had been a false sense of security, could only stare back at him in wide-eyed disbelief.

The thought of the well-dressing celebrations being held at Castonbury Park, and so necessitating Lily spend more time here than she might ever have wished or asked for, seemed dreadful enough, but having Giles Montague offer his personal help with the organisation of those celebrations was unthinkable!

Nor did she believe for one moment that the haughty and arrogant Lord Giles would ever agree to do anything 'under her direction.'

'I really could not ask that of you, my lord, when you obviously have so many other calls upon your time now that you are home at last.' She gave another of those sweet smiles.

Amusement—no doubt at Lily's expense!—gleamed briefly in those grey eyes. 'But you did not ask it, Miss Seagrove, it was I who offered,' Giles Montague drawled dismissively.

'But—'

'As far as I am concerned, the matter is settled, Miss Seagrove.' He rose abruptly to his feet as an indication that their visit was also at an end.

A dismissal Mr Seagrove, his real purpose in calling having now been settled to his satisfaction, was only too ready to accept as he rose to his feet. 'I am sure you have made the right decision, my lord, for both the family and village as a whole.' He beamed his pleasure at the younger man.

For once in her young life Lily could not help but wholeheartedly disagree with her adoptive father. Oh, she had no doubts that the rest of the village would see the reestablishment of the celebrations to Castonbury Park as a positive thing, a return to normality after almost a year of uncertainty.

But as the person who would be required to consult with Giles Montague, Lily could not help but feel a sense of dread....

Three

'I do believe this particular shade would complement your colouring admirably.' Mrs Hall laid out a swatch of deep pink material upon the counter top of her establishment, where several other bolts of material already lay discarded after having been rejected by Lily as not quite what she wanted.

In truth, Lily was not absolutely sure what she did want, only that she had decided to purchase some material to make up a new day gown, and Mrs Hall's establishment in the village was so much more convenient than having to travel all the way to the nearest town of Buxton. Luckily, that lady had several new selections of material in stock, and Lily's needlework was also excellent due to Mrs Seagrove's tutelage in earlier years. Besides which, with the celebrations less than two weeks away, Lily was sorely in need of a new gown—

Lily drew her thoughts up sharply as she realised she was not only prevaricating but actually practising a deception upon herself; her reason for deciding she needed a new gown for the day of the well-dressing celebrations could be summed up in just three words—Lord Giles Montague! Which was a ridiculous vanity on Lily's part, when she had no doubts that the haughty Lord Giles would have taken absolutely no note of the gowns she had been wearing on the two occasions on which they had last met.

'Or perhaps this one…?' Mrs Hall held up another swatch, having obviously drawn a wrong conclusion as to the reason for Lily's present distraction.

'I think perhaps— Oh, how beautiful!' Lily gasped in pleasure as she focused her attention on the material which she was sure had to be a match in colour for the green of her eyes.

If styled correctly, it could be prettied up with cream lace at the neck and short sleeves to wear in the evenings. Not that Lily had attended any of the local assemblies since Edward died, but even so…

'It is perfect,' she breathed in satisfaction. 'But no doubt costly?' she added with a self-conscious grimace; she was, after all, only a vicar's adopted daughter, and as such it would not do for her to look anything other than what she was, and this material had a richness about it that was unmistakable to the eye.

As she had grown to adulthood Lily had often found herself wondering if, as so many in the village so obviously suspected, she really could be the daughter of one of the dramatically beautiful Romany women who stayed in the grounds of Castonbury Park during the summer months.

Several years ago Lily had even plucked up the courage to question one of them, a Mrs Lovell, the oldest and friendliest of the Romany women. The old lady had seemed taken aback by the question at first, and then she had chuckled as she assured Lily that the tribes took care of their own, and that no true Romany child would ever have been left behind to live with a gorjer. It had been said in such a contemptuous way that Lily had no difficulty discerning that the old lady meant a non-Romany person.

Even so, Lily had still sometimes found herself daydreaming as to how different her life would have been if, despite Mrs Lovell's denials, her mother really had been one of those lovely Romany women....

No doubt once she was grown she would have worn those same dresses in rich and gaudy colours that she had seen the Romany women wearing, with her long and wildly curling black hair loose about her shoulders as she danced about the campfire in the evenings, enticing and beguiling the swarthy-skinned Gypsy men who watched her with hot and desirous eyes.

Her daydreams had always come to an abrupt and disillusioned end at that point, as Lily acknowledged that might possibly be the exact way in which her mother had conceived the child she had abandoned on the Seagroves' doorstep twenty years ago!

'Perhaps it is not quite...suitable.' She sighed wistfully as she touched the beautiful moss-green material longingly. 'A serviceable grey would be more practical, do you not think?' Her liking for the material in front of her was so immediate and so strong, it was impossible to prevent the wistfulness from entering her tone.

The other woman laughed lightly. 'Like the gown you are wearing today, you mean?'

Lily glanced down at her gown, one of her older ones, chuckling softly as she realised the other woman was quite correct and that the gown was indeed grey, and that it was also eminently serviceable in style. 'Do forgive me.' She smiled at the other woman in rueful apology. 'My head is so filled with arrangements for the well-dressing I did not even take note of which gown I had put on this morning!'

Mrs Hall nodded. 'I have noticed that everyone in the village is excited at the prospect of the May celebrations returning to Castonbury Park this year.'

Everyone but Lily, it seemed….

How different it would have been if Lord Giles had not currently been in residence at Castonbury Park.

Ridiculous—if Lord Giles Montague was not at home, then Lily very much doubted that the May celebrations would have returned to Castonbury Park at all.

And as Mrs Hall had already stated, news that the garden party was once again to take place at Castonbury Park had quickly spread throughout the village in the two days since Giles Montague had told the vicar of his decision. Not that Mr Seagrove had spread that news himself. No, he would only have needed to mention the arrangements to Mrs Crutchley, the wife of the local butcher, for that to have occurred.

Mrs Crutchley had been in charge of arranging the flowers in the church for the Sunday services since the death of Mrs Seagrove, Lily having been considered by that lady as far too young to take on such an onerous task. As such, Mrs Crutchley also put herself in charge of orchestrating the floral decorations each year for the well-dressing ceremony.

One word from Mr Seagrove to this garrulous lady as to the change of venue to Castonbury Park for the celebrations after the ceremony, and that knowledge had spread quickly throughout the whole village. Indeed, everyone Lily had chanced to speak with in the past two days had talked of nothing else but the prospect of an afternoon and evening enjoying the Duke of Rothermere's hospitality.

Everyone except Lily, for reasons she had not shared with anyone this past year....

But if she was to be forced to suffer a day in the company of Lord Giles—and it seemed that she was—then she really must have a new gown in which to do it! 'Yes, I believe I will take this material, after all,' she announced firmly as she stood up decisively, turning to admire the arrangement of ribbons in the window as Mrs Hall cut the appropriate amount of fabric. 'I believe I would like this also.' Lily had plucked a long length of dark green ribbon from the display and now handed it to Mrs Hall to be included in the package, knowing the ribbon would make a fine contrast to the lighter green of the material, as well as giving the gown a festive look for the well-dressing.

'Is that everything?' Mrs Hall proceeded to wrap and tie Lily's purchases in brown paper after her reassuring nod.

'You will send me the bill, as usual?' At which time Lily would no doubt learn that there would be none of her allowance left with which to make any other purchases, either this month or the next!

It would be worth going without, if only to show Lord Giles that she could be just as elegantly dressed as any of the fashionable women he might know in London, Lily told herself as she walked briskly back to the vicarage, her parcel clutched tightly to her chest. Giles Montague enjoyed looking down his arrogant nose at her far too much—

'You are looking mightily pleased with yourself,' drawled that gentleman's superior voice. 'Can it be that you are on your way to an assignation, or have perhaps just left one…?'

Lily was frowning as she turned sharply to face Lord Giles.

'I am finding your habit of appearing out of nowhere most irritating, my lord!'

He made no reply as he raised dark brows beneath his tall

hat, once again the epitome of the fashionable gentleman, the tailored black jacket and plain grey waistcoat he wore today very much in the understated elegance of the most stylish of gentlemen, like the cane he carried of black ebony tipped with silver.

Lily's chin was high as she met that mocking silver-grey gaze. 'And in answer to your question, I was neither on my way to an assignation nor leaving one, but merely visiting one of the shops in the village.'

Giles's expression was deliberately noncommittal as he looked at Lily Seagrove between narrowed lids, noting the flash of temper in those moss-green eyes and the colour in her cheeks as she answered his query. Quite why he felt the need to constantly challenge this particular young woman he had not the slightest idea, but the result, he noted—those flashing green eyes and the flush in her cheeks—was more than pleasing to a gentleman's eyes.

His mouth thinned with displeasure at the realisation that it was more than pleasing to his own eye! 'You have completed your purchases, and are now on your way back to the vicarage, perhaps?'

'I am.' She tilted her chin, as if daring him to challenge her claim.

Giles nodded tersely. 'As I am on my way to visit with your father, I shall walk along with you.'

No 'please' or 'may I,' Lily noted irritably, just that arrogant 'I shall.'

But it was an arrogance she knew from experience it would do no good to challenge. Just as she knew it would serve no purpose for her to enquire as to the reason he intended visiting with her father; it would certainly be too much to hope that Giles Montague was finding the annual celebrations at Castonbury Park too much of a bother, after all.

'By all means, my lord.' Lily nodded graciously before continuing her walk without sparing a second glance to see whether or not Giles Montague fell into step beside her.

Which was not to say she was not completely aware of his tall and dominating presence beside her as he easily matched his much longer strides to her shorter ones. Or the speculation with which several of her neighbours eyed them as they passed, even as they curtseyed or bowed in recognition of the man at her side.

Lily had no doubt those curious eyes continued to watch the two of them as they strolled along the village street towards the vicarage. 'His Grace is a little better, I trust?' After several minutes of suffering what she knew would be the avid speculation of her neighbours, Lily felt self-conscious enough to feel forced into making some sort of conversation. She turned to glance up curiously at Giles Montague when he did not immediately reply. A frown had appeared between his eyes, his mouth had become a thinned line and his jaw was tight. All of which Lily found most unreassuring. 'My lord?' she prompted uncertainly.

Lily's long friendship with Edward had resulted in her having spent a considerable amount of time at Castonbury Park itself, and so she had often chanced to meet the Duke of Rothermere whilst in Edward's company. She had come to know His Grace as a pleasant and charming man, one who was capable of showing a fondness for his children. He had a genuine affection for Lily's father which had included Mrs Seagrove when she was alive and, as a consequence, Lily too. Certainly there had never been any sign in either His Grace's speech or demeanour towards her to imply that he considered her as anything less than the true daughter of Mr and Mrs Seagrove.

Unlike the grim-faced gentleman now striding along so confidently beside her!

But that did not infringe upon Lily's regard for the Duke of Rothermere. The poor man had suffered so these past years, losing first Lord James and then Edward, that it was no wonder he had withdrawn from the world to become but a shell of his former robust and charming self!

'You are alarming me with your delay in making a reply, my lord,' she said.

In truth, Giles was not sure what to say in answer to Lily's query. 'My father seems much the same in physical health as when I arrived three days ago.'

Which was to say his father was both frail in stature and looking so much older than his sixty-odd years. The duke did have periods when his vagueness of purpose did not seem quite so noticeable, when he appeared to listen attentively as Giles told him of the work he had instructed to be carried out about the estate. But it had quickly become apparent to Giles that it was a feigned interest.

This was worrying enough in itself, but was made all the more so because the legalities of his father's successor were still in a state of flux. His brother Jamie had been swept away in a Spanish river, and his body never recovered. It was not an unusual occurrence admittedly—so many English soldiers had died during the years of fighting Napoleon, never to be seen or heard of again by their families. But, in the case of the heir to the Duke of Rothermere, the lack of physical evidence had resulted in a delay with regard to the naming of Giles as the duke's successor.

His father's strangeness aside, there was something not

quite…right about the current state of affairs at Castonbury Park, and now that he was here Giles fully intended, before too much more time had elapsed, to find out exactly what it was.

Perhaps he would know more when he'd had a chance to thoroughly review the estate account books which Everett, the estate manager, was having delivered to him later today.

Lily frowned at Giles's reply. 'I believe my own father had hoped that your return might bring about some improvement to His Grace.'

Giles's mouth twisted humourlessly. 'No doubt you did not share Mr Seagrove's optimism?'

'I, my lord?' She raised surprised brows. 'I cannot say that I had given the subject of your return any thought whatsoever.'

Giles found himself chuckling huskily. 'I am finding your lack of a good opinion of me to be a great leveller, Miss Seagrove!' he explained as she regarded him questioningly.

Lily, finding herself once again distracted by the difference a smile made to Giles Montague's countenance, now felt the warmth of colour enter her cheeks at his drawled rebuke. 'I am sure I meant you no insult, my lord.'

He continued to smile ruefully. 'Perhaps that is what I find most telling of all!'

Lily gave a pained frown. 'I merely meant, as your return to Castonbury was in no way assured, that I tried not to— that I did not consider at any length what effect, if any,' she said, her cheeks now ablaze, 'it might have upon His Grace's health or the people here.' Only, she recalled guiltily, in regard to how selfish it was of her to wish that Giles Montague might never return at all!

This, she now accepted, had been a childish hope on her part; Lord Giles Montague was now, to all intents and purposes, the future Duke of Rothermere, so it was only to be expected that he would come back to Castonbury Park, if only for the purpose of ensuring that his future inheritance continued to flourish.

'I believe you have instructed a great deal of work to be done about the estate…?' Indeed, village gossip had been rife with nothing else but the 'doings of Lord Giles' these past two days.

He raised dark brows. 'Work, I might remind you, which you yourself pointed out to me only days ago, was in need of my immediate attention.'

'I was not criticising, my lord—'

'No?' He looked down at her.

'Certainly not.' Lily had absolutely no doubt that Giles Montague would make a very capable Duke of Rothermere when that time came, his years as an officer in the army having given him an air of authority totally in keeping with the lofty position. Yes, the arrogantly disdainful Giles Montague was more than suited to becoming the future Duke of Rothermere. Lily simply could not see herself remaining in Castonbury once that dreadful day came.

Quite where she would go, or what she would do, or how she would explain her departure to Mr Seagrove if he was still with them—and she prayed that he would be—Lily had no idea. She only knew that she would find remaining in Castonbury, under the charitable auspices of the hateful Giles Montague, absolutely intolerable!

'I am gratified to hear it,' the infuriating man drawled. He paused beside the gate into the vicarage garden.

Lily frowned her irritation as she was also forced to pause. 'I do not believe I care to continue this conversation, my lord.'

His mouth quirked with derision. 'And I do not believe it is really necessary for you to do so, when I already know, after our conversation a year ago, with what horror you must have viewed the thought of my returning for even a short visit.'

'Then why did you bother to ask?' Lily eyed him impatiently.

He shrugged those broad shoulders. 'I thought to amuse myself, perhaps.'

'Indeed, my lord? And did you not find enough "amusements" in London these past nine months?'

His eyes narrowed. 'And what would you know of my movements these past months?'

Lily felt the warmth of colour in her cheeks. 'No matter what you might consider to the contrary, my lord, Castonbury is not completely cut off from civilisation!' And besides, it was his sister Phaedra who had confided, in a whisper, that her brother was reputed to be enjoying the favours of many beautiful women, as well as frequenting the gambling and drinking dens!

The present Duke of Rothermere was rumoured to have once been a man who enjoyed all of the…amusements London had to offer, as well as some of the more local ones, so perhaps his second son was taking after him in enjoying those often less than respectable pursuits?

He gave an exasperated shake of his head. 'Unless you have forgotten, I spent my early years growing up here.'

Lily tilted her chin proudly. 'I have not forgotten anything about you, my lord.'

His mouth thinned. 'Including, no doubt, my words to you a year ago!'

'Most especially I will never forget those, my lord,' she assured him before turning to push open the gate for herself as Giles Montague made no effort to do so.

'Never is a very long time, Lily.'

'You— Oh, bother!' Lily had turned sharply back to face him, catching her parcel on the gatepost as she did so, and succeeding in knocking it from her arms and to the ground. She huffed at her own clumsiness even as she bent down to retrieve the parcel.

Giles, having intended on doing the same, instead found himself wincing as their two heads met painfully together, Lily's brow coming into sharp contact with the hardness of his chin. Unfortunately it was in the exact same spot as his friend Milburn's fist had landed six days previously!

'Oh, my word!' The dropped parcel forgotten, Lily now raised a gloved hand to her obviously painful brow, those moss-green eyes having filled with tears.

Giles pushed aside his own discomfort to quickly discard his cane and reach out to grasp the tops of her arms as he looked down at her anxiously. 'Let me see!' He pushed her hand aside, a frown darkening his own brow as he saw the bump that was already forming under her delicate skin. 'Do not poke and prod at it!' he instructed sternly as he clasped her gloved fingers firmly in his own even as they crept to the painful spot.

Giles tensed as he became aware of the warmth of Lily's fingers through the thin lace of her glove, the rapid rise and fall of her breasts against the bodice of her grey gown, her pulse beating rapidly at the base of her slender neck, and when Giles raised his gaze it was to see Lily catch the full redness of her bottom lip between tiny white teeth.

Because of the painful bump to her forehead? Or something else…?

Green eyes now looked up at him in questioning confusion from between long and silky black lashes. 'My lord…?' she breathed huskily.

The very air about them seemed to have stilled, even the

birds in the trees seemed to have ceased their singing to look down, watchful, expectant, upon the two people standing in a frozen tableau beneath them.

Giles drew a ragged breath into his starved lungs, aware as he did so of his own rapidly beating heart pounding in his ears. Because he could feel the warmth of Lily's hand against his own? Look down upon the rapid rise and fall of her creamy breasts above the curved neckline of her gown? Smell the lightness of her floral perfume on her smooth, ivory skin?

Giles's nostrils flared at this sudden, unwelcome awareness as he released her before stepping back abruptly. 'We should go in now, your brow will need the application of a cold compress to stop the worst of the swelling,' he told her grimly.

'My parcel…!' She attempted to retrieve it.

'Hang your parcel—'

Glistening green eyes glared up at Giles as he would have prevented her from reaching for the parcel. 'It is the material for my new gown, and I do not intend to leave it outside for the birds to peck at or the rain to fall upon—'

'Oh, very well.' Giles made no effort to hide his impatience as he bent down to gather up the parcel before handing it to her. 'Now can we go inside?' he prompted harshly as he picked up his ebony cane, his expression grim.

Lily had absolutely no idea what had happened, only knowing that something most assuredly had.

Giles Montague had looked at her just now as if seeing her for the first time, his eyes no longer that cold silver-grey but instead burning a deep and unfathomable colour of pewter. They were eyes that had swept across the swell of her breasts, the pale column of her throat, before coming to rest on the fullness of her lips. The intensity of his gaze had caused Lily to catch at her bottom lip with her teeth.

Even more puzzling had been her own response to the intensity of that gaze....

For several moments it had seemed as if they might be the only two people in the world, even breathing had been too much of an effort; the blood in Lily's veins had seemed to burn, her breasts had felt full and sensitive inside her gown.

She had taken note of every hard plane of his aristocratic face—the intelligent brow, those heated grey eyes, a long slash of a nose between high cheekbones, those firm and sculptured lips slightly parted above the square strength of his jaw. Considering all of these attributes, Lily found herself acknowledging Giles Montague as being a breathtakingly handsome man!

Giles Montague.

The arrogant and disdainful Giles Montague.

The hated and despised Lord Giles Montague.

It was unbelievable, unacceptable, that Lily should have such thoughts about a man who had never made any effort to hide the contempt he felt towards her.

She clutched her parcel tightly to her breasts as she turned and walked the small distance down the pathway before opening the door and entering the vicarage. 'My father is no doubt in his study writing his sermon for Sunday,' she dismissed with a complete lack of manners as she stared at the top button of Giles Montague's waistcoat rather than at the hard planes of his face.

'You will see to putting a cold compress on your forehead immediately.' Again there was no question or suggestion from Giles Montague, only that cold inflexibility of will that Lily had come to expect from him.

Her chin rose as she looked up at him. 'I will decide what I will or will not do, my lord!'

His grey eyes narrowed to silver slits. 'You already have a

bump on your forehead half the size of a hen's egg. Do not make it any worse out of stubborn defiance of me!'

Lily drew her breath in sharply. 'You are arrogant, sir, to assume your opinion on anything would ever affect my own behaviour one way or the other!'

'Arrogant? Possibly,' Giles acknowledged with a derisive inclination of his head. 'But, in this particular case, I have no doubt I am necessarily so,' he added drily, heartily relieved to realise that he and Lily Seagrove had returned to the natural state of affairs between them.

Her cheeks flushed with irritation and her eyes flashed. 'You—'

'What on earth is— Oh, Lord Giles?' Mr Seagrove looked slightly perplexed as he stood in the now-open doorway to the family parlour and recognised the gentleman standing in the darkness of his hallway. 'And Lily...' The vicar looked even more puzzled as he saw his daughter standing slightly behind Lord Giles.

'Lord Montague and I met outside, Father,' Lily spoke up firmly before 'Lord Montague' had any opportunity to say anything that might add to her father's air of confusion.

Once seated at the kitchen table in order to allow the clucking Mrs Jeffries to apply a cold compress to the bump on her forehead—not because Giles Montague had instructed that she do so but because it was the right and sensible thing to do!—Lily could not help but think again of those few minutes of awareness as she stood outside the vicarage with Giles Montague....

Four

· ·

'So exciting! I am sure Monsieur André is beside himself at the thought of baking all those delicious cakes for the garden party! And Mrs Stratton has us all polishing and cleaning the silver until we can see our faces in it,' Daisy, a plump and pretty housemaid at Castonbury Park, chattered on excitedly. 'Do you think the old Gypsy woman will be there again this year to tell our fortunes? Oh, I do hope so! Last year she said a tall, dark and handsome stranger would sweep me off my feet. I haven't chanced to meet him yet, but I live in hopes—'

It was now two days since Lily had literally clashed heads with Giles Montague outside the vicarage, and having already made several calls in the village on her way to Castonbury Park today, she was now only half listening to Daisy as the maid chattered non-stop on the walk down the hallway in the direction of Mrs Stratton's parlour.

'She prefers to be called a Romany. And her name is Mrs Lovell,' Lily supplied, the making of her new gown and the well-dressing celebrations having taken up more of her own thoughts and time than she would have believed possible, as she dealt with the wealth of arrangements to be put in place before the ceremony next week.

She had also, after more enquiries from curious neighbours than she cared to answer, found a style for her hair which managed to cover the discolouration which still remained upon her brow despite the swelling having disappeared.

Daisy's 'tall, dark and handsome stranger' could easily be a description of Giles Montague. Lily's own dislike of that gentleman did not appear to have prevented her from acknowledging that he was indeed tall, dark and very handsome. After twelve years away from home, with only infrequent visits back to Derbyshire, he could also be considered something of a 'stranger' to most of the people in Castonbury. Daisy was certainly young enough not to have too many recollections of him.

Giles Montague's return had now resulted in the whole of the estate and household staff being 'swept off their feet,' as he began to issue orders and instructions for the work he considered needed to be done before Castonbury Park opened its gates to the village for the well-dressing celebrations the following week.

'Oh, I hope I did not cause offence, Lily!' Daisy's embarrassed expression revealed that she was aware of the things said in the village concerning Lily's true parents. 'It's just that Agnes said she saw one of the pretty Gypsy caravans on the other side of the lake yesterday. And the Gypsy—the Romany, Mrs Lovell,' she corrected with a self-conscious giggle, 'is so wonderful at telling fortunes, that I hoped it was her. It's my afternoon off today, so maybe I'll take a walk over that way and see for myself—'

Lily also wondered if the caravan might belong to Mrs Lovell, that elderly lady usually arriving at Castonbury several weeks ahead of her tribe, and so giving her the opportunity to go about the village selling the clothes pegs and baskets she had made through the winter months. Her fortune-telling had also been a feature of the well-dressing celebrations ever since Lily could remember. Whether or not those fortunes ever came true did not seem to matter to the people in the village, as they, like Daisy, simply enjoyed the possibility that they might—

Lily's wandering thoughts came to an abrupt end as she heard the sound of raised voices from down the hallway. Or rather, a single raised voice....

'—do not say I did not warn you all! And do not come crying to me when he succeeds in killing His Grace!' There was the sound of a door being forcibly slammed.

'Uh-oh, it's Mr Smithins, and he sounds as if he's on the warpath again!' Daisy whispered in alarm as she clutched Lily's arm. 'I'd better get back to me polishing!' She beat a hasty retreat back to the kitchen just as Smithins appeared at the end of the hallway, the scowl on his face evidence of his bad temper.

A short, thin and balding man, he possessed an elegance of style about his demeanour and dress that some might consider foppish. Lily had observed that he was also something of a despot in regard to the other household servants at Castonbury Park, considering himself far above them in his position as personal valet to the Duke of Rothermere. Hence Daisy's hurried departure back to her work in the kitchen; Smithins was perfectly capable of boxing the young maid's ears if he felt so inclined!

His scowl deepened as he strode down the hallway and caught sight of Lily watching him.

She grimaced self-consciously as she felt herself forced into speech. 'Is anything amiss, Mr Smithins?'

His eyes narrowed. 'Mark my words, it will all end in tears!' he muttered as he pushed past her before continuing on his way without apology.

Lily felt slightly unnerved as she turned to look at the valet, but more by his angry claim of some unnamed person 'killing His Grace' than his rude behaviour to her just now. What on earth could have happened for Smithins to—

'Ah, Lily,' Mrs Stratton sighed wearily as she appeared in the doorway of her parlour and saw Lily standing outside in the hallway. 'Do please come in,' she invited softly.

Lily hesitated. 'I have obviously called at a bad time....'

'Not at all,' the older woman assured wryly. 'Smithins is volatile of temperament, I am afraid,' she continued as Lily slowly entered the cosy parlour.

'But...he seemed so vehement...?'

Mrs Stratton shook her head. 'He is merely annoyed because Lord Giles refuses to heed his advice concerning His Grace.'

Lord Giles? Smithins's warning just now had been a reference to Giles Montague's behaviour in regard to his father?

The housekeeper sighed. 'His latest concern seems to be the carriage ride His Grace is to take with Lord Giles this afternoon.'

Lily's eyes widened. 'Is His Grace well enough for a carriage ride?'

'He has seemed much improved this past day or so,' Mrs Stratton assured. 'I am sure that a change of scenery will be far more beneficial to him than sitting alone in his rooms day after day, and allowing his nerves to get the better of him.'

Possibly, but it was only the end of April, and the chill wind blew off the Derbyshire hills still. 'My father has been invited to dine with His Grace and Lord Giles this evening.' Indeed, the invitation to dine at Castonbury Park this evening had been the only thing Mr Seagrove had been willing to impart to Lily concerning Giles Montague's visit to him two days ago!

The older woman frowned slightly. 'I understood the invitation was for both you and Mr Seagrove....'

It had been. It still was. But as Lily could not imagine Giles Montague really wanting to spend an evening in her company—as she had no desire to spend an evening in his—she had been sure that her inclusion in the invitation had only been made out of politeness to her father, and as such she had intended making the excuse of having a headache this evening when it came time to leave for Castonbury Park.

But having heard Smithins's warning just now, perhaps she should reconsider that decision?

'I really should pay no mind to Smithins if I were you, Lily.' Mrs Stratton gave a rueful grimace as she seemed to read Lily's hesitation, even if she had misunderstood the reason for it. 'I am afraid he has been allowed to become far too overbearingly protective this past year where His Grace is concerned.' She gave a weary sigh. 'I have long been forced to listen to his ravings for one reason or another.'

That may be so, but Lily seriously doubted that those 'ravings' had ever been about Lord Giles Montague before this week, or involved an accusation of him 'succeeding in killing' his own father. 'Do you think there is any basis for truth in Mr Smithins's concerns for His Grace?'

'None at all,' the housekeeper dismissed briskly. 'Lord Giles has always been the most dutiful of sons.'

Had it been 'dutiful' of Giles Montague to remain in London these past nine months when he had been needed here at Castonbury Park? Was it 'dutiful' of him, now that he had at last returned, to be seen to take his father, a man who was obviously fragile in health, out on a carriage ride? Admittedly, he now seemed to be taking a belated interest in the estate, but—

'Besides, you will see for yourself this evening how His Grace fares.' Mrs Stratton smiled. 'And I know that Monsieur André is greatly looking forward to preparing some more of the meringues after I told him how much you enjoyed them when you were here last,' she added with a twinkle in her eye.

Lily felt the colour warm her cheeks at Mrs Stratton's more than obvious attempt at matchmaking. She had only seen the new French chef once or twice since his arrival at Caston-bury Park, although she had noticed on those occasions that he was handsome. Even so, Lily very much doubted that even a French chef would be willing to overlook her questionable pedigree.

'But I am sure you did not come here to discuss this evening's menu with me…?' Mrs Stratton prompted lightly.

Lily gave herself a mental shake as she was reminded of her reason for calling. 'I was in the village and was waylaid by Mr Crutchley as I passed the butcher's shop. He said he has not yet received an order from you for the traditional pig to roast.' The ladies of the village would no doubt enjoy par-taking of the delicacies provided by Monsieur André, but the men were all of hardy farming stock, and as such required a heartier repast for their tea than the sandwiches and cakes the French chef would be providing.

The housekeeper looked slightly perplexed. 'I understood from Lord Giles that he intended to talk to Mr Crutchley personally.'

'Lord Giles?' Lily repeated slowly. 'But…I do not understand.'

Mrs Stratton smiled indulgently. 'I believe the pig roast is to be his own gift to the celebrations.'

'I— Well. That is very generous of him.' Lily still frowned her puzzlement.

'Indeed,' the housekeeper agreed warmly. 'He has stated that he also intends to provide the liquid refreshment for the gentlemen.'

To say Lily was surprised at Giles Montague's personal largesse would be putting it mildly; as far as she was aware, he had not shown any interest before now in the welfare and happiness of the people living in the village of Castonbury.

But he had not become his father's heir until Lord Jamie's demise either.

Was she being completely fair to Giles Montague, Lily wondered as she walked back to the vicarage, or was she perhaps allowing her own prejudice of feelings towards that gentleman to colour her thoughts and emotions?

Thankfully she had not seen Giles Montague again in the past two days, but he had been the subject of much discussion in the village.

She had heard from several of the women how their eldest sons had been taken on for the summer months so that the fallow fields at the Park might be prepared for a winter crop. Another had commented that her carpenter husband had been employed to effect repairs upon several of the barns to ready them for the storing of the harvest to come. A builder had been seen up on the roof of Castonbury Park itself to repair several tiles that had fallen off in the severe winter storms.

All of it was work that Giles Montague had apparently instructed to be carried out.

Perhaps her criticisms of him had had some effect, after all—

No, a more likely explanation was that Giles Montague already considered himself master here!

Could there, after all, be some truth in Smithins's earlier

warning to Mrs Stratton regarding the Duke of Rothermere? Was Giles Montague deliberately endangering his father's already precarious health, in the hopes that he might become the presumptive Duke of Rothermere sooner rather than later?

Lily had no answer to those questions. One thing she was certain of, however; she no longer intended suffering so much as the twinge of a headache to prevent her from dining at Castonbury Park this evening!

'I must thank you for sending John and the carriage for us, Lord Giles.' Mr Seagrove beamed as Lumsden showed the vicar and his daughter into the formal salon that evening. He was wearing his usual clerical black, his daughter looking slender and graceful in a gown of deep blue. 'I am afraid my open carriage is not at all suitable for going out in the evenings, and our horse now so old that he is not inclined to go out after dark either.'

'Not at all,' Giles drawled dismissively. 'I could not risk Miss Seagrove suffering a chill.'

A chill which was all in those moss-green eyes, Giles discovered with a frown as he bent formally over Lily's gloved hand before glancing up to see her looking back at him with icy coldness. Not a particularly good omen for what Giles had hoped would be an evening free of the tensions he had been forced to suffer earlier today whilst out visiting with his father!

'Besides which,' he added dismissively as he stepped back from the immediate glare of those chilling green eyes, 'my father and I took the carriage out earlier today, so it was no bother for John to set out again this evening.'

'And how did your father enjoy his carriage ride, my lord?' Lily prompted evenly, the curls arranged on her brow in such a way as to cover the discolouration of skin Giles was sure she would have suffered from their clashing of heads two days ago, although he could see no sign of a bump still being there, indicating she may—but only may!—have taken his advice, after all, and applied the cold compress.

'You appear to be very well informed of the movements at Castonbury Park, Miss Seagrove.' Giles regarded her through narrowed lids, his own jaw having ached for several hours after coming into contact with her brow, but thankfully having suffered no further visible bruising.

She shrugged creamy shoulders. 'Mrs Stratton happened to mention the outing when I called on her earlier today.'

'Indeed?' Giles murmured drily.

'Yes.' Lily's cheeks became slightly flushed at the derision she heard in Giles Montague's tone at hearing she had once again called upon the housekeeper at Castonbury Park. 'You omitted to answer my query concerning your father's enjoyment of his carriage ride, my lord…' she reminded determinedly.

He looked down at her with shrewd grey eyes. 'Did I?' he drawled.

'Yes.' Lily glared her frustration, feeling at that moment much like a mouse must when being played with by a cat. In the case of Giles Montague, a large and arrogant cat!

'How remiss of me.' He turned away to look at Mr Seagrove.

'Would you care for a glass of claret before dinner, sir?'

'I would, thank you, Lord Giles.' Her father beamed at the younger man, as usual seeming unaware of the tension that existed between Giles Montague and his daughter.

'May I get you a glass of sherry, or perhaps lemonade, Miss Seagrove?' Giles Montague raised dark and mocking brows as he glanced in her direction.

He was a very large and arrogant cat whom Lily was nevertheless forced to acknowledge looked extremely handsome in black evening clothes and snowy white linen! 'No, thank you,' Lily refused stiffly, more than slightly annoyed with herself for having noticed how handsome Giles Montague looked this evening.

Giles turned to dismiss Lumsden with a terse nod before crossing the room himself to pour the claret into two crystal glasses, a frown low on his brow as his thoughts turned once again to the events of this afternoon. Not the most enjoyable time he had spent in his father's company since his return, and Lord knows those previous visits to his father's rooms had not been conducive to Giles sleeping comfortably at night!

Calling to talk with the family lawyers in Buxton earlier today had succeeded in helping Giles to slowly, very slowly, unravel the tangle his father appeared to have made of things since Jamie had perished. A tangle that the duke had only made worse during that last battle with Napoleon at Waterloo, when it had seemed as if Wellington might not prevail. Indeed, the Duke of Rothermere's actions at that time had been so extreme that Giles was still uncertain, even with the help of the lawyers, as to whether or not he would ever be able to set things to rights.

Wise investments of his own over the past ten years had enabled Giles to accrue his own personal fortune, and it was these finances which were currently allowing the estate and other Montague households to run with their usual smoothness and largesse. Although how long that could continue would depend upon how long Giles's money lasted....

Making it doubly infuriating that he now had to suffer the irritating Lily Seagrove prodding and poking at him as if he were an unfeeling son who had dragged his frail and ailing

father out on a needless carriage ride. All the more so when
the visit to the family lawyers had been made at his father's
insistence!

'My lord—'

'I believe my father is about to join us now,' Giles bit out as
he heard voices out in the hallway. 'Perhaps you would care
to ask him yourself as to how he enjoyed his outing this afternoon?' He looked expectantly towards the door.

Lily's eyes widened as the Duke of Rothermere entered the
room. She had seen His Grace rarely these past six months but
had noted his increasing frailness on each of those occasions,
but it was possible to see that there was colour in his cheeks
this evening, and a faint sparkle of life in his eyes.

'Ah, the pretty Miss Seagrove!' he greeted her with obvious pleasure as he slowly crossed the room to bend gallantly
over her gloved hand. 'And Reginald!' He turned to greet his
old friend warmly.

'Your Grace.' Mr Seagrove beamed. 'May I say how well
you are looking this evening!'

'I am feeling well.' The duke nodded. 'So much so that I
hope you are feeling up to the possibility of a game of chess
after dinner?'

'I should enjoy that very much.' Mr Seagrove accepted one
of the glasses of claret from Giles Montague whilst the duke
accepted the other, the two older gentlemen continuing their
conversation as he returned to pour a third glass for himself.

'You are positive I cannot provide you with refreshment,
Miss Seagrove?' He quirked a brow as he moved to stand beside her, glass of claret in hand.

It was a mockery Lily knew she justly deserved, when the
Duke of Rothermere had so obviously suffered no ill effects
from going out into the countryside earlier. Indeed, appear-

ances would seem to imply the opposite! 'No, thank you, my lord,' she said stiffly.

'I believe you wished to enquire of my father as to whether or not he enjoyed his outing today...?' he reminded softly.

Lily frowned. 'There is obviously no need when His Grace is in such good spirits.'

'Much to your disappointment?' Giles Montague prompted softly.

Her cheeks warmed as she gave him a startled glance. 'Why on earth should you think that?'

'Perhaps because earlier you all but accused me of putting my father's health in danger by taking him out for a carriage ride.' Giles knew one only had to look at the Duke of Rothermere to see that the outing had been beneficial. Indeed, his father, having had the direness of the family's financial situation revealed to Giles by the family lawyers, now seemed like a man who had had a heavy weight removed from his frail shoulders!

A heavy weight which now pressed upon Giles's shoulders instead.

'I— You— I did no such thing!' Lily spluttered even as the guilty colour deepened in her cheeks.

Giles grimaced, knowing his conversation was not at all polite to a guest in his family home, but he found it impossible to resist challenging Lily when she seemed so set on seeking reasons to dislike him. More reasons... The frankness of their conversation a year ago had undoubtedly already ensured that dislike!

It was an animosity of feelings Giles could well do without when he already had so many other problems to deal with. 'Perhaps it was I who misunderstood the reason for your concern,' he dismissed curtly.

Lily knew that Giles Montague had not misunderstood her in the slightest, and that she had, with the aid of the bad-tempered Smithins, drawn a completely wrong conclusion. But there was no way Giles Montague could have known that when he—

Stop it, Lily, she instructed herself sternly. There were no two ways about it—she was guilty of listening to gossip, and of drawing a hasty conclusion as to Giles Montague's motivations for the afternoon outing with his father. Worse than that, she had all but made a false accusation of heartlessness towards him because of it!

'I apologise if I seemed…overconcerned earlier, in regard to His Grace's health,' she spoke stiffly, her gaze fixed upon the buttons on Giles's waistcoat as she found herself unable to look up and meet what she suspected would be chilling displeasure in those icy grey eyes.

Giles scowled as he looked down at that bent head, irritated beyond measure that he should once again note the fineness of Lily Seagrove's looks—the dark silkiness of her curls, that delicate nape, the long dark lashes downcast against cheeks of ivory-white, those full and ruby-red lips. As for the creamy swell of her breasts just visible above the low neckline of her blue gown…!

Damn it, was his life not complicated enough at present without his noting the attractions of a young woman whose position in life, and questionable antecedents, rendered her unsuitable as being anything more to him than a gentleman's mistress? At the same time, Giles's acquaintance with her adoptive parents made the offer of such a role in his own life impossible.

And where that particular idea had come from Giles had absolutely no idea. Nor, having thought of it, did he wish to pursue it!

Five

'As it is a warm evening, Miss Seagrove, perhaps you would care to take a walk on the terrace whilst our fathers retire to play their game of chess?'

Lily looked up at Giles Montague from beneath thick black lashes as he walked over to where she was still seated at the dinner table, his arm extended in silent invitation as he waited for her to rise.

As could be expected of the duke's French chef, it had been a magnificent dinner—made more enjoyable for Lily by the fact that Giles Montague, seated at the opposite end of the table to his father, had remained broodingly silent for most of it!—but Lily's pleasure in the evening could no longer continue now that her father and the Duke of Rothermere had decided to retire to the duke's rooms and enjoy their brandy and cigars over the promised game of chess. And so leaving Lily, and Lord Giles, one presumed, to find their own amusement....

'Would you not prefer to remain here and enjoy your own brandy and cigar?' she prompted restlessly, her father and the

Duke of Rothermere having already made their excuses and left the dining room together.

'Only if you will agree to remain also…?' Giles Montague arched dark brows.

Lily smiled dismissively. 'I am afraid I do not drink brandy or enjoy cigars!'

He gave a tight smile at her irony. 'And I could not possibly be so rude as to enjoy them either when to do so would abandon you to your own amusements.'

Perhaps a walk outside would be preferable to the two of them retiring to the salon for the next hour or so and attempting to make polite conversation.

'Then I believe I should enjoy taking a walk outside in the fresh air, thank you.' Lily gave a gracious nod of her head before standing as Giles Montague moved to pull back her chair, ignoring the arm he offered to instead turn and walk alone to where Lumsden had opened the French doors in anticipation of their stepping outside onto the terrace.

Giles regretted his suggestion as he realised—too late!—that it may not be altogether wise to venture outside in the moonlight with Lily so soon after his earlier acknowledgement of her physical attributes.

Moonlight…?

Damn it, he had never considered himself to be a romantic man, and in the past had only ever taken a woman to his bed when he felt a physical need to do so, and always in the clear understanding that the encounter meant no more to him than a passing fancy.

Whether he 'fancied' Lily Seagrove or not, her position as the adopted daughter of the local vicar meant she was not a woman Giles could ever seriously consider taking to his bed. Not the ideal circumstances under which he should follow her as she strolled outside into the moonlight, before crossing to stand beside the balustrade of the terrace and gaze out across the parklands. Her dark blue gown and ebony hair allowed her to meld into the darkness, and so made a stark contrast to the ivory paleness of her skin. Soft and silky skin dappled in moonlight, and which surely begged to be touched and caressed—

'Everything looks so much more beautiful in the moonlight, does it not?' she remarked on a wistful sigh.

'What?' Giles scowled darkly as he tried to force any idea of intimacy with this young woman, either now or in the future, firmly from his thoughts.

Lily turned to glance across at where Giles Montague stood so tense and still in the shadows of the house, her breath catching in her throat as the moonlight caught the sharp angles of his face to give him an almost satanic appearance, and making a pale glitter of those silver-grey eyes. She moistened her lips before speaking. 'I was remarking on how much more beautiful everything looks at night, my lord.'

'Yes…' Those grey eyes glittered more brightly than ever as he stepped out of the shadows; the darkness of his clothing added to his dark and predatory appearance.

Lily quickly turned away, feeling herself tremble slightly even as she reached out to tightly grip the balustrade before her, totally aware of Giles Montague as he crossed the terrace in sure but soft strides until she sensed he stood just behind her. Indeed, he was standing so close to her that Lily was sure she could feel the warmth of his breath against her nape!

'Is it too cold for you out here, after all?' he prompted huskily. He obviously saw her tremble and mistook the reason for it.

Cold? Lily had never felt warmer!

But it was the sort of warmth that came from within, a

deep and compelling heat as the blood seemed to rush more quickly through her veins, and her breasts felt suddenly constricted beneath the fitted bodice of her gown, and so making breathing even more difficult.

Was she ill?

Perhaps coming down with a cold or the influenza?

Certainly her limbs felt aching and trembling, her palms damp inside the lace of her gloves and her cheeks warm as if with a fever. 'Perhaps a little,' she acknowledged softly, resisting the urge to turn and look at Giles Montague as she caught a rustle of movement behind her. She could not prevent her gasp as she felt the warmth of his evening jacket being placed about her shoulders. 'Oh, please, I could not possibly—'

'Oh, but you must.' His hands came to rest on her now-covered shoulders in a light and yet compelling grip as she would have attempted to remove his jacket, his breath now every bit as warm against her nape as Lily had imagined it might be.

She stood tense and stiff as she knew herself completely aware of Giles Montague's touch, from the tips of her toes to the top of her ebony head. As she was aware of how the heat of Giles Montague's body had been absorbed into the material of the jacket that now warmed her. Just as she was also aware of inhaling the lightness of his cologne—sandalwood and lime?—every time she attempted to draw breath. It invaded her senses, and caused Lily's trembling to intensify as she now felt uncomfortably hot inside the confines of his jacket. It was a heat and discomfort she was sure would only deepen if she were to turn and actually look at Giles Montague!

'Better?' he breathed huskily.

Heavens, no, it was much worse to be so aware of everything about Giles Montague, of all men, and yet seemingly unable to break the spell of that awareness!

She must, after all, be suffering from a malaise, a life-threatening fever, one that made it impossible for her to breathe, and would surely carry her off completely if she did not soon find some relief from lack of breath and the heat that coursed through her veins!

'Lily…?'

'I—' She halted her protest as she heard how husky her voice sounded, her breasts quickly rising and falling as she once again attempted to breathe. 'Perhaps we should go back inside….' She finally chanced a glance over her left shoulder at him. And instantly wished that she had not!

Giles Montague's face was lean and shadowed beneath dark hair ruffled onto his forehead by the gentle brush of the breeze, his shoulders appearing very broad in the white evening shirt, his stomach taut and flat beneath his waistcoat.

Lily quickly averted her gaze. 'I think perhaps I will not wait for my father to finish his game of chess, after all, but rather I will leave now…. My lord?' she prompted sharply, as instead of releasing her, she felt his hands tighten their grip upon her shoulders. 'You are hurting me, my lord,' she protested softly as she tried to extricate herself from his clasp.

For several long seconds it seemed as if Giles Montague would not allow her to be released, and then just as suddenly the heat of his hands was removed, allowing Lily to slip away before taking the jacket from her shoulders, resisting the slight shiver at the loss of its warmth as she turned to hold the garment out to him. 'My lord?' she prompted firmly when he made no effort to take it from her but continued to scowl down at her broodingly in the moonlight.

Giles's hands were clenched at his sides, a nerve pulsing in his tensed jaw as he fought an inner battle with himself not to give in to the demand that he take Lily in his arms and—

And what?

If he should kiss Lily Seagrove, even once, then he would be openly acknowledging his desire for her. An unwanted desire, and one which Giles had no reason to believe Lily returned. In fact, her every word and gesture towards him implied the opposite!

He stepped back abruptly. 'I will instruct John to bring the carriage round,' he bit out tersely, a frown darkening his brow as he reached out and took his jacket from Lily's gloved fingers before shrugging his shoulders into its tailored perfection, determinedly straightening his cuffs in an effort not to look at her again.

'That will not be necessary—'

'It is very necessary,' Giles assured firmly as he turned to stride across the terrace and open the door for her to enter. 'Not only do I insist you return home in the carriage, but I shall accompany you.'

Her chin was raised in challenge as she joined him at the open door. 'You perhaps fear that if I were to walk home alone at night I might be set upon by the Gypsies?'

Giles's jaw was tightly clenched at her deliberate challenge towards what most—what he, certainly—believed to be her antecedents. 'The elderly Mrs Lovell is the only one of the Romany to have arrived so far, and I somehow doubt you have anything to fear from her!'

Lily raised dark brows. 'I am surprised you were even aware of her presence….'

He gave a tight and humourless smile. 'Since my return a week ago I have made it my business to know all that transpires on the Rothermere estate.'

'So many have remarked,' Lily acknowledged ruefully as she swept past him to enter the warmth of the dining room.

'You sound disapproving, when only days ago I believe you urged me to take an interest.'

'I, my lord?' Lily raised her brows as he stepped into the dining room. 'You are mistaken.'

'I do not believe so, no,' he bit out tightly.

Lily frowned. 'It must be somewhat…tedious for you that the law does not as yet allow you to officially claim the title of Marquis of Hatherton.'

'Tedious?' Giles Montague echoed softly as he carefully closed the door behind him before turning, the grey of his eyes now like shards of opaque glass as he looked down the lean length of his nose at her. 'You believe I must consider the death of my elder brother as being tedious?'

Lily had spoken hastily, still totally unnerved by the strange turmoil of her feelings towards Giles Montague. 'I meant no disrespect to Lord James's memory.'

'No?'

'Certainly not,' she insisted sharply.

Giles Montague gave a haughty acknowledgement of his head. 'In that case I must consider any intended disrespect to have been directed towards me. And if so, then I believe I should warn you that the last person to accuse me of wishing my brother James dead, so that I might inherit his title, no doubt still has the bruises about his throat to show for it!'

Lily's startled gaze instantly moved to that spot on the arrogant, square jaw where Giles Montague had sported a bruise the week before.

'Yes,' he confirmed as he saw her glance. 'That very same gentleman,' he drawled self-derisively.

'Oh,' she breathed softly.

He raised mocking brows. 'You had perhaps imagined, having heard of my exploits in London, that I received my injury for a…less respectable reason?'

Having given some thought to that bruise after their initial meeting in the woods, Lily had thought exactly that, she now acknowledged guiltily. In fact, she knew she had quite enjoyed imagining the arrogant Giles Montague to have perhaps been struck on the chin by a jealous husband or lover shortly before leaving London!

Except…

It now transpired that Giles Montague had received that blow whilst defending the affection he had for his dead brother.

That Lord James had died far away in Spain, swept away in the torrent of a fast-flowing river, his body never recovered, had, Lily knew, been a painful blow to the members of the Montague family residing in Derbyshire. Her own prejudice of feelings towards Giles Montague had not allowed her to see that, although he had been away from home when the news arrived, he must have been just as wounded, if not more so, by the loss of his older brother.

'I apologise,' she spoke huskily. 'I meant you no insult. I—' She gave a self-disgusted shake of her head. 'I spoke out of turn, and I apologise.'

Giles slowly allowed the tension to ease from his shoulders. 'One apology would have sufficed,' he assured drily. 'Now, if you are quite ready to leave, I will ring for Lumsden and have the carriage brought round.'

'I really do not want to be any trouble—'

'My dear Lily, it is now my belief that you have been nothing but trouble since the moment your baby basket was left upon the Seagroves' doorstep twenty years ago!'

Green eyes opened wide with shock at the unexpectedness

of his attack. 'I— You— That was completely uncalled for!' she gasped faintly.

Yes, it was, Giles acknowledged wearily. Uncalled for, and deliberately cruel. But, in truth, he was feeling cruel. A combination of physical frustration and inner turmoil had most definitely rendered him cruel!

He grimaced. 'It would seem that it is my turn to apologise to you.' He gave a self-disgusted shake of his head. 'Obviously the carriage ride earlier today was not as beneficial to my own temperament as it was to my father's!'

Lily looked up at Giles searchingly, but saw only that hard implacability about the firmness of his mouth, and the icy disgust in his eyes. Whether that disgust was directed towards her or himself Lily was unsure. 'No doubt you have noticed, my lord, that we do not seem able to converse for two minutes at a time without insulting each other.'

He gave a humourless smile. 'Then might I suggest that the answer would seem to be for us not to converse at all?'

Lily could find no argument with that suggestion; in fact, after the strangeness of her feelings whilst outside on the terrace just now, she would welcome never having to see or speak with Giles Montague ever again....

'So you've come to see me at last, have ye?'

Mrs Lovell ceased stirring the coals of the fire, over which her cast-iron cooking pot was suspended by a shepherd's crook. She turned to look across to where Lily stood at the edge of the small clearing situated between the lake and the river, the place where the elderly Romany usually made her camp. Lily took absolutely no offence at the elderly lady's accusing tone, knowing from years of making such visits that it was merely Mrs Lovell's way. 'I thought to give you a few days to settle before calling.' She smiled as she stepped further into the clearing, wearing one of her older gowns of serviceable blue cotton, with a straw bonnet over her curls.

'Did ye now?' The elderly Romany straightened. She was a small and wizened lady of indeterminate years, her complexion weathered by years of suffering the extremes of either the heat of the sun or the bitterness of the cold. Her eyes were hazel, a strange mixture of brown, blue and green, and her mouth slightly folded in on itself where she had lost most of her front teeth. Her greying black hair was secured beneath its usual black scarf; her gown was also black, but covered from waist to toe by a white pinafore. 'You've grown even taller than when I saw ye last year,' she added bluntly.

Lily laughed softly. 'I fear that I have, yes.'

'Why be afeared?' Mrs Lovell began to drop the ingredients for her stew into the pot as the water began to boil—several diced carrots and a parsnip or two, some potatoes, a few herbs, followed by what looked to be a skinned and boned rabbit.

'It would seem that the fashion is for the fair and delicate this Season,' Lily explained ruefully as she sat down on one of the logs of wood the other woman had gathered and would no doubt place upon the fire later.

'Fair and delicate!' Mrs Lovell's snort of disgust was indicative of exactly what she thought of that insipidness. 'Ask any man and he'll tell ye he prefers to be able to feel a bit of shape to the woman as warms his bed at night.'

Lily knew she would never ask any gentleman such a thing! And the colour that now warmed her cheek owed nothing to the flames of the fire but to memories of the liquid heat that had consumed her on the terrace yesterday evening, as Giles Montague had stood so close to her that for several moments she had imagined he might actually be about to kiss her!

Which, in the light of day, Lily could clearly see as being fanciful nonsense; Giles Montague disliked her far too much even to think about kissing her let alone attempting to do so!

True to his word, last night he had ordered one of the Rothermere carriages be brought round before accompanying her on the short drive back to the vicarage. It had been a carriage ride that had seemed excruciatingly long as, abiding by his suggestion, neither of them had spoken so much as a word to the other until they made their goodbyes at the vicarage door. It had turned into a tense and stiffly polite parting, during which Lily's gaze had remained firmly fixed upon Giles Montague's neck cloth rather than risk another glance at his face.

To now be so vividly reminded of that time alone with him on the terrace at Castonbury Park, when Lily had been trying so hard all morning not to think of him at all, caused her to speak hastily lest Mrs Lovell see her blushes and attempt to tease the reason for them from her. 'I see that Samson is still with you.' She looked admiringly at the piebald horse tethered a short distance from the brightly coloured caravan which Mrs Lovell called a vardo and which he had pulled faithfully these past ten years.

'No doubt he'll see me out,' the elderly Romany dismissed practically, her shrewd gaze still focused on Lily. 'Have you found yourself a young man yet?'

'No,' Lily dismissed lightly—nor was she ever likely to do so when she stood so uncertainly between one world and another, neither Quality nor peasant, fish nor fowl.

'Are all the men blind in these parts, then?' Mrs Lovell gave the stew a last stir before resuming her seat on the small stool that stood to one side of the fire.

'I do not believe so, no,' Lily laughed softly. 'Mrs Jeffries sent you this.' She held out the apple pie she had brought with her wrapped in muslin.

'Kind of her.' The elderly Romany nodded as she accepted the gift, sniffing appreciatively. 'Mmm, cinnamon,' she murmured with satisfaction before placing it carefully to one side. 'If the men here are not blind, then they must surely be senile,' she continued with her usual asperity.

'No, I do not believe they are senile either,' Lily dismissed patiently when her attempt at diversion obviously failed. 'I am merely—I am afraid my lack of position in Society does not encourage many suitors,' she finally explained with a sigh, knowing of old that Mrs Lovell was too direct in manner to tolerate any attempt at prevarication from others.

'What does that mean, your "lack of position in Society"?' the old lady repeated with obvious scorn.

'Exactly as it sounds.' Lily smiled ruefully. 'It is well known in these parts that I am a foundling. It is not what a gentleman might expect of his wife and the future mother of his children.' She shrugged without rancour.

'I never heard of such a thing!' Mrs Lovell gave another dismissive snort. 'In my day a pretty face and child-bearing hips was all as was required to be a wife and mother!'

Lily held back another smile with effort, knowing that the old lady had not intended to cause amusement with the bluntness of her remark. 'Do you have children of your own, Mrs Lovell?' The old lady had been a widow for as long as Lily had known her, nor did she recall ever having been introduced to any children from that marriage.

'I did.' The other woman busied herself stirring more herbs into her stew pot. 'As fine a son as any woman ever had.'

Lily sensed sadness beneath the statement. 'He is not with you any more…?' she prompted gently.

'He died right here in Castonbury almost twenty-one years ago,' Mrs Lovell revealed gruffly.

A pained frown appeared on Lily's brow. 'I had no idea—Oh!' She gave a breathless gasp as memory stirred; she had heard tales of a young Romany man who had met with an accident in the woods here twenty or so years ago, believed to have been shot by mistake by the then Rothermere game-keeper, and buried in the churchyard across the lane from the vicarage. She had never seen the grave, nor the name carved upon it, but it seemed too much of a coincidence for it not to have been Mrs Lovell's son.

'It will be exactly twenty-one years in two days' time.' The old lady's gaze met hers unflinchingly.

Lily's eyes were wide. 'Is that the reason you always arrive here some days or weeks ahead of your tribe?'

'Maybe,' the other woman conceded gruffly.

She gave a pained wince. 'I am so sorry for your loss—'

'It was long ago and a different time.' Mrs Lovell straightened with brisk dismissal. 'But I don't recall him as being stupid enough not to marry the pretty woman he fell in love with, no matter what her breeding,' she added caustically.

Lily smiled gently, moved by the things Mrs Lovell had not said, able to see the pain of the loss of her only child still raw in that lady's expressive hazel eyes. 'I am afraid that a gentleman requires a little more than prettiness and child-bearing hips in his wife.'

'There ye go again with that "I am afraid."' Mrs Lovell frowned her disapproval. 'What is there for one as beautiful as you to be afraid of, except the stupidity of men?'

This time Lily could not hold back her laughter. 'You are very good for my self-esteem, Mrs Lovell.' She chuckled merrily.

'Self-esteem, is it?' The elderly woman gave a disgusted shake of her head. 'The men in these parts must be stupid, as well as blind and senile, is all I can say!'

'Your assessment appears to be harsh, Mrs Lovell, but quite possibly a correct one!'

Lily turned so sharply in the direction of that familiar, mocking voice that she was in danger of falling off the log on which she sat, only just managing to catch herself in time, and feeling the colour drain from her cheeks as she stared wide-eyed at where Giles Montague stood on the edge of the clearing, his tall hat once again throwing his face into shadow.

But Lily was more concerned about how long he had been standing there, rather than how he looked. And exactly how much of the frankness of Mrs Lovell's conversation he may have overheard....

Six

Lily gathered her wits enough to stand up awkwardly before making an abrupt curtsey. 'My lord.'

Giles nodded briefly in response, his smile humourless as he easily discerned the emotions that had flickered across Lily's expressive face at the unexpectedness of his appearance at Mrs Lovell's fireside—alarm, quickly followed by surprise. The former could be—and no doubt was!—attributed to seeing him again so soon after their stilted parting yesterday evening, and the surprise was no doubt due to finding Giles visiting Mrs Lovell at all, when Lily made no secret of the fact that she considered him to be not only arrogant but toplofty.

He quirked his brow before turning his attention to the elderly Romany as he stepped forward into the clearing. 'I brought over some tea and honey for you, Mrs Lovell, and Tom Anderson also sent over some of the liniment for your horse that he says you covet.' He presented her with the sack he carried.

'Kind of ye both, I'm sure.' The elderly woman nodded her thanks as she checked the contents of the sack. 'Perhaps the two of ye would like to join me in a cup of the tea?' she prompted even as she sat forward to hook the stew pot from over the fire and replace it with a blackened kettle.

'I believe my father will be expecting me back at the vicar-age.' Lily instantly refused the invitation, having no real wish to cut short her visit with Mrs Lovell but also having no de-sire to spend any more time in Giles's unpleasant—and un-settling—company.

'Nonsense.' Mrs Lovell briskly dismissed her excuses. 'I am sure Mr Seagrove enjoys yer company enough that he can spare ye for the short time it will take to drink some tea with me.'

How could Lily refuse when Mrs Lovell put forward her argument in such reproving tones! 'Well, of course, if you in-sist…' she agreed weakly.

'I do,' the old lady said firmly.

Lily sank back down upon the log, keeping her gaze averted from Giles…even if she was completely aware of his presence only feet away from her!

Giles had walked over from the house, checking to make sure the work he had ordered to be done at the lake was in progress on the way, only realising that his approach to Rosa Lovell's camp must have been masked by the undergrowth as he heard the two ladies in candid conversation.

And he had not particularly liked what he had overheard, knowing that in all probability he was responsible for the opin-ion Lily obviously now had of herself. A less than flattering opinion, which Giles had expressed a year ago when he had told Lily of all the reasons she was unsuited to being the wife of his brother Edward, or any other gentleman of Quality.…

'Sit ye down beside the yag, lad, and stop making the place look untidy!' Mrs Lovell's eyes twinkled merrily as she gave

Giles a gap-toothed smile and drew up another log with the obvious intention of having him sit down upon it. 'And afterwards I'll do a little dukkering, if'n it pleases ye both,' she added with a sly glance at first Lily and then Giles.

The elderly lady looked so mischievous that Giles could not help but chuckle. 'Do we have to "cross your palm with silver" first?'

'Gold would be better,' Mrs Lovell came back cheekily.

'No doubt.' Giles smiled ruefully.

'Unless Miss Lily thinks that Mr Seagrove would not approve of her indulging in such pagan practices as fortune-telling…' the elderly lady added teasingly.

Lily gave a rueful smile. 'I am sure my father's clerical profession dictates that he should not approve, at the same time as he would admit that his innate curiosity makes him eager for any and all knowledge!' she conceded affectionately.

Giles's gaze was guarded as he turned to her. 'You would not consider it an intrusion if I were to join the two of you?'

She barely glanced at him from beneath her straw bonnet as she shrugged dismissively. 'I believe we decided some time ago that I am the intruder here, and that it is your property to stay or go as you see fit.'

Giles should have expected to receive such a reproof after all that had passed between them, but even so his mouth firmed at the flat disinterest in Lily's tone. 'It would only please me to join the two of you if you were to assure me I am welcome to stay.'

Then go, Lily wished to tell him, *and go now*. Her nerves were already frayed to breaking at this unexpected encounter with the man whose very presence now caused her discomfort, and moreover a man who had made it more than obvious he could not abide to be in her company for any length of time either.

But she could not speak so bluntly to the future Duke of Rothermere with the ever-curious Mrs Lovell as watchful witness to the exchange. 'Mrs Lovell made the invitation, not I,' she answered huskily.

'Even so...'

'Will you stop dithering, lad, and sit ye down!' Mrs Lovell lost all patience with their stilted politeness. 'The tea's made now, and I'll not have it go to waste. I'll not be a minute finding the mugs.' She left the two of them alone as she disappeared off to her brightly coloured caravan.

Lily smiled at hearing the haughty Giles Montague referred to as 'lad'—anyone less like a lad she could not imagine! But no doubt it was how Mrs Lovell thought of him, having been coming to stay at Castonbury Park since before he'd been born. No doubt the elderly Romany probably also remembered him as being the 'mischievous scamp' Mrs Stratton had referred to some days ago.

It led Lily to question how long he had been in the habit of visiting Mrs Lovell's fireside; Lily would never have believed it of the disdainful Giles Montague if she had not witnessed it with her own eyes. Perhaps she did not know the haughty Giles Montague as well as she had thought....

Giles knew that he really should not have intruded once he became aware of Lily's presence at Rosa Lovell's fireside, and instead returned later in the day when he was sure the elderly lady was alone. Except, having heard the husky warmth in Lily's voice as she chatted so easily and warmly with Mrs Lovell, he had been unable to resist joining them. In the hopes, perhaps, that some of that warmth might spill over onto him.

Even wearing that unfashionable gown of faded blue cotton and an unbecoming straw bonnet that had also seen better days, Giles knew he could not look at Lily without feeling the same stirrings of desire that had kept him awake long into the previous night, stirrings which now resulted in him shifting restlessly upon the log as he sought a more comfortable position that would not expose the direction of his thoughts.

'Here ye are!' Mrs Lovell returned triumphant with three mismatched metal mugs before proceeding to pour the tea, all in apparent ignorance of the strained silence between her two guests. 'Drink it all down, my chivvies,' she encouraged gleefully as she handed them their steaming mugs of honey-sweetened tea. 'And then I'll look at your palms and see what the future holds in store for the both of you!'

Giles did not need a crystal ball to 'see' that his immediate future held a soaking in the coldness of either the lake or bath in order to cool his thoughts.

'One of my reasons for visiting was to ask if you will kindly do the fortune-telling at the well-dressing again this year.' Lily concentrated all of her attention on Mrs Lovell.

Which was not to say she was not still entirely aware of Giles sitting on the log beside her own. Or immune to that faint hint of sandalwood and lime of his cologne, that same masculine smell which had surrounded her the evening before when he had wrapped his jacket about her for warmth. A warmth which, seconds later, and for totally different reasons, Lily had found almost unbearable!

She had every reason to dislike the man intensely, and yet still she could not deny the heat and trembling she had felt at his close proximity yesterday evening, or that sudden sensitivity of her breasts pressing against the bodice of her gown. An aching sensitivity that still made Lily blush to think of it!

'Of course.' Mrs Lovell nodded in answer to her request. 'Some of the tribe have decided to resume the pilgrimage to Saintes-Maries-de-la-Mer this year, now that the fighting is over and we can travel across to France again, but I'm too old for such things.' She grimaced dismissively.

And, Lily realised after their earlier conversation, if the elderly lady had gone on the pilgrimage to France with the rest of her tribe, then she would not have been able to visit her son's grave on the anniversary of his death.

'I am sure we will appreciate your company all the more because of it.' Lily smiled warmly at the older woman, determined to visit the grave of Mrs Lovell's son herself, and place some wildflowers upon it, now that she was aware of its existence.

'Get on with you!' Mrs Lovell snorted at the compliment. 'Put aside your tea now, my chivvy, and let me take a look at your palm and tell ye what the future holds.'

Lily had a certain reluctance to know what was in store for her—she would much rather have had foreknowledge of Giles arriving at Mrs Lovell's fireside today than anything that may or may not be about to happen in her distant future!

A surreptitious glance at Giles beneath lowered lashes revealed that he did not seem in the least put out that he was not sipping tea from his usual fine china. Instead that silver-grey gaze rested on her broodingly, and in doing so made Lily even more aware of how her old blue serge gown had become a little tight about the breasts from constant washing, and how the shortness of the hem revealed her ankles in scuffed and muddied brown boots.

Her less than fashionable appearance prompted her into hurried speech. 'Your father has suffered no ill effects from his late evening?' It had been almost midnight when she heard her father arrive back at the vicarage.

Giles frowned darkly as the question forced him to recall the visit to his father's rooms this morning. The duke was indeed suffering from exhaustion after his carriage ride yesterday afternoon and the burst of social largesse in the evening, resulting in the overattentive Smithins treating Giles with more than his usual coolness. The valet was merely an irritant Giles had no trouble ignoring, but he could not dismiss his father's obvious lack of physical stamina with the same disinterest.

'If he did I am sure he will be fully recovered by tomorrow,' he assured her.

'I have a sarsaparilla tonic you might take for your father when you leave. Very good for cleansing the blood.' Mrs Lovell nodded sagely.

'Thank you.' Giles accepted gracefully, already knowing that Rosa Lovell's tonic would suffer the same fate as the doctor's appeared to have done—placed on the shelf beside his father's bedside before being completely ignored.

Mrs Lovell seemed satisfied with his answer, however, as she turned briskly to Lily. 'Time to remove yer glove and let me take a look at yer palm.'

'Perhaps His Lordship might like to be first...?' she prompted with a cool glance in Giles's direction.

His gaze narrowed as he easily guessed that Lily believed he would refuse to be a part of such nonsense as fortune-telling. 'By all means...' He held out his left hand for Mrs Lovell's inspection.

'The other's yer dominant hand.' The elderly lady chuckled dismissively and waited while Giles replaced his left hand with his right. 'And I don't really need to look too closely to know as your square fingertips indicate an orderly and methodical nature. That the length of your index finger says ye are a leader and maker of decisions.' She turned his hand over. 'Or that these—' she chuckled again as she touched the dark hair on the back of his hand '—show ye to have a passionate nature, for all ye would rather not.' She bent over his palm once again. 'Your love line is strong and true—'

'Perhaps you should take a look at Miss Seagrove's hand now,' he suggested lightly as he firmly removed his hand from further perusal.

His parents' marriage had, as far as Giles was aware, been one of mutual respect and liking, and as content as any of the arranged marriages of the *ton*. But even so, he did not believe that contentment to have prevented his father from occasionally enjoying the company of other women, and so giving Giles the rather jaundiced view that a wife was taken in order to provide the necessary heirs, a mistress for physical enjoyment, and the two were never to be found with the same woman.

Mrs Lovell gave him one of those piercing looks that saw far too much before turning to look at Lily. 'Let me take a look,' she prompted eagerly.

Giles could not remember having seen Lily's hands bare since she had reached adulthood, and now found himself looking on interestedly as she slowly removed her glove to reveal long and slender fingers, the nails kept short, no doubt in deference to the work she did about the parish. Nevertheless, her skin appeared pale and delicate in contrast to Rosa Lovell's brown and work-roughened hands as the old lady gazed down at Lily's palm.

'A long and uninterrupted lifeline, which is good,' Mrs Lovell said softly. 'A determination of nature. A yearning for travel...' She looked up as Lily's breath caught in her throat. 'A well-hidden yearning for travel,' she amended lightly. 'Again, a passionate nature,' she murmured distractedly as she touched the mound at the base of Lily's thumb. 'No man is going to be left wanting in your bed, that's for su—'

'I believe I really must be going now!' Lily's cheeks burned as she snatched her hand from the elderly lady's grasp before standing up abruptly, only to give a grimace of dismay as she realised she had accidentally knocked her booted foot against the metal mug she had previously placed upon the ground, and succeeding in tipping out the last of the tea.

The ever-watchful Mrs Lovell instantly scooped up the mug to look at the contents. 'What do we have here…?' she murmured softly.

'I thought the Romany considered the reading of tea leaves to be beneath them?' Giles Montague prompted drily.

'Not at all, there's just no money to be had from it!' the old lady dismissed scornfully. 'No one's going to part with their silver, let alone gold, to have the tea leaves read! There is something here, though.…' Her frowning attention returned to the contents of the mug.

Lily gave a firm shake of her head. 'I really do not think—'

'I see a darkness in your future,' the elderly Romany said slowly.

'A man of darkness. One who means to do you harm—' Mrs Lovell broke off her dire predictions as Lily lightly lifted the mug from her fingers. 'I was nowhere near finished.' She scowled her disapproval as Lily emptied the last of the tea dregs into the grass.

'I am sure it is better if we do not know too much about what the future may bring, Mrs Lovell, else we should all go mad with worrying about it,' Lily dismissed lightly as she set down the mug before replacing her glove, sure that she already knew which gentleman that 'darkness' referred to! 'I may rely on your presence at the well-dressing celebrations next week, Mrs Lovell?' she added briskly.

'I have said ye may….' The elderly lady still looked troubled as she rose less spryly to her feet. 'Ye will take care, Lily—'

'You must not worry about me, my dear Mrs Lovell.' She laughed dismissively as she bent instinctively to kiss one leathered brown cheek. 'I am perfectly capable of ensuring that no harm comes to me. From any gentleman,' she added firmly.

'I do not recall saying as it would be a gentleman—'

'Gentleman or otherwise, there is no one in Castonbury who wishes me harm, I do assure you,' Lily repeated before turning coolly to Giles Montague. 'My lord.' She nodded dismissively before turning quickly on her booted heel and hurrying away.

Nevertheless she felt the weight of that gentleman's gaze following her with the same heaviness as she might feel a rain cloud over her head.

'Well, laddie…?'

Giles had stood up the moment Lily fled. Now he turned to look down enquiringly at the much shorter Rosa Lovell. '"Well," Mrs Lovell…?'

Hazel-coloured eyes glittered up at him mockingly. 'I trust you have sense enough to chase a pretty lass ye desire when the opportunity arises?'

He gave a rueful shake of his head. 'I assure you I have no wish to chase Lily Seagrove, or any other "pretty lass"!' Mrs Lovell raised sceptical brows. 'You really are an outrageous rogue, Mrs Lovell!'

She gave a wry chuckle. 'I'm not so old yet as I can't see

when a handsome man desires a pretty woman. Go after her, laddie. If only to see that she comes to no harm,' she added worriedly. 'The tea leaves are never wrong, my lord. Someone means to do Lily harm. And soon, if I'm not mistaken.' A frown darkened her furrowed brow.

'And what if Lily believes that "someone" to be me?' Giles prompted drily.

Shrewd dark eyes gazed searchingly up into his before Mrs Lovell gave a slow shake of her head. 'Then she would be wrong.'

He gave a mocking acknowledgement of his head. 'I doubt Miss Seagrove would agree with you!'

'She's too young as yet to realise that a man's passion all too often leads him to behave like a fool,' the old Romany dismissed bluntly.

Giles gave a rueful burst of laughter. 'I have no idea why it is I continue to like you, Mrs Lovell!'

She eyed him teasingly. 'No?'

'No,' he confirmed drily. 'But I will do as you ask, and follow Lily. If only to set your mind at rest concerning her safe arrival back at the vicarage.'

'You tell yourself that's the reason, by all means, laddie.' Mrs Lovell gave him a condescending pat on the arm.

Giles gave another self-derisive laugh before setting out to follow Lily through the woods.

'Lily? Lily, wait!'

Lily's instinct was to increase her pace rather than reduce it as she heard Giles calling after her. She had no desire to engage in further conversation with him.

'Lily, I asked you to wait, damn it!'

Hearing that customary arrogance in Giles Montague's

voice only succeeded in making Lily all the more determined that he should not catch her, as she all but ran through the dense woodland. But she was aware of the increasingly loud crackle of the dry undergrowth as indication that Giles's much longer strides meant he was gaining on her with every step.

Giles's gaze was narrowed on his quarry as he hurried after Lily's lithe form flitting between the trees with a familiarity which spoke of her having done so many times before. As indeed she no doubt had, when she and Edward were children.

The haste needed to catch his quarry gave him sharp cause to remember the injuries he had sustained in battle as his thigh began to ache from a deep sabre wound he had received at Talavera, the scars upon his chest from Salamanca unsightly, but no longer as painful. 'Lily!' His fingers finally curled about her arm as he pulled her to a halt, glowering down at her as he swung her about to face him. 'Running away will not—'

'I am not "running away"!' She glared her indignation. 'I have merely tarried too long at Mrs Lovell's fireside and now must hurry if I am to return to the vicarage in time for lunch.' She gave a pained wince. 'You are hurting me—'

'And you were running away,' Giles repeated grimly even as he relaxed his grip on her arm.

Those green eyes flashed her displeasure as she gazed up at him challengingly. 'That would seem to imply that there is something I feel the need to run away from.'

He shrugged. 'Is there not?'

A frown appeared between those magnificent eyes. 'You think far too much of yourself, sir.'

'Perhaps that is because you choose to think far too little of me!' Giles bit out harshly.

Lily did not want to think of this gentleman at all. In any way. At any time. Ever again. She had spent far too many hours the previous night doing exactly that as she lay awake in her bed. And had succeeded in finding very few answers to the unsettling questions such thoughts had posed.

She tilted her chin. 'What is it you want from me, my lord?'

What did Giles want from Lily Seagrove?

All and everything that the astute and blunt Mrs Lovell had minutes ago stated that he did!

Seven

Giles's total awareness of Lily the evening before, and again today, now told—warned!—him that he desired nothing more at this moment than to lay her down on the soft green moss on the forest floor, an exact match in colour to her eyes, before slowly removing every article of her clothing until she lay pale and naked before him. After which he wished to remove all the pins from her hair before releasing that long cascade of ebony silk down onto her shoulders and draping it across her breasts, leaving those rosy-red tips peaking temptingly through that darkness as he lowered his head—

Oh, good heavens!

Giles's hands began to shake as he desperately tried to resist that temptation, but it was a battle he lost, as rather than releasing her and moving away, he instead began to pull Lily towards him with a determination which far surpassed any and all warnings of inner caution.

Lily's eyes widened in alarm as Giles Montague pulled her ever closer. 'What are you about...?' she managed to gasp breathlessly even as his heat once again enveloped and drew her closer.

He gave a grim smile. 'Madness,' he bit out harshly. 'Complete and utter madness!'

'Giles—'

'Say it again!' Those silver-grey eyes burned down at her with an intensity that was frightening.

'What…?' Lily could no longer think as she was pulled against the hard heat of Giles's muscled chest and the flatness of his stomach, before his arms moved about her with the implacability of steel bands.

'Say my name again, Lily!' he encouraged gruffly. 'Say it!' he repeated fiercely, his eyes now glowing with that same fervour of emotion.

This was indeed madness. But of a kind Lily had never encountered before. A madness which robbed her of all will, as she knew she could no more resist the allure of Giles Montague than he seemed to be able to resist her.

The stiffness drained from her as her body softened intimately into and against his much harder one. 'Giles,' she murmured softly.

'Again!'

'Giles,' she repeated breathlessly.

'Oh, dear God…!' Giles groaned achingly even as he lowered his head towards hers.

Her lips were soft, and she tasted of the honey she had taken in her tea, Giles very quickly discovered. He kissed her fiercely, urgently, his lips and tongue exploring the moist heat of her mouth, even as he revelled in the softness of her curves arched against him, her hands clasped onto the lapels of his jacket, as if she feared she might fall if they did not.

Giles was hungry for her. Hungry for the taste of her. The

feel of her. And it was a hunger that he knew had begun that first day they had met here in the woods, and it had only grown deeper with each subsequent meeting, until Giles knew he could no longer deny that aching hunger.

He held her tightly against him, groaning low in his throat as he moved his hands down to cup the firmness of her bottom before pulling her up and into him, her lush and slightly parted thighs becoming a tortuous friction against him.

The blood began to pump hotly, feverishly, through Giles's body, and he dragged his mouth from hers to bury his face against her throat, tasting her there even as one of his hands moved up to cup the lushness of her breast, the material of her cotton gown thin enough that he could feel the tight nipple pressing into his palm. He tasted the lobe of her ear, her cheek, before his mouth was once again on Lily's to claim her soft gasps of pleasure as the soft pad of his thumb laid siege to her breast.

Lily became lost in that same madness as Giles kissed her deeply, feverishly. Burning, consuming heat. And pleasure. An aching, pulling pleasure as Giles grasped the tip of her breast between finger and thumb, the heat building between her thighs as his lips and tongue explored the deep recesses of her mouth, evoking feelings, sensations, unlike anything she had ever known or experienced before. An aching burning heat that consumed even as it begged, pleaded, for—

For she knew not what!

Lily only knew that this pleasure was so intense, so all-consuming, that she wanted…something more. Needed… something more.

She felt she might truly go mad if she did not find relief from the pressures building ever higher inside her hot and aching body.

She gasped as she felt Giles's fingers against her flesh as he deftly unfastened the buttons at the front of her gown to pull the chemise aside and bare her breasts to his ministrations, her nipple captured between thumb and finger as he began to tug gently, rhythmically, causing a hot pool of moisture to flood between Lily's thighs.

She drew in a ragged breath as Giles wrenched his mouth from hers to once again bury the heat of his lips against her throat before moving slowly downwards, his lips and tongue a fiery caress against the slope of her other breast before she felt that heat close over the aching tip to suck deeply, the drawing, pulling sensation on her breast causing Lily's knees to buckle.

Giles followed as Lily sank to the forest floor, laying his long length down beside her on the soft moss as he continued to taste the fullness of her nipple even as his other hand moved down the slope of her slender waist, across the full curve of her hips and lower still as he gently pulled up her gown to discover she wore stockings held up with ribbons, and soft cotton drawers.

'Giles…?' She gave a strangled gasp as his hand nudged her legs apart to allow him to cup her there, that gasp turning to a groan—of pleasure, Giles hoped—as he pulled fiercely on her nipple with his lips even as he sought her silken folds amongst the fabric of her drawers.

Those silken folds parted to the caress of his fingers, a deep well of moisture dampening him as he began to stroke her, lingering as he felt her pulse and swell to his ministrations, and heard Lily's panting breaths as her pleasure deepened and grew, her hips now moving up to meet those caresses.

Giles parted those wet folds to plunge one moist finger inside her opening even as his thumb continued to stroke the bud above. He drew hungrily on her nipple, thrusting his finger, and then two, deep into her as he felt the inner walls quiver in a way which he knew signalled she was hurtling towards climax.

'Giles...!' Lily gazed up at him in alarm as she felt herself overwhelmed by unimaginable pleasure.

'Let go, damn it!' he demanded fiercely. 'Now, Lily!'

As if the encouragement was all she had needed, Lily felt as if a dam suddenly burst inside her, pulsing inward and then outward, her breath coming in aching sobs as wave after wave of that pleasure engulfed her before ripping her apart and then slowly putting her back together again.

She buried her face against Giles's chest as those waves slowly, oh-so-slowly, subsided. She felt overwhelmed and her body shook as those tremors continued to quiver through her body.

'Would you touch me now, Lily?' Giles encouraged throatily even as he grasped one of her hands in his and began to move it slowly down between their two bodies.

Lily, still weak and gasping from that overwhelming pleasure, now gasped anew as Giles cupped her hand against the lengthy bulge beneath his breeches. A living, pulsing bulge, which moved enticingly against her fingers....

A burning curiosity to know more overcame her own feelings of uncertainty as she heard Giles groan low in his throat at her touch, his head resting against her breasts as she continued to move caressing fingers against him to feel its insistent throbbing in response to her actions.

'Oh, God, again, Lily!' he pleaded gutturally as he fell back onto the mossy ground, his eyes closed, his cheeks flushed, lips slightly parted, his breathing becoming increasingly laboured.

Lily sat up, unconcerned by her bared breasts as she caressed that hard and throbbing length from root to tip, slowly, tenderly, and was rewarded by Giles's groans of pleasure. She had never dreamed, never even guessed at the pleasure Giles had just shown her, let alone realised that she might be able to give him that same pleasure....

'Touch me, Lily!' Silver eyes blazed fiercely into her own.

Lily hesitated only briefly, her curiosity once again winning out over embarrassment, her hands shaking slightly as she unfastened the buttons at the sides of his breeches to reveal white drawers beneath, her eyes opening wide as she looked down upon that pulsing hardness she had so recently caressed as it jutted through the opening at the front.

Lily found herself watching in fascination as it seemed to grow even longer and thicker under her regard, as if in silent invitation.

Giles groaned low in this throat as he watched Lily's tongue move moistly over the parted plumpness of her lips, and easily imagined how that hot little tongue might feel against him. His hot gaze moved to her bared and pert breasts, the nipples red as berries as they stood firm and puckered.

Aching, unable to resist, Giles reached up to cup one of those tempting globes, watching Lily's flushed face as he took the nipple between his thumb and finger, squeezing gently, and was instantly rewarded by her sharp intake of breath as she began to tremble and shake. 'Place your other breast in my mouth, Lily,' he encouraged throatily as he lay back against the mossy ground.

Her eyes were wide green orbs as she slowly bent over him, her breast now hanging temptingly above his mouth as he continued to caress its twin, watching the pleasure that lit her eyes and flushed her cheeks as he parted his lips to draw the plump nipple into the heat of his mouth. He continued to hold her heated gaze as he caressed, gently at first, and then deeper, harder, as he felt the fingers of her gloved hand close about him, and the rasp of those lace-covered fingers moving up and down.

'Grip me tighter, Lily.' He released her breast to groan, 'Oh, God…!' His head fell back against the moss, eyes closed, back arching, knowing he was close to reaching his own climax—

He froze, his eyes opening wide as he felt a hot, moist caress and looked down to find Lily bent over him. He was about to lose control from simply watching her tongue caressing him. 'You have to stop now, Lily!' he pleaded fiercely, but he knew his plea came too late as he felt himself pulse and release.

Lily pulled back slightly and with a hoarse cry Giles reached out to hold her gloved hand firmly in place.

Giles's throat was dry and he felt completely spent after the deepest and most satisfying climax he had ever known in his life. It was an intensity of pleasure he owed completely to Lily's ministrations and this strange and deep attraction they had for each other.

Lily's heart thundered in her chest, not breathing at all as she knew herself completely mortified by what had just transpired, as she recalled—in shocking detail!—the intimacies the two of them had just indulged in together.

'Lily…?'

She could not even look at Giles again as she drew back sharply, turning her face away to stand up and turn her back towards him with the intention of refastening her gown, only to give a low groan as she saw the state of her lace glove.

Had her actions been purely instinctive? A desire to please Giles, as he had undoubtedly pleased her? Or was her behaviour due to something else, something much more fundamental, and inherited from the mother who had given birth to her before abandoning her?

'Lily?'

She kept her back turned towards Giles as she peeled off her glove and dropped it to the ground before attempting to refasten her gown with fingers that shook uncontrollably as they refused to do her bidding.

'Here, let me,' Giles prompted huskily, his own clothing straightened to decency as he stepped forward to push Lily's hands aside so that he might refasten the buttons at the front of her gown. Her head was bent so that he could not see her features, but he was nevertheless able to feel the way she had stiffened as his fingers brushed lightly against her breasts. 'Lily?' He raised a hand with the intention of lifting her chin so that he might see her expression.

'Please…do not touch me.' She flinched before stepping away from him, her face deathly pale as she continued to stare down at the ground.

Giles gave a pained frown as his hands dropped back to his sides. 'We did nothing wrong—'

'Nothing wrong!' she repeated incredulously as she finally looked up at him, those moss-coloured eyes glittering brightly.

Whether with tears or anger, Giles was as yet unsure…

She gave a jerky shake of her head and groaned. 'If our shocking behaviour just now were ever to become public knowledge…!'

'I have no intention of telling anyone,' he said quietly. 'Have you?'

She began to pace agitatedly. 'The Duke of Rothermere has always made these woods available for the use of the people in the village, and as such any one of them could have… could have—'

'Chanced to walk by whilst we were lost to the throes of passion?' Giles supplied evenly, wishing to know for certain this conversation was going in the direction he believed it was before he gave suitable reaction to it.

'Exactly!' Lily groaned.

His mouth twisted derisively. 'The chances of that are minimal.'

'But not impossible!'

'No...' he accepted abruptly.

She gave a low and keening wail as she continued to pace. 'What little standing I have in the village will be destroyed—destroyed!—if our indiscretion should ever become known!'

Giles drew himself up warily. 'Exactly what is it that you require of me, Lily?'

Lily ceased her pacing to look across at him as she heard the chill in his tone, not in the least encouraged by the ice she also detected in his gaze, or the firm set of his jaw and thinned lips. Those very same lips which had kissed and known her so intimately only minutes ago....

She gave a slow and wary shake of her head. 'I do not remember saying that I required anything of you.'

Those sculptured lips twisted derisively. 'But I sense that you do, nevertheless.'

'I—' She swallowed, her throat having gone dry. 'I cannot think what to do or say at this moment.' She could only feel! And her feelings were ones of humiliation and regret.

Humiliation that she had succumbed so quickly and so completely to Giles's seduction.

Regret that her actions, if they should become known, would reflect badly on the kind and gentle Mr and Mrs Seagrove, for having taken one such as her into their hearts and home.

'Enlighten me, Lily,' Giles bit out harshly. 'Can this possibly be the same manner in which you persuaded the more gullible Edward into offering you marriage?'

'I— What…?' Lily gave a dazed shake of her head.

'I believe my words were clear enough, Lily.' Giles's mouth had thinned as he looked disdainfully down the long length of his nose at her. 'If not, let me reiterate that I am curious to know if this was the way in which you secured a marriage proposal from my brother Edward? By allowing him to make love to you, and afterwards suggesting a scandal?' he said coldly.

What little colour had returned to her cheeks as she paced so agitatedly now drained away completely, the only colour in her face now being those huge moss-green eyes that looked up at him in disbelief. 'How dare you? How could you even suggest such a thing?' she finally gasped. 'You think that I—? You believe that I have behaved in that shameless manner before today? With Edward, of all people!' she added incredulously. 'And that I did so in order to entrap him into marriage?'

What else was Giles to think, when Lily's first concern had been for her own good reputation if their indiscretion today should ever be realised? A reputation which Giles already had serious reasons to doubt.

His jaw tightened. 'I believe I asked if that was the manner in which his marriage proposal came about.'

Her chin rose challengingly as she informed him, 'I received no marriage proposal from Edward!'

If that had indeed been the case, Giles thought, then the omission had only been because Edward had had the foresight to first inform Giles of his intentions towards Lily. Intentions Giles had spoken firmly against, advising Edward, if he must, to make the woman his mistress but never his wife. The heated manner of their own lovemaking just now, and Lily's less than virginal responses—surely no virgin could have touched him as Lily had?—would seem to indicate that Edward had taken that advice, after all.

At least Edward had had carnal knowledge of the woman he had claimed to love before he died, but at the same time that put Giles in the position of having made love to his brother's lover! A young and beautiful woman who now seemed intent upon using her sensual charms to ensnare yet another Montague into marriage, this time the heir presumptive to the dukedom!

'Nor will you receive one from me,' Giles informed her coldly. 'But the position as my mistress may be available if you are at all interested in taking up that role.'

And if she said yes, what would he do then? Would he take her to mistress, after all, or do the sensible thing and turn away from the temptation she so obviously represented to him?

With his body still satiated from the pleasure he had known at Lily's touch, Giles had no immediate answer.

Lily recoiled as if she had been struck. Indeed, she felt as if she had. This man, a man whom she had allowed to make love to her and whom she had made love to, dared to insult her still further by offering her a position as his mistress!

'You are sensual enough.' Giles seemed to take her silence as indication she was considering his suggestion. 'And with a little tutoring as to my personal preferences, I am sure that we would deal very well together in the bedchamber. Your adoptive father's friendship with mine poses something of a problem, of course, but as long as we are both discreet I see no reason why either of them needs ever know of the arrangement. There are several empty cottages on the estate in which we might meet—'

'Stop!' Lily managed to gasp when she finally recovered her breath enough to speak, her emotions in turmoil. 'I do not— You—' She gave a protesting shake of her head. 'How dare you even suggest such a demeaning arrangement to me!' she accused. 'How dare you!'

He shrugged those broad shoulders. 'It is all you will ever receive from me. My wife, when I choose to take one, will certainly not have been used by my brother first, nor be the illegitimate offspring of a Gypsy!' His top lip curled back disdainfully.

Lily felt as if she might faint. Or scream. Or hit something. Preferably Giles Montague, for daring to stand there looking at her so contemptuously as he offered her the position as his mistress!

'I do not think so!' Giles reached out and grasped Lily's slender wrist as her hand swung upwards with the obvious intention of slapping him on the cheek, just as she had done a year ago. 'Shall I take it from your response that your answer is no?' He looked down at her with hard mockery as he continued to hold her immobile.

'You may—because my answer is most certainly no!' She wrenched her arm out of his grasp, and no doubt bruised her delicate flesh in the process.

'Then there would appear to be nothing further for the two of us to discuss.' Giles gave an abrupt inclination of his head before bending down to pick up his hat from where he had dropped it earlier, and then turned on his heel to stride away in the direction of home.

But in full knowledge that it had been Lily, rather he, who had been the one to turn down the role as his mistress.

Eight

'You have seemed very quiet these past few days, my dear....' Mr Seagrove looked across the luncheon table at Lily. 'The arrangements for the well-dressing are not proving too much for you, I hope, on top of all the other work you do about the parish?'

It was that very work about the parish which Lily believed to have kept her sane these past three days!

Ordinarily she would have shared her confused feelings by speaking, or writing of them, to her friend Lady Phaedra, but as Phaedra was Giles's sister, Lily had no one in whom she might confide.

Instead she had kept herself too busy to think during the day, and too tired to do anything other than fall straight to sleep in her bedchamber at night. Because she dare not allow herself the time to think, refused to think, about Giles Montague, or the things that had transpired between them the last time they had been alone together. Something which had proved somewhat difficult the day following their lovemaking, when the tips of her breasts had felt sensitive, and between her thighs had suffered a similar soreness.

She had seen Giles several times whilst she was out and about in the village, but thankfully always at a distance, either riding about the estate on his black steed, or in one of the ducal carriages, no doubt on his way to Buxton in pursuit of business, or possibly pleasure. And each time she had chanced to see him Lily had inwardly shrivelled with mortification as she was once again reminded of their lovemaking, and the humiliating conversation which had followed.

'Not at all, Father,' she now answered her adoptive father evenly. 'Indeed, once Mrs Stratton and I have discussed the last details this evening all arrangements for the well-dressing celebrations should be well in hand.'

Mr Seagrove nodded. 'Then perhaps there is some other reason for the air of…melancholy I have sensed in you these past three days?'

The fact that her adoptive father was aware of exactly how long Lily had been less than her cheerful self was cause for concern; his curiosity would certainly be piqued if he were ever to learn that it was the same day upon which she had last visited with Mrs Lovell, and Giles Montague had joined the two women shortly thereafter!

'I believe there has been thunder in the air as a precursor to the storm, and I have merely suffered a headache because of it,' she dismissed lightly. 'I am sure I shall be completely recovered now that the weather has broken.' The unseasonal rain was currently lashing down outside their cottage, with the occasional flash of lightning, quickly followed by a crash of thunder.

'Let us hope that there will not be too much damage to crops or property,' the vicar remarked ruefully as he glanced out of the window at the storm raging outside. 'No doubt Sir Nathan will enjoy regaling me with news of it over dinner this evening, if that should prove to be the case,' he added with less than his usual forebearance.

Lily could not help but smile at Mr Seagrove's obvious lack of enthusiasm for the dinner he was to take this evening at the home of Sir Nathan Samuelson, a single and eligible gentleman of forty or so years who owned a small estate in the area, but also a man who was known to be rather a dull, dour character.

Indeed, Sir Nathan was twice Lily's age at least, and had such an unappealing nature, she had felt less than enthusiastic when several times during the past year Sir Nathan had appeared to show a preference for her company. She had certainly been relieved to have the excuse of her previous engagement with Mrs Stratton this evening, as a polite way of refusing Sir Nathan's invitation for her to join her father and him for dinner!

Sir Nathan did possibly have one thing in his favour, however, in that he made no secret of the fact that he was no more enamoured of the male members of the Montague family than she now was—in Lily's case, one member of that family in particular!

'No doubt,' Lily agreed softly. 'And now, if you will excuse me, Father, I believe the rain is lessening at last, and I should perhaps call upon Mrs Lovell to ensure all is well with her.'

Aware of Mrs Lovell's shrewdness of nature, and wishing to avoid any questions that elderly lady might have in regard to Lily's previous visit, she had avoided returning to the Romany camp, but knew she could delay no longer, knowing that whilst the elderly lady stayed here Mr Seagrove considered her as much one of his parishioners as any who lived in the village.

Besides which, yesterday had been the anniversary of the death of Mrs Lovell's son, and Lily wished to reassure herself that the elderly lady had not suffered any ill effects from that sad day. Out of respect for her grief Lily had herself visited the graveyard beside the church yesterday and placed daffodils on the grave of Matthew Lovell, presuming the wildflowers already arranged there to be from Mrs Lovell.

She stood up now, somewhat relieved they were at the end of their meal rather than the beginning of it; she had no wish for her father to delve further into the reasons for her preoccupation. 'I believe I will take Mrs Lovell some fresh milk and eggs.'

'I am sure she and her nephew will appreciate your thoughtfulness.' Mr Seagrove smiled his approval of the suggestion.

'Her nephew…?' Lily raised surprised brows as she recalled the elderly Romany telling her that the rest of her tribe had travelled on a pilgrimage to France, and would not be joining her for several weeks.

'Judah Lovell.' The vicar nodded. 'I chanced to meet him in the village yesterday. He informed me it is many years since he returned to Castonbury, so you perhaps will not remember him. A very friendly and cheerful young man. He is the son of Mrs Lovell's deceased brother-in-law, I believe.'

'No, I cannot say I ever remember meeting a Judah Lovell… But it is very kind of him to join his aunt,' Lily approved warmly, pleased to know that Judah Lovell had arrived in time to be with his aunt on the anniversary of her son's death. 'I will take some extra eggs and milk, in that case.' She nodded decisively; hopefully the presence of Mrs Lovell's nephew would also help to discourage that lady from

asking Lily any personal questions concerning her abrupt departure three days ago and Giles Montague's pursuit of her
only minutes later!

The rain had stopped falling some time ago. Giles's gaze
narrowed as he sat atop his horse and looked in satisfaction
at the men preparing the fields for the winter crop, having
found himself drawn into matters about the estate in spite of
himself. Indeed, he had been kept very busy about the estate
over the past few days, and had also made another visit alone
to the family lawyers in Buxton, so that he might further
discuss the Montague family's financial situation with them
without his father being present.

The news Giles had received from those gentlemen was
every bit as dire as he had initially feared it to be, with his father having made the same mistake as so many other members
of the *ton* the previous year, when news had reached London
that Wellington was in retreat in Brussels and may possibly
lose the battle completely. Fearing large government expen-
diture on a continuing war, or possibly even a French inva-
sion of England itself, many—including Giles's father, it now
transpired—had sold off their investments in 'consols,' and at
a tremendous loss.

It was these very investments which had provided the Montague family with its twice-yearly income, the loss of which
had now left the estate almost bankrupt, and also accounted
for the money not being available for work to be carried out
about the estate as usual.

There was still the considerable inheritance left to Jamie
by their mother, as the eldest son, of course, but the same law
governed the retrieval of that as it did the inheritance of the

title of Marquis of Hatherton; neither one could be claimed until irrefutable proof of Jamie's death could be produced.

And through all of these worries, Giles also had the added burden of the memory of that last encounter with Lily Seagrove....

Just to think of what he now believed to have been her machinations and manipulations was enough to bring about a return of those feelings of revulsion Giles had experienced upon realising they had not been indulging a shared passion, as he had believed at the time, but that he had been deliberately and shamelessly manoeuvred into a position where Lily Seagrove had believed he would have no choice but to make her an offer of marriage or risk possible exposure as her seducer.

His prompt and cold response to those less than subtle hints had put paid to any such idea of blackmail, he hoped!

Certainly Giles had so far not received a visit from a shocked and distressed Mr Seagrove, with that gentleman demanding Giles make suitable amends—namely by an offer of marriage—for having brought possible disgrace upon his adopted daughter.

Neither, surprisingly, had Giles heard anything further from that young woman herself.

Which he had quite expected to at any moment during the past three days. After all, there were only two of the Montague sons left alive and unmarried, and Harry's responsibilities in London meant that for the main part he remained well out of range of Miss Seagrove's reach. Giles could only wish that he had remained so too!

Instead of which he was here and available at Castonbury, and circumstances now dictated he had no choice but to remain here for some time to come. Quite how he and Lily

Seagrove were to conduct themselves towards each other for the duration of that time Giles could not even begin to guess, most especially when they were in the presence of the amiable Mr Seagrove. He—

A flash of colour—grey or possibly blue?—to the right of his vision, caught and held his attention, his gaze frosting over, mouth thinning, jaw tightening, as he recognised Lily Seagrove walking along the lane which edged the Castonbury woods.

And looking for all intents and purposes as if, following the rain, she were on a pleasurable stroll and enjoying the beauty of the freshened countryside!

Lily avoided going through the woods at Castonbury Park and instead took the much longer way along the still-dampened lane to the Romany encampment, carrying in a basket the eggs and pitcher of milk intended for Mrs Lovell and her nephew; Lily had no wish to ever again enter those woods, let alone see or visit the place of her seduction and humiliation.

Just to think of Giles's coldness when he had insulted her was enough to make Lily shudder and tremble in mortification.

She was still unsure as to why he should believe she had seduced Edward, but his disparaging reference to her supposed Romany heritage had been unmistakable. And how she hated him for it! Indeed, Lily now wondered what demon could possibly have taken possession of her for her ever to have behaved in such a shameless fashion in Giles's arms three days ago. She—

'And what's a pretty maid like you doing wandering about the countryside all on yer lonesome?'

Lily's expression was curious rather than alarmed as she

turned to face the owner of that cheerfully teasing voice, finding herself looking at a young man dressed in a shabby brown jacket, a collarless white shirt and thick black trousers over heavy, worn boots. His overlong hair glinted in the sunshine that had appeared after the rain and his dark eyes twinkled merrily in his boyishly handsome face as he stepped out of the woods directly in front of her.

The fact that Lily did not recognise him, or he her, would seem to imply he was a stranger to these parts. Mrs Lovell's nephew, perhaps? 'Good day to you, sir,' she returned politely. 'Do I have the pleasure of addressing Mrs Lovell's nephew?'

'Ye do, indeed,' he confirmed lightly, the slightest hint of an Irish accent in his tone. 'Judah Lovell's the name. And who might you be, my lovely?'

Such familiarity would certainly not be acceptable in a gentleman, but Lily took no offence, used as she was to Mrs Lovell's often less than respectful manner. 'Miss Lily Seagrove, daughter of the Reverend Mr Seagrove, whom I believe you met yesterday,' she supplied softly. 'And I am on my way to visit with your aunt.'

'Then it's fortuitous that the two of us chanced to meet, so it is,' Judah Lovell came back cheerfully. 'Would ye care to take my arm so that I might ensure you don't trip over any tree roots on the way there?' The sleeve of his shabby jacket looked less than clean as he offered her his arm.

It placed Lily in something of a quandary. It was not really seemly for her to be alone with this handsome young Romany, but Mr Seagrove had mentioned meeting Mr Lovell yesterday, and had seemed to find him acceptable. And as they were both on their way to Mrs Lovell's camp it would surely be rude of Lily to refuse to accompany him.... 'That is very kind of you, Mr Lovell, thank you.' She maintained a suitable distance as she tucked her hand lightly into the crook of his arm.

★ ★ ★

Giles instinctively urged Genghis forward as he saw a brawny man step out of the woods in front of Lily Seagrove, only to then check his restless mount as he belatedly recognised the young man as Mrs Lovell's nephew Judah, who Giles had encountered yesterday when that young man came to enquire about work on the estate, employment the young Romany should be about at the present moment.

Giles continued to watch as the two appeared to converse pleasantly together for a minute or two, before Lily took that young gentleman's arm and happily accompanied him into the darkness of the woods.

Indicating, perhaps, that the meeting between the handsome young Romany and Lily Seagrove was an arranged one?

A case of like calling to like?

Certainly, if Lily Seagrove's true heritage was indeed that of the Romany, then the young and roguishly handsome Judah Lovell was far more suited to being her lover than Giles could ever be.

A realisation which left a surprisingly sour taste in Giles's mouth.

Lily was disappointed to find Mrs Lovell was not in her usual place beside the fire when she and Judah entered the encampment a short time later. Disappointed, and not a little uncomfortable. Walking alone through the woods with Judah would no doubt be considered improper by some, but remaining alone with him here, when his aunt was not present, was entirely unacceptable.

'Aunt Rosa has no doubt gone to gather some herbs for her medicines and potions while the stew cooks,' Judah said. 'Would you care for some tea while we wait for her return?'

The stew bubbling in a pot over the fire seemed to suggest that Judah's assertion was correct, but even so… 'I—'

'What are you doing back here so soon?'

Lily's relief at Mrs Lovell's return, which spared her from the embarrassment of explaining to Judah that she could not stay, was tempered somewhat by the harshness she detected in the old lady's tone. She had always welcomed Lily's visits in the past.

Did she know something of what had transpired between Giles and Lily following her last visit?

Her cheeks were ablaze with those memories as she turned to face the elderly Romany, her guilty expression turning to one of puzzlement as she saw that Mrs Lovell was looking accusingly at her nephew rather than at Lily.

'I thought you said as His Lordship had given you work in the fields today,' the elderly woman added sharply.

'I came back for some of yer stew for me lunch.' Judah shrugged unconcernedly. 'And 'ad the good fortune to meet the beautiful Miss Seagrove on the way,' he added flirtatiously, that merry twinkle once again in his dark eyes as he looked at her admiringly.

Mrs Lovell's gaze narrowed disapprovingly. 'See about your lunch, lad, and leave Miss Seagrove to me,' she instructed gruffly.

Her nephew gave a shrug. 'The fields'll still be there whether I return in ten minutes or an hour.'

'Lord Giles may not see it in quite the same way,' his aunt said drily.

Judah Lovell grinned unabashedly. 'What Lord Giles don't know ain't gonna hurt him!'

'It's that attitude that gets us a bad name!' Mrs Lovell gave an exasperated shake of her head as she moved to ladle some of the delicious-smelling stew into a wooden bowl. 'Take that with you and get along back to work!' She thrust the bowl into her nephew's work-roughened hands.

'Da always said ye were a terrible slave-driver!' Judah grinned unrepentantly as he easily ducked the swipe his aunt took at him with the ladle from the stew. 'No doubt I'll be seeing ye again soon, Miss Seagrove,' he added cheekily, before turning to whistle a merry tune as he went on his way.

Lily had not known what to think as she listened to the exchange between aunt and nephew, never having heard Mrs Lovell speak quite that harshly to anyone before, although Judah had not seemed at all abashed by it.

She turned to look curiously at Mrs Lovell, who muttered to herself as she banged and clashed pots together for what seemed no apparent reason. 'You seem somewhat…agitated today, Mrs Lovell,' Lily prompted after several minutes of this pointless exercise.

'I seems agitated because it's what I am!' Piercing eyes, which appeared more brown today than blue or green, glared across the fire at Lily. 'What do you think the Reverend Seagrove would have to say to me if'n he was to learn I returned to me fireside to find his daughter alone here with me nephew?'

Lily could not even pretend not to be taken aback by the force of the elderly lady's accusing tone. She gave a pained frown as she answered calmly. 'My father knows and trusts me well enough to realise that the circumstances of our being together were perfectly innocent.'

'Your father, mebbe.' Mrs Lovell nodded impatiently. 'But what of others in the village? What sort of scandal do ye think there'd be if'n it became known you've been alone here with my young rogue of a nephew?' She gave an exasperated shake of her head.

Lily blinked. 'I assure you that nothing untoward happened—'

'It's not me as needs reassuring.' Mrs Lovell gave an exasperated sigh. 'Gossip is gossip, and it's been known in the past to bring disgrace upon a lovely lass such as yourself.'

Lily sat down abruptly on one of the logs placed about the fireside. They were much as they had been three days ago when Giles had sat down beside her, before the two of them had indulged in exactly the sort of scandalous behaviour Mrs Lovell was now saying that people might suspect had occurred between her nephew and Lily, if their time here alone together were ever to become known!

'Now there's no need to look so downhearted.' Mrs Lovell obviously regretted her earlier sharpness as she reached over to pat Lily's clenched hands together upon her knees. 'It's yourself as I'm thinking of, and no one else. Judah has been across the sea in Ireland with his da since he was a boy, and I has no doubts as there's a bairn or two over there with his yellow hair and wicked black eyes!'

'Mrs Lovell!' Lily felt the warmth of colour enter her cheeks.

'Just promise me you'll stay well away from the likes of him,' the older woman pressured firmly.

'As Mr Lovell has already stated, the two of us only met today by chance,' Lily assured huskily.

Mrs Lovell nodded. 'Promise me it won't happen again.'

Lily grimaced. 'Good manners would prevent me from being rude to Mr Lovell if we were to meet again by chance.'

'Hmmph!' The elderly Romany gave a dismissive snort. 'With Black Jack Lovell as a father Judah's got no more idea of what's mannerly than the cows in the fields!'

Lily smiled ruefully. 'But Mr and Mrs Seagrove have ensured that I do.'

'Now just ye take heed of me, young lady!' Mrs Lovell gave

a firm shake of her head. 'Good manners or no, ye must stay away from him, or I has no doubts as you'll live to regret it, the same as a lot of other beautiful young women have likely had reason to!'

Lily gave a surprised laugh. 'That is not a particularly…familial warning, Mrs Lovell.'

'Familial, be dem——!' The elderly Romany's mouth tightened as she broke off abruptly. 'If'n ye won't give me your promise, then I'll have to insist ye don't come visiting me no more.'

'Mrs Lovell!' Lily straightened in shock at the other woman's obvious vehemence of purpose. 'If it bothers you so much, then yes, of course I must give you my promise, my dear Mrs Lovell.'

Those shrewd eyes brightened. 'As you'll stay away from Judah.'

She gave a gracious inclination of her head. 'I promise I will do everything I may to avoid finding myself alone in the company of your nephew, yes.'

The older woman visibly relaxed. 'I don't mean to be——' She gave a shake of her head. 'It's just—he's a young rogue, and too much like his father to be trusted alone with any pretty maid, you understand?'

'I believe so…' Lily nodded slowly.

Just thinking of the intimacies she had shared in the woods three days ago with Giles Montague was more than enough reason for Lily to understand the dangers Mrs Lovell alluded to.

If that occurrence was anything to go by, Lily could not be trusted at all. She would do well to mind Mrs Lovell's advice with respect to *all* men, whether gentleman or not!

Nine

....

'Would you care to explain exactly what it is you are doing here alone and so late at night?'

Lily halted as if frozen. Which it felt as if she truly might be, in blood as well as in body and spirit, as she easily recognised Giles Montague's voice speaking to her in the darkness.

Her meeting with Mrs Stratton having passed satisfactorily, it had indeed been Lily's intention to now walk back to the vicarage alone, just as she had walked here earlier, Mr Seagrove having required their ancient carriage this evening to take him to Sir Nathan's home for dinner.

But Lily had not realised quite how late it was, or how dark it had become, whilst she and Mrs Stratton talked so amiably together. She would certainly have hoped, as she left quietly and unobtrusively through the servants' entrance at the back of Castonbury Park, before hurrying in the direction of the path and gate opening out to the lane, not to find herself face to face with Giles Montague, of all people!

Although 'face to face' was not an accurate description as

yet, when Lily had still to turn in order to look at that gentleman!

'Well?' Giles prompted harshly as Lily Seagrove kept her
back firmly turned towards him, her shoulders appearing stiff
beneath the darkness of her cloak, with a pale bonnet covering her dark curls.

He had decided to take a stroll towards the stables as he
smoked his cigar after enjoying an early dinner with his father, lingering there to chat with head groom Tom Anderson
before walking back to the house, only to come to an abrupt
halt in the shadows as he had spied Lily Seagrove leaving by
the back of the house, her movements appearing almost furtive
as she looked first one way and then the other, before dash-
ing across the yard towards the pathway leading down to the
lane. A lane which was so dark and shadowed it was impossible to distinguish from the surrounding trees!

Giles's mouth tightened ominously. 'I swear, Lily, if you do
not soon answer me—'

'I have every intention of answering you, my lord.' She
turned abruptly, her face appearing very pale in the moonlight, lashes downcast rather than turned up at him, although
her chin was raised at its usual stubborn angle. 'I am here because I have called on Mrs Stratton and now intend to walk
back to the vicarage.'

'In the dark and alone?'

She shrugged dismissively. 'My father had need of the carriage this evening, and it is no hardship at all for me to walk
down a lane I have known for the whole of my life.'

'A lane which at this moment is very dark and deserted,'
Giles bit out impatiently. 'But perhaps it will not remain the
latter for long if you have arranged to meet someone along
the way...' he added scornfully.

Those dark lashes rose as Lily Seagrove gave him a startled look. 'And why might I have done that?'

Giles looked down at her coldly as he resisted the hurt reproach in her pale eyes, knowing his anger was directed towards himself as much as Lily. He had fallen as much into a tangle over this particular young woman as his brother Edward had a year ago.

Unlike Edward, Giles did not believe there to be anything more than desires involved in his intentions towards Lily, but there was no denying that he did desire her. Still. Even after discovering her pretty performance yesterday was an act, and seeing her with Judah Lovell earlier today...

There was just something too appealing about the wild passion he knew burned beneath the innocent beauty of Lily's eyes and the fineness of her features. A passion which had resulted in her reaching a physical climax in his arms, and which Giles had answered in kind beneath the caress of her fingers. Those same caresses which Giles had recalled and relived ever since in an effort to rid himself of this ridiculous desire he felt to possess her completely!

He had no intention of becoming involved with any of the local women whilst he was here, although he could perhaps have sought release by riding over to Buxton and seeking out some willing woman there. But somehow the thought of making love to any woman but Lily Seagrove had not appealed.

And still did not, if the tightening in his breeches, just at sight and smell of her light and floral perfume as she shook those dark curls, was any indication!

He eyed her impatiently. 'It is quite useless for you to attempt to deny the possibility of such a tryst, Lily, when earlier today I saw you enter the woods with Judah Lovell!'

She gasped. 'I— You—' She gave another shake of her head,

those dark curls caressing the paleness of her cheeks. 'I am sure there was nothing for you to see, my lord.' Her voice was low and husky when she finally managed to speak.

'No?' He raised dark brows. 'The two of you seemed to be…well acquainted.'

A frown appeared between her eyes. 'I had never met him before today, and no doubt when you saw the two of us together he was merely offering to accompany me on my visit to his aunt.'

'Indeed?'

'Yes—indeed!' Lily felt stung into snapping indignantly, irritated beyond words that it should have been Giles Montague, of all people, to see her at that moment. He had clearly drawn his own condemning conclusions, which she already knew he would have been only too pleased to make where she was concerned.

'At a time when Mr Lovell should, by rights, have been at work in the fields at Castonbury Park,' he added impatiently.

'Your arrangement with Mr Lovell is not my concern,' Lily dismissed. 'I only know that he behaved the perfect gentleman throughout our own meeting earlier today.'

'As opposed to…?' Giles's voice was dangerously soft.

A danger Lily chose not to heed. 'As opposed to those who should, but obviously choose not to, behave as such!'

His mouth thinned with displeasure. 'You are referring to me, no doubt?'

'No doubt,' she confirmed coldly.

A derisive smile curved those sculptured lips, the darkness of his clothing and the snowy white linen seeming to indicate he was dressed for dinner. 'Oh, I assure you, Lily, I have no difficulty whatsoever in behaving the gentleman—when I believe the lady to whom I am talking warrants such niceties!'

Lily's eyes widened indignantly. 'You—'

'I believe I have advised against repeating this once before,' Giles warned between gritted teeth even as he reached out and grasped the wrist of the hand Lily Seagrove had once again raised with the obvious intention of striking him. 'Unless you are goading me into retaliating?'

She gasped. 'You would strike a woman?'

'No,' he assured softly, eyes narrowed. 'But if you were to strike me, I should very much enjoy putting you over my shoulder before carrying you into the stables, throwing you down upon the straw in one of the stalls before making love to you with all the enthusiasm the stallion shows the mare!'

Lily had felt herself go deathly pale as each successive—and shocking!—word left Giles Montague's scornful lips, so much so that her own lips now felt numb, and her mouth and throat so dry that she could not have spoken even if she had been able to think of anything she might say in answer to such deliberate crudeness of speech.

A crudeness which had nevertheless caused a rush of liquid heat between her thighs, and also rendered her breasts hot and aching.

'Nothing to say?' Giles Montague raised one arrogantly mocking brow. 'Perhaps that is because you find the idea of such a…wild coupling to be arousing?'

To her everlasting shame, Lily knew that was exactly how his words had affected her!

To a degree that her breasts now felt so swollen and aching she could barely breathe, and the hot dampness between her thighs had become a veritable flood as she began to throb and ache with a desire to know the same completion she had experienced once before under the expert attentions of this gentleman's caressing fingers.

Lily attempted to swallow and then moisten the dryness of her lips, and instead shook her head in denial as her tongue refused to do her bidding.

Grey eyes glittered down at her knowingly and hard lips smiled in satisfaction at her silence. 'Indeed, I assure you I would be only too happy to oblige, Miss Seagrove—' he managed to invest a wealth of insult into the formality '—but having just come from the stables myself, I am fully aware that Tom Anderson is still there tending to one of the horses. Unless, of course, you would find having Old Tom as audience to our lovemaking to be even more…stimulating?'

'You are being both disgusting and crude!' Lily finally managed to gasp her outrage.

Yes, that was exactly what he was being, Giles acknowledged, disgusted with himself. Just as he was also aware that it had been Lily's disparaging remarks to him that were responsible, in part, for goading him into being so drawn into the problems now besetting the Castonbury estate, when his initial intention had been to visit briefly before leaving again for the entertainments of London.

He drew himself up to his full height. 'I apologise, Miss Seagrove,' he bit out curtly. 'A single…taste of your passions does not entitle me to insult and abuse you simply because I do not approve of the next man upon whom you choose to bestow those same favours.'

She released an incredulous gasp. 'Only you could possibly contrive to make an apology sound even more insulting than the original slight!'

He gave a humourless smile. 'Perhaps that is because only I know of your true nature, Miss Seagrove?'

She gave a slow shake of her head. 'And perhaps you do

not know me at all, my lord,' she spoke quietly. 'Now, if you will excuse me—'

'I asked if it is your intention to meet with Judah Lovell on your way home?' he demanded harshly as he reached out and clasped her arm.

'Not that it is any of your business, but no, it is not!' Her eyes flashed in the darkness before she looked down at that restraining hand. 'Now release me, sir, before I am forced to scream and alert Tom Anderson, and no doubt others of your household staff, to my imminent danger.' She glared up at him in challenge.

Giles's hand dropped slowly back to his side as he looked down at her in grudging admiration. 'You are in no danger from me, I assure you. Of a repeat of our time together three days ago, or anything else. Which is not to say,' he continued firmly, 'that you would not find yourself in such danger from others if you are allowed to walk home alone in the dark. Did you not heed anything of what Mrs Lovell told you with regard to the "dark and dangerous man" who means to "do you harm"?' he added derisively.

'Why should I, when it is clear the only person who is a danger to me stands before me right now?' Lily came back challengingly.

'I am?' Giles's mouth was tight with displeasure.

'Do not look so surprised by my deductions, my lord,' she taunted. 'Your crudeness this evening is but another example of how much you enjoy hurting me. As such,' she continued over his protestations, 'Mrs Lovell's dire predictions or otherwise, I would still prefer to face alone whatever dangers may lie in wait in the darkness for me, than be forced to suffer your insulting company another moment longer!' She turned firmly on her heel before marching away.

Admiration gleamed grudgingly in Giles's eyes and he continued to watch Lily until she had disappeared into the darkness. A totally futile gesture of defiance, of course, when his own father's friendship with Mr Seagrove at least dictated that Giles could not allow that gentleman's daughter to roam about the darkness of the countryside alone.

Nor did he like the idea that Lily had so obviously decided that he was a danger to her safety.

As to Giles enjoying hurting her—he knew he would far rather pleasure Lily than hurt her....

Lily barely had time to stumble blindly along the pathway and out onto the lane, as hot tears tracked down her cheeks, before she heard the sound of something moving stealthily through the forest beside her, accompanied by the sound of loud and laboured breathing.

One of the deer allowed to roam the Park, perhaps?

Or possibly a fox, or a badger?

Or perhaps one of the cows had escaped from the field?

Whatever it was it appeared to be coming ever closer!

Lily's tears ceased and she stumbled slightly as she continued walking whilst turning to look nervously into the depths of the woodland that now seemed so much darker and more menacing than it had in daylight. She wished she had not so rashly refused Giles Montague's offer to accompany her home; she may have every reason to consider him the most obnoxious gentleman she had ever met, but she had no doubt that his presence would have ensured that no harm came to her. From anyone but himself, at least!

None of which was at all comforting when Lily was now so obviously alone and vulnerable to whatever might be chasing her...

She gasped, unable to move, even her heart seeming to stop beating, as she saw a pair of glittering eyes fast approaching before a huge black beast rushed out of the forest towards her, snorting loudly, and slathering at the mouth, before it rose up on its back legs and—

'Down, Genghis!'

Lily's eyes widened even further at the harsh sound of Giles Montague's voice in the darkness, and she stumbled back as she realised that voice was coming from the back of that huge and glittery-eyed black beast.

But she had no time to think further, even to attempt to turn and run, as hands reached down to painfully grasp the tops of her arms and she was lifted up to sit sideways on the back of that huge black beast as it began to heave and buck beneath her!

'Easy, Genghis,' Giles softly soothed his mount again. 'Genghis only eats stubbornly unaccompanied young ladies on Fridays, and today is Thursday, I believe,' he drawled tauntingly as he now easily held the skittish Genghis in check with one hand on the reins whilst holding the warmth of Lily Seagrove against his chest with the other.

Lily only seemed to cling to the lapels of Giles's jacket all the tighter as she turned her face into his waistcoat. 'Please put me down at once…' she instructed shakily, her voice barely more than a whisper.

Giles scowled in the darkness. 'Stop being ridiculous, Lily—'

'It is not ridiculous when I have never learnt to ride!' She raised her head to glare up at him, her eyes large in the pale oval of her face.

'Then that is clearly an oversight in your education which is about to be remedied.' Giles ignored her protest, his arm tightening about her slender waist as he turned Genghis in the direction of the village. The muscles in his thigh began to ache from the effort of controlling Genghis and the old sabre wound he had sustained on the Continent.

'I insist you return me to the ground, at once!' Lily repeated fiercely as she began to struggle in his arms, only to still again as the horse beneath her showed his displeasure by tossing back his head, and causing the heavy black mane to whip lightly across her cheek. 'Giles, please…!' She looked up at him in appeal.

He scowled down at her, his face appearing all hard planes and angles in the moonlight. 'You are completely mistaken if you think I intend to walk to the village when I might ride. As it is I had to leave the stables so quickly I am without benefit of the comfort of a saddle!'

'I did not ask that you accompany me to the village.'

'And yet here I am,' he pointed out as he looked grimly ahead.

Lily gave an impatient shake of her head. 'If you insist on accompanying me—'

'I do.'

She heaved a shaky sigh. 'Then by all means you must ride. I shall walk beside you.'

'That is utterly preposterous when we have a perfectly good horse we might both ride!' he bit out scathingly as he urged the mount into a slow trot.

It was a move which instantly prompted Lily to cling all the tighter to Giles's lapels as that heated horseflesh surged and dipped precariously beneath her thighs. 'I…admire horses tremendously,' she spoke huskily. 'Have always believed them to be splendid, beautiful creatures—'

'I am sure Genghis will be pleased to hear it!'

'—but I have never wished, have no wish still, ever to be upon the back of one,' she continued raggedly. 'Edward tried several times to encourage me to learn to ride, but I—I could not…cannot…bring myself to do so. The truth is…' She drew in a deep breath. 'The truth is I have always been rather nervous of being too close to all that—that uncontrolled power!' she admitted huskily, at the same time aware that she was now just as nervous of being near Giles Montague's uncontrolled power! Her sudden embarrassment caused her to rush into further speech. 'Mabel is the only horse I have ever been able to dare approach—'

'Mabel…?'

'My father's old mare.'

Giles easily recalled the nondescript brown mare which he had seen in front of the vicar's equally as decrepit carriage. 'There is no comparison between a docile nag of that kind and a fine hunter like Genghis!' he snorted dismissively.

'Which is why I have asked that you put me down—'

'We will arrive back at the vicarage in less time than it would take me to halt and lower you to the ground.'

'Please…!'

A frown darkened Giles's brow as he felt Lily trembling in his arms, her face turned pleadingly up to his as he glanced down at her in the moonlight. 'You truly are frightened…' he realised slowly.

'Yes.' She gave an involuntary shudder.

That the normally indomitable Lily was willing to admit as much to him was, Giles knew, a testament to the depth of that fear. Just as he knew that his displeasure earlier at being thought the 'dark and dangerous' man Mrs Lovell had predicted in Lily's future had rendered him less than understanding in regard to that fear. 'I was always taught that the best way to overcome fear is to face it—'

'And I am sure that for you that is true,' she acknowledged softly. 'I am obviously made of poorer stuff!'

Giles knew that to be untrue, in as much as he had learnt these past ten days that Lily was more than a match for him, both in obstinacy and determination. Nor—no matter what Lily may think to the contrary!—was he a deliberately cruel man. He remembered now that as a small child one of his sisters—he did not recall now which of them it had been, Kate or Phaedra—had had an irrational fear of spiders, and he or Jamie had always been only too happy to rid their sister of the offending arachnid. His upbringing now demanded that he could not be less considerate of Lily's nervousness in regard to Genghis.

'If that truly is the case…' He halted Genghis before gathering Lily more firmly against him, her face once again turned into his chest as he kept one arm behind her back and placed the other beneath her thighs as he swung his uninjured leg over the hunter's sleek back before sliding them both down onto the ground. 'You may look now, Lily,' he drawled, as she kept her face buried against his chest.

Lily raised her head tentatively before looking around, relieved to see that she was no longer up on the back of that fierce-looking horse. Although she was not sure she considered her present position as being any safer than she had been on the hunter's back!

'I am capable of walking now if you would care to release me,' she assured huskily.

He glanced down at her only briefly as he began to stride down the lane to the vicarage visible in the distance, grimly ignoring the twinges of discomfort in his thigh. 'And I am perfectly capable of continuing to carry you in my arms.'

Lily's cheeks blazed with colour. 'If someone should see us together like this—'

'Such as the baker's cat? Or Mrs Crutchley's overweight pug unexpectedly out for an evening stroll, perhaps?' he dismissed scornfully.

Admittedly, it was very late for anyone to be abroad in this part of the village, but even so… 'You are the one who earlier seemed concerned about my reputation,' Lily reminded him, her voice sharp as she recalled how offensive Giles had been in his hurtful accusations.

Not that her precarious social position rendered the young Romany as an unsuitable match for her. Perhaps the opposite. But she liked Judah Lovell no more than she did Sir Nathan Samuelson and felt no romantic interest in either man.

How could she possibly, when despite her own dislike of Giles Montague and his less than flattering opinion of her, simply being held in his arms now was enough to make her heart beat faster and her body to feel fevered?

Ten

· ·

'They do not appear to have left a candle burning in anticipation of your return,' Giles observed gruffly as he lowered
Lily to the ground at the front door of the vicarage several
minutes later.

She finished smoothing and straightening her cloak over
her pale gown, and righting the bonnet upon her curls, before
looking up at him. 'It is an unnecessary expense in a household where every penny must be accounted for,' she dismissed
without complaint.

Giles had lived all of his life at Castonbury Park, the only
hardships he had ever suffered being his years spent abroad
fighting the French, and even then his comfort had still been
far greater than that of the enlisted men. That the situation
might soon change at Castonbury Park, if the family finances
did not improve in some way, did not seem so important when
Giles considered that Lily had lived all of her young life with
a lack of the comforts he had always taken for granted as his
right.

A fact that perhaps went some way to explaining—to excusing—her wish to marry well?

It certainly rendered Lily's behaviour in regard to an advantageous marriage as no more ambitious and designing than that of the dozens of young debutantes who appeared in London each Season, having been tutored and polished for the sole purpose of finding themselves a rich or titled husband, preferably both.

'My lord…?' Lily prompted at his continued silence.

Giles gave himself a mental shake. 'I seem to remember you called me "Giles" earlier.'

'Amongst other things, yes.' Her lips twitched as she repressed a smile.

'Amongst other things,' he conceded drily. 'Such as "insufferable" and "crude." Names, which I am sure you feel no regret at having used in regard to me?' He frowned darkly.

Lily knew that at the time he had most certainly deserved them, that Giles was more inclined to judge her on what he believed to be her nature rather than attempting to see her as she truly was. 'No, I do not regret them in the least. Indeed, your manner towards me since your return to Castonbury has, for the most part, been inexcusable and offensive.' Her cheeks felt warm as she thought of that single occasion upon which his behaviour—and her own!—had been something else entirely! 'But— You said something to me…when last we met.' Lily's gaze dropped from his at the mention of their time together in the woods. 'Something which has… troubled me ever since.'

'I said many things to you that day which, as with the things I said to you earlier this evening, may perhaps have been better left unsaid,' he acknowledged harshly.

She frowned. 'But this— It is not the first time that you

have said something in a similar vein.' She looked up at Giles searchingly in the darkness, but the moon was not shining brightly enough this evening for her to be able to discern his features properly. Which was perhaps part of the reason why she felt able to talk with him so frankly...? 'You implied— seem to be under the misapprehension—that I meant to marry Edward.'

Lack of light to see by or not, there was no missing the stiffening of Giles's shoulders as he straightened before look- ing down the long length of his nose at her, a nerve visibly pulsing in his clenched jaw.

'I seem to recall we had a more than frank discussion on that very subject a year ago!'

'A conversation which, at the time and since, has left me completely bewildered as to why you should ever have thought I might have desired to marry Edward,' she owned huskily.

'You would have been a fool not to have wished to marry him when he was the son of a duke!' he rasped harshly.

'Then I must indeed be a fool,' Lily murmured ruefully.

Giles frowned darkly. 'You are saying that you did not de- liberately set out a year ago to entice my brother into offer- ing you marriage?'

She drew in a sharp breath. 'That is exactly what I am say- ing, yes,' she confirmed softly.

He gave an impatient shake of his head. 'Do not make the mistake of thinking me a fool too, Lily—'

'But it is foolish to have believed I could ever have consid- ered taking Edward as my husband,' she insisted exasperatedly.

'You told me yourself only days ago that you loved Edward.'

'But not in the way one should love a husband,' Lily de- nied earnestly. 'I did love Edward, I love him still, but as my brother. As he loved me as his sister.'

'In that you are completely wrong.'

'No, I am not, Giles, and I must insist you hear me out before you make any more false accusations,' she said.

'You must insist…?' he repeated, steely soft.

'Yes.' She remained determined in the face of his haughtiness. 'Edward and I grew up together, played together as children, danced and gossiped together at the local assemblies—usually as to which of the young ladies present was attempting to attract Edward's interest!' she acknowledged ruefully. 'We were as brother and sister, always. And our affection for each other was exactly that, as one sibling for another.'

Giles stared down at her wordlessly. When he and Edward had spoken on the subject a year ago his brother had declared that he was in love with Lily Seagrove and wished to make her his wife. A marriage Giles had felt no hesitation in firmly advising his brother against.

Yet, Lily now denied there had ever been such a relationship between herself and Edward, nor had there ever been any suggestion of marriage between them. Because, she claimed, she had loved Edward as a brother, and not as her future husband.

A truth—if indeed it was the truth!—which would have rendered Giles's behaviour towards Lily a year ago as completely incomprehensible, and the depth of his lovemaking, and offer to make her his mistress three days ago, as truly scandalous!

But it could not be the truth—could it? Edward had been so certain that he was in love with Lily, that he wished to make her his wife, and surely no man could be that certain of his feelings if he had not received some sort of encouragement from the lady whom he professed to love?

Besides, Lily had returned the intimacy of Giles's lovemaking three days ago, before then talking of the scandal which would ensue if they had been seen by anyone. And Giles had certainly seen her disappearing into the woods earlier today with Judah Lovell!

No, Lily's actions proved that she was—that she had to be!—exactly the devious young woman Giles had always thought her, and that this claim of innocence on her part was just a deliberate attempt to bewitch him into believing her lies. 'It makes a very pretty story, Lily,' he acknowledged derisively. 'But it does not stand against all evidence to the contrary.'

Her eyes widened. 'What evidence?'

His mouth twisted mockingly. 'Edward himself told me of the love he felt for you—'

'I have told you—'

'—and of his intention of asking you to become his wife,' Giles continued harshly. 'A marriage proposal I advised most strongly against, I assure you,' he added scathingly.

Lily felt the colour drain from her cheeks even as she stared up at Giles, sure he could not be telling her the truth, that he must just be saying these things to further hurt and confuse her. She and Edward had only ever shared a friendship. A friendship Lily had treasured all the more for its not being in any way romantic, and so never necessitating her to be anything other than herself when in Edward's company. Edward could not have told his brother that he was in love with her and wanted to marry her. She—

She had not loved Edward in that way, certainly, but was it possible that Edward could have been in love with her? Enough, and in such a way, as he really had told Giles of his wish to make her his wife?

Giles certainly seemed convinced this was the case. Just as his disapproval of such a match, and his conviction that Lily had used her feminine wiles in order to ensnare Edward, would also explain the hateful things Giles had said to her a year ago.

It would also go a long way towards explaining his less than respectful behaviour towards her—his scandalous behaviour towards her!—since his return to Castonbury ten days ago.

Could it really be true that Edward had loved her, not as a sister but as a woman? To the extent that he had wished to marry her and make her his wife…?

Certainly Edward had never shown any interest in the young ladies who lived locally, and who always made such a fuss of him at the assemblies or if they happened to meet in the village. But Lily had always assumed that to be because Edward preferred the more sophisticated young ladies to be found during his visits to London, and her own lack of interest in any romantic attachment between the two of them merely another reason Edward had liked to spend so much time with her whenever he was at Castonbury.

But what if she had been wrong? What if she was the one who had misunderstood, and Edward's disinterest in those other young ladies had been because he actually preferred to be with Lily for another reason entirely than mere friendship—

No!

It was not— It could not be true! It was impossible for Lily even to consider the possibility that for all of those years Edward had desired her as a man desires a woman. The very same desire Giles had shown for her three days ago…

Lily could not bear to think of indulging in those same intimacies with Edward. Nor did she want to believe that Edward had ever wanted that sort of intimacy with her.

'You are truly a cruel and hateful man to say such things to me merely in an attempt to spoil my own sweet memories of my friendship with Edward!' She glared up at Giles, her gloved hands clenched into fists at her sides as she fought back the tears, of anger as well as pain.

That frown still darkened his brow. 'Lily—'

She evaded his reaching hands. 'I— You— And I am sure I never hated anyone as much in my life before as I now hate you!' She turned to open the door to the vicarage, hurrying inside and closing the door firmly behind her before collapsing back against it. Her breathing was loud and ragged in the silence of the hallway as the hot tears fell unchecked down her cheeks for the second time that evening.

It was a lie!

Everything Giles Montague had just said to her had to have been a cruel and hateful lie, deliberately intended to hurt her.

As much of a lie as Lily's claim of hating Giles....

Giles stood unmoving outside on the doorstep for several long minutes after Lily had entered the vicarage so suddenly, too surprised at her vehemence, her obvious and genuine distress, to be able to make sense of what had just occurred. To comprehend why she had found it so upsetting for him to talk of Edward's feelings for her.

Her distress had seemed so genuine, her anger towards Giles so heated, that he was now forced at least to consider the unpleasant possibility that his conclusions of a year ago, of Lily being a designing female out to ensnare herself a rich and titled husband, may have been wrong, and that her distress, at the thought of their own discovery three days ago, had also been genuine rather than a deliberate ploy to force an offer of marriage from him.

Edward had talked to Giles of his feelings for Lily, of his desire to make her his wife, but what if Lily herself had been completely ignorant of those feelings, of that desire, as she now claimed to be?

She stated she had found Giles's conversation a year ago bewildering, his less than respectful behaviour towards her since his return to Castonbury highly offensive. Which it truly would be if Lily was as innocent in her dealings with Edward—with him!—as she now claimed to be!

Dear God, what if he had been wrong…?

'You are out and about very late this evening, Lord Giles? There is nothing amiss with His Grace, I hope?' Mr Seagrove's voice sharpened with concern.

Giles had been so deep in thought, so lost to the possibility of Lily's complete ignorance of Edward's feelings for her—of the depth of his own insulting behaviour towards her, if that were true!—that he had been completely unaware of Mr Seagrove's return until the other gentleman spoke to him.

He drew in a deep and steadying breath before turning to face the older man. 'No, there is nothing at all amiss at Castonbury Park, Mr Seagrove,' he assured him. 'I merely escorted Miss Seagrove home after she had visited with Mrs Stratton,' he explained economically.

'That was very kind of you, my lord.' Mr Seagrove beamed up at him approvingly. 'Perhaps, if you are in no hurry to return home, you would care to come inside and join me in my study for a glass of brandy?'

Did Giles wish to sit with Mr Seagrove and enjoy a glass of brandy, aware as he did so that Lily was in one of the bedchambers overhead? To imagine how she would slowly remove all of her hairpins to release those glorious ebony curls over her shoulders and down the length of her spine, before taking off all her clothes, to stand barefoot and naked before donning a sheer nightgown to slip between the warmth of the bedcovers?

With an almost painful throb in his breeches Giles answered a very firm no, he could not think of staying. 'It is late, Mr Seagrove,' Giles excused lightly. 'And you must be very tired after your evening out.'

'Not at all,' the other gentleman assured unhelpfully. 'Indeed, I would more than welcome your company, after an evening spent listening to Sir Nathan talk of his crops and the necessity of him taking a wife to grace his estate.' He gave a delicate grimace.

Giles had no doubt that Mr Seagrove had to be referring to the less than stimulating company of Sir Nathan Samuelson, a gentleman who owned an estate in the area, and as such was known to Giles, but whom he had never been able to muster a partiality for. 'I had not heard that Sir Nathan was betrothed, let alone about to be married.'

'He is not either as yet.' Mr Seagrove sighed heavily. 'Indeed, I have noticed that the ladies of marriageable age in the area seem to avoid him, and he does not care for London, apparently. I myself find him to be— Forgive me.' The reverend waved a hand, as he clearly realised he was being less than discreet about one of his flock. 'I am afraid I am a little out of sorts this evening after learning that Sir Nathan's marital intentions may, for lack of interest elsewhere, have turned towards my darling Lily.'

Sir Nathan Samuelson and *Lily*?

Why, the man was twice her age, and a pompously self-important bore to boot.

What did it matter what the man's character was; Lily's questionable parentage rendered marriage to a man of Sir Nathan Samuelson's standing as nothing less than advantageous from her perspective. Once married to him, she would become Lady Samuelson and mistress of a modest estate, future mother to the son who would one day inherit that title and estate.

And Giles felt nauseous just thinking of Sir Nathan Samuelson going to Lily's bed each night, imagining the other man touching and caressing every inch of her smooth and silky skin, before nudging her legs apart and—

He scowled darkly. 'Would such a marriage find favour with you, Mr Seagrove?'

'It would not be for me to choose, but Lily.' The older man avoided a direct answer.

'But you think she might be willing to accept if Samuelson were to offer?' If Lily were the things Giles believed her to be, had accused her of being, surely she would be a fool not to accept such an offer of marriage.

Mr Seagrove looked pained. 'If the offer were to be formally made it would be my duty to advise that she do so, certainly. Such a marriage would be…more than Mrs Seagrove and I could ever have hoped for, given the lack of knowledge of Lily's forebears.' He looked even more distressed. 'Indeed, Sir Nathan informed me that he would be willing to…overlook that lack once she has produced his heir.'

Giles scowled. 'And how does he intend to regard her until that day occurs?'

'He did not care to say….' Mr Seagrove looked less than happy at that omission.

As well he might not! Giles's dislike and distrust of Sir Nathan had not been made indiscriminately. As a child he had chanced to see Sir Nathan whip a disobedient horse into submission, and the other man's behaviour in regard to the people who worked on his estate was also said to be less than kind. The thoughts that Sir Nathan might privately use that same harshness on his wife—on Lily!—did not even bear thinking about!

It also posed the question—despite Lily's own opinion on the subject!—as to whether Sir Nathan Samuelson's interest in Lily might not make him that 'dark and dangerous man' Mrs Lovell had predicted in Lily's future....

'Perhaps I will join you in a glass of brandy, after all, Mr Seagrove,' Giles rasped harshly, his expression pained as he followed the older man inside. A pain which he knew had very little to do with the throbbing of the muscles in his injured thigh.

'Yes...?' Lily bristled warily as she opened the door of the vicarage the following morning to discover Giles Montague standing outside on the doorstep.

Mrs Jeffries had gone to shop in the village this morning, so making it necessary for Lily to answer the brisk knocking on the door herself. But, following their conversation the previous evening, the last person Lily would have expected to call this morning had been Lord Giles Montague!

Especially as she had overheard him and Mr Seagrove in muted conversation in her father's study for half the night, and found the decanter of brandy in there to be completely empty this morning. Her father's headache at breakfast had testified to his having consumed his fair share of its contents! Under the circumstances, Lily would not have expected Giles Montague to be out and about at all this morning, let alone looking every inch his normal arrogant self in a tall hat, brown tailed jacket over a darker brown waistcoat and white linen, with cream buckskin pantaloons above brown-topped black Hessians, the latter seeming to indicate that he had once again ridden his horse here.

She continued to hold the door partially closed. 'I am afraid that my father is not at home this morning.'

He looked down the length of his nose at her. 'I have not called with the intention of speaking with Mr Seagrove.'

Lily raised surprised brows. 'Oh…?'

Giles smiled bleakly as he saw her increased wariness. No doubt a perfectly justified wariness, following the abrupt end of their own conversation the previous evening. After Lily had professed to now hate him more than she had ever hated anyone in her life before! 'Your father and I talked at great length together last night,' he admitted ruefully.

Indeed, only the disgusting concoction produced by his valet—the contents of which Giles had no desire to know!—had saved him from the blinding brandy-induced hangover which, upon awakening, had threatened to incapacitate him for the rest of the day!

'So I understand.' Lily's frosty tone implied that her father had suffered that same fate, no doubt without the benefit of the same remedy. Her next comment confirmed that to have been the case. 'I am sure it is not seemly for a man of the cloth to feel so ill from overimbibing! Perhaps in future you might limit your shared libations to one or two glasses of the fine brandy which your own father provides for mine?'

Giles gave a tight smile. 'Surely it is preferable that I was present than that Mr Seagrove should have indulged alone?'

'I am sure it would have been better if he had not indulged at all!' she came back tartly. 'Which I am sure he would not have done without the encouragement of your own company.'

That may be so, although somehow Giles doubted it. Mr Seagrove had been most despondent concerning Sir Nathan's interest in Lily—no doubt some of that misery could be attributed to the thought of having the old bore as a son-in-law for the rest of his life!—and Giles had found himself to be equally as disturbed by the thought of Lily marrying Sir Nathan. Most especially at the thought of that dour and taciturn gentleman exercising his marital rights in her bed every night.

That Giles's own less than respectful behaviour towards Lily should have precluded his feeling murderous at the mere thought of Lily in Sir Nathan's bed, his to do with as he wished, whenever he wished, made absolutely no difference to Giles feeling exactly that excess of emotion!

Which, following a night lacking in restful sleep despite imbibing a vast quantity of brandy, was the reason Giles had been quite unable to interest himself in anything else this morning other than riding over to the vicarage so that he might see and speak with Lily again, aware as he was that there were still many things left unsaid between them.

The fact that Lily looked so pale this morning, her eyes appearing dark and haunted, would seem to indicate that she had not spent a restful night either. 'I feel our conversation yesterday evening was left unfinished,' he bit out tautly. 'So much so that I feel we must talk on the subject further.'

'I do not see why.' Her chin rose proudly, the pink that had entered her cheeks a perfect match for her high-waisted gown. 'I believe I was more than clear as to my feelings towards… towards certain members of your family, as well as towards yourself!' She clenched her hands together in front of her.

Those same slender and graceful hands that only days ago had caressed Giles until he climaxed.

It was an unprecedented loss of control Giles would not have believed possible until he had experienced the excitement of having Lily's hands upon his naked flesh. An excitement he had been unable to put completely from his mind, let alone forget entirely.

'You implied yesterday evening that we may have been speaking somewhat at odds with each other this past year, an implication I feel merits further discussion—'

'I believe I have said all I wish to say to you, on that subject, or any other!'

Giles drew in a harsh breath at her vehemence of feeling. 'If I were to ask nicely might you not reconsider, and take a short walk outside with me?'

Lily's eyes widened at the unexpectedly pleasant tone of voice. 'Why should I wish to do that?'

'After stating so frankly yesterday evening how much you hate me?' he prompted ruefully.

'Perhaps *hate* was too strong a word.' Lily gave a pained frown as she inwardly acknowledged that it was the things Giles had said to her which she had so hated and not the man who had said them, in that his comments now made her question the nature of Edward's friendship with her.

Oh, she was still angry with Giles, resented him for causing her to question the cherished memories she held of her friendship with Edward. But as she'd lain awake in her bed last night she had realised that she was more troubled by those remarks than angry.

It had not helped that she had also been aware of her body once again feeling hot and feverish just from listening to the deep tenor of Giles's voice as he and her father conversed in the room beneath her, forcing her once again to acknowledge that it was not dislike alone she felt for Giles Montague....

'Will you not reconsider, Lily?' he now prompted huskily. 'If only for the sake of the friendship and regard our fathers bear for each other?'

She gave a pained wince. 'Is it not a little unfair of you to bring that friendship into our own disagreement?'

'More than a little,' he conceded grimly. 'Which should only serve to show you how much I wish to continue our conversation.'

Lily knew she should refuse. To do anything else, aware of her attraction to this man in spite of the bad feeling between them, would not only be unwise on her part but possibly reckless too.

Why, despite everything Giles had said and done to her since returning to Castonbury, did Lily so much want to accept his invitation?

Eleven

. . . .

'I would consider it a great service to me if you were to agree to take a walk with me, Lily.'

Her heart skipped a beat at the husky entreaty she now heard in Giles's tone. An entreaty she at least tried to resist. 'I have so many other things to do this morning….'

'We need not be gone long,' he encouraged softly.

'If you really feel we must talk together, then could we not just sit in the parlour here?' she prompted impatiently.

'The fact that you opened the door to me yourself just now would seem to imply that Mrs Jeffries is also away from the vicarage?' He raised dark brows.

Lily nodded in confirmation. 'She has gone to the butcher's.'

Giles felt his desire quicken just at the thought of being alone in the vicarage with Lily. A desire which was totally inappropriate given their previous conversations. 'Then we cannot remain alone here.'

Lily hesitated only a moment longer as she looked up at him searchingly before stepping back to fully open the door. 'Perhaps you would like to wait in the parlour whilst I go upstairs and collect my gloves and bonnet.'

Giles allowed himself a brief moment of triumph at Lily's acquiescence even as he gave a shake of his head in refusal of the belated invitation to enter the vicarage; he was feeling too restless of spirit this morning, too aware of everything about Lily, if truth be told, to be able to suffer the confines of the vicarage alone with her, even for so short a time. 'I will stay out here and ensure that my horse remains securely tethered in our absence.'

'Very well.' She gave a cool nod of her head, leaving the door open as she turned away.

Giles remained standing where he was for several minutes after Lily had disappeared down the hallway to ascend the stairs, the lingering aroma of her perfume once again invading his senses, the stirring of his arousal serving as confirmation that his decision not to remain alone here in the vicarage with Lily had been the sensible one.

Which did not prevent him from pausing in the doorway, hard and aching, hands clenched at his sides, as he fought the totally inappropriate urge he felt to follow Lily up the stairs and finish what they had started four days ago.

Giles finally gathered enough control over his desire to be able to move down the pathway and step out into the lane and secure Genghis's reins to the fence, talking softly as the stallion nudged him affectionately in the shoulder. 'I agree, Genghis, this is indeed a madness, but I cannot seem to—'

'Do you speak often to your horse, my— Oh, my goodness!' Lily gave a gasp as, having locked the vicarage behind her and placed the key beneath one of the flower boxes in the window as was the family custom when everyone was out, she now reached Giles's side and saw for the first time the long scar which ran the length of the horse's long silky neck, from ear to wither. 'What on earth can have happened to him?' One lace-gloved hand was raised to her throat at the thought of what could have caused such a grievous injury to such a magnificent animal, her earlier feelings of reluctance, at the thought of spending any time alone with Giles, completely forgotten as she stared compassionately at the scarred horse.

Giles gave the beast a reassuring and affectionate stroke down the length of that long and glistening neck. 'I will tell you as we walk, if you really care to know.'

'I should, very much.' Lily may have no inclination to learn to ride a horse but that did not prevent her from appreciating and empathising with the serious nature of an injury which could have resulted in such an horrific scar. 'I believe I have heard you call him Genghis?' She looked at the silky black horse admiringly.

'Yes.'

'Like the Mongol emperor?'

Giles smiled slightly. 'Exactly like.'

'He was with you during the battles against Napoleon's army,' Lily guessed huskily.

'Some of them, yes,' Giles confirmed grimly. 'He belonged to a fellow officer who named him that, no doubt because Genghis proved himself to be fearless in the face of the enemy.' He fell into step beside her as they walked across the lane and into the churchyard.

'And that fellow officer…?'

His jaw tightened. 'Cut down and killed.'

'I am sorry. Did you know that this is the grave of Mrs Lovell's son?' She paused beside the mound upon which the two arrangements of flowers, her own and Mrs Lovell's, had been placed two days ago.

Giles frowned as he read the inscription on the weath-ered gravestone: *Matthew Lovell, Beloved Son and Husband, 1768-1795*. 'Can it be that he was the Romany killed here on the estate twenty-one years ago?'

'So I am told, yes,' Lily confirmed softly.

'I was only seven at the time, but still I remember it well.' He nodded. 'The Romany were beside themselves with grief, and my father utterly distraught that one of his employees was thought to be responsible for the death.'

She raised surprised brows. 'The estate gamekeeper was only "thought to be responsible"?'

Giles shrugged broad shoulders. 'I believe the man denied that he had been anywhere near the woods that day. Nor could it be proven otherwise. His claim of innocence made no difference to my father having to dismiss him, of course,' he added grimly. 'He could not allow a possible murderer to continue to live and work on the Castonbury estate.'

Lily nodded heavily. 'I had no idea, until a few days ago, that Mrs Lovell had ever had a son.'

Giles's mouth tightened as he recalled that Mrs Lovell also had a nephew. A very handsome and flirtatious nephew whom Giles had chanced to find chatting and laughing with one of the housemaids near the stables at Castonbury Park earlier this morning! The same handsome young nephew he had seen Lily meet and enter the woods with the previous day....

'Shall we go on?' he prompted abruptly.

'Of course.' Lily nodded graciously as she continued walk-ing through the graveyard towards the meadow on the other side. 'You were about to tell me about Genghis's injury,' she reminded him huskily.

Giles grimaced. 'Well, to answer your earlier question—yes, I can often be found speaking to my horse!'

She eyed him mischievously as she tried to shake off her earlier sadness for Mrs Lovell's loss. 'Could that possibly be because he is incapable of answering you back?'

Giles grinned appreciatively. 'I had not thought of it in quite that way before now, but perhaps you are right!' He laughed and inclined his head. 'Although I have no doubt that Genghis would find a way to let me know of his displeasure if needs be.'

'He is such a beautiful and fearsome creature!'

Giles sobered as he held open the gate so that they might walk out into the meadow. 'You would not have thought so if you had seen him shortly after he was cut down.'

'Tell me,' she invited softly as they walked down the grassy slope towards the river.

Giles's expression became grim as he thought back to that day two years ago. 'I was with my regiment, and we were preparing to go into battle against Napoleon's troops once more. Not one of the bigger battles, but what we would normally have called a skirmish.' He gave a pained grimace. 'We were wrong. It more resembled a slaughterhouse— I am sorry, Lily.' He turned to her apologetically as she gave a soft gasp. 'Perhaps it would be best if I did not tell you any of this.'

'But of course you must tell me.' She frowned crossly. 'I assure you, I am not some simpering miss who runs away from hearing the truth!'

'I never thought that you were.' In fact, the opposite; Lily had demonstrated several times—including agreeing to walk with him today—that she preferred to face unpleasant situations rather than run away from them.

She nodded briskly. 'That I am shocked is due only to my own ignorance of such things. You, on the other hand, and so many others like you, actually lived and fought your way through times so terrible that those of us at home cannot even begin to imagine the horror of it all. I wish for you to tell me, Giles,' she encouraged huskily. 'If it will not distress you....'

It was not that final plea which encouraged him to comply with Lily's request—although goodness knew Giles had given her little or no reason this past year to feel in the least considerate towards his own feelings—but the fact that for the first time she had called him Giles without his bidding...

He straightened. 'Then I must start at the beginning of the day, and not the end. I had received word that morning that my brother Jamie had been lost to us, drowned at Salamanca.' His jaw tightened as he heard Lily's sharply indrawn breath. 'It was too immense, too sudden, for me to comprehend. I simply could not believe that Jamie was truly gone.'

Lily frowned. 'I well remember how devastated your father and other members of your family were when they received the news at Castonbury Park. But at least they had one another. I can only imagine how awful it must have been for you to be so far away from your family when news of Lord Jamie's death was brought to you.' Her eyes had darkened in sympathy.

Giles nodded grimly. 'It certainly put me in the mood to fight that day.' He scowled. 'Unfortunately we were outnumbered and outgunned, and after several bloody hours of fighting on horseback and foot we looked defeat in the face. Somehow a last rallying of the troops secured the victory. But so many of my comrades were already dead or dying, and I myself was left for dead after receiving a blow to the head which had rendered me unconscious. When I awoke some hours later it was to find all unnaturally still about me, with no noise to be heard except for the low moans of dying men and the pained whinnying of the horses as they, too, lay injured and dying.'

He had described the scene so well and so vividly that Lily was almost able to hear the guns firing, the shouts of the fighting men and the terrified snorting of the horses, to smell the lingering odour of gunpowder and the blood of so many dying men and horses.

Giles gave a grimly humourless smile as he continued. 'I lay there on the ground, numb from the waist down, all of me covered over in blood, and for several moments believed that I had only woken in order that I might die too.'

Lily instinctively reached out a hand and placed it upon his muscled forearm. 'Please…you have said enough. I insist you not talk of it any more when it is so obviously painful for you to do so!'

He gave a perplexed frown as he looked down at her. 'Should you not be rejoicing at my suffering rather than sympathising, when time and time again I have demonstrated such a lack of understanding in regard to your own feelings?'

'I could never be glad at another's suffering,' she assured him huskily.

Giles gave a pained smile. 'Even my own?'

'Even yours,' Lily conceded softly.

He gave a puzzled shake of his head. 'You are very generous of heart.'

Lily returned his gaze quizzically. 'And that surprises you?'

In truth, everything Giles had learnt about this particular young woman, since returning to Derbyshire, had succeeded in surprising him—her genuine concern for his father's deteriorating health, even if that concern had on one memorable occasion reflected so badly upon him; the care he had heard many in the village say that Lily gave so unselfishly to her father's parishioners; the affection Lily so obviously felt for the roguish Mrs Lovell, and the compassion she felt for the loss of that lady's son, a man who must have died before Lily was even born.

It was the same compassion she now felt for Genghis's injury, even though she had admitted to being somewhat afraid of horses.

And the concern she now showed for Giles, in regard to Jamie's death, and the bloody battle he had fought only hours after that terrible news had been brought to him, showed a capacity for empathy Giles believed few to be capable of, and certainly none that had been so deliberately mocked and insulted by the very object of her compassion.

'You truly are Mr Seagrove's daughter,' he acknowledged huskily.

'I only wish that were true—' She broke off abruptly to look up uncertainly at Giles as he lifted one of his hands to cover her gloved one as it rested on his forearm.

He shrugged. 'It is true, in as much as we are all surely a result of our upbringing rather than those who are physically our parents.'

Her throat moved convulsively as she swallowed before speaking. 'If you continue being kind to me, Giles, then I fear there is the distinct possibility that I may actually come to like you—an occurrence which I am sure would not be pleasing to either one of us!'

Giles looked down at her wordlessly for several stunned moments, before bursting into throaty laughter. Something he had not felt in the least inclined to do since his return to Castonbury ten days ago.

It caused Giles to acknowledge that Lily's ability to ignite his sense of humour, when onerous financial and family problems gave him very little reason to find anything in the least amusing, was yet another thing which surprised him about this young woman.

'I doubt there is any real danger of that ever happening, Lily,' he finally drawled, 'when I am just as likely to insult you—either intentionally or unintentionally—with my very next breath!'

She looked up at him from beneath long, dark lashes. 'Something you might perhaps avoid doing for more than two minutes at a time if you were to accept that my feelings for Edward were only ever that of a sister?'

Giles scowled darkly. 'And are your feelings towards Judah Lovell as innocent?'

'You were right, it was almost with your next breath!' Lily acknowledged with a snort as she purposefully removed her hand from beneath his, her face flushed as she continued to look up at him. 'As I have informed you, I only met that young man for the first time yesterday. I can honestly claim not to have any feelings whatsoever towards him beyond the politeness of acknowledging him as Mrs Lovell's nephew.'

Giles gave a disbelieving snort. 'And what of Sir Nathan?'

'Can you possibly be talking of Sir Nathan Samuelson?' She looked up at him with obvious puzzlement.

Giles nodded haughtily. 'He is a single and eligible gentleman.'

'And I barely know him!' Lily did not know whether she should laugh or feel angry at the unlikely introduction of Sir Nathan Samuelson into their conversation.

Not only was Sir Nathan old enough to be her father, but he was also portly, red-faced and bewhiskered—and pompous and bad-tempered to boot. Lily had certainly never looked at that gentleman as being anything other than one of her father's less pleasant parishioners—

She stilled as an unpleasant idea occurred to her. 'My father dined with Sir Nathan at Grantby Manor yesterday evening.'

'So he informed me.' Giles's teeth were now so tightly clenched he could feel the throb of his own pulse in the tautness of his jaw.

'Can it be possible that he—? Could he have—? No, surely even Sir Nathan cannot have—' She broke off with a shudder. 'He cannot!'

Her distaste for even the idea of Sir Nathan as anything more than one of her father's parishioners was so obvious that Giles felt discomforted at having allowed his own feelings of distaste for the man to have prompted him to usurp Mr Seagrove's role as Lily's father. To such a degree that he had sounded like a jealous suitor himself!

Which was utterly preposterous. Admittedly, their conversations yesterday evening and again today had made Giles question his summation of Lily's character a year ago, but that did not imply he felt any romantic interest in her himself.

'Perhaps, if Mr Seagrove has not yet found opportunity to discuss the matter with you, I should not have spoken on the subject either.'

'Mr Seagrove seems to have found opportunity to discuss the subject with you—no doubt while the two of you indulged in an excess of brandy last evening!' Her eyes flashed a deep warning.

Hers was now a glittering and angry gaze which Giles found he no longer had any wish to meet. 'Perhaps we should return to discussing how Genghis suffered his injuries—'

'It can wait until you have fully explained what you meant by your remarks regarding Sir Nathan,' Lily insisted firmly.

Giles winced as he heard the anger in her voice. Even if that anger did give a sparkle to Lily's fine green eyes, and add becoming colour to the ivory perfection of her cheeks! 'I really cannot—'

'Oh, but you really can, Giles!' she assured with controlled determination.

He grimaced, finding it did not please him at all to hear Lily say his name in that angry tone. 'Mr Seagrove merely mentioned yesterday evening that Sir Nathan had talked in a…complimentary fashion about you, over dinner.'

'And in what manner did I even enter into their conversation, let alone have Sir Nathan talk about me in a "complimentary fashion"?' she repeated with dangerous softness.

Giles shifted restlessly, wishing he had never begun this particular conversation. 'I am sure Mr Seagrove will happily explain all when next you see him.'

'But you are with me now, Giles, and so may save me the bother of the wait,' Lily reasoned sweetly.

What Lily suspected could not possibly be true, could it? That Sir Nathan Samuelson, a man of plain if not unattractive looks, of an unpleasantness of manner which Lily knew had already caused at least one lady in the county to refuse his offer of marriage, had now turned his lecherous gaze in her direction?

Lily would rather remain an old maid for the rest of her life than marry a man she could not even bring herself to like, let alone love! Indeed, given her circumstances, she had long ago decided that in all probability an old maid was exactly what she would one day become….

She breathed out shallowly. 'When you and Mr Seagrove spoke on the subject yesterday evening, did he also say whether or not he would approve of such an offer?'

Giles shifted uncomfortably. 'He…implied it would be your own decision, not his.'

'That would appear to settle the matter, then.' Lily felt some of the tension ease from her shoulders, having been aware that if Mr Seagrove had approved of the match, then she would at least have had to appear to give the matter some thought before refusing. Indeed, she would much prefer it if Sir Nathan could somehow be persuaded into not asking at all!

'It does?' Giles eyed her questioningly.

'Undoubtedly,' she dismissed briskly. 'When—if my father asks, I will simply state that I would not be willing to accept Sir Nathan as my husband if he were the very last gentleman upon this earth!' She repressed a delicate shudder of distaste.

'Poor Sir Nathan!' Giles felt as if a heavy weight had been lifted from his shoulders. But it was quickly followed by a frown appearing on his brow at his acknowledgement of those feelings of relief to be even more ridiculous than the ones he had earlier attributed to jealousy.

Lily eyed him critically. 'You do not sound very sympathetic.'

Possibly because Giles did not feel in the least sympathetic towards the gentleman who had caused him to spend the past twelve hours gnashing and grinding his teeth in frustration at the very thought of that gentleman sharing Lily's bed and body.

'Nor,' Lily continued tartly, 'do I appreciate my father having discussed this matter with you before it has even been mentioned to me!'

Giles winced at what he knew to be her perfectly justified feelings of resentment. 'Mr Seagrove did not so much discuss it with me as mention it to me casually as we enjoyed a glass of brandy together—' He broke off to catch Lily's disbelieving snort. 'A glass or six of brandy together,' he allowed drily.

She gave him a reproving glance. 'You are obviously a bad influence upon each other and should be kept apart in future!'

In truth Giles had very much enjoyed his conversation and brandy with Mr Seagrove the night before, had found that gentleman to be both learned and well informed, and he now perfectly understood his father's long and warm friendship with the man. Being a duke had long set his father apart from all but his peers, in the same way Giles would also find himself set apart were he to one day inherit the title from his father.

If he inherited the title from his father, Giles reminded himself grimly, the manner of Jamie's death, and the lack of a body as proof of that death, meaning that as a family they still had to find physical evidence before the succession could be secured, along with Jamie's considerable inheritance from their mother. It was—

'I was only jesting, Giles.'

He blinked, realising that he had allowed his thoughts to wander to the other problem which had begun to plague him day and night since his return to Castonbury.

The *other* problem?

Lily had become something of a problem to him, Giles now acknowledged, as just looking down into the exotic beauty of her face once again reminded him that she was not Mr Seagrove's daughter at all.

As such, an offer from someone of Sir Nathan's ilk was far more than Lily could ever, or should ever, have hoped for. Moreover, it was an offer Giles should be encouraging her to accept in his role as the future Duke of Rothermere.

Instead he found himself raising a hand to cup the warmth of one of Lily's ivory cheeks as he continued to gaze down into that lovely face; those green, slightly uptilted eyes, and the full and berry-red of her lips were an enticement Giles was finding more and more difficult to resist. 'You are so very beautiful, Lily.'

She looked slightly alarmed. 'Perhaps we should, after all, resume our walk whilst you continue to talk of Genghis?'

Yes, that is exactly what they should do.

Should?

Must!

And yet just the feel of Lily's silken skin beneath Giles's fingertips, her warmth, made it impossible for Giles to think of anything else but the need he felt to make love to her again.

Twelve

Lily's heart began to beat wildly in her chest as she saw the intensity of Giles's silver gaze fixed firmly, hungrily even, upon her slightly parted lips, instantly making her aware of how very alone the two of them were out here in the meadow together amongst the scented wildflowers, the only sounds their own soft and husky breathing and the twittering of the birds.

A pleasurable lethargy descended over Lily's body, an aching heaviness in her breasts, and heat between her thighs. A heat and aching heaviness that she acknowledged were becoming all too familiar when she was anywhere in the vicinity of Giles Montague!

'We really should continue our walk, Giles,' she prompted with a sharpness she was far from feeling.

He blinked as if waking from a dream, or perhaps the same sensual spell under which Lily had felt herself falling. His hand dropped away from her cheek as he straightened abruptly. 'Yes, of course.' His expression became remote as he indicated she should precede him.

Even Lily's legs felt unwieldy as she turned to walk down

to where the river tripped and gurgled over rocks smoothed by years of the water's caress, at the same time completely aware of Giles as he matched his much longer strides to her own. A glance from beneath lowered lashes revealed that he now looked every inch the grimly forbidding Giles Montague, rather than the man who had made love to Lily so passionately four days ago, and touched her again so gently only moments ago whilst his eyes had sought to bore into her very soul.

She could not forget the look, no matter how hard she tried.

'I remember playing here as a child,' she remarked abruptly, having reached the riverside, in an attempt to try to ease the tension between them.

Giles nodded. 'Before we went away to school Jamie and I would often hide from our tutor beneath that willow.' He looked at the magnificent tree as its branches draped down even heavier and thicker than he remembered, creating what he remembered to be a cool and shadowed den beneath.

Lily looked up at him. 'As did Edward and I….'

His smile was tinged with sadness. 'And now there is only the two of us left to remember those happy times.'

'Yes.'

'You really did not love or wish to marry Edward, did you.' It was a statement rather than a question.

Lily turned back to look at the river. 'I loved him as my very best friend in all the world. I always will.' She had realised, as she lay unable to sleep the night before, that her friendship with Edward was not spoilt, after all, and that Edward had gone to his death with hope still alive in his heart that she might return his love. There was some comfort in knowing that.

'But never as your lover.'

She continued to stare down at the flowing water. 'No, never as a lover.'

Giles drew in a sharp breath. 'I needed to talk to you today, Lily, because I—I have realised that I owe you an apology.'

Her face remained averted. 'Just one?' She couldn't resist the taunt.

'I— You were so insistent yesterday concerning your feelings for Edward, and your father also spoke last night of your sisterly regard for Edward.'

Her profile showed the sadness of her smile. 'And you have chosen to believe my father when you did not believe me.'

'I— It was—' Giles shook his head. 'Please understand, Edward was so firm in his declaration of love for you that I felt sure you must be aware of those feelings.'

'I was not.' Her eyes were wet with tears as she turned to look at him. 'Could you not—? Please—please do not break my heart again, by talking of a love I could never have returned!'

Giles straightened, cut to the quick by sight of those tears. Tears for which he knew he was responsible. 'Perhaps, for now, we could continue our conversation of Genghis?'

'If you please,' Lily encouraged softly.

If Giles pleased…!

His shoulders ached almost as much as that old wound to his thigh as he fought to keep his hands from once again reaching out and taking Lily into his arms before kissing her. Except Giles knew he did not want to stop at taking her in his arms and kissing her; he wanted so very much more.

Lily's fierce denial the evening before, of loving Edward as anything more than a brother, and Mr Seagrove's fond memories of his daughter and Edward's friendship since childhood, had caused Giles to think long and hard on the subject once he returned to Castonbury Park. It was hard for him to acknowledge the possibility that, no matter what Edward may have told him a year ago of his feelings for Lily, she may not have returned those feelings. Nor would she have accepted his offer of marriage if he had ever made one.

As she had today rejected the suggestion that she might ever accept such an offer from Sir Nathan Samuelson—

'Giles?'

It was now his turn to stare blindly at the river as he forced his memories back to the day two years ago rather than give in to the urge to take Lily in his arms. 'Genghis had fallen across my lower body when he was cut down, and so gave me the mistaken impression that I had lost the use of my legs. Once I realised that the blood over me was not mine but his, I was able to crawl out, inch by inch, from beneath his weight. And, as I did so, I realised that Genghis still lived.'

Giles had forgotten his own discomfort completely that day as he was instead filled with elation at seeing that slight rise and fall of Genghis's heavy barrel chest, something he would not have believed possible once he saw the extent of the stallion's injuries. A French sabre had sliced him open from ear to wither, and the blood still seeped from the wound.

'It was—' Giles shook his head, knowing that his behaviour towards Lily this past year dictated he could not be less than honest with her now concerning his own feelings and emotions in regard to the events of two years ago. 'The extent of Genghis's injuries dictated it would have been a kindness on my part to shoot him then and there. But I—I could not bring myself to do it. Jamie was gone. My fellow officers and most of my men were also slain. To allow this magnificent creature to suffer that same fate seemed beyond bearing.'

'What did you do?' Lily prompted huskily.

He sighed. 'I tried to get help for him, but the medics were far too busy dealing with the injuries of the men to bother with a mere horse.'

'You tended him yourself?'

Giles nodded abruptly. 'I did what I could for him—cleaned the wound, sewed it up as best I could with the supplies I had—and then sat down beside him and simply willed him to live.' He frowned grimly as he recalled those hours—days—during which he had sat at Genghis's side, ignoring his own wound as he ensured that the horse's wounds remained clean and free of the flies that swarmed constantly over the battle-ground soaked with blood.

Hours and days when Giles had not left the horse's side except to collect water from a nearby stream, occasionally dribbling some of that water into his own mouth once he had seen to Genghis's needs, but taking no other food or sustenance as he concentrated all of his attention on willing the fallen horse to recover.

The same hours and days when Giles had also come to accept the loss of his elder brother, and to the knowledge that there was nothing he could do or say which could ever bring Jamie back to them.

They had been the bleakest and loneliest hours and days of Giles's life, his only companion the seriously wounded horse whom he had refused to allow to die. Lonely hours and days, when the loss of Jamie and his fellow soldiers had left scars inside him which had healed but would never be forgotten....

Lily could only imagine the scene Giles described to her, but even that was horrific enough; to have lived through it was beyond her comprehension. 'You obviously succeeded.'

He smiled grimly. 'Something Genghis did not at all thank

me for once he began to regain his strength, I assure you. His suffering then was immense.' The bleakness in those silver-grey eyes revealed that Giles's own suffering had been almost as severe. 'He several times tried to show his displeasure by attempting to bite me.'

Having seen the affection which now existed between this man and that fierce warrior of a horse, Lily had no doubt that Genghis had long ago forgiven Giles for the pain he had suffered because of this man's stubborn determination that he should live.

Giles grimaced. 'I think— I have come to believe since, that Genghis had somehow come to represent the whole of those bloody years of war to me, and that if he were allowed to die, then all of it—Jamie's death, the deaths of all those other brothers and sons and fathers and husbands—would be rendered utterly meaningless.'

'And yet I can tell that you now miss your life in the army.' Lily knew with a certainty that this was so.

His jaw firmed. 'It is what I was brought up to be. What I have always known I was meant to do.'

And if not for the unexpected death of his older brother, no doubt what he would still be doing. 'And is that the reason you found it so...so difficult to come back here nine months ago after you had resigned your commission?' Lily prompted huskily.

He drew in a harsh breath. 'No. That was due to something else entirely.'

Lily looked at him enquiringly, adding nothing, just waiting silently for him to speak again.

'The thought of coming back to Castonbury,' Giles continued forcefully, 'of being here, where I knew I would feel Jamie and Edward's loss more deeply than anywhere else, was unbearable to me! Of course, I had not realised quite how my father's health had deteriorated, else I should have been here sooner, my own feelings of loss be damned!' He looked grim.

And this, Lily acknowledged achingly, was the same man for whom she had harboured such anger and resentment this past year.

Even more so in the almost eleven months since Edward had been struck down at Waterloo.

Giles was a man Lily could now see she had judged as harshly as he had judged her, in that she had chosen to see only what she had perceived to be Giles's cold and arrogant nature, rather than attempting to see him as he truly was: a man who felt emotions so strongly, and so deeply, that he must hide them beneath a veneer of cold arrogance lest he be thought weak or vulnerable.

Lily now believed he had deliberately chosen to share his vulnerability with her today, as a way of atoning, apologising, for his previous behaviour to her.

And in doing so he allowed Lily at last to see that Giles was indeed a man who had more than deserved Edward's hero-worship. That if he bore any responsibility at all for Edward's premature death, then it was only in having been the man that he was, a man of strength and loyalty whom Edward had wished to emulate.

The anger and resentment Lily had felt towards Giles for so long melted like the winter snow in the warmth of spring, as she knew she looked up into the face of a man who was still tormented by the death of both his brothers, as well as the men who had served with and under him. Giles had now confided that torment to her in a way she doubted he had ever done with anyone else, and in doing so allowed her to see that he was not a man lacking in emotions at all.

Her face was full of compassion as she reached up to gently curve her hand about one of Giles's rigidly tensed cheeks—

'Do not, Lily!' he bit out harshly, every part of him having tensed, his eyes a glittering silver as he looked down at her.

She stilled with her fingers against that tensed cheek. 'Why should I not?'

A nerve pulsed in Giles's rigidly clenched jaw. 'I am not in full control of— You should know that our conversation has left me with few defences. I have nothing left with which to resist taking you in my arms and kissing you, as I so long to do!' He looked down at her hungrily as he fought that inner battle.

A battle which Lily's beauty would surely ensure he was destined to lose?

That nerve once again pulsed in the rigidity of his jaw. 'Lily—'

'Giles?'

His breath caught in his throat as he saw the tears glistening in those beautiful green eyes. Were those tears for him? 'I did not tell you any of those things with the intention of arousing your pity—' He broke off as she laughed softly.

She gave a gentle shake of her head. 'Giles, you are not a man for whom I or anyone else could ever feel pity,' she assured huskily.

Giles continued to look down at her searchingly but found none of the mockery in her expression that he might have expected from her words. 'It is a fact that during times of war women would…allow soldiers to make love to them, for the simple reason they believed it might be their last such memory.'

She moistened her lips with the tip of her tongue. 'And did you personally…accept many of those offers?'

His mouth tightened as he answered her honestly. 'Too many for me now to recall any of their faces!'

Lily drew her breath in sharply at the bluntness of Giles's reply, even as she knew with certainty that it had been his intention to shock her, perhaps to disgust her, in an effort, no doubt, to regain the shield over his emotions which he had lost during those minutes of baring his soul to her.

But Lily knew she was no longer capable of feeling shock and disgust where Giles was concerned.

She again ran the tip of her tongue over her full lips. 'You underestimate your…attraction, Giles, if you believe that to have been the only motivation for those women to have invited you into their beds.'

His throat moved as he swallowed before answering her harshly. 'We are venturing onto dangerous ground, Lily.'

Lily had known the moment she opened the door to Giles this morning that she should not be alone with him today, that to do so, after her longings of the night before—when just to hear the low rumble of his voice, as he talked with her father in the room beneath her bedchamber, had been enough to arouse her—would be to flirt with danger. An irresistible danger, which Lily knew had only intensified as Giles talked of his despair and determination on the day Genghis had been so mortally injured.

She looked up at him quizzically. 'Is it so very dangerous?'

'Very.' Giles was totally aware of the light caress of Lily's fingers still resting against his cheek, of her soft floral perfume, of the swell of her breasts above the neckline of her gown, of the temptation of her red and delectable lips!

'And if I were to tell you that I am not afraid?' she prompted huskily.

His mouth thinned. 'Then I would advise you to think again!'

She shook her head in gentle reproof. 'You may try all you wish, Giles, but I can no longer be fooled by your air of coldness or arrogance.'

'But I am cold and arrogant—'

'Yes, you are,' she conceded softly. 'But you are also the man who obviously loves his family deeply. The same man who refused to allow the fearsome Genghis to die.'

He gave a pained frown. 'I am also the man who might insult you again with his very next breath,' he reminded harshly.

'And if that occurs, I shall think of our conversation just now, and refuse to take insult at anything you have said to me.'

Giles drew in a harsh breath as Lily gazed up at him with those clear and trusting green eyes, knowing that, for the moment at least, he had no defences with which to resist her. 'You are a very stubborn young woman—' He broke off as she laughed huskily.

'I believe us to be as stubborn as each other,' she explained ruefully.

He grimaced. 'Perhaps.'

'There is no "perhaps" about it.' She chuckled as she shook her head. 'If not for that stubbornness, that set opinion of each other that we refused to let go, we might have become friends much earlier than this.'

Friends? Giles pondered. Did Lily really consider them to have now become friends? In the same way that she and Edward had been friends? 'I already have two sisters, Lily,' he bit out harshly. 'I have no need of another.'

She breathed softly. 'My regard for you is not in the least sisterly!'

Giles looked searchingly into those clear and candid green

eyes, knowing himself to be without armour to resist their unwavering glow. 'I am not a man deserving of your admiration, Lily,' he rasped harshly.

'Nevertheless, you have it.'

He gave an impatient shake of his head. 'And have you considered that perhaps that was my intention all along? That I may have told you these things merely as a way of persuading you into thinking more kindly of me?'

She regarded him quizzically for several long moments. 'Do you wish me to think more kindly of you?'

'What I wish is for you to remove your bonnet and release your hair!'

Those green eyes widened at the vehemence of his tone. 'Release my hair?'

He nodded abruptly. 'I have imagined—' He shook his head, knowing he could not tell Lily the amount of times he had lain on his bed aroused and throbbing, imagining the fingers about him were hers, and the silkiness of her hair was draped across the nakedness of his chest and thighs! 'I have long wondered as to its length and thickness,' he rasped throatily.

She continued to look up at him for several long seconds before raising her gloved hands to untie her bonnet, removing it completely to allow it to fall to the grassy riverbank at their feet before peeling her gloves down her arms and allowing them, too, to flutter to the ground next to her bonnet. Her slender, bare hands now moved up to seek out the pins holding her dark curls in place.

'Good heavens…!' Giles's breath caught in his throat as Lily at last shook her head and allowed her curls to fall about her shoulders and down her back, a glossy, ebony tumble so long and thick as it fell all the way down to the gentle curve of her bottom. 'Lily...!' He reached up to touch those curls wonderingly before allowing their silky softness to fall and cascade through his fingers. 'I have never seen anything so beautiful.'

Her cheeks were flushed. 'My mother always said it would be sacrilege to cut it.'

Giles could not stop touching the ebony softness. 'Mrs Seagrove was a very wise woman.'

Lily laughed softly. 'It takes hours to dry when it is washed.'

Giles's breath caught in his throat as an image of a naked Lily instantly filled his head, her hair a wet and silky curtain over that nakedness, her breasts full and pert, the rosy nipples peeping out temptingly through those dark curls. 'You must never cut it, Lily.' His fingers became entangled in the rich darkness as he pulled her unerringly towards him.

Lily could barely breathe, let alone speak, her proximity to Giles now such that she could feel the soft warmth of his breath against her cheek, and see the dark pewter ring of colour edging the paler iris of his glittering grey eyes. Piercing grey eyes which now held her own captive....

'Promise me, Lily!' His fingers tightened painfully in her curls as he tilted her head back, exposing the creamy column of her throat. At the same time, his other arm curled about her waist and pulled her against his parted thighs, making her aware of the hard length of his arousal even as the solidity of his chest pushed up the full swell of her breasts.

Lily's palms lay warmly against the waistcoat covering that muscled chest. 'If it is your wish—'

'It is!'

'Then I promise you never to cut my hair.'

His breath caught in his throat. 'Thank you.'

She looked up at him, so very aware of the throb of Giles's

swollen arousal pressing into her own heat. 'Is it now your intention to kiss me again?'

Was it—?

Good heavens, Giles wanted nothing more than to kiss the wild and exotically lovely creature he held in his arms. To kiss Lily, to touch and caress her, to hold her wildness to him, if only for the short time she might allow it.

Every muscle and sinew in his body was tense with that need as he answered her gruffly. 'I will not take anything you do not give willingly, Lily.'

'I—' She broke off abruptly, tensing at the sound of someone whistling.

'Stop dawdling back there, boy!' The harsh tones of Mrs Lovell's voice were unmistakable.

The whistling stopped. 'Sure an' it's a fine day for a walk, Aunt Rosa,' Judah Lovell answered her unconcernedly.

'Carry this basket of herbs for me if ye can't be useful in any other way,' his aunt snapped her impatience as those two voices came steadily closer to where Lily and Giles stood.

Lily looked up at Giles with wide eyes, her cheeks having paled. 'We should not be found here together like this!'

A brief wave of…something washed over Giles, as he wondered if Lily's panic was thoughts of discovery by Mrs Lovell or her nephew. He quickly dismissed the emotion; there had been so many misunderstandings between him and Lily already, without his jumping to yet more.

'Come!' Giles urged softly as he released Lily to remove his hat before taking a firm hold of her hand and leading her quickly beneath the branches of the overhanging willow, the two of them at once enclosed inside its dark cavern of foliage, allowing them to hear the approach of Mrs Lovell and her nephew if not actually see them. And if Giles and Lily could not see Judah and Mrs Lovell, then hopefully the pair could not see them either....

'There's usually mushrooms hereabouts,' Mrs Lovell could be heard announcing cheerfully.

'Can't we get 'em on the way back?' her nephew grumbled.

Giles knew he should have been at work in the fields of the estate but he had obviously decided not to bother.

'You're a lazy good-for-nothing.' Mrs Lovell obviously echoed Giles's sentiments. 'Just like your father before ye.'

'And 'ow would you know what me da were like, when ye never troubled yourself to set eyes on 'im again after we left for Ireland twenty years ago?' Judah Lovell came back dismissively.

'Black Jack was a lazy good-for-nothing then, and I has no reason to believe that changed afore he died,' the elderly Gypsy returned scathingly. 'And don't look at me like that, Judah. You know as well as I what a wastrel ya da were, and from what I've seen since ye got back you're just like him,' she added remorselessly.

Her nephew gave a merry laugh. 'Why bother meself working for something when it sits there for the taking!'

'We'll have none of your thieving ways round here, Judah-me-lad,' Mrs Lovell warned harshly. 'No, nor none of your wicked ways with the lasses neither. You'll leave no tow-headed chivvies here when ye go.'

'There's only one lassie in these parts beautiful enough to waste me time on,' her nephew informed her with youthful dismissal.

'Oh?'

'That vicar's daughter is—*ow*! What the 'ell was that for?' Judah exclaimed, following the loud sound of flesh meeting flesh.

'Keep ya trap shut about Lily Seagrove!' Mrs Lovell hissed fiercely. 'You hear me, boy?'

'I 'ears you,' her nephew confirmed disgruntledly. 'Weren't no need for ye to 'it me just because I said Lily—'

'I said as you weren't to talk of her again,' Mrs Lovell warned angrily. 'You'll stay well away from her if'n you know what's good for ye.'

'The only time I've even spoken to her was when I brought 'er to your yag yesterday.'

'Well, make sure as you don't see or speak to her again. Now pick up ya feet, boy, and get a move on before I decides I feel like hitting ye again—hello, what's this?'

'Looks like a lady's bonnet and gloves to me,' her nephew answered drily.

'Well, I can see that for meself!' his aunt snapped her impatience with his cheekiness. 'I wonder what they're doin' here?'

Giles had felt Lily's tension as Judah had remarked on her beauty, but he was now aware of Lily's dismay at the realisation that her bonnet and gloves had been discovered on the grassy bank where she had left them in their haste to duck beneath the willow.

'What does it matter what they's doing 'ere?' Judah had obviously reached the end of his patience. 'Take the bonnet and gloves wi' ye, if you're that worried about 'em, and let's get on to the village!'

'If'n your poor mother were alive she'd turn over in her grave to listen to the way you speak to your elders and betters.'

'If'n she were alive she wouldn't be in her grave.'

'I believe it is safe now, Lily,' Giles murmured reassuringly several minutes later as the Lovells' voices became fainter and then faded away entirely. He finally heard the closing of the gate going into the churchyard as evidence that they had indeed gone on their way to the village.

Only Giles immediately realised, as he looked down at the pale oval of Lily's beautiful face in the cool darkness, that he now faced a much more serious—and immediate!—danger than discovery by the Lovells.

Thirteen

'I fail to understand what you find so amusing?' It had taken Giles some seconds to realise that Lily was not trembling with fear as he had originally surmised, but was instead laughing, her eyes now glowing with amusement in the strange half-light beneath the branches of the willow.

That laughter still trembled on her lips as she shook her head. 'I was only thinking of how all your misconceptions of my behaviour must now be shattered.'

'Oh?'

She nodded. 'In one morning you have accepted that I loved Edward only as a brother, learnt that I would not consider taking Sir Nathan Samuelson as a husband if he were the last man on earth and that the only time I chanced to meet Judah Lovell was yesterday, when you happened to see him escorting me to Mrs Lovell's campsite.'

Yes, Giles had indeed come to a realisation of all those things. 'Which would seem to leave me as the only man in your life....'

Lily's amusement faded as she became aware of how very

alone they now were beneath the silence of the willow's thick branches, and that Giles's arms still circled the slenderness of her waist. 'You?'

His eyes glowed down at her in the darkness. 'You must know that I desire you, Lily. How could you not?' he added. The evidence of that desire was all too evident to them both.

She moistened her lips with the tip of her tongue, suddenly very aware of the pulsing heat of Giles's desire as it pressed against her soft abdomen.

Urgently.

Temptingly!

'Dare I hope you feel that same desire for me, Lily?'

She breathed shallowly. 'I—'

'Please tell me the truth of it, Lily,' Giles urged huskily, his arms tightening about her waist. 'For I will not frighten or disgust you with the depth of my…my arousal, a second time.'

Lily stared up at him in the gloom, able to see the fierce glitter of Giles's gaze upon her, and the sharp blades of his cheekbones, the firmness of his jaw clenched so tightly beneath the sensuality of his sculptured lips.

Did she desire Giles?

It seemed now as if Lily could not remember a time when she had not.

Their conversation today meant she could no longer see him as Edward's cold and arrogant older brother. Or as the man who had insulted and reviled her because he believed her guilty of trying to ensnare his besotted younger brother into matrimony. Neither could she any longer believe him to be coldly callous about the estate or his father's health.

Lily had now seen him as a man who loved his family deeply, and in such a way that he was willing to do anything, say anything, in order that he might protect them from all that he thought might harm or threaten them. He was a man who had given up his life in the army, a life he was so suited to and a career which he had loved, in order to take his place here at Castonbury as his father's heir.

He was, in fact, all that Lily admired in a man.

And the man that she knew she desired with every particle of her being.

And as surely as Giles's doubts had been dispelled, in regard to her intentions towards Edward, Sir Nathan Samuelson and even Judah Lovell, so had Lily accepted she would, by necessity, one day become that old maid she had imagined.

Despite being adopted by Mr and Mrs Seagrove, she was, and would always be, a foundling, her only choice to marry someone like Sir Nathan, an unpleasant man whom no other woman wished to take for her husband, or to become the plaything of a man like Judah Lovell, a good-natured wastrel, who would take and use her body and emotions before discarding them.

If that truly was to be her fate, then Lily would rather choose the man who might one day discard her.

She now took a determined breath. 'I was not frightened or disgusted the other day, Giles.'

'No?' He looked down at her searchingly.

'No. I—I thought it beautiful,' she admitted softly. 'I thought *you* beautiful.'

Giles stilled, momentarily stunned into silence by Lily's words, by the unmistakable sincerity of her husky tone. 'Men are not beautiful, Lily.' He finally regained his own voice ruefully. 'We are brutal, selfish creatures, more often than not led by our—' His harsh words ceased abruptly as Lily placed her fingertips against his lips.

'Giles, if your intention is to succeed in shocking me into

running away from you, from this, then do not even try.' She pulled out of his arms to step away from him, her gaze meeting his unwaveringly as she reached behind her.

Her intention of unbuttoning the back of her gown was so achingly obvious that Giles could only watch in mute fascination as she finished unfastening the buttons before the bodice of her gown slid down the slender length of her arms and she allowed the gown to fall to the ground, leaving her dressed only in a thin chemise and white stockings secured in place by two pretty blue garters about her thighs, the heavy length of her ebony hair flowing seductively over her bare shoulders and down the slender length of her spine.

Giles sucked a gasp of air into his lungs as he gazed at the full plumpness of her breasts beneath her chemise, the tips hard and red as berries, her waist slender, with a dark triangle of curls visible between the gentle curve of her thighs.

She looked, in fact, so beautiful, so like Giles had thought of her so many times in his tortured nights, that he felt a moment of light-headedness as all the blood in his body seemed to rush to one single location. 'You are so very lovely, Lily,' he groaned, his hands clenched and trembling at his sides.

'As are you,' she assured softly as she stepped forward to slide his jacket from his shoulders before her fingers moved to the buttons of his waistcoat.

'No.' Giles placed one of his hands over hers to still those questing fingers. 'Before you do that you must know that I have— That I have many scars from battle…'

'And, if I am not mistaken, many that are not visible to the eye,' she guessed huskily.

'Perhaps,' he allowed gruffly.

'Then, if you allow it, I shall kiss each and every one of the scars that I do see.' She looked up at him in mute appeal.

It was a plea Giles was unable to resist, groaning his acquiescence even as his hand dropped back to his side and he stood tense and shaking as Lily removed his waistcoat, before untying and discarding his neck cloth, the slow unfastening of the buttons of his shirt revealing the first of those scars.

Giles drew in a ragged breath as he felt the softness of Lily's lips against his hot and sensitised flesh as she gently kissed the length of the first scar, the silky curtain of her hair as warm against his skin as he had imagined it might be.

He offered no further resistance as Lily freed his shirt from his breeches before lifting the garment over his head, her gaze darkening as she viewed the half-dozen or so scars that criss-crossed his chest before her fingers traced caressingly the lines and planes of his torso.

'You must have been very brave—'

'I am not brave, Lily, I am—was…merely a soldier,' he corrected gruffly.

Lily's hands were warm against his flesh as she glanced up at him in gentle rebuke. 'Can you never return to that life?'

'It would be better for my own peace of mind if I were to accept that this, being heir to the Castonbury estate, is now my fate.' His voice sounded harsh in the silence.

She looked up at him as her fingers once again began to lightly trace the scars upon his chest. 'It is not all bad, surely?'

'Not all, no.' Giles drew in a sharp breath even as he forced the tension from his shoulders and felt the pleasure of those caresses. 'Indeed, I am slowly learning it has unexpected… compensations.'

She chuckled huskily. 'And are those compensations to your liking, my lord?' Her lips were once again light as a butterfly as she kissed the long scar on his belly that he had received some four years ago and which had put him on his back in the hospital for months following the battle.

'Oh, yes.' Lily was to his liking! Her hands and lips traced that scar down to where his long, hot length tented the front of his breeches. 'Not yet!' Giles reached out to clasp the tops of her arms as she would have unfastened the buttons which would release that hardness to the caress of her lips and tongue. 'I wish to kiss and touch you first, Lily.' He wanted to worship at her feet. To touch and kiss every inch of her silken body before claiming her as his own.

For he intended to claim every part of her. Would make love to Lily in such a way she would never be able to forget how it felt to have him touching her, or dispel the taste of him from her lips and tongue, and the feel of him moving inside her hot and silken sheath.

His eyes were fully accustomed to the half-light now, allowing him to step back slightly and gaze his fill of Lily's pale ivory skin. He slipped the straps of her chemise from her shoulders before it fell softly to her waist, leaving bare her full, pert breasts tipped with those ripe buds on which he had long ached to feast.

Lily gasped softly, her hands moving up to rest on Giles's shoulders for balance as one of his hands lightly cupped her breast, his gaze continuing to hold hers as his head lowered and he began to lick and tease that full and sensitive tip. Long, arousing sweeps of his tongue swept against aching flesh, teeth gently biting, tasting, before he finally parted his lips and pulled her nipple deeply, hungrily, into the moist and encompassing fire of his mouth.

She felt the rush of heat between her thighs as Giles moved his other hand up to cup her other breast before rolling the sensitive peak between thumb and forefinger, setting a rhythm that caused a point between her thighs to swell and moisten. To ache with need. To burn.

Lily's hands rose from Giles's broad shoulders to become entwined in the heavy silkiness of his hair. 'Please…! Oh, please!' She felt the heat of the increasing moisture between her legs as she moved restlessly, groaning softly, trembling uncontrollably, as Giles's other hand stroked between her thighs and pressed gently against the sensitive throbbing bud there.

She felt cool air brushing against the dampness of her nipple as Giles released her before dropping down onto his knees in front of her to slowly slide her chemise down over her hips and allow it to fall to the ground beside her gown, her stockings and garters now her only adornment. 'Have you touched and caressed yourself since we were last together, Lily?' His fingers lightly parted the dark curls between her thighs, the warmth of his breath a teasing caress against her skin.

Lily felt the burn of colour in her cheeks. 'I—'

'There must be truth between us from now on, Lily.'

The truth. The truth was that until four days ago, until Giles had touched her so intimately, Lily had known nothing of the pleasures of her own body. Had never dreamt… imagined—

'Did you touch your breasts, Lily? Did you caress your breasts until you ached with need?' he pressured huskily.

'I cannot—'

'You can!'

'I— Yes, yes, I did that!' she admitted breathlessly.

'And did you touch yourself here, where you ached the most?'

Giles swept his tongue across the aching place between her thighs, causing Lily's legs to tremble so much she would have fallen if not for her hands gripping Giles's warm shoulders. 'Lily?' His tongue rasped against her a second time.

'Yes!' She shuddered uncontrollably as the pleasure became almost unbearable.

'And here?' That marauding tongue swept lower, caressing, building the need until she thought she could take it no longer.

'Yes…'

'And did you put your fingers here?' He gently nudged her legs apart before moving closer, his fingers taking Lily to the edge of that plateau of hot and overwhelming pleasure. 'Lily, answer me,' he urged fiercely.

She felt bereft, empty, without Giles's mouth on her. 'Yes!' she groaned achingly. 'Yes. Oh, yes! I did all of those things. All of them!' And she had. Every night since Giles had made love to her she had moved restlessly in her bed, until, with a groan, she had had no choice but to give in to the temptation to caress her breasts, to rub the throbbing ache between her thighs, her own fingers in place of him.

'And did you climax, Lily? Did you rub and caress yourself until you reached completion?'

'Yes!'

'And did you think of me when the pleasure came, Lily? Did you imagine it was me touching you?' he pressed urgently.

'Yes…' she sobbed.

'I have thought of you too, Lily,' he admitted gruffly. 'Each and every time I have brought myself to the same point, I have closed my eyes and imagined it was your hands touching and caressing me.' He smiled ruefully as she looked down at him in surprise. 'Oh, yes, Lily, I have needed to find a release for my desire for you too. Many times over. But none of my imaginings measured up to the reality of touching your silken skin, to tasting you, and holding you.' He buried his face between her thighs once more.

She gave a low cry of rapture as Giles sent her over the edge of that plateau and into the deep and overwhelming sea of wave after wave of uncontrollable pleasure.

Again, and yet again, he took her to that plateau and then over its edge, until Lily answered only to the relentless caress of Giles's mouth and hands. 'Please! No more!' she finally begged as she swayed weakly. 'I cannot again, Giles. Please, no more.'

He ran his tongue lazily over the sensitivity of her inner thigh. 'Do you want me, Lily? All of me?'

She was mindless with that need. She knew that a hundred Mrs Lovells, and a dozen Judah Lovells, could now be outside on the riverbank, and she would not care. Only Giles existed for her at this moment in time.

'Lily?'

Her knees buckled as another wave of pleasure overwhelmed her, and she knew she would have fallen if Giles had not held her so tightly. 'Yes, I want you,' she gasped, her voice raw.

'Then you shall have me.' His eyes glittered in the gloom of the weeping willow as he moved to smooth his jacket on the ground before lowering her onto it. 'But first I have to kiss you,' he groaned before his mouth claimed hers.

Minutes, hours, days could have passed as Giles kissed her, lingering to play and stroke once that first hunger had been assuaged, the heat of his tongue seeking out every sweet curve of her lips and mouth, the smooth column of her throat, the slope of her breasts, allowing her the time to recover from his earlier onslaught, when he had been unwilling to give her respite as he brought her again and again to climax just so that he might hear her gasps of pleasure and mewling cries as she shuddered and trembled to completion.

Giles had never before known a woman who responded so readily, so completely, or gave that response so honestly. So much so that he ached to be inside her just so that he might hear those groans again as she reached orgasm.

'Will you help me take off the rest of my things?' He sat up to begin pulling off his boots, for once cursing his boot-maker for having made them such a perfect fit.

Lily chuckled huskily as she moved up on her haunches to aid him, completely unconcerned with her near-nakedness, and rendering Giles temporarily still as he gazed hungrily at the gentle sway of her bared breasts as she pulled off one boot after the other before her deft fingers moved to the fastening of his breeches.

She gasped slightly as she saw that last scar etched deep into his muscled thigh, her lips as soft and tender as butterfly wings against his puckered flesh.

Giles reached up to touch either side of her face. 'You truly are a wonder to me, Lily.' He kissed her again hungrily, only to break off that kiss as he felt her cool fingers close about him. His hands closed about those caressing fingers. 'Not this time, Lily. I—I am too far beyond control to hold,' he acknowledged gruffly as he gently pushed her back onto his jacket before moving over and between her parted thighs.

He rested on his arms as he paused to look down at her in the dappled darkness. He saw her dark curls, wild and wanton, about her bare shoulders. Her eyes were languid with longing. Her lips were full and swollen from his kisses. The dark triangle of her curls was a sharp contrast to the long length of him as he shifted to slowly guide himself into her.

'You will not get me with child as my father did my mother?'

Giles drew in a harsh and rasping breath at the sound of her

husky plea. 'No, I—I will be careful,' he assured her gruffly
as he began to enter her inch by slow inch, the pleasure of
it so overwhelming that Giles began to doubt his ability to
control himself. 'Lily?' He looked down at her as he heard
her sharply indrawn breath, very aware that there was still an
equal amount not yet inside her. 'I do not want to hurt you—'

'I do not want you to stop!' She reached down to clasp his
buttocks as he would have pulled back. 'It is only—' She shook
her head. 'You feel so silky and smooth and yet so hard and
big at the same time.'

It took every ounce of Giles's self-control to raise his head
from looking down at their two joined bodies to instead look
at Lily's face in an effort not to give in to the need he felt to
thrust fully inside her, until he was totally surrounded by her
moist heat. 'I am not hurting you?'

'No,' Lily assured, never having imagined that having a
man inside her would feel like this, so full, so much pressure,
the long length of him seeming like wood encased in velvet as
he slowly entered her. 'Well, perhaps it feels a little…strange,'
she conceded as he continued to look down at her. 'But I do
not want you to stop.'

'Then we will go slowly. Very slowly,' he promised gruffly.
'And if it becomes too much for you, then you must tell me
and I will stop immediately.'

Lily was not sure that going slowly would ease the pressure building inside her; in fact, she was sure it would not.
She knew only that she needed—wanted—something, and
it only increased, intensified, at his slow and tortuous entry.

She gasped as she raised her legs and wrapped them about
Giles's waist, lifting, bringing him fully into her and resulting in a momentary pain, a ripping, as that long and velvet
length surged fully inside her, filling her completely. With a

groan, Giles drove forward, touching something deep inside her, a place that had never been touched before, and which once again sent her spiralling up to that plateau of pleasure.

His eyes glittered in the darkness as he raised his head sharply. 'God, Lily!'

'Do not stop, Giles,' she pleaded, and her legs tightened about him as she began to move, working herself along his pulsing length and causing herself to quiver and contract. 'Please do not stop!'

Giles knew he would not have been able to stop if his life had depended upon it, groaning even as he lowered his head to take one tight nipple into his mouth as he plunged into her, again and again, not even the shock of knowing he had pierced Lily's innocence enough to bring him to his senses as she undulated rhythmically beneath him.

Only the remembrance of her earlier plea made him pull out as he felt her pulsing in orgasm at the same time as his own climax began to explode.

He let out a roar of ecstasy as his release burst from him, until he knew himself completely spent, and could only collapse against the heat of her breasts.

And only just in time, as the faint sound of voices—Mrs Lovell and her nephew returning from the village?—could once again be heard heading towards the river!

Fourteen

· ·

'And I thought I told ye not to mess with the lasses about here.' Mrs Lovell could be heard scolding her nephew as the voices drew closer. 'I'll have ye know that Mrs Hall is a re-spectable widow.'

'It's usually the respectable ones as is most grateful for a bit of attention!' Judah came back cheekily. ''Specially when they's as pretty as Mrs Hall.'

His aunt gave a disgusted snort. 'You'll meet your match one day, Judah-me-lad, mark my words, and it can't come soon enough for me. Now hold on to this here basket whilst I go and see if there's any mushrooms beneath this willow.'

Which was the only warning Lily and Giles had of Mrs Lovell pushing aside the willow branches and poking her head inside where they still lay together in a naked tangle!

Lily's eyes were wide with shock as she hurriedly reached out to pull Giles's discarded shirt over their nakedness before looking pleadingly across at the Gypsy woman.

Mrs Lovell seemed completely at a loss for words for several long seconds as she took in the scene before her, her expression one of open-mouthed incredulity. Then she clamped her lips together noisily before speaking weakly. 'No, it seems as if someone has been here before me....' She ducked quickly back out of the branches—hopefully before her nephew could catch a glimpse of Lily and Giles entwined together. 'Let's get along, boy, I has things to do back at the yag. And I reckon some young lady might be along later to collect her bonnet and gloves,' she added pointedly, followed by the sound of them both making their way along the riverbank.

Lily was unsure if she had even remembered to breathe, for what had seemed to last for hours could in reality have only been a few brief seconds. She was now absolutely mortified that Mrs Lovell should have found her and Giles in such a compromising position.

'What are you doing?' Giles could only stare up at Lily in confusion as she slipped quickly out of his arms before standing to begin hurriedly collecting up her clothes.

She pulled her chemise on over her head before releasing the long cascade of her hair from the neckline. 'Surely it is obvious?'

Giles sat up to rest his arm on one bent knee. 'You cannot just dress and leave as if nothing has happened!'

'I must leave now if I am to go and retrieve my bonnet and gloves from Mrs Lovell before returning to the vicarage in time for luncheon.' She shook out her gown before stepping into it and pulling it up over her arms to settle it on her shoulders before reaching back to refasten the buttons. 'And now that she has—has discovered the two of us together, I feel that I really should go and offer her at least some sort of explanation for—for what she has just witnessed.' Her face was very pale in the sun-dappled gloom.

'Would you like me to come with you?'

'Certainly not!' She turned to protest forcefully. 'It will be…awkward enough, without having you present too!'

Giles stood up abruptly. 'We need to talk before you leave—'

'Did you not hear me just say that I have to go immediately if I am to visit Mrs Lovell and return home in time to eat luncheon with my father?' Lily avoided meeting Giles's gaze as she stepped away to smooth her crumpled gown in preparation for emerging from what she had thought to be the privacy of the willow branches.

'I heard you.' His hands reached out to grasp her shoulders as she would have turned to leave. 'Look at me, Lily,' he instructed firmly. 'I said look at me!' He shook her slightly as she instead kept her gaze levelled on the silky dark hair covering his scarred and naked chest. A naked chest which Lily had so enjoyed kissing and caressing only minutes ago….

But to raise her gaze to look at Giles's face would, she knew, be to see the condemnation of his expression, and to look down lower, to where his shaft was still visibly semi-aroused against his body, would be even more embarrassing.

How did one usually go about bringing an end to an encounter such as theirs had been? Lily had no experience upon which to base her actions; she only knew she found the aftermath of their spent passion to be awkward in the extreme.

Her closest friends were Lady Kate and Lady Phaedra, the three women often confiding in one another, but once again Lily knew she absolutely could not discuss this with either of them!

She shook her head. 'As I am sure Mrs Lovell is only too well aware, it would only give rise to speculation if I were to return home without my bonnet and gloves. Surely we can talk another time, if you really feel we must.'

His fingers tightened painfully on her shoulders. 'Oh, I

definitely feel that we must!' he grated forcefully. 'What on earth did you think you were doing?' he added exasperatedly as he gave her another shake. 'Damn it, Lily, did you not think it might be important to inform me that…that I would be your first lover?'

'And why should I have told you that?' Lily did look up at him now, her gaze wary.

'Because I could have hurt you. More than I obviously did,' he added.

'I am not hurt, Giles,' she assured softly. 'You were…extremely considerate with me.' Once again she could not meet his gaze. 'I…enjoyed the experience very much.' She had more than enjoyed it; for her, it had been a life-changing experience. But in such a way that she could not even bear to think about it now, let alone discuss it with this angrily impatient Giles.

'You enjoyed—!' Giles stared down at her in exasperation, still reeling from the shock of knowing that minutes ago he had taken Lily's innocence. He had thought— Had assumed— Her enthusiastic response to his lovemaking, four days ago as well as today, had led him to believe…

What had it led him to believe? That he had been right about her character all along, and that Lily had taken other lovers before him?

Their actions today had shown him that those thoughts, beliefs and assumptions had been mistaken.

He should have known, should have guessed the truth, when their conversation earlier today had succeeded in eliminating each and every one of the men living locally with whom Lily might possibly have been intimately involved in the past. His brother Edward. Sir Nathan. Even that rascal Judah Lovell.

Yes, Giles should have realised the truth of Lily's innocence, but he had not, and now she—

'I have no idea what you are thinking behind that fierce scowl.' Lily looked up at him warily in the dappled darkness. 'But I trust that whatever it is, you do not intend to make any more foul or false accusations…?'

Giles could feel the tension in her shoulders, as if she were preparing for a verbal blow. A blow she obviously expected him to deliver. 'Why?' he groaned huskily instead.

She blinked long dark lashes. 'Why what?'

He frowned. 'Why me?'

She breathed softly. 'I do not understand.'

'You must!' Giles could feel the rapid beat of her pulse beneath his fingertips as he looked searchingly into her eyes. 'You are young and beautiful. Desirable—'

'And totally unsuited to being anything more than wife to a man such as Sir Nathan Samuelson, or mistress to a man of my own choosing,' she finished bluntly. 'I chose you.'

'You wish to take up the offer of becoming my mistress?' Giles echoed incredulously.

In truth, Lily had not thought beyond the here and now, beneath this willow with Giles. And, her own emotions aside—and the awkwardness of being discovered by Mrs Lovell—she could not in truth feel regret for the choice she had made.

Well…she could perhaps have wished the embarrassment of their present conversation had not occurred.

Her own emotions were something Lily would have plenty of time—hours, days, weeks, months ahead!—in which she might consider the folly of not having come to a realisation of those feelings earlier.

For Giles's part, she had no cause for complaint; as she had already stated, he had proven to be considerate as well as passionate in his attentions towards her. Everything and more, in fact, that any woman might wish for in a lover.

As the pleasurable ache between Lily's thighs surely testified!

She straightened. 'Could we not just agree that we both… enjoyed our time together, and leave it at that?'

'No, we damn well—!' Giles broke off his ferocious outburst as he saw the way Lily flinched at his vehemence. 'Lily—' he deliberately gentled his tone '—surely you cannot expect to…to give me your innocence, and then just walk away as if nothing has occurred?'

'Why can I not?'

'Because—' Once again Giles had to make a deliberate effort to bite back his frustration with Lily's calm composure. A composure he found all the more baffling because of his own lack of it! 'I cannot talk to you when I am not even dressed!' He moved to gather up his drawers, cursing under his breath as he pulled them on. 'Damn it, Lily, can you not see that we at least must discuss what will happen now!' He straightened impatiently.

'I have told you of my intention to go and collect my bonnet and gloves from Mrs Lovell—'

'I did not mean literally!' Giles glared.

Lily knew that, of course; she would just rather the two of them did not have this conversation, particularly now. Facing the curious Mrs Lovell already promised to be embarrassing enough! She also felt a little discomforted and damp between her thighs, and her legs were feeling decidedly unsteady.

There was also, she realised, a heaviness where her heart should be….

None of which she wished to reveal to this impatiently angry man who was the cause of that discomfort! 'I do not have time for this now, Giles.'

'When do you expect you will have time for it?' he cut in harshly.

Never, if Lily had her way. 'Do you regret what happened?'

His face darkened. 'Of course I regret it!'

Lily flinched at his vehemence. 'Then there is nothing more to be said.' She held her shoulders stiffly.

His expression softened. 'Lily—'

'If you will excuse me?' She avoided the hand he lifted with the obvious intention of grasping her arm. 'I have Mrs Lovell to visit, and lunch to eat with my father.' In her present mood, it would probably choke her! 'And this afternoon I still have several things to do ahead of the well-dressing celebrations.' Her back was straight and uninviting as she moved the branches of the willow aside.

Giles's expression was pained as he stood bare-chested beneath the shadows of the willow, knowing the evidence of their lovemaking was unmistakable for any who cared to look at Lily; her ebony curls fell in a loose tangle down the length of her spine, there was a slightly dreamy look to her eyes, and her lips looked full and a little swollen. There was also a slight redness to the skin visible above the scooped neckline of her gown, no doubt caused by the stubble upon Giles's chin. 'Lily, please—'

'Goodbye, Giles.' She spared him a last cursory glance before setting out along the riverbank, no doubt in the direction of Mrs Lovell's campsite.

Giles cursed the fact that he could not follow her without causing a scandal if he were seen by anyone dressed only in his breeches and with his own hair no doubt in disarray.

Instead he returned to collect the rest of his clothes, only to bestow instead a frustrated punch of his fist into the trunk of the tree, uncaring—welcoming, even—the pain of the cuts and grazes he received to his knuckles for his trouble.

If Lily seriously thought this was an end to their conversation then she was in for a sharp awakening!

Lily did not, as she had said she would, go straight to Mrs Lovell's campsite. The tears that fell hotly down her cheeks prevented her from being in anyone's company for some time after she had left Giles. Instead she managed to stumble blindly a safe distance away from the willow tree, making sure she was off the main path and collapsing beneath a tall oak, before allowing the deep sobs to rack her body.

Giles was quite correct to ask her what on earth she had thought she was doing!

Had she really thought that she might behave as so many gentlemen did, by taking her pleasure with Giles, without consequence? Oh, not the consequence of an unwanted pregnancy; she believed Giles when he assured her there would be no consequences of that nature. But had she really believed that she could make love with him and her emotions would remain unengaged?

Had she not realised that her emotions must already be engaged for her to wish to make love with Giles in the first place?

If she had not, then she was a fool. A blind, stupid fool.

Because now she knew beyond a shadow of doubt that she had fallen in love with Giles Montague!

No girlish infatuation—she was far too old for that—but a deep and abiding love.

In these past few hours she had come to admire everything about him: his deep love for his family; his obvious bravery as a soldier; his caring and consideration for the people who lived and worked on the Castonbury estate, despite his earlier reluctance to assume his role as heir, even including the comfort and well-being of the transitory Mrs Lovell. And as for his looks…!

Lily had only to gaze upon Giles's harshly chiselled features and firmly muscled body for her pulse to race and her skin to feel hot and fevered!

What must he think of her now?

Did Giles hate and despise her for being the temptress he had thought her to be a year ago? More so, perhaps, because she had ultimately displayed that wantonness with him?

How would she ever be able to face him again knowing how he must now despise her?

She could not.

She would not!

She must find a way to leave Castonbury in the near future, and it must be in such a way that her father would find acceptable. For Lily would not, could not, remain in Castonbury and suffer the pain of seeing on a daily basis how Giles must now feel towards her.

Mrs Lovell looked up from poking her fire as Lily silently entered the campsite some minutes later, her sharp gaze roving critically over Lily's dishevelled appearance. 'Sit ye down, lass, an' I'll brew some tea.'

Lily cast a wary look at Judah as he lazed on the other side of the fire. 'I really cannot stop—'

'I said sit ye down, lass. You, boy.' She turned to her nephew. 'Take the pail and go and collect some fresh water for the tea.'

He rose languidly to his feet, his dark gaze fixed questioningly on Lily. 'You look just like—'

'And is it for you to comment on how a lady does or doesn't look?' His aunt gave him a disapproving glare.

His handsome face flushed resentfully. 'I was only saying—'

'Well, don't.' Mrs Lovell thrust the bucket at him.

Judah seemed distracted as he slowly took the bucket, his narrowed gaze still fixed on Lily as she stood at the edge of the campsite. 'She looks different with her 'air down like that. Almost as if she might be one of u—'

'Will you just go and get the water, Judah Lovell, afore I clip yer ear for the second time today!' his aunt rounded on him fiercely.

Judah shot his aunt a resentful glare. 'I'm going, ain't I?'

'Not as quick as I'd like, no.' Mrs Lovell watched her nephew until he had sauntered well out of earshot. 'Sit ye down, lass.' She turned to Lily. 'Before ye fall down,' she added firmly as she straightened to collect up mugs for the tea.

Lily sat. Or rather, she collapsed weakly onto one of the logs upended beside the fireside, but unable to feel any of the warmth emitted by its flames. It caused her to wonder if the ice about her heart was not taking over her whole body. She moistened dry lips before speaking. 'I am sorry for being the cause of discord between you and your nephew—'

'Ye ain't,' the old lady assured her bluntly. 'I hadn't set eyes on him for twenty years until he turned up here again—nor wanted to—and the sooner he goes off again about his own business the better I shall like it.' Her expression was grim as she picked up a cloth to lift the kettle from over the fire.

Lily blinked as the elderly lady poured the boiling water into the waiting teapot. 'But I thought you sent Judah for more water?'

'Menfolk has no place in our conversation. 'Specially ones as nosey as Judah.' Mrs Lovell frowned her disapproval in the direction her nephew had taken to the riverside.

Lily chewed on her bottom lip. 'I am sorry for—for what you saw earlier.'

'Here's your bonnet, gloves and hairpins.' Mrs Lovell placed them beside Lily as she handed her a steaming mug of the hastily brewed tea. 'Drink that down ye, lass, and maybe you'll feel a little better.'

Lily gave a choked and humourless laugh. 'I somehow doubt that, Mrs Lovell.'

'Nothing's ever as bad as ye think it is.' The elderly lady made herself comfortable on the stool facing Lily across the fire, her sharp gaze fixed on Lily's face.

'I believe this might possibly be worse, so much worse, than I think it is!' she assured emotionally, but sipped her tea obediently anyway. But she could not taste the brew, nor did she feel any melting of that inner ice.

Mrs Lovell eyed her curiously. 'Do ye love him?'

Lily glanced up and then as quickly looked away again as she saw the speculation in the other woman's curiously sharp gaze. 'Would a more pertinent question not be what Lord Giles's feelings might now be towards me?' She would not insult the elderly lady by even attempting to pretend she did not know exactly to whom Mrs Lovell was referring.

'It's obvious to anyone with eyes in their head that he's fond of ye.' The older woman gave a dismissive snort. 'And that you're fond of him. You'd have to be stupid as well as blind not to see the way the two of ye were looking at each other when ye were here together a couple of days past.'

'No—'

'Oh, yes,' the older woman confirmed with satisfaction. 'So what's got you so upset about it all that you're as white as a ghost?'

Lily gave a rueful shake of her head. 'Do you really need to ask me that?'

'Well, as long as there'll be no chivvy as a result—'

'There will not,' Lily assured hastily.

Mrs Lovell nodded. 'Then I would say that the two of you were only doing what comes naturally.'

Lily gave a slightly bitter laugh. 'My behaviour today has been shocking, Mrs Lovell. Absolutely scandalous.' She trembled slightly as she avoided meeting that shrewd hazel-coloured gaze. 'I do not suppose you would care for a travelling companion when you leave Castonbury? No, I do not suppose you would.' She answered her own question dully as the elderly woman looked taken aback by the request. 'I am afraid I have been extremely stupid, Mrs Lovell, and must now find some way in which to salvage a scrap of my pride, at least.'

'Well, you won't succeed in doing that by running away.' The older woman tutted disapprovingly. 'And for what it's worth, whatever you did ye weren't alone when ye did it.'

No, Lily certainly had not been alone when she had behaved so shamelessly. If she had been alone, then it would not have been so shameless! 'I am afraid that sort of—of behaviour may be acceptable for a gentleman, but it is certainly not the case for a single lady.'

'I got no time for such nonsense,' Mrs Lovell scorned.

Lily, unfortunately, did not have that same freedom of choice. Something she should surely have thought of before making love with Giles! Maybe she had thought of it, but at the time had just not cared? However, it had been a rash moment she would no doubt have plenty of time to regret during the coming days and weeks!

Her more immediate problem was to find some way—although goodness knew how it was to be found—of getting through the next few days at least, without finding herself alone again in Giles's company. Something which, Lily knew, with the well-dressing celebrations to take place at Castonbury Park in two days' time, was going to be extremely difficult to achieve.

'Would you like me to help ye rearrange your pretty hair?'

Lily gave a pained wince at the kindness she heard in Mrs Lovell's gentle tone. 'I would, thank you.' She distractedly gathered up her hair and coiled it up onto her crown.

The older woman moved round the fire to begin putting in the pins to hold it in place. 'I can't believe— Lord Giles is a good man. An honourable man…'

'Oh, he is,' Lily assured hastily, having seen the genuine fondness between Giles and the elderly Romany on her previous visit here.

'Then I don't see what the problem is.' Mrs Lovell moved back to her seat on the opposite side of the fire.

Lily imagined that life must be so much simpler for Mrs Lovell, stopping to camp when and where she liked, travelling on when she became bored or restless, eating and sleeping to no other clock but her own.

Unfortunately Lily's life was not the same, the stigma of her birth having already given her a precarious position socially, as well as having attached preconceived expectations to her character. Expectations which she had surely only confirmed with her behaviour today with Giles.

'I am sure you are right, and I am worrying unnecessarily.' She stood up dismissively. 'I really must go now, my dear Mrs Lovell. But I will see you at Castonbury Park for the well-dressing?'

'Ye will. But—'

'I really must make haste.' Lily secured her bonnet about

her now-tidy hair. 'Father will be expecting me.' She hurried off before Mrs Lovell had a chance to say anything further.

With any luck, by the time she returned to the vicarage Giles would already have been back to collect Genghis and would by now be safely on his way to Castonbury Park.

Fifteen

....

It did not take a glance into Mrs Lovell's crystal ball—if indeed she possessed one—for Giles to realise that Lily was deliberately avoiding him. That she had been successfully avoiding him for the whole of the two days since they had made love together beneath the willow.

Not that Giles had too many hours to spend brooding over the reasons for that. He had found the time to visit the vicarage yesterday, only to learn that Lily was not at home, and so he had spent an hour talking with Mr Seagrove instead. Otherwise Giles's attentions had been completely taken up by the problem of the increasingly pressing financial situation now besetting the whole of the Montague family. A problem his father seemed to have chosen to ignore by once again withdrawing to his rooms and retreating into silence.

Giles had paid another visit to the lawyers on the day following his lovemaking with Lily, after which he had been forced to once again send word to his man in London to advance more of his personal funds.

But the letter which had been delivered to him earlier this

morning, if it should prove to be genuine, made all of those other problems pale into insignificance!

None of which Giles could allow, or would allow, to be seen during the well-dressing celebrations. His instructions to Mrs Stratton, as well as Monsieur André, were that all arrangements for those celebrations were to proceed with the Duke of Rothermere's usual largesse.

But beneath all of those other problems was still the knowledge that Lily was deliberately avoiding him.

Even now, on the day of the well-dressing, she had managed to stay away from him by keeping herself busy outside in the garden, helping to put up the tables and chairs, as well as preparing the numerous stalls necessary for the celebrations later today.

It did not please Giles in the least that when he did finally chance to meet up with her it was in the company of that charming rascal Judah Lovell!

The two of them appeared to be arranging the covers over the poles for the tent where Mrs Lovell was to do her fortune-telling; Lily was laughing softly at something the young, handsome and—damn him—flirtatious Romany had just said to her.

That humour faded the moment she looked up and saw Giles standing several feet away watching the two of them. 'Lord Montague.' Her curtsey was as formal as her words, her gaze lowered demurely.

His mouth tightened as he nodded in curt acknowledgement of her greeting. 'Lily.' His gaze was icy as he turned to the younger man. 'I wonder if you would mind leaving us for a few moments so that I might talk privately to Miss Seagrove?'

'Sure an' that's up to Lily 'erself, don't ye think?' Judah's expression bordered on the insolent as he met Giles's gaze in open challenge.

Giles's eyes narrowed upon hearing Judah refer to Lily by her Christian name, his voice dangerously soft. 'Whether you choose to go or stay is your own decision, surely.' The threat in his tone was unmistakable.

Judah held his gaze for several seconds longer before he turned to look down at Lily. 'What do you think, Lily?'

What Lily thought was that the tension between the two men was palpable, so much so that she was forced to repress a shiver of apprehension as she looked from one to the other and saw the unspoken challenge as their gazes met and clashed.

Having managed to avoid seeing Giles for the past two days, she had no wish to speak with him now, either privately or in the company of others, but the contest for her attention was such that she was sure only her acquiescence to Giles's request would succeed in putting an end to it without the possibility of blood being shed. 'Perhaps, if Mr Lovell does not mind continuing on alone for a few minutes, the two of us might stroll about the garden together, Lord Montague.' She gave a gracious bow of her head as she preceded Giles in the direction of one of the rose beds.

She was so aware of Giles, as he first walked behind her and then at her side as he easily caught up with her, his strides being so much longer than her own.

The past two days had been nothing short of purgatory for Lily.

Not only had she gone out of her way to avoid any situation in which she might find herself face to face with Giles, but as he had also warned, her father had spoken to her concerning Sir Nathan's interest. An interest she had no hesitation in assuring her father she did not, and would not ever, return. That her father had been relieved by her answer she had no doubt, but he had also felt duty bound to point out the advantages of such a marriage.

And all the time he had done so Lily had been aware of the fact that not only was such an alliance wholly repugnant to her, but coming so soon after her lovemaking with Giles, it was now also totally out of the question for her to accept a proposal of marriage from any gentleman, repugnant or otherwise.

Leading her to question whether she had not consciously known that all along, and if it had not contributed to her recklessness that day.... Certainly she could no longer offer herself to any decent man as an innocent bride.

'Are you well?'

She glanced sideways at Giles upon hearing his softly spoken query, but was unable to read any of his thoughts from the remoteness of his expression.

This did not stop Lily from being wholly appreciative of his handsome ensemble. He wore a dark grey superfine over a paler waistcoat and white linen, with dove-grey breeches and black Hessians, his dark hair having been blown across his brow by the warmth of the light breeze.

She turned away from that breathtaking handsomeness. 'I am very well, thank you, Lord Montague. And you?'

'As well as can be expected when my lover calls me "Lord Montague" in that cold tone and has been avoiding my company for two days!'

Lily gasped softly at the directness of Giles's attack, colour burning her cheeks as she came to an abrupt halt in order to glare up at him. 'How dare you speak to me of such things here?' she hissed fiercely, very aware of the dozens of other people milling around the gardens and grounds of Castonbury Park, all helping to prepare for this afternoon's celebrations.

'Where else should I speak of them, when I have not so much as managed to set eyes upon you?' he came back unapologetically.

Lily turned to glare at him, the warmth of her embarrassment still high in her cheeks. 'I believe it would be best for all concerned if you did not speak of it at all, but rather tried to forget it ever happened!'

'And is that what you have been attempting to do?'

'We were not talking about my feelings on the matter!'

'Oh, no, Lily, this avoidance really will not do at all.' Giles shook his head, more than pleased to have her full attention, no matter what the reason.

She had looked pale when he had approached her earlier, the grey of her gown doing little to add to that colour, but the angry blush now in her cheeks, and the glitter in those clear green eyes as she glared up at him, made her appear more like the beautiful woman he had made love to beneath the willow.

'Do you really imagine that I could ever forget—ever want to forget—our lovemaking, Lily?' he prompted huskily.

Her hands were clasped tightly together in front of her. 'I wish that you would try!'

Giles gave a pained wince at her vehemence. 'Why?'

'Because—' She gave a disbelieving shake of her head. 'You said that you regretted what had happened.'

His eyes narrowed. 'Are you saying you now regret it too?'

She glared her exasperation. 'Has my avoidance of you since not indicated as much?'

Giles looked down searchingly into the beauty of her face—dark lashes surrounding those extraordinary green eyes, her small nose, those wide, lush lips above a small and determined chin. It was a face which had haunted Giles's days as well as his nights since they had last met. 'I regret very much taking your innocence, Lily,' he told her softly. 'But it is only the timing I regret, not the deed itself.'

'You talk in riddles!'

'Do I?'

Lily gave an agitated shake of her head. 'I do not have the time to deal with your mockery today, Giles—'

'And if it is not mockery?' he prompted huskily. 'If my reason for wanting to see you again was so that I might ask if you would consider becoming my wife?'

Lily's gaze flew to his face, her expression startled. She saw only that same wide forehead, dark brows over grey eyes, high cheekbones either side of the arrogant slash of a nose, his lips sculptured perfection above a stubbornly relentless jaw.

Except...

There was something different about his eyes. A softness? An uncertainty, perhaps?

If that was so, then it was a softness and uncertainty which did not in the least detract from the fact that he must once again be mocking her!

She shook her head. 'The silly cat may look at a king, my lord, may perhaps even make love with him, but never any more than that.' She turned away with the intention of returning to her previous task.

Only to have her arm firmly grasped by Giles's fingers as he halted that departure. 'You are referring to yourself as a silly cat?'

'What else?' She sighed her impatience with his persistence. 'You are Lord Montague, and heir to the Duke of Rothermere, and I am merely the vicar's adopted daughter, an abandoned child of questionable parentage at best.'

'And the heir to the Duke of Rothermere may marry where and with whom he wishes!'

'And a sensible heir would never wish to find himself married to the penniless adopted daughter of the parish vicar!'

Giles mouth twisted as he thought of the state of his family's finances, and the letter he had received earlier that morning. 'We may be more equal in that than you can ever imagine, Lily.'

'Somehow I doubt it very much!'

He frowned. 'Does that mean you would not even consider me if I were to offer you marriage?'

'So that you might once again accuse me of plotting and planning such an outcome? I think not, Giles!' Lily eyed him scathingly.

'I offer no such accusations—'

'Then perhaps that will come later!' She gave an impatient shake of her head. 'Now if you are quite finished playing with the cat, my lord, she is wishful of returning to help prepare for the celebrations later today.' She gave his restraining fingers about her arm a pointed look.

If Giles had needed any further confirmation of Lily's lack of deception in regard to her reasons for making love with him—which he did not—then her refusal to even take seriously his offer of marriage left him in no doubt as to her innocence; the designing and scheming woman he had once believed her to be would have had no hesitation in greedily accepting even the suggestion of a proposal of marriage from the future Duke of Rothermere!

He drew in a harsh breath. 'Mr Seagrove informed me, when I called at the vicarage yesterday, that you have refused any suggestion of a marriage between yourself and Sir Nathan Samuelson.'

Her chin rose. 'And is that why you have chosen to hint at an offer of marriage yourself today? Because you wished to bedevil and taunt me with the possibility of it?'

Giles searched the proud beauty of her face. 'Does the possibility bedevil and taunt you, Lily?'

It did, more than Lily would ever allow Giles to see, when she knew an offer of marriage from him was much like an elusive and beautiful butterfly, fluttering just beyond her reach, beguiling and tempting her to scoop it up in her hands and hold it tightly to her, only to find when she opened up her fingers that her hands were empty.

'No, it does not,' she answered him flatly. 'I have not now, nor will I ever, have any desire to receive a marriage proposal from you, let alone trouble myself giving an answer to it. Now, if you will excuse me?' She looked at him haughtily. 'As I have said, I still have much work to do.'

Giles slowly uncurled his fingers from about her arm, remaining beside the rose bed as Lily instantly turned and walked back in the direction of where she had been working earlier with Judah Lovell.

He had not dared to imagine what Lily's reaction might be to the suggestion of marriage between the two of them, but he had hoped—he had certainly hoped—that it might be favourable. To have the first proposal of marriage he had ever made in his life thrown back in his face without thought or consideration would have been humiliating if Giles did not find it so amusing at the same time.

A burst of laughter overtook him as he gave in to that amusement; Lily was, without a shadow of a doubt, the most unpredictable, beautiful and enchanting woman he had ever met. Or ever hoped to meet....

And if she believed their conversation over in regard to a marriage between the two of them, then she was very much mistaken.

'—cannot imagine what has happened to Mrs Lovell, can you?' Mrs Stratton frowned as she looked pointedly towards the line of people from the village already gathered outside the tent where the elderly Romany should have been waiting to begin telling their fortunes.

Should have been waiting, because as Lily and the housekeeper of Castonbury Park could clearly see, Mrs Lovell had not as yet arrived at the celebrations. Lily had not expected her to attend the well-dressing ceremonies—she never had in the past—but she never missed the party afterwards. 'She assured me that she would be here in time....' Lily voiced her own concern. 'I wonder what can have happened to delay her?'

Hannah Stratton shook her head. 'Shall I send one of the maids over to check, do you think?'

Lily placed a reassuring hand on the older woman's arm. 'I will go myself.' In truth, she would welcome the time such a task might enable her to spend away from the crowd of people milling about the gardens of the estate. And from the overwhelming presence of Giles Montague, especially....

She had assisted her father earlier during the ceremonies at the three wells in the village, murmured polite approval to Mrs Crutchley as to the splendour of the floral arrangements at each of the wells, invented amusement for some of the village children when they had become a little restless—and all of that time been completely aware of Giles as he stood attentively at her father's other side in representation of the Montague family.

Indeed, his appearance, in blue velvet and grey silk, had been of such magnificence that Lily challenged any woman, in love with him or otherwise, not to be affected by such a proud display of male elegance!

Certainly Lily had been far from immune to such splendour, her gaze returning again and again to the arresting handsomeness of Giles's face, as she looked at him from beneath the brim of her cream bonnet which she had prettied up with the same dark green ribbon which adorned the high waist of the new moss-green gown she had made especially for the occasion.

At the time of choosing the material and ribbon for the new gown—a mere two weeks ago, although it seemed so much longer!—Lily knew she had done so in the hopes of impressing Giles. A forlorn hope now, if ever there was one!

Nevertheless, Lily had chosen to wear her new gown anyway, aware that she was in need of all the self-confidence she possessed if she were to get through the rest of the day.

She could see him across the garden even now, as he talked with his father, who had decided to make a brief appearance in order to welcome everyone to his home. Giles looked so handsome and aristocratic next to his much frailer father. A breathtaking and disturbing handsomeness which Lily would indeed welcome escaping from, if only for the short time it took her to find and bring back Mrs Lovell.

'I will not be long.' She smiled reassuringly at Mrs Stratton now. 'With any luck, I may meet Mrs Lovell coming along the towpath.'

'Let us hope so.' The housekeeper nodded distractedly as she obviously spotted something occurring in the tea tent not to her liking or satisfaction.

Lily took advantage of that distraction to hurry away,

slipping quietly from the throng of people towards the direction of Mrs Lovell's campsite.

'Have you seen Miss Seagrove?' Giles frowned his displeasure as he stood beside Mrs Stratton, having spent the past hour escorting his father about the garden, then returning the exhausted duke to his rooms and the attentions of Smithins. He now found himself free to seek out and speak to Lily, only to discover she was nowhere to be found in the gardens or the kitchens, and no one he had questioned had seen her either.

Giles had been fully aware of Lily's efforts to avoid conversation with him during the well-dressing ceremonies this afternoon—indeed, each time he had so much as dared a glance at her, she had quickly turned away in an effort not to meet his gaze. And if she had now decided to absent herself from the celebrations at Castonbury Park as another means of avoiding him, then Giles very much feared he would have to go to the vicarage and bring her back here by force, if necessary!

Everyone he and his father had spoken to as the two of them moved slowly amongst their guests had only complimentary words to describe how capably Lily had organised today's event, and the last thing Giles wanted was to deprive her of the enjoyment of all her hard work because she felt such a pressing need to avoid his own company.

'She went to look for Mrs Lovell—' Mrs Stratton glanced down at the fob watch pinned on the white collar lapel of her black gown. 'Oh, dear, I had not noticed how the time had flown by, but I believe it is now more than an hour since Lily left to seek out the Gypsy woman. What do you think could have happened to delay them both?' She frowned.

Giles had no idea, but he certainly intended on finding

out. Especially after a narrow-eyed glance about the milling crowds showed that Judah Lovell was not currently present amongst the guests either! 'Do not concern yourself, my dear Mrs Stratton.' He smiled reassuringly at the housekeeper. 'I am sure that all will be well.'

'Perhaps Mrs Lovell has fallen ill? Do you think perhaps I ought to accompany you?' She looked flustered at the mere idea of abandoning her duties here.

Giles patted her arm reassuringly. 'I am sure you have quite enough to do, Mrs Stratton, without concerning yourself about this matter too,' he assured dismissively.

'Well…I do still have to oversee the entrance of Monsieur André's delicious cakes and delicacies.'

'Then do not let me delay you, Mrs Stratton.' Giles nodded approvingly, keeping his smile firmly fixed in place until the housekeeper had hurried away to cluck over the French chef's confectionaries, his expression only becoming grim as he turned to stride off in the direction of Mrs Lovell's campsite.

The whole way there he knew that if he discovered that rascal Judah Lovell anywhere within Lily's vicinity, he was like to turn violent with jealousy!

The scene that met Giles's gaze when he reached Mrs Lovell's campsite seemed to imply that someone had already beaten him to those feelings of violence.

Mrs Lovell's belongings were scattered haphazardly about the clearing—furniture and utensils thrown from the brightly coloured caravan and lying broken, clothes and other fabrics ripped into unrecognisable rags; even the fire, which Giles knew was never allowed to go out, lay in a heap of cold ashes in the centre of all the other chaos.

But he could see no sign of Lily, or Mrs Lovell or even Judah Lovell.

It took Giles some minutes more to realise that Judah's much shabbier caravan and horse were no longer parked alongside his aunt's....

Sixteen

Lily lay with her hands and feet tied, a dirty handkerchief stuffed in her mouth. She had been bundled into the back of a not very clean Gypsy caravan, and the lurching movement of that vehicle only seconds later gave testament to it being driven away from the campsite at great speed. What was happening to her?

One minute she had been standing looking in astonishment at the shambles that was Mrs Lovell's campsite, and wondering where on earth that elderly lady could be, and the next Lily had found herself grabbed from behind, a rope quickly tied about her wrists, before she was turned to face her captor.

Judah Lovell!

'What—'

'There's no time for talking now.' His expression had been grimly determined as he'd pulled a filthy handkerchief from the pocket of his baggy trousers and pushed it into her mouth.

Lily gagged at the taste and smell of that ragged piece of material, her eyes starting to water, but whether from the smell or shocked tears, she was unsure.

Cruel humour glittered in those dark eyes as the young Romany saw her response. 'Not what you're used to, is it, missy? Never mind, we'll soon 'ave plenty of gold for ye to buy a dozen new silk 'andkerchiefs if ye want 'em! In the meantime—' he turned Lily roughly and pushed her towards the back of his caravan '—we'd best be away from 'ere smartish, afore someone—probably that snooty Lord as keeps sniffing about your drawers—decides to come looking for you.'

Giles? He was referring in that derogatory way to Lord Giles Montague? The man that Lily loved with all her heart....

'Thought I didn't notice how cosy the two of you were, aye?' Judah had eyed her tauntingly as he bundled her inside his caravan and tied her feet together with another piece of rope. 'Never mind, you'll forget 'im soon as you 'ave me between your legs, and then we'll see who's the better man!'

Lily had no doubt as to who was the better man as she kicked out with furious indignation, but Judah only pushed her the rest of the way inside his caravan.

He laughed cruelly as he saw how easily he managed to suppress that show of anger. 'Don't you worry, lass, I likes 'em feisty!' The door had been closed, shutting Lily into complete darkness.

And here she had remained, being bounced uncomfortably against the bare wooden floor for what seemed like hours, but was in all probability only half an hour or so, all the time hoping that snooty lord would indeed realise she had gone missing and come looking for her.

'Well, don't just stand there looking, lad, untie me!' Mrs Lovell glared up.

Giles had no idea how long he had been standing lost in shocked disbelief at the destruction all around him, when he heard the sound of a groan coming from the other side of Mrs Lovell's brightly coloured caravan, his years of battle instantly telling him that it was a moan of pain. Striding hurriedly about the caravan he had come across Mrs Lovell, seated on the ground, her wrists tied to the huge wooden wheel of the caravan, the blood and bruising about her face indicative of the violence she had suffered.

He moved quickly down onto one knee now, to begin untying the bonds about her wrists, his expression coldly grim as the elderly lady gave another groan of pain. 'Who did this to you? Whoever it was I will see that they are—'

'Never you mind about me.' Mrs Lovell winced as she slowly lowered her hands, the unnatural position of two of the fingers on her left hand indicating that they might be broken. The split on her swollen bottom lip made her words slightly slurred. 'He's taken Lily—'

'Who has taken Lily?' Giles sat abruptly back on his haunches, his eyes turning glacial.

'Who do you think has taken her?' The elderly woman got awkwardly to her feet with Giles's hand beneath her elbow— the only part of her that did not seem to be bruised or broken! 'That black-hearted, no good, thieving, son of a murdering—'

'Your nephew?' Giles removed his handkerchief from his pocket and moved hastily to the bucket of water, dampening the silk material before wiping away the worst of the blood on Mrs Lovell's face. 'Are you saying that Lily has gone with Judah Lovell?'

The old lady looked up at him with eyes as sharp and dark as a bird's. 'Lily wouldn't go anywhere willingly with that evil—'

Giles stilled. 'You are saying that Lily has been kidnapped by your nephew?'

'Tied up and bundled into the back of his vardo is what she's been!' Mrs Lovell, obviously tired of his careful dabbing at her cuts and bruises, grabbed the handkerchief from his hand and impatiently wiped the blood away herself.

Giles's eyes narrowed as he saw the amount of swelling and bruising the elderly lady had suffered. 'Those look like the result of someone's fists.'

Her mouth set determinedly. 'Oh, don't you worry, laddie, he'll be made to pay for every one o' these hurts when I next sees him. In the meantime, you'd best go after him. Now. Afore any real harm befalls Lily.'

'Explain, if you please.' The years Giles had spent as an officer in the army were the only thing preventing him from reaching out and shaking Mrs Lovell within an inch of her life, and if she did not soon explain to him when and for what reason Judah had tied Lily up and taken her away with him, then he would forget those years of training and give in to his instincts.

'There's no time for that now,' the elderly woman snapped her impatience. 'It's enough for you to know he's taken Lily against her will, heading Buxton way, and that he means to marry her as soon as possible.'

Giles staggered a step back. 'Marry her!'

'Thought that might get your attention.' Mrs Lovell eyed him knowingly. 'Yes, he means to marry her. But she don't want to marry him. So if you want to put a stop to it you'd best follow on pretty smartish. 'Cos once he's made her his wife there'll be no stopping him. Now go and get that big horse of your'n and get after him. Now!' she added grimly.

Giles still had absolutely no idea why Judah Lovell should have taken Lily, or why he meant to marry her; it was enough for now to know that she had not gone willingly. 'You will be all right alone here whilst I am gone?'

Mrs Lovell gave a grimace. 'I don't know of anyone else as wants to punch and kick me, if that's what you mean!'

For beating up a lone elderly lady, Judah Lovell deserved to be thrashed. For daring to tie up and take an unwilling Lily, he deserved, and would receive, so much more!

Bounced and jostled, every inch of her battered and bruised, Lily had no idea how much longer she could bear to suffer the darkness and discomfort of the caravan, along with the worry about Mrs Lovell's condition, let alone not knowing the reason for any of it.

Surely Giles—someone—would have noticed by now that she was missing, and attempt to seek her out? To find Mrs Lovell too....

Surely Judah was not so low, so base, as to have harmed his own aunt? The state of that dear lady's belongings, broken and ripped, along with the fact that she was nowhere to be seen, would seem to indicate that he had.

As he meant to harm Lily?

But why?

What possible reason could Judah Lovell have for kidnapping her? Was it possible that he was somehow mentally deranged? Lily could think of no other reason—

All thoughts ceased as Lily heard the sound of shouting outside, accompanied by the caravan surging forward as the horse was encouraged to speed up, several painful splinters going into her bare arms as she was once again thrown across the rough wooden floor, only to be tossed back in the other direction as the caravan came to a lurching stop.

There was the sound of more shouting—could one of those voices possibly be Giles's or was that just wishful thinking on Lily's part?—followed by a brief silence, before the door at the back of the caravan was wrenched open and the blinding sunlight streamed inside to where she lay.

Giles's earlier anger was as nothing compared to the blinding rage that consumed him as he wrenched open the door at the back of Judah's caravan and saw Lily lying on the dirty floor, her hands and feet tied, a dirty gag filling her pretty mouth, all making Giles wish that he had inflicted mortal damage on Judah Lovell rather than just landing a blow which had rendered him unconscious.

His fury abated slightly—but only slightly—as he saw the way Lily's eyes lit up at the sight of him, before those green eyes instantly became awash with tears. Hopefully ones of relief at being rescued, rather than from physical pain, else Giles really would be pushed into committing an act of violence from which Judah Lovell might not recover!

'Lily!' Giles climbed into the caravan to lift her quickly up into his arms and cradle her against him as he untied the rope from her wrists and removed the gag from her mouth. 'You— I— Thank God I found you in time!' His arms tightened about her and he buried his face against her throat once he had discarded the rope and filthy rag, no longer sure whose tears were dampening her skin, her own or his. He rocked her backwards and forwards in his arms as if he never wanted to let her go again.

In time for what, Lily was unsure; she only knew she was so glad to see Giles, to be held safely in his arms. She no longer cared if she revealed her feelings for him as she threw her arms about his neck and clung to him as if she never wished to let him go.

'Do you feel up to receiving a visitor?'

Lily looked over to where Giles stood in the doorway of one of the guest bedchambers at Castonbury Park.

In truth she was still slightly disorientated at having been brought here at all, once Giles had issued orders for the grooms who had accompanied him to follow on behind and bring the unconscious Judah Lovell back with them to the house, before then sitting astride Genghis with Lily cradled gently in his arms.

They had entered Castonbury Park along the front driveway rather than the back, well away from the curious eyes of the people attending the well-dressing celebrations in the gardens. Giles had refused to relinquish her even once he had slid down from Genghis's back, but instead carried her into the house and up the stairs to this magnificent bedchamber, all the time issuing orders to the servants for hot water to be brought up for a bath, and soothing lotions, all to be delivered immediately if not sooner. Indeed, Lily felt sure Giles would have remained in the bedchamber whilst she took her much-needed bath—and that Lily would have let him—if Mrs Stratton had not shooed him out of the room!

An hour later, freshly bathed, with her hair washed and still damp about her shoulders, she was dressed in one of Phaedra's night-rails. Mrs Stratton tucked her into the warm bed before disappearing along with the bathwater, and Lily now felt as if being tied up and carried away by Judah Lovell must have been a dream. Or a nightmare.

At least, she might have thought that, if not for the soreness of her wrists and ankles where the ropes had chaffed her skin, and the aches and pains in her body from being thrown uncomfortably about the floor of the dirty caravan.

She felt a little shy now as she faced Giles across the width of the bedchamber. 'Of course you must come in, Giles.' Her voice was huskily inviting. 'I have yet to thank you for rescuing me, and—'

'I am not in need of thanks,' he assured her gruffly as he entered, closing the door behind him but making no effort to cross the bedchamber to her bedside.

Lily drank in her fill of him, noting that he had changed out of the clothing he had worn earlier—no doubt it was as filthy as Lily's gown had been. He appeared to Lily now as every dear and beloved inch the aristocratically handsome Lord Giles Montague.

'Nevertheless, I do thank you.' Lily looked down at the gold-coloured brocade coverlet under which she lay. 'I do not know why Mr Lovell behaved in the way that he did, but I am grateful for your rescue. If not for you, I am sure I would have suffered a much worse fate.' She repressed a shiver of revulsion as she recalled the physical threat the golden-haired Romany had made to her before he closed her inside the confines of his caravan.

'Do not think of that now, Lily!' Giles crossed the room in three long strides until he reached her bedside, and was able to take one of her hands firmly within his grasp as he looked down at how tiny and fragile she looked as she sat propped up against the pile of lace pillows.

Tears once again flooded those moss-green eyes. 'I could not find Mrs Lovell earlier. Do you think it possible—?'

'She is safe in the bedchamber next to this one,' Giles assured quickly.

A look of relief instantly came over her pale features. 'I was so worried. I saw the destruction of her home and belongings, and feared that—' She gave a pained frown. 'He did not harm her?'

Giles's expression was grim. 'He beat and kicked her cruelly, and deliberately broke two of her fingers, but the doctor has seen her and says she will recover in time.' He would not soften the blow by lying to Lily after all that she had already suffered.

She gasped. 'I must go to her—'

'And so you shall.' Giles released her hand to firmly grasp her shoulders instead as he looked down into the pale beauty of her face.

'Lily, I thought I had lost you earlier today!'

Her throat moved convulsively as she swallowed before speaking softly. 'I, too, thought I was lost.'

Giles looked down at her searchingly. 'It must not be allowed to happen again.'

'No.' After the ordeal Lily had suffered today, of believing herself to have been taken away from Giles for ever, of that wicked young man carrying out his threat to claim her for his own, she no longer cared in what capacity she might remain in Giles's life, lover or mistress, only that she should never be parted from him again.

'Heavens, how I love you, Lily!' Giles gathered her up into his arms. 'I love you so very much that I will not allow anyone or anything to take you from me ever again!'

Giles loved her?

He *loved* her?

He raised his head to look down at her as he sensed how she had stilled with shock. 'You did not listen to me properly earlier today, Lily, when I spoke of marriage between the two of us. I love you, I am in love with you and I wish—above and beyond all else—to have you for my wife!'

Lily stared up at him, not sure she could have heard him correctly. Had Giles really just said—? Had he just stated—?

His laugh was husky—and slightly uncertain? 'Is there any hope for me, Lily? After all that I have said and done, my abominable treatment of you, is there any chance you might possibly one day come to return my feelings for you?'

It was uncertainty, Lily realised dazedly. The haughtily self-confident Lord Giles Montague was uncertain of *her*. Of her feelings for him!

How could it be possible? What had she ever done to deserve that a man like Giles, a man she now knew to be honourable and true, should fall in love with her and wish to make her his wife?

The latter was impossible, of course, given the differences in their stations, but the fact that he loved her, that he wanted—that he had asked—her to be his wife, was so incredible to Lily that she could only stare up at him with all the love she felt for him glowing in her overbright eyes.

'Lily?'

She melted at the uncertainty she still heard in his dear strong voice. 'Oh, Giles, do you not know how much I—' She broke off as a knock sounded softly on the door of the bedchamber before it was opened and Lumsden stood stiffly in the doorway.

The butler swiftly averted his gaze from where Lily, wearing only the borrowed night-rail, was still held firmly in Giles's grasp. 'Mrs Lovell is becoming agitated at your delay, Lord Giles.'

'I had forgotten all about Mrs Lovell!' Giles shook his head. 'Please assure her that Miss Seagrove and I will be with her immediately, Lumsden.'

'Certainly, my lord.' The butler bowed stiffly before his downcast gaze was once again raised to look at Lily. 'I am pleased to see you feeling so much better, Miss Seagrove.'

'Thank you, Lumsden.' She smiled at him warmly. 'I am pleased to be so!'

He nodded stiffly. 'I will tell Mrs Lovell that you will be with her shortly, my lord.'

'Oh, dear.' Lily chuckled softly once the butler had left, closing the door quietly behind him. 'He is no doubt scandalised to find the two of us alone together and so close in this bedchamber, and me in a borrowed shift.'

They weren't close enough, as far as Giles was concerned, nor would they be until he had Lily as his wife, safely sharing his own bed. 'You were about to say, "Giles, do you not know how much I..."' he prompted huskily.

She avoided meeting his gaze. 'Should we not go to Mrs Lovell?'

Yes, they should. And they would. As soon as Lily had completed that sentence. No matter what it might be! 'Please, Lily?' he groaned achingly.

After all that the two of them had shared, the intimacy of their relationship, it did not seem possible that Lily should once again feel shy in Giles's company. And yet she did.

'Lily, please!'

She could not bear it, could not bear to see the suffering upon his dear and handsome face a moment longer! 'I am already in love with you, Giles.' Her voice was husky but firm. 'I could not have made love with you if I had not already been in love with you, my darling Giles!' she assured him when he seemed able only to stare down at her in stunned disbelief.

'You— I—' He turned to scowl at the door as there was a second knock upon it in as many minutes. 'What is it, Mrs Stratton?' he prompted impatiently as it was she who this time entered the bedchamber uninvited.

The housekeeper looked uncomfortable. 'Mrs Lovell is threatening to get out of bed and come to see Lily for herself if you do not both go to her in the next few seconds.'

'We are coming right now, dear Mrs Stratton.' Lily laughed as she climbed out of bed to pull on the robe which matched her night-rail.

Giles reached out to grasp her hand before she could follow the housekeeper from the bedchamber. 'This conversation is not over, Lily,' he warned determinedly.

'I hope not, Giles.' She stood up on her tiptoes to kiss him lightly on the lips. 'Oh, I do so hope not!' Lily could feel the warmth in her cheeks as she continued to hold his hand as they left the bedchamber together.

Her good humour faded the instant she saw Mrs Lovell looking frail and every inch her seventy-six years as she sat propped up against the pillows in the adjoining bedchamber, her long dark hair shown to be liberally sprinkled with grey as it lay loosely across her narrow shoulders, her poor face battered and bruised. 'Oh, my dear!' Lily released Giles's hand to run across the room, hesitating only as she reached the bed, unwilling to take the elderly woman in her arms, as she so longed to do, for fear she might somehow increase her suffering. 'Judah Lovell is a foul and unfeeling monster!' she cried.

The last time Lily had seen Judah Lovell he had been unconscious, thrown across the saddle of one of the grooms' horses. But looking down at the many bruises and cuts that young man had inflicted upon his own aunt—with his fists?—and the splints supporting her two broken fingers, Lily wished vehemently that he had not merely been knocked unconscious but dead!

Mrs Lovell gave a wan smile as she reached out with her uninjured hand and grasped one of Lily's. 'He has truly been revealed as the "dark and dangerous man" that the tea leaves warned us of, my love. He may have the face and hair of an angel, but his heart is as black as the deepest night,' she added in answer to Lily's puzzled frown.

And Lily had feared—fleetingly—that it might be Giles who was that 'dark and dangerous man' who wished to harm her.

How ridiculous that fear now seemed, when he had become the dearest person in the world to her, and the truest friend. Indeed, he was so dear to her, so much a man that she had come to admire as well as love, that it seemed impossible now to think she had ever thought of him in any other way.

'I do not understand why—why your nephew behaved in this way.' She shook her head. 'What could he possibly hope to gain by injuring you and carrying me off in that way?'

She gave another shudder at the thought of what her fate might have been if Giles had not rescued her.

A shiver which Giles saw and responded to by putting his arm about her waist and drawing her near.

'So it's like that, is it?' Mrs Lovell looked pleased by the possessive gesture. 'I had hoped that it might be, but ye never can be sure.'

'You may be very sure, Mrs Lovell.' Giles spoke quietly but firmly. 'I intend to make Lily my wife and ensure that no harm will come to her ever again.'

The elderly woman nodded. 'In that case, there's a tale I must tell the both of you.'

'You really must not trouble yourself with this now—'

'Oh, yes, my chivvy, I must.' Mrs Lovell assured Lily gruffly. 'Today has shown it's a tale that's long overdue.'

'But—'

'Sit ye down, lass, and listen to what I has to say,' the elderly woman instructed firmly.

Giles released Lily only long enough to fetch the stool from in front of the dressing table, and a chair from beside the window, waiting until Lily was seated in the chair before perching on the stool beside her and taking her hand back into his; if he had his way he would never allow Lily out of his sight or out of reach of his touch ever again!

He turned to look at Mrs Lovell, his expression one of gentle enquiry. 'Unless I am very mistaken, one of the things you wish to tell us is that Lily is your granddaughter?'

Seventeen

'What—?' Lily gasped breathlessly, her eyes wide and shocked as she stared down at the sunken figure in the bed.

'Ah.' Mrs Lovell gave Giles an appreciative glance. 'So you've guessed that, have you?'

'Not until a few minutes ago,' Giles conceded. 'But the likeness between the two of you, now that I see you together with your hair loose about your shoulders, is unmistakable to someone who cares to look.'

'Hard to believe I was once as beautiful as Lily, hmm?' The old lady cackled at her own joke before sobering. 'Judah Lovell saw that same likeness when Lily arrived at the yag with her hair down two days ago!' Her gaze had hardened.

'You—'

'Could the two of you please, please, be silent for just a moment?' Lily regained her breath enough to be able to gasp. 'I am really your granddaughter, Mrs Lovell?' She looked down at the other woman uncertainly.

The elderly woman's expression softened as she steadily returned that gaze. 'You really are.'

'But I— You had only a son, I thought.' Lily was still too stunned to be able to make any sense out of Giles's statement and Mrs Lovell's confirmation of it.

'Matthew,' the elderly lady confirmed gruffly.

Lily nodded abruptly. 'And when I asked you several years ago, you said that I was not the daughter of one of the young ladies in your tribe.'

'And I didn't lie to you.' The older woman nodded. 'It was my son, Matthew, who was your father.'

Lily's throat moved convulsively, and she barely breathed. 'And my mother?'

Mrs Lovell smiled emotionally. 'Thea. Dorothea. Matthew's wife, and my own daughter-in-law.'

Lily blinked. 'But— Then I am not— The two of them were married when I was born?'

'For a year or more.' The old lady nodded as she gave Lily's hand a squeeze with her uninjured one.

Lily turned dazedly to Giles. 'I am not illegitimate, after all….'

'No, my love.' He smiled at her reassuringly. 'And it would not have mattered to me if you were. I love you, and would still have wanted you for my wife, no matter who your parents were.'

Lily smiled at him lovingly through her tears. Tears of happiness. Not only did Giles love her and want to marry her, but she was the daughter of Matthew and Dorothea Lovell, the granddaughter of Rosa Lovell. She had a family. She belonged!

She had loved Mr and Mrs Seagrove all of her life, and always would. They were, and always would be, the mother and father of her heart, who had loved and cherished Lily as their own.

But ever since she had been called 'Gypsy' as a child, and

Mrs Seagrove had explained when and how she had been left to them as a gift to their childless marriage, Lily had felt a certain sense of displacement, of not quite belonging any-where. To finally learn who her real parents were, who her grandmother was, meant more to her than she had ever re-alised. It was—

Lily turned quickly back to Mrs Lovell. 'Where is my mother now?'

'Ah, my chivvy.' Tears filled the elderly lady's eyes. 'She died long ago. It was—'

'No!' Lily groaned achingly. 'When did she die? How did she die?'

It was impossible for Giles to miss the silent plea for help in Mrs Lovell's eyes as she turned to him. 'Shall we let Mrs Lovell—your grandmother—tell us all in her own way, my love?' he urged Lily gently, wishing there was some way he might spare her any more anguish, but knowing that she needed to learn the truth of her parents and her birth. The strong and determined Lily whom he had come to love would accept nothing less!

She seemed to mentally shake herself. 'Of course. I am sorry, Mrs— Grandmother,' she corrected shyly.

Tears glistened in those wily hazel eyes. 'Ah, and it does my old heart good to hear you call me that at last!'

'I will call you nothing else from this moment on.' Lily nodded firmly.

Mrs Lovell settled herself further up the pillows. 'Then I must begin at the beginning of this tale and not the end.' She nodded decisively. 'Your mother's name was Dorothea Sutherland. She was the daughter of Sir Thomas Sutherland, from Yorkshire. He was a very wealthy and widowed gentle-man who had arranged for his only daughter, Dorothea, to marry a lord or an earl or some such—I forgets now. Anyway.' She drew in a deep breath. 'Dorothea, being an independent young lady of twenty-three, and with a definite mind of her own, weren't having none of it.' Mrs Lovell turned to smile affectionately at Lily. 'It's obvious where your own stubborn nature comes from!'

Giles chuckled softly at the slight indignation in Lily's expression. 'You are very stubborn, my love. And I am thankful for it,' he added gruffly. 'I believe I might have continued to wallow in my own arrogant assumptions if not for your determination to convince me otherwise.'

'Very nicely done, Lord Giles.' Mrs Lovell shot him a mischievous glance.

'I thought so.' He nodded ruefully.

'Well, as I say, Thea were a stubborn one. And besides, she already had her eye set on the handsome young Gypsy that was visiting the village with his tribe.' She chuckled wryly. 'My Matthew didn't stand a chance against such a determined young woman, and afore any of us knew about it the two of them had run off together and were married.'

'Were they very much in love?' Lily prompted huskily.

'Very,' Mrs Lovell had no hesitation in confirming firmly. 'Thea's father were none too pleased, o' course, and refused to have any more to do with her once he knew of the marriage. But Thea weren't bothered one little bit. She and Matthew were happy, and she took to the travelling life like one born to it.' Her eyes glowed with pride for the young lady who had been her daughter-in-law. 'Some o' the tribe were none too happy about bringing in an outsider either. Black Jack Lovell, Judah's da, were one o' them.' Her mouth tightened. 'Until he ferreted out that Thea had an inheritance, that is, and decided he might like a bit o' that for himself.'

'An inheritance?' Lily looked puzzled. 'I thought you said her father had disowned her?'

'He did.' Mrs Lovell nodded abruptly. 'But her ma, being a forward-thinking lady, had left some money when she died for Thea to inherit when she turned twenty-one. Once Black Jack found out about it my Matthew and Thea were doomed,' she added heavily.

Lily swallowed down the nausea that had risen suddenly to her throat. 'The shooting accident in the woods?'

'Weren't no accident.' Her grandmother snorted. 'Nor were it the gamekeeper as done it neither.' She scowled. 'I were never able to prove it, but Black Jack Lovell killed my Matthew, your father, as sure as I'm laying here!'

Lily gave a dazed shake of her head. 'But why? What could he possibly have hoped to gain by doing such a thing?'

'Ten thousand pounds.'

'Ten thousand pounds?' Lily gasped.

Her grandmother nodded. 'That were the sum of Thea's inheritance.'

Lily looked stunned. 'But I do not see how? How did your brother-in-law intend to take possession of my mother's money?'

'Could he possibly have intended to marry Matthew's widow?' Giles prompted softly.

'Aye.' Mrs Lovell scowled darkly. 'Thea, being a woman of sense, saw through him. Besides being well along with you, Lily, she were heartbroken at Matthew's death.' She sighed deeply. 'We both were.'

Lily fell back against her chair, so bombarded with information—with emotions—that she could only cling tightly to Giles's hand as her world shifted and settled, before as suddenly shifting again.

Her father had been Mrs Lovell's son, Matthew, her mother Dorothea, a lady, and the daughter of Sir Thomas Sutherland.

Except that was not the end of the story. It seemed that Mrs Lovell—her grandmother—believed that Matthew had been murdered by her own brother-in-law, for the sole purpose of marrying Thea himself and taking possession of her inheritance.

She swallowed hard. 'And is—is my grandfather, Sir Thomas, still alive?'

'No, my chivvy.' Her grandmother looked regretful. 'I found out shortly after Thea died that he'd been killed in a hunting accident six months after Thea ran off with my Matthew.'

Lily looked searchingly at the elderly lady. 'You discovered this shortly after my mother died?'

Mrs Lovell winced. 'You're far too clever fer your own good! Yes, it were after Thea died. I—I had the idea that perhaps your grandfather might be willing to take in his newborn granddaughter and bring her up as his own. But it weren't to be.' She sighed heavily. 'Sir Thomas had been dead almost a year by that time, and wi'out any sign of forgiveness for his only daughter.'

Lily drew in a ragged breath. 'My mother died giving birth to me.' It was a statement rather than a question, and was the only explanation Lily could think of for Mrs Lovell hoping that her maternal grandfather might take in a newborn baby.

'Aye, she did,' her grandmother confirmed quietly. 'But not afore she had named you Lily Rosa, after her own mother and Matthew's.' She smiled tearfully. 'You were such a beauty, Lily, and Thea was so proud o' you.'

Lily gave a pained frown. 'You did not consider keeping me yourself?'

'O' course I considered it.' The old lady bristled. 'I would have liked nothing better. But I daren't.'

'Black Jack?' Giles frowned darkly.

Mrs Lovell nodded. 'As I said, I had no proof that he'd killed my Matthew, but I let him know that I knew, and advised that he take himself off to other climes, and never come back if'n he didn't want me to go to the authorities and leave them to decide what had really happened that day. I told the duke o' my suspicions too, as to who had really slain Matthew—I couldn't let some poor innocent take the blame.' She looked at Giles. 'Your da saw my predicament, and instead of dismissing the gamekeeper he moved him to another o' the Montague estates.'

Giles shook his head. 'I never knew that....'

'No reason why anyone else should know,' the elderly lady dismissed briskly. 'It was between your da and me.'

'It was indeed.' He nodded. 'Black Jack would appear to have confirmed your suspicions by taking his son and going to Ireland.'

The elderly lady sighed. 'But even that weren't far enough away for me. Not when there was a vulnerable babe to consider. The tribe moved on at the end of the summer as usual, but Thea was near her time, so we stayed a few miles from Castonbury until the babe was born. When Thea died giving birth to Lily I knew I had to protect her in some way.'

'By leaving her with the Seagroves once you had discovered that her grandfather was dead, and then returning to your tribe and telling them that both Thea and the baby had died.' Giles looked anxiously at Lily as he spoke, heartsick on her behalf for having learnt who her real parents were, only to as quickly find that they were both lost to her for ever.

'Yes.' Mrs Lovell's voice quavered with emotion. 'I didn't

want to give you up, Lily.' She clutched anxiously at her grand-daughter's hand. 'I just didn't know how else to protect ye. If Black Jack ever found out that ye were alive, none of my threats would have made an happerth of difference to his one day coming back and claiming ye for himself, or his son.'

Lily still felt completely overwhelmed by all that Mrs Lovell had told her. 'But why? I do not understand. And what possible reason could Judah have had for carrying me off in that way today? Why did he attack you so viciously? Break up your beautiful home and destroy all your things?'

The elderly lady grimaced. 'Because he was looking for something.'

Lily blinked. 'But what? And what can it possibly have to do with me?'

Her grandmother smiled. 'Can you have forgotten your mother's ten thousand pounds?'

'I—' She gave a confused shake of her head.

'I was going to tell you all afore I left Castonbury this summer.' The elderly woman nodded. 'You'll be twenty-one come October, Lily. And on the day of your twenty-first birthday, or the day ye marry, you'll inherit Thea's fortune.'

Lily looked stunned once again. 'I will?'

'Judah couldn't know it, o' course, but your inheritance is all nice and safe in the bank waiting for you, exactly where Thea left it.' Mrs Lovell nodded with satisfaction.

Giles drew in a sharp breath as he realised his worst fear had just become realised. Lily was to be an heiress, whereas he—he was nothing more than the precarious heir of a dukedom which was almost bankrupt!

'Judah told me his da were rambling in his fever when he died a year ago—and may his soul rot in hell!' Mrs Lovell added hardly. 'He told Judah the real reason they went to Ireland, of Thea and Matthew, and the fortune he had lost when Thea and the babe died. It were our misfortune that there were nothing to hold Judah in Ireland once his da were dead, and that he decided to look up his old aunt in Castonbury.' She shook her head impatiently.

'When he recognised the likeness between us the other day, and realised the truth of it, Judah decided to take your fortune for himself.' She gave another disgusted snort. 'That boy's as stupid as his da. Thought I carried the money about with me in my varda. As if!'

'And that is why he beat you?'

'Yes, my chivvy. But he didn't get nothing out o' me.' Her grandmother squeezed her hand reassuringly. 'I told him your money was in a bank where he couldn't get his dirty hands on it.' Her face darkened. 'That's when he decided to carry ye off and marry ye.'

Lily now understood only too well those remarks Judah Lovell had made to her concerning silk handkerchiefs.

Just as she now realised that not only did she have a grand-mother, but a fortune too. A fortune which would make her more Giles's equal, and as such able to accept his proposal of marriage….

'Giles?'

He looked up from where he had once again been reading the letter delivered to him only this morning, his expression softening as he saw Lily standing in the doorway of his fa-ther's study, and still wearing the borrowed robe and night-rail. 'Is all now settled between you and your grandmother?' Giles had excused himself from the ladies' company shortly after the revelation about Lily's fortune, needing to be alone with his thoughts for a while.

With the knowledge that he was no longer in a position to ask Lily to become his wife.

'For now.' She nodded, smiling as she entered the room and closed the door softly behind her. 'I have left my grandmother and my father to speak privately together.' Her smile widened. 'I believe a considerable amount of that conversation will be memories of what a little hellion I was as a child!'

Giles chuckled huskily. 'I remember you being an enchanting hellion.'

Her eyes widened as she moved to stand in front of the desk where he sat. 'You do?'

He nodded. 'Very much so.'

'And I always believed you never even noticed that I was alive!'

'You were far too impishly entertaining to ignore,' Giles assured softly.

Lily tilted her head as she studied him quizzically. 'You seemed to…leave us rather abruptly, earlier.'

Giles's gaze could no longer meet her probing one. 'Sir Rufus had arrived to deal with Mr Lovell.' He referred to the local magistrate. 'And I thought to allow you and Mrs Lovell some time alone together.'

Her eyes glowed. 'Is it not wonderful news, Giles?' She clasped her hands together. 'Not only do I have a grandmother, but a fortune too!'

'Wonderful news,' he echoed softly.

She frowned. 'You do not seem particularly pleased?'

Perhaps because he was not. Which was totally selfish of him!

And he did not mean to be selfish; it was only that Lily's change in circumstances, when placed beside the now-dire ones of all the Montague family, made it impossible for him to repeat his proposal of marriage to her. 'I am very pleased for you, Lily. I can only imagine how relieved you must be to know the truth after all these years.'

'But…?'

He gave a pained frown at her intuitiveness. 'What makes you think there is a "but"?'

Lily looked down at him searchingly. She had come to know this man very well in the past two weeks—to love him—and although Giles had not returned to that haughtily arrogant gentleman she had known previously, neither was he the loving man he had been but a few hours ago.

'There is a "but," Giles.' She deliberately moved about the desk as she spoke, standing so close to him now that her thigh touched his, and knowing that he was affected by her proximity as a flush darkened his cheeks and his gaze burned hotly as he looked up at her. 'Tell me what is wrong?'

He drew in a ragged breath. 'Could you perhaps return to the other side of the desk?'

'No.' She smiled confidently, knowing that whatever was wrong it had nothing to do with Giles falling out of love with her.

That flush deepened in his cheeks. 'I cannot think logically when you are standing next to me, Lily!'

'And if I have no wish for you to "think logically"?' Lily looked at him teasingly.

'I must!' He stood up abruptly to stand some distance away in front of the window, his hands clasped tightly together behind his back. 'Lily, I— There is a letter atop the desk. I think you should read it.'

Lily looked down curiously at the desktop. 'This letter?' She picked up a single sheet of white notepaper.

Giles glanced back at her. 'Yes.'

'But it is addressed to the Duke of Rothermere.'

He grimaced. 'And my father would have a heart attack and die if he had been allowed to read it before I did!'

'And yet you wish *me* to read it?'

Giles smiled grimly. 'You will see why once you have done so.'

Lily frowned as she turned her attention to the letter, quickly reading the words written there, and the signature of Alicia Montague at the bottom of the sheet of paper. 'This lady says that she is your brother Jamie's widow? And that there is a child!' Lily raised a hand to her throat.

'A boy of eighteen months.' Giles nodded abruptly. 'Named Crispin for my father.'

Lily blinked. 'You had no knowledge of your brother having married before the receipt of this letter?'

Giles shook his head. 'None.'

Lily allowed the letter to flutter back to the desktop before moving quickly to Giles's side. 'She states the marriage took place in Spain some two years ago, shortly before Lord James's death.'

'She states that, yes.'

'But would Lord James not have told his family, told you, if that had been the case?'

'I would like to think so, yes.' His expression was grim. 'I find it…curious indeed, that this woman has waited all this time to declare herself my brother's widow, and her son his heir.'

Lily looked at him searchingly. 'What do you intend to do about it?'

'I had thought to go down to London immediately and speak with this lady myself— What is it?' Giles prompted softly as she gasped.

She chewed on her bottom lip. 'I had not imagined the two of us would be parted so soon after our betrothal?'

Giles drew in a sharp breath. 'There can be no betrothal between us now, Lily.'

'What?' She stared up at him dazedly, her face having gone pale. 'I do not understand, Giles. Earlier today you said— You asked— You do not for one moment think—? Giles, it makes no difference to my love for you whether you are heir to the dukedom or not.'

He shook his head. 'I did not for one moment think that it would.'

She looked uncertain. 'You no longer wish to marry me?'

Giles groaned as he saw the pain in her green eyes, awash with unshed tears. 'Of course I wish to marry you, Lily.' He grasped both her hands tightly in his. 'There is nothing I want more! But— There are several other things you are as yet unaware of.'

'What things?' Her expression was distraught. 'Do you have a secret wife hidden away somewhere too? A son of your own your family is unaware of?'

'No, of course I do not,' he dismissed impatiently. 'Lily, last year my father—' He shook his head. 'All you need know of that is that because of an unwise decision he made a year ago, the Montague family is all but bankrupt.'

She stilled. 'And this is the reason that the estate was allowed to become run-down? And why you personally paid for several of the refreshments at today's celebrations?'

Giles nodded. 'And why my father and I visited the lawyers together last week—on the occasion you believed I was endangering his health by taking him out for a carriage ride,' he added drily. 'And why I have myself called upon them again earlier this week.' His expression was grim. 'All to no avail. The family coffers are all but empty, and Jamie's inheritance from our mother is caught up in the same legality as the naming of the heir to the Duke of Rothermere. Although the latter may not be quite so urgent now that it seems a child who is only eighteen months old may eventually become that legal heir.'

Lily gave a slow shake of her head. 'I am sorry for all of that, of course. I can appreciate how worrying it must have been for you. But I do not see why it should affect our own plans to marry. In fact—' her expression brightened '—once I am in possession of my own inheritance I will be able to—'

'No, Lily!' Giles's hands tightened painfully on hers, his eyes glittering with intent. 'I will not hear of you putting a single penny of your inheritance towards saving the Montague family!'

'And I will not hear of you being so noble as to renege on our betrothal because your family's finances are unsettled and my own are suddenly changed!' Her eyes glittered just as intently.

Giles's expression softened slightly as he saw that determination in her expression. 'You truly are magnificent when you are angry, Lily.'

'Do not attempt to flatter me out of my present mood, Giles.' She glared up at him. 'If you so much as attempt to back out of our betrothal, out of a false sense of pride, then I shall be forced to visit lawyers of my own with a view to suing you for breech of promise!'

He smiled. 'It is not false pride, Lily. Nor, if you recall, did you ever formally accept my marriage proposal.'

'I am accepting now!' There were two bright spots of angry colour in her cheeks as she continued to glare up at him. 'I love you, Giles, and I have every intention of marrying you!'

Giles's heart had leapt at her declaration, only to sink again as he thought of all the reasons he should refuse. If Lily were to marry him, then she would be marrying a man whose position in life was no longer secure; Giles's personal fortune was dwindling by the day in an effort to keep the Montague family in the luxury to which they were accustomed, and if Alicia Montague's claim should prove true, then he was no longer the future Duke of Rothermere either. It might mean that he could eventually rejoin the army, of course, but would Lily really want that sort of life for herself now that she had the money to do whatever she wished?

'I can imagine nothing I would enjoy more!' Lily's reply was the first indication Giles had that he had asked that last question out loud. 'Mrs Lo— My grandmother—' her face flushed with pleasure '—was quite correct when she predicted that I have always wished to see more of the world. It must be my Romany blood, but I am sure I should enjoy nothing more than accompanying my husband, Lord Giles Montague, when he travels with his regiment.'

Giles felt his earlier resolve weakening in the face of Lily's enthusiasm. In the face of the love for him that shone in the clear green brilliance of her eyes....

'Oh, my darling Giles.' Lily clasped his hands tightly as she glowed up at him. 'Can you not see how wonderful it will be? The two of us married and together always?'

Giles could see. And how he hungered for it. Hungered for Lily! 'You are an heiress now, Lily, a very wealthy young lady, and may have your choice of husbands—'

'Then I choose you.' Her mouth was set stubbornly. 'If you will have me?'

'If I will have you!' He released her hands to crush her tightly in his arms. 'How can I possibly resist you?' He groaned.

'It is my hope that you cannot.' She smiled confidently.

He sighed his defeat in the face of her determination and his deep love for her. 'Then we shall only be married on two conditions.'

She eyed him quizzically. 'Which are?'

'Firstly, that we will not marry until the identity of the heir to the Duke of Rothermere has been decided upon.'

'But does that mean you will not make love to me again either, until after that matter has been settled?'

How could Giles possibly be with Lily, be in love with Lily and know that love was returned, without making love with her? 'I will make love to you again in but a few minutes if you agree to my second condition!' Giles assured vehemently.

'Very well, I agree.' She grinned up at him impishly.

He shook his head. 'Secondly, that when you come into your inheritance in a few months' time, not a penny of it is to be put at the disposal of the Montague family. That condition is more important to me than the first, Lily,' he insisted as she would have protested.

Lily gazed up at him searchingly, noting the pride in Giles's expression, the determination in his gaze and the stubborn set of his jaw. 'Very well, I agree to your second condition, also. For now,' she added warningly. 'If circumstances should change, then I also reserve the right to change my mind and help in any way that I can.'

'Just knowing that you love me and intend on becoming my wife will be enough to help me to get through this,' he assured huskily.

She reached up and cupped either side of his face as she gazed up at him with all the love she felt for him shining in her eyes. 'I will love you always, Giles. Always.'

'As I will always love you, my darling, darling Lily!' Having believed such a short time ago that he must, in honour, let Lily go, Giles now found himself totally lost to the warmth of her love.

A love for each other that he had no doubt would last a lifetime.

★ ★ ★ ★ ★

The Housemaid's *Scandalous* Secret

HELEN DICKSON

Prologue

Cholera had killed Lisette's parents. Suddenly, at nineteen years old, she found herself homeless, penniless, with no family and no purpose in life. She was adrift but she would survive. She could survive anywhere, but she belonged nowhere.

Unable to remain in her beloved India, she was to travel to Bombay, where she hoped to work her passage on board a ship bound for England.

Lisette had enjoyed living in an Anglo-Indian society in Delhi. Her father had been an eccentric academic, a linguist and a botanist, working for the University of Oxford in India. It was through her father's friendship with the Rajah Jahana Sumana of the state of Rhuna that she had met and become a close friend of the Rajah's daughter, Princess Messalina.

Messalina was being escorted to her wedding in Bhopal and suggested Lisette travel part of the way with her as one of her attendants. Not wishing to draw attention to herself Lisette was dressed as a native girl, for to travel openly as an unescorted English girl was unthinkable.

Lisette had parted from her friend when the rains came. It was a light sprinkling at first that washed the dust from the air. Then, as the lightning pranced closer in a flashing, sizzling display of the storm's power, a torrential downpour marched across the land, turning the roads to mud and causing the rivers to overflow. The people Lisette was travelling with reached the banks of a wide, fast-flowing river at the only point of safe crossing for twenty miles upstream and down. Usually the banks here were lined with *dhobis* busy with piles of washing, *mahouts* bathing their elephants and children playing and splashing in the shallows.

The rain had stopped some time ago. The last rays of the sinking sun catching the river glittered on the rushing water in a haze of gold. The bridge creaked and swayed with the pull of the current. It was almost dark, but rather than wait until morning by which time the bridge could have been washed away or become impossible to cross, the travellers decided not to postpone their crossing.

There were so many people and conveyances and bullocks milling about the bridgehead that Lisette was in danger of being crushed to death. Panicking she tried to turn back but she was carried forward by the frenzied crowd. She saw the red uniforms of British soldiers trying to bring some kind of order to the chaos but to no avail. One of them, an exceedingly handsome and masculine British officer, was familiar to her, although they had never been introduced. He and his orderly had ridden part of the way with the rajah's procession— the presence of British soldiers had provided added protection against marauding bandits.

Trying to keep his horse from bolting from the melee ahead, Colonel Ross Montague watched the unruly multitude push onto the bridge. Light was fading fast but when he caught sight of a star-spangled bright pink sari he was transfixed. He recognised it as belonging to one of Princess Messalina's attendants. He could just make out her slender figure crushed against the rails and trying desperately to hang on. What she was doing there he did not stop to wonder at, for at that moment she was in serious danger of falling off the bridge that was dipping precariously under the weight of the crowd.

The next minute, to her horror, Lisette found herself flung into the raging torrent. With night drawing in it was difficult for the majority on the bridge to see what had happened, but looking down on the scene, Ross had a clear picture of it and immediately flung himself out of the saddle, quickly shedding his red jacket.

'Leave her, man,' his companion shouted above the din. 'There'll be many more in the water before this evening's done.'

'Hold my horse, Blackstock. The life of a soldier calls for a far greater degree of proficiency in dealing with the unexpected than is required of the average man.'

'But to jump into a fast-flowing river is in excess of your official duties. It's insane—suicidal.'

With a grin, Ross tossed him the reins and his jacket. 'I'll be back.'

Pushing his way towards the bridge, he shouted to make himself heard above the tumult of yelling voices and the thunder of the water rushing below.

The current sucked Lisette deep into the river. Breaking the surface, choking in the thick, muddy water, she didn't see the figure that dove off the bridge after her. She tried to swim but hampered by the weight of her sari it was impossible. Desperately she tried to grasp at anything that would prevent her from being washed away, but the force of the water defeated her and swept her a hundred yards or more downstream until she crashed into a tree. The bank had been washed away but mercifully the tree's roots were still secured. Grabbing at a branch she groaned when it cracked and gave way. Somehow she managed to grab another, but the long green leaves slipped between her fingers. Her heart wrenched with despair. She couldn't drown, not when she had come so far.

Suddenly she felt something slide about her waist, then knock against her legs. For one horrified second she thought she was about to be eaten by a crocodile, but then hope flared when she felt a hard body pressed to her own.

'Cling on to me,' a voice yelled in Urdu above the roar of the water.

Spluttering and thrashing Lisette desperately tried to do as he asked. Again she reached out to take a fresh grip on the tree and this time she managed to grasp a branch and hold on. Dragging herself and her companion towards it she emerged through a canopy of leaves, her sopping wet veil wrapped around her, half covering her face. The man managed to half drag himself into the branches and hauled her up beside him. Exhausted from their exertions and panting for breath, they were still for a moment. Then, seeing she was in danger of slipping back into the water, the man's arms were about her once more.

Eventually he managed to edge along the tree towards the bank. Feeling sand beneath his feet, he pulled the woman he had rescued along with him and lay down with her on the sandbank, out of the water. The night was now pitch-black and he daren't move any further. His breathing was laboured and his arms and legs ached, his body battered and bruised.

The woman clung to him in a frenzy of terror. 'Are you all right?' he asked, his mouth close to her ear.

Though she made no sound he could feel the rise and fall of her breast against his own, while the feel of her warm, wet body and every slender curve and line of it spoke eloquently of a woman, not a child.

'Are you hurt?'

She did not reply, but she shook her head in a helpless gesture that might have been either agreement or dissent, and for some reason, that small despairing gesture cut him to the heart and he tightened his arms about her, whispering foolish words of comfort. For a moment her body shuddered and she lay her head against his shoulder. Wrapped together, the darkness of the night and the danger of falling back into the river forced them to remain where they were. The night wind arose and blew strongly off the water, and the girl in his arms began to shiver in the cold air.

After a while Lisette ceased to shiver. It was strangely comforting to lean her aching head against her rescuer's shoulder. With his arms tight about her, she was conscious only of an unfamiliar and inexplicable feeling of being safe—a feeling she had longed for since the day her parents had died and she had left the safe and familiar walls of her home. She did not know why the presence and the touch of this man should give her this warm feeling of safety, and she was too battered and bruised and physically exhausted to figure it out. It was enough to feel protected.

In fact, the closeness of him was dizzying, so much so that she hardly knew her own thoughts. She felt pleasurably wan-

ton feelings rippling through her, and instead of trying hard
to stifle the feelings, she allowed them to flood through her.
They were overwhelming sensations, so new and strong that
they frightened her. She moved slightly, as though to pull away
from him, and his arms tightened in response.

It was a long time since Ross had held a woman in his arms,
and though he could not see her face distinctly, the feel of her
firm young body moulded against his made his blood throb
through his veins. 'Hold still, my lovely. It's not safe for us to
move until we have light. Until then we have no choice but
to cling on to each other and keep ourselves warm.'

Had it not been for that softly rich voice, Lisette would not
have relaxed into his secure embrace once more, little realising the devastating effect her thinly clad body was having on
him. Her heart was racing now, part of his heart, his body…
Her face was uplifted and she strained her eyes to see her rescuer. His lean features were starkly etched, his eyes translucent
in the ghostly light. It was impossible to make out anything
more, but she knew it was the soldier who had accompanied
the rajah's procession.

Ross held her firm. He felt the softness of her silken hair,
the stirring pressure of her small, round breasts against his
chest, and even in this dire situation, he ached to sample this
woman more thoroughly.

Lisette's mind reeled and the next moment she felt the
warmth of his mouth on hers. She gave herself up to this, her
first kiss, savouring it with a sensual awakening as the stranger's arms held her captive. It lasted no more than a moment,
but it was enough to stir the strange feelings until she became
acutely conscious of her innocence. The trembling weakness in
her body attested to its potency. She found her lips entrapped

with his once more, and though they were soft and gentle, they flamed with a fiery heat that warmed her whole body. Her eyes closed, and the strength of his embrace, the hard pressure of his loins and his hand cupping her breast made her all too aware that this was a strong, living, healthy man, and that he was treating her like a woman, indeed desiring her.

In that moment Lisette tried to still the violent tremor that had seized her, but his powerful, animal-like masculinity was an assault on her senses. She was unable to resist him and she felt her body offer itself to this man, this stranger, and in that instant they both acknowledged the forbidden flame that had ignited between them. Right there, with the river raging all around them, they exchanged a carnal promise as binding as any spoken vow.

When her leg slid sideways and she felt the cold lap of water against her flesh, reason flooded back to her. She had no doubt that this man would take her there and then if she did not halt things now. Having been properly brought up and having consorted with an Indian princess, no one should treat her like this. This man thought she was a native girl, so as a native girl she must behave.

Sliding her lips away from his, with her mouth against his ear she managed to say, 'Please don't do this. Would you take advantage of an innocent woman when she has nothing with which to defend herself? Am I fair sport to be ravished like this? Would you make me an outcast for the rest of my days?'

Hearing her words Ross shook his head and gathered her to him again. With an effort he restrained the urge to take her lips once more for he must not. 'You are right. I have no wish to take you—not here, not like this—delightful though the prospect might be. I go too fast. What you are doing away from the royal procession is not my concern—and you do seem to have a penchant for getting yourself into trouble—but now that I have found you I contemplate a much grander bedding for you and me. We will talk about it when we get out of this damned river.'

Hearing the male arrogance edging his voice, Lisette swallowed drily. 'Then tell me where you plan this bedding so that I can avoid it,' she exclaimed, knowing that what he was saying was wrong…and yet it was so wickedly exciting, like nothing she had ever experienced before.

Ross gave a small sensual laugh, sending shivering pulse beats through her body. 'Nay, my lovely girl. Do not think you can avoid your destiny. I am a soldier, but I have been in India long enough to know your culture is full of the mysteries of destiny and fate and other fantasies. When we kissed I felt the desire in you. Deny it if you can.'

Lisette was helpless in denying it. How could she, when she had felt it too?

'Rest easy,' Ross said, his arms gathering her against him, 'while we wait out the night.'

With nowhere to rest her arm Lisette placed it around his waist and closed her eyes.

As the water continued to rush around them, Ross did the same, knowing there was the danger of the water rising. If it did, they would not survive the night.

When dawn broke up the darkness of the sky, Ross opened his eyes to find his arms empty of his companion's soft warmth. Panic seized him and he cursed himself for allowing himself to fall asleep, but he had truly believed she would be safe in his arms. Standing up, his eyes did a frantic search of the water round about, but there was no sign of her.

Thankfully the river level had fallen during the night and the bridge hadn't been washed away. Without any difficulty he managed to make it to the bank. On reaching it and looking at the ground, he saw the small footprints of a woman coming out of the river. This in itself put paid to the theory that she had been washed away. But there the trail ended. She had vanished as if spirited into thin air.

He was astounded at the strength of his relief that she was alive, but then he felt a strange sensation come over him and he could hardly believe it himself when he realised it was pique and a helpless, futile sick anger against fate and himself and the foolish instinct of his kind that had driven him to leap unthinkingly to the rescue of a drowning native girl. And now the ungrateful girl had simply got up and left him; the sense of loss and disappointment would come later.

He was affronted because having endangered his life to rescue her, she had left without so much as a farewell, slipped from his hands as unexpectedly as she had been placed into them. He set off to look for his horse and young Blackstock, determined to banish the native girl from his mind. But all the way to Bombay he did not stop looking for the girl in the pink, star-spangled sari.

The events of that night were a hideous jumble in Lisette's mind, and reaction had her in its grip. On opening her eyes and seeing the river level had fallen, careful not to disturb her companion, she had gotten to her feet and looked down into his deeply tanned and undeniably good-looking face. His closed eyes were fringed with black lashes and he was tall, his chest broad and hard muscled. His luxuriant dark brown hair and clean-shaven face enhanced his masculine good looks.

Her heart stirred. How she would like to get to know him better, but there was something inside her telling her to flee, not to become entangled with this man whose only thought when they had been locked together had been to bed her. And so, shaking so violently she could barely walk, troubled by doubts and fears and a haunting sense of insecurity, she had left her handsome rescuer and made it to the riverbank.

Fortunately she spotted the people she was travelling with encamped on the other side of the river. Reclaiming her bundle she carried on with her journey to Bombay.

One

. . . .

Surviving tropical storms, pirates and a thousand other dis-
comforts in the cramped quarters allotted to her on board ship,
Lisette was relieved when she arrived in England, a country
of bucks and beaux, Corinthians and macaronis. It was said
that the old King George III had lapsed into incurable madness and his son 'Prinny' had been made regent. As the ship
made its way up the river Thames, she went on deck. Against
a marbled sky of grey and white, London was spread out before her—streets and houses, church spires and the dome of
St Paul's.

Lisette felt no attachment to England. It was a long way
from the India that she loved, with its tiger hunts and elephants, oriental princes and potentates glittering with fabu-
lous jewels living in medieval state in fantastic marble palaces.
India had been her world for so long that England on this
grey morning was a pale comparison. A swift vision of that
lovely, mysterious country with all its smells, its vibrancy and
blistering heat sprang into her mind with a mixture of plea-

sure and pain and she choked a little, and then swallowed. It was no time to be self-pitying, when she was on the brink of a new life.

Stepping onto dry land her legs shook like those of a new-born colt. After the relative quiet of the small cabin, the noise and bustle of the East India dock was jarring and chaotic. The Company was rich and powerful and well organised, owning the largest ships that used the port of London. The dock was a scene of great variety. The smell of tar and coffee beans, timber and hemp, permeated the air, along with other aromas which titillated her nostrils. Another ship of the fleet, the *Diligence*, had already docked and its cargo of tea, silks and spices from India and porcelain from China was being unloaded.

Although Lisette had seen many a dark face in Bombay and heard all manner of languages spoken, she was dazzled by the spectacle of foreigners and shouting sailors, uniformed men and those in styles of dress she had never seen before. That was the moment that the enormity of her undertaking came over her. She was in a country that held nothing for her. Even the faces looked alien. Fear sank into her but it was too late to do anything about it.

Stevedores carrying crates and trunks swarmed up and down the gangplank. One of them struggled to carry a barrel. On reaching the bottom of the gangplank he lost the battle and it rolled away in the direction of a prancing horse. The horse sidestepped to avoid it, causing its young handler to leap back or risk being struck by a flying hoof. The horse rose up on its hind legs with a snort of alarm, dragging the short rein from the man's grip. Finding itself unexpectedly free, with stirrups dancing, it then began to rear and prance with its hooves flailing, scattering everyone in its path. Raising a noisy furore amongst the crowds it was heading straight for Lisette.

She watched as it came closer. The horse had its ears back and nostrils flared, but it seemed to her that its head was still well up, which was a sign that it was not completely out of control. The only thing she could think of was to try to slow the horse. Unafraid, stepping into its path she began to walk towards the charging beast, holding her arms wide. When it was close she uttered a gasp of admiration, for it was the most beautiful chestnut horse and it was galloping straight at her.

'Oh, my God! Get back, woman! Get back!' the horse's handler shouted.

Standing only a few feet from the danger, Lisette heard the warning but stood her ground, not out of bravado but from sheer fascination as the magnificent animal reared up. 'Oh, you beautiful creature!' she whispered. Then, as if she were urging a child to do her bidding, 'Stop, stop, you'll hurt yourself if you're not careful.'

Reaching into her pocket for a sugared sweet, she held out a flat palm to the horse, which ground to a halt, snorting wildly and rolling big hazel eyes. 'Come on, you adorable thing. I'm sure you're going to like it.' The horse decided he would. He accepted the sweet as Lisette calmly took hold of the short rein and proceeded to stroke his quivering, satiny neck. With huge hindquarters and a barrel chest, he was a splendid sight. 'You're so lovely.' She sighed as the horse nudged her pocket for another sweet. 'But where have you come from?'

Suddenly a swift, agile figure appeared from nowhere.

'It's all right, Blackstock,' the figure shouted to the man who had brought the horse off the ship. 'I'll handle him. Give me that horse,' he demanded of Lisette, holding out his hand for the rein. But as he made to grab it, the horse flattened his ears, stamped his foot and lunged at him, knocking the man sideways so that he collided with Lisette and she started to topple back. Acting so swiftly his movement was a blur, he gripped her upper arms and hauled her forward.

She landed against him, her breasts pressed to his chest, her hips welded to his hard thighs which felt as resilient as tempered steel. The breath was knocked out of her, leaving her gasping. His hands held her upright, his long fingers gripping her arms. His lips thinned, the austere planes of his face hardened and his fingers tightened about her arms. To Lisette's stunned amazement, he lifted her easily and carefully set her down a couple of feet away from him. When he released her arms she turned to the restless horse.

'Stop that,' she scolded, reaching out and jerking the rein reprovingly. 'You mustn't stamp your feet. Here, have another sweet.' The man, a soldier, stared at her. The expression his eyes contained—intensely concentrated—sent a most peculiar thrill through her. She blinked and stared back, and then it was as if she was seeing a dream awake before her. She knew this man. Her body and all its senses remembered him. She knew him by the rich, hypnotically deep voice, and the icy, needle-like chills that were her own response to him.

'Stepping in front of an out of control horse is a dangerous and extremely foolish thing to do,' he reproached sternly. 'Do you make a habit of it?'

'No, and nor do I make a habit of talking to strangers—and never to gentlemen in uniform,' she replied, her light mockery laced with gentle humour.

He scowled down at her averted face. 'And that is your rule, is it?'

For the first time she turned her head and faced him fully. A salvo was fired. It struck home with a crushing weight. Lisette couldn't have realised that Ross Montague could not trust himself to speak. Her beauty was such that his breath caught in his chest. It brought home to him the starvation of his need to feel a woman's touch.

'Oh, absolutely,' she replied calmly.

With a will of iron, Ross clamped a grip upon himself. 'Rules are made to be broken—at least mine are. By me,' he said with an ease he little felt. 'You could have been maimed for life or worse. But it is clear that you seem to have a way with horses.'

'I was brought up with them in India where I have lived since I was a child. I love them and they seem to like me— and this is such a beautiful horse. If he's been confined on board ship for weeks on end no wonder he bolted like he did. I would say he could do with a good gallop.'

Beginning to relax as he looked at this enticing young woman in a dark grey, unadorned gown, his interest growing by the second, Ross gave her a slow smile. 'I agree, but he will have to be patient a while longer.' Having witnessed the entire incident and relieved no one had been hurt, this girl had amazed him. 'I've never seen anyone stand in front of a charging horse before. I am impressed. But you do realise that the horse could have killed you, don't you?' She gave him a look that was almost condescending, a look that told him she had known precisely what she was doing and that she was more than capable of dealing with a runaway horse. He was indeed relieved that she was unharmed, though he was a little surprised at the strength of his emotions.

Taking the rein, the horse jerked back and for a moment he

wrestled with the animal, speaking to him in a soothing voice until he calmed down. Fascinated, Lisette watched him. She didn't know men could move like that. His coordination was faultless. He was so tall, large and lean but strongly muscled beneath the splendid scarlet-and-gold regimentals that hugged his broad shoulders and narrow waist without a wrinkle or a crease. She felt she should leave him now, this stranger—yet he wasn't a stranger, not to her. Was this really the same man who had saved her life, the man in whose arms she had spent an entire night, clinging on to him for dear life lest she fall into a raging river?

Tall and arrogant looking, he was olive skinned, almost the colour of a native of India. His hair was dark brown, thick and curling vigorously at the nape of his neck. His eyebrows were inclined to dip in a frown of perplexity over eyes that were watchful. It was his eyes that held her. They were vivid and startling blue, a shade of blue she had never seen on a man or woman before. It was the deep blue of the Indian Ocean—or was it the colour of the peacocks' feathers that strutted cock-sure in the grounds of the rajah's palace? His face was too strong, his jaw too stubborn and too arrogant to be called classically handsome. His features were clear cut, hard edged. Only his lips, with a hint of humour to relieve their auster-ity, his intelligence and the wickedness that lit his blue eyes, gave any hint of mortal personality.

'His name is Bengal,' Ross informed her, 'and he was given to me by a maharajah of that place. Sometimes I wonder if he's a horse at all and not Nimrod in disguise. The Hindus believe in the transmigration of souls and I'm not convinced that in some previous incarnation this horse wasn't a noble prince dedicated to hunting wild boar.'

'Then for the love of his sins it would appear he has now descended into the body of a horse with his love of the chase unaltered,' Lisette said laughingly as the horse nuzzled at her pocket.

Ross met her wide gaze and looked at her long and deliberately, studying the young and guarded face, noting the wariness and schooled immobility with interest. There was something about her, something vaguely familiar that attracted his attention. He had the impression that he had seen her before, but he could not imagine where. He saw a girl slightly above average height, graceful and as slender as a young willow. Beneath her bonnet her blue-black hair was drawn straight back and confined in a black net so that its shining, luxuriant weight tilted her little pointed chin up as though with pride.

When he looked into her eyes which were surrounded by a thick fringe of jet-black lashes, he felt an unexplainable pang of desire. They were intense, large eyes of an unusual honey-gold colour—or was it amber?—and they gave her whole face a magical look. In them were golden flecks of light, reminding him of the tigers of India. She had also acquired the lovely honey-gold skin that no longer looked quite English, yet could never be termed foreign. In fact, she seemed to radiate a feminine perfection, with all the qualities he most admired. Her soft pink lips were tantalising and gracefully curved, full and simply begged to be kissed—in fact, he'd come within a whisker of kissing them already today, but kissing a young woman before being properly introduced was simply not good form.

A flush of colour rose into Lisette's cheeks, embarrassed as this man studied her with such cool and speculative interest.

'So you have just returned from India.'

'Yes. My mistress has instructed me to look for a conveyance. Her husband, Mr Arbuthnot, has recently retired as a factor from the Company.'

'I see. And you are?'

'Lisette Napier. I am lady's maid to Mrs Arbuthnot.'

'And where is home, Lisette Napier?' Ross was intrigued and he wondered why, for he didn't often make conversation with maids.

'Wherever I happen to be—with my work, you understand.' Her voice was low and somewhat strained. 'Before that I lived with my parents in India since I was a small child. But after India—well…'

She felt his interest quicken. Ross bent his head to look into her face. 'Yes?'

'Well—it will be…different here in London.'

His teeth flashed in a sudden infectious grin. 'You will find it very different indeed from India's hot clime.'

'Yes,' she said, trying not to let herself sound too regretful.

'And your employer? Does she live in London?'

She nodded. 'Somewhere in Chelsea, I believe.'

He grinned. 'You will find it dull in comparison to India.' Ross knew he should take his horse and move on but he was curiously reluctant to do so. Goodness, what was wrong with him, standing here talking to a servant girl when he had things to do. Again his horse nudged the girl's pocket and with a laugh she produced another sweet, her hand stroking his neck to the horse's evident delight.

'You'll spoil the beast,' Ross found himself saying.

Lisette saw that in the place of idle amusement was a look of awakened concentration. As their eyes met she shivered with an involuntary surge of excitement. She felt that this was the moment when she should remind him of their previous encounter, and with a multitude of ways of doing so on the tip of her tongue, thought better of it and bit back the words. Explaining her reasons for travelling to Bombay dressed as an Indian girl might prove difficult and tedious, and since they were unlikely to meet again there was nothing to be gained by doing so.

'He deserves to be made a fuss of after enduring such a long journey. I knew someone who had a similar horse once. She...'

Her voice trailed away. Ross waited for her to speak, to tell him more, but she didn't. She merely stared into the distance as though she were alone, or he were no more important than his horse. Less so, for she evidently loved horses. He felt a strange sensation come over him and he could hardly believe it himself when he realised he was affronted because she was unconcerned whether he moved on or stayed.

He tried again. 'How long have you been a lady's maid?' he asked, doing his best to be patient, though it was not really in his nature. He had her attention again and she smiled.

'Oh—long enough,' she replied, studying him covertly, her gaze sliding over him.

Ross felt the touch of her gaze, felt the hunter within him rise in response to that artless glance. He almost groaned. 'And is it your intention to always be a lady's maid? Would you not like to return to India?'

A glow appeared in her eyes. 'Oh, yes—and perhaps I will, one day, but I have to make my own way in the world, sir...'

'Colonel. Colonel Ross Montague.'

Ross studied her for a moment, frowning. She was looking at him, silent and unblinking, in the same way the dark-eyed Indian women stared in that unfathomable way. Having lived there for some considerable time, he suspected it was something she had developed almost unconsciously over the years, through her association with some of those doe-eyed women.

Spending many years in India had shaped Ross's ideal of feminine beauty. He was no great admirer of European standards—the pink and white belles who had begun to invade India, accompanying parents attached in some form to the East India Company. With their insipid colouring, their simpering ways and carefully arranged ringlets, they set their caps at him, attracting him not one whit.

Ross sought his pleasures with the dusky, dark-eyed maidens, who offered a chance of escape from the stifling rounds of British social life, although there had been singularly few of late. This, it may be added, was not from lack of opportunity. Ross Montague was no celibate, but two things obsessed him—India, with its beauty and glamour and its cruel mystery, and the East India Company, with its precious collection of merchant traders from London who were conquering a subcontinent and maintained their own army administering justice and laws to the Indians.

In India fortune had done nothing but smile on Ross. Young men with ambition and ability could go far. He had served with distinction; working his way up through the ranks he had now been rewarded with a promotion to colonel. But on receiving a letter from home, he had felt the sands of his good fortune were running out.

One of his cousins had been killed in the bloody shambles of the battle at Waterloo and another of his cousins, the heir to the Montague dukedom, had been listed as missing somewhere in Spain. Bound by the ties of present and future relationships to the house of Montague, Ross had returned to

England at a time when his presence was likely to be of great comfort to his relatives there.

But India held his heart and imagination and he had little time for anything else—and certainly not marriage. He hadn't wanted a wife before he'd joined the army. Nothing had changed.

'How old are you?' he inquired abruptly.

The unexpectedness of the question appeared to take Lisette by surprise, and she answered in unconscious obedience to the authority in his voice. 'Twenty,' she replied, having reached that age as the ship sailed round the Cape of Africa.

He raised an intrigued eyebrow, choosing to ignore her awkward response. 'And you have a place.'

Her mouth quivered, but then she looked away, rather awkwardly. She felt her heart tighten. 'Not beyond three weeks. Now my employer's husband has retired from the Company he is to move his family to Brighton where they have a full complement of staff already. I have been told I must seek another situation.'

As she stood there she looked vulnerable for the first time. Her air of impregnable self-sufficiency vanished and Ross saw her troubled and rather desperate. 'You have references?'

'Oh, yes—well, just the one. I can only hope it will secure me another position—even that of a scullery maid would be better than nothing at all.'

'Even though it would be a blow to your pride?'

'I'm truly not proud,' she said with a bewitching smile. 'I'm wilful, I suppose. Stubborn too. And headstrong. But not, I think, proud.'

At that moment appeared Lottie Arbuthnot, her employer's daughter, treading with care over obstacles and holding her skirts to her sides so as not to mark them on the many barrels and casks piled up on the dock. On reaching Lisette she pricked her with her needle-like eyes.

'Lisette! Here you are. Mama is becoming quite vexed. How long you have been in securing a carriage.'

Ross turned and looked at her with an apologetic gesture. 'The fault is all mine—or perhaps I should say it was my horse who waylaid her. Having been released from the confines of his quarters on board, he ran amok when he reached the dock. Had Miss Napier not been so adept at handling horses there is no telling what damage he might have done.'

Staring up at the handsome colonel, Lottie disregarded his comment about Lisette and with a simpering smile fluttered her eyelashes in what Lisette consider to be an appallingly fast manner. 'Then you are forgiven, sir. I am Miss Lottie Arbuthnot. Miss Napier is servant to my ma and me.'

'So I understand,' Ross replied with a wry smile, beginning to feel pity for Miss Napier.

Lottie's arrival rudely shook Lisette out of the trance that seemed to have taken over her. It wasn't until that moment that she realised she had lost all sense of propriety. Colonel Montague must think her forward and impertinent. Embarrassment swept over her, washing her face in colour. Lottie was a moody, spiteful girl who had made her life extremely difficult on board ship as she had tried to do her best for both her and Mrs Arbuthnot, to whom she owed much gratitude.

Mrs Arbuthnot had taught her the refinements of being a lady's maid. She wore a smart black or dark grey dress and starched muslin apron and cap and could dip a curtsey as gracefully as a debutante. But all through the voyage she had been at the mercy of Lottie's every whim. It must be Lisette who helped her dress, Lisette who brought her tea. Oh, that she would never have to see the girl again!

'Lisette.' Lottie spoke peevishly. 'See, your face is quite red. Are you unwell?'

'No, I—I think it must be the heat,' she stammered. 'Excuse me. I'll go in search of a conveyance.'

'Allow me,' Ross said, handing the horse to Blackstock, who appeared at that moment. In no time at all he had secured a conveyance to take Miss Napier and the Arbuthnot family to Chelsea.

As Lottie continued to prattle on, Lisette saw Colonel Montague was watching her steadily, and she sensed the unbidden, unspoken communication between them. *He knows what I'm thinking*, she thought. It may be all imagination but she knew he was as bored and irritated by Lottie as she was. She felt instantly ashamed, knowing that Lottie could not help being the person she was.

Feeling in her pocket for some sweets, she handed them to him.

He smiled at her. 'Are these for me or the horse?'

A gentle flush mantled her cheeks. 'For Bengal, of course. If he should prove difficult you might be glad of them.'

Lowering her head she bade Colonel Montague a polite goodbye and walked back to the ship, a step behind Miss Arbuthnot. Yet she continued to feel his presence behind her, large and intensely masculine. Her senses skittered—she clamped a firm hold on them and lifted her chin, but she felt a cool tingle slither down her spine and the touch of his blue gaze on the sensitive skin on her nape.

As she walked, Ross thought she did so with the grace and presence of a dancer. As she had told him of her circumstances, he had been taken aback when her look became one of nervous apprehension. How different she'd suddenly appeared from the girl who had stepped in front of his horse, when her proud, self-possession had raised his interest. At first, not knowing what was the matter, he had thought that perhaps she was ill, but then he'd realised that she was afraid. Though her assurance and confidence had aroused him, that glimpse of vulnerability had drawn forth emotions he had only felt once before—in India—with a girl and a raging river... A girl who had also moved like a dancer.

Emerging from the river and seeing her small footprints in the mud, assured that she had survived the night, he had determined to banish the native girl from his mind. But all the way to Bombay he had not stopped looking for the girl in the pink, star-spangled sari and thick, black oiled plait hanging to her waist. The memory of that night and the girl had stayed with him, the way the hot heat of a candle flame stared at for a few moments would burn behind closed eyelids.

Those same emotions made him want to protect this girl, to keep her from harm. His fancy took flight and he imagined himself as her champion, secretly carrying her colours beneath his armour next to his heart, watching that proud smile on her face turn inward to a sweet, imploring look of appeal. Before his imagination could propel him to even more exquisitely poignant pangs of desire, Blackstock told him he would make the necessary arrangements for his baggage to be sent on to Lady Mannering's house in Bloomsbury.

Ross immediately mounted his restive horse and nosed him away from the dock, the clip-clopping of the horse's shoes ringing sharp and clear in the bright morning air. But he had made a mental note of where Miss Napier could be located, tucking the information into a corner of his mind to be resurrected when he so desired.

Light streaming through the long windows fell in bright shafts upon the black-and-white marble floor. Ross felt a warm glow. The house belonged to his widowed maternal aunt, Lady Grace Mannering. In his absence the house had lost neither its old appeal nor its very special associations with those happy years he had spent as a boy in London with his sister, Araminta.

Drawn by the bittersweet memories stirred by hearing lilting strains of a merry tune being played on the piano, he strode across the hall to the door of the music room and pushed it open to find Araminta seated at the instrument.

She stopped playing and turned towards the door and the man who stood there. Joyous disbelief held her immobilised for a split second, then she shouted, 'Ross!' and amid squeals of laughter and ecstatic shrieks, she bounced off the stool and burst into an unladylike run. Almost knocking him over she flung her arms around his neck in a fierce hug, laughing with joy and nearly choking him in her enthusiasm. Embracing her in return, a full moment passed before Araminta relaxed her stranglehold.

'Oh, Ross, dear brother, is it really you? You look wonderful. I've missed you so much. I don't know what I would have done without your letters,' she gushed, hugging him again.

Pulling him down onto the sofa, his legs disappearing amid a flurry of skirts, all at once she launched into a torrent of questions ranging from where he had been, what he had been doing and how long was he going to stay, hardly giving him time to reply.

When he had the chance he studied her closely. Five years

had gone by since he had last seen her and the girl he had known had been replaced by a lovely young woman. Her shining light brown hair was a tumble of rebellious curls and her eyes as deeply blue as his own.

'I'm happy to see you looking so well, Araminta,' he said, realising just how much he had missed his only sibling. 'I hardly recognised you. Why, you must have grown taller by half a head in the time I've been gone. You look so mature.'

'And you are very handsome, Ross,' Araminta declared breathlessly, 'and so distinguished in your military uniform. You are a colonel now?'

He nodded. 'I was promoted just before I left India.'

'Will you go back there?'

'Of course. I'm home on extended leave—for how long depends on what I find when I get to Castonbury Park.'

Learning of her nephew's arrival Lady Mannering entered. Her small, rotund figure was encased in deep rose silk and a widow's cap was atop her sprightly brown hair liberally streaked with grey. As she went to greet her nephew, her eyes were bright with intelligence, set in a soft, lined face.

After greeting his aunt affectionately, Ross sat across from her and looked at her homely face and the light blue eyes that had scolded and teased him and Araminta and loved them so well. His look became sombre.

'Cousin Giles wrote and told me about young Edward.'

Grace's eyes filled with sadness. 'Yes, it was quite dreadful when we heard he'd been killed. There was great relief when Giles came back. As you will remember Edward was so attached to his older brother, but now Giles has resigned his commission. What happened to Edward has affected him rather badly, I'm afraid. And if that weren't bad enough Jamie is still missing.'

Ross stared at her in stunned disbelief. His cousin Jamie Montague, heir to the magnificent Castonbury Park in Derbyshire, had been listed as missing in Spain a year before Waterloo. 'Good heavens! I was hoping he'd been found by now. Is there still no word?'

'I'm afraid not.'

'No body has been found?'

She shook her head. 'It's thought that he was washed away when crossing a swollen river before the push for Toulouse.'

'Then Giles stands next in line. Knowing of his love for the military life, he will be a reluctant heir.'

'He was in London recently. It would have been good for you to have seen him before he left for Castonbury. Still, I suppose you've been fighting your own battles in India.'

'I'll catch up with him there. Castonbury is still my home and I am eager to see my uncle. Giles must be feeling pretty wretched right now. With Edward dead and Jamie missing—and of course Harry busy with his work here in London, he's going to need someone close.'

'Family support is always a good thing at a time like this, Ross. All things considered, the Montagues aren't as invincible as they thought.'

Having been raised with the Montague children, Ross had come to look on the six siblings as his brothers and sisters, and his concern over the disappearance of one and the death of another affected him deeply. Added to this was the financial crisis that had hit the family following the Napoleonic wars. Although the Montagues courted danger, they were his family, to be defended to the death.

'On top of Jamie's disappearance, Edward's death will have affected my uncle very badly.'

'I'm afraid it has. Everyone is quite worried about him. The letters that Phaedra writes to Araminta tell of his declining health and that his mind is not what it was, that at times he seems to be a little…unhinged I believe was the term she used. Which reminds me. A letter has been delivered from Castonbury Park. It's from Giles. Would you like to read it now?'

'I'll do that when I go and change.' Ross frowned with concern. 'I shall not delay in leaving for Castonbury. But first I shall have to visit my tailor—which I shall do first thing tomorrow. After that I shall be free to go.'

'The Season is almost over. Araminta can go with you.'

'Are you to accompany us too, Aunt?'

'You know how I prefer to be in town. However, I will give you the loan of my travelling chaise to take you to Castonbury. It could do with an outing and it will give the grooms something to do. Do you require a valet, Ross?'

'I've brought my own man with me, Blackstock, a young subaltern in my regiment. I left him at the dock sorting out the baggage. He should be here shortly.'

In the privacy of his room, Ross opened the letter from his cousin Giles, and found he was greatly disturbed by its contents. It contained a hurried account of a mysterious woman claiming her son was Jamie's heir, and that the family was in dire financial straits. Indeed, the news was so dire it seemed as if the house of Montague was about to come crashing down. Giles asked Ross to go and see this woman, who was in lodgings in Cheapside, for himself, and afterwards to seek out his brother Harry while he was in London and explain the situation. Ross must also emphasise to Harry the importance of finding out what had happened to Jamie, and that it was imperative that Harry left for Spain as soon as he was able.

Folding the letter, Ross sat down to draft a note to his cousin Harry.

Before sitting down to dinner, Ross sought his aunt's company in order to see what other troubles might have befallen the Montagues in his absence. He was shocked to discover that his sister had broken her betrothal to Lord Antony Bennington, son and heir of the Earl of Cawood in Cambridgeshire. Ross was disappointed. From what he remembered of young Bennington the man was an agreeable sort. Was there any good news to be had? he wondered to himself.

'Araminta must have had good reason to cry off her betrothal to young Bennington,' Ross said with a troubled frown. Having played nursemaid, surrogate father and guardian to Araminta all her life, she was in part the reason why he had returned to England, to provide the final direction she needed to cross the threshold into matrimony. It would seem he was going to have his work cut out to have her settled before he could return to India. 'How has it affected her?'

'Araminta is a girl of too much resolution and energy of character to allow herself to dwell on useless and unseemly sorrow for the past,' Aunt Grace said. 'Naturally she was regretful for a while, but she has wisely turned her attention towards the future, which is vastly more important to her than pining for what is lost.'

'Do you know what happened to make her break off the betrothal? Did she not speak of it to you?'

'No, she did not. The only reason she would give was that

they did not suit—but I heard from a reliable source that Araminta caught him in a dalliance with a young woman by the name of Elizabeth Walton.'

Ross looked at Araminta with concern when she walked in and sat beside her aunt on the sofa. Looking at her now he noted her eyes held a certain sadness, and Ross was not at all convinced that she had put her broken betrothal behind her.

'You haven't forgotten that we're going shopping tomorrow, have you, Araminta?' Grace said as they settled down to dinner. 'I thought we might start by visiting the Exchange. Of course, all the best shops are on Bond or Bruton Street. If we have the time we can go there after.'

'You may have to go alone. I swear I have the onset of a headache. I think I shall lie in, if you don't mind.'

'But I do mind. Fresh air will be more beneficial to you than lying in bed all day. I'll send Sarah in to pamper you if you like.'

'How very generous of you, Aunt Grace. You know I'm in need of a maid of my own, for while Sarah is diligent, she has so much to do. She is always in a hurry and knows nothing of dressing me properly. Little wonder I appear at dinner looking half dressed and my hair all mussed up,' Araminta complained.

Ross pricked up his ears and looked at his sister, an image of the delectable Miss Napier drifting into his mind. 'You require a maid?'

'I most certainly do,' Araminta replied adamantly. 'I've mentioned it to Aunt Grace before but she never seems to get round to it.'

'That's true,' Grace said. 'There always seems to be so much to think about. But I agree, Araminta, you really do need a maid of your own.'

'Then might I suggest someone?' Ross said, feeling a strange lift to his heart. 'I met a young woman yesterday. She's been in India and is employed as maid to a lady and her daughter who reside in Chelsea. Her position is to be terminated in three weeks and she is looking for another post.'

'Why?' Araminta asked suspiciously. 'What has she done?'

'Nothing. Her employers are moving to Brighton and she will no longer be required.'

Ross's suggestion cheered Araminta somewhat. She studied the almost fond smile upon her brother's face as he spoke of the girl and noted the gleam in his eyes. He seldom smiled, she knew, unless the smile was seductive or cynical, and when he was in the presence of his uncle, the Duke of Rothermere, he rarely laughed. It was almost as though he believed sentimentality silly and anything that was silly was abhorrent and made a man vulnerable. She was intrigued. Was it possible that he'd developed a special fondness for this maid?

'What is this extraordinary female's name and what does she look like?' Araminta asked, anxious to discover more about the girl who'd had such an unusual effect on her brother.

'Her name is Lisette Napier. She is quite tall, slender and dark haired. Her speech is as cultured as yours and mine. Her manners are impeccable and she is presentable.'

'And how old is she?'

'I believe she is twenty.'

'I see. Isn't that a little young to be a lady's maid?'

'And will she make a suitable maid?' Aunt Grace asked.

'I really have no idea about such things, but I'm sure Mrs Arbuthnot would not employ her if she wasn't any good at her job.'

'Well, heaven forbid if she's prettier than Araminta. It would never do for a maid to be more becoming than her mistress.'

'Oh, that doesn't matter,' Araminta remarked happily, having already decided to take Miss Napier on—for her brother's sake as well as her own need and curiosity. 'I should very much like for you to hire her, Ross.'

'I expect you could do worse than give her a chance—perhaps for a trial period of a month. See how she gets on.'

'Yes—yes, I will. Decent servants are neither easy to find, cheap to train, nor simple to keep. I would like to meet her first.'

Ross nodded and began to attack the roast lamb with renewed relish. 'I'll do my best. I have no doubt that Mr Arbuthnot's address can be located through East India House.'

The Arbuthnot family had been at home in Chelsea for a few days when Lottie dressed early and told Lisette to prepare for a trip to the Royal Exchange to do some shopping. There were some items she wished to purchase before she left for Brighton. Glad of the opportunity to escape the stilted confines of the house, where she found the work hard for both Mrs Arbuthnot and Lottie demanded their pound of flesh, and eager to see more of London, Lisette put on her coat and bonnet and prepared to enjoy herself for a couple of hours or so.

When the carriage turned in to Cornhill, both girls were in good spirits. They stared with excitement at the immense stone front of the facade of the Exchange with its high arcades and column and the clock tower reaching skyward.

Alighting from the carriage they went through the archway where the arcade square of the Exchange opened up before them. It was filled with merchants and traders and hawkers of wares, mingling with people of all occupations and positions and gentlemen in military uniforms. It was a fashionable place to shop and used as a rendezvous, much frequented by beaux waiting to meet a lady bent on flirtation.

'Oh, what a wonderful place,' Lisette murmured, breathing in the different smells that reached her, from roasting chestnuts to hot pies and horse dung. She was captivated by the sight and would have stopped, but Lottie was moving on through the yard. She hurried after her.

Taking hold of Lisette's arm, Lottie was unable to conceal her excitement, blushing delightedly when a handsome young soldier touched his hat and winked at her. 'I think I would like to have a look round the little stalls in the yard first but the shops upstairs are always the best.'

And so they passed a pleasant half-hour browsing among the stalls with Lottie dipping into her silk purse for coins to buy fripperies and handing them to Lisette to place in her basket. They mounted the staircase and strolled along the upper gallery. It was thronged with shoppers and Lisette found it difficult to keep Lottie within her sight at times. When she disappeared inside a shop to purchase some gloves, telling Lisette that she would probably be a while since she wished to browse, Lisette slipped in after her. She was distracted when some beautiful lace collars caught her eye. Pausing to take a look, she could only wish she had the money to buy one. It would certainly enhance the grey dress she wore day in and day out.

She had not been inside the shop very long when she had an odd feeling that she was being watched. The short hairs on the nape of her neck rose on end and her spine tingled. As she began to turn slowly to see if her suspicions were correct, she was half expecting to see Lottie behind her for she was sure now that she was only being fanciful.

Her eyes flicked round the shop and turning round she passed the stranger with hardly more than a glance, not even pausing for the sake of politeness as the man swept his hat from his dark head. Instead she lifted her skirts to descend a step.

Ross leaned back against the fixtures and smiled his appreciation as his eyes caressed her trim back. Suddenly Lisette stopped, and sensing his eyes on her she whirled to gape at him, her amber eyes wide in disbelief on finding herself face to face with Colonel Montague—tall, lean and strikingly handsome, recklessly so, with magnificent dark brows that curved neatly, a straight nose and a firm but almost sensuous mouth. The lean line of his jaw showed strength and flexed with the movement of the muscles there.

'Colonel Montague?' the question burst from her.

'The same, Miss Napier.' Now having her full attention, he held his hat before his chest in a bow of exaggerated politeness, before taking her arm and drawing her aside.

He had appeared too suddenly for Lisette to prepare herself, so the heady surge of pleasure she experienced on seeing him again was clearly evident, stamped like an unbidden confession on her lovely face. For a long, joyous interval they held each other with their eyes, savouring the moment, enjoying afresh the powerful force that sprang between them. Then he smiled.

'Miss Napier! How odd to find you here.' Desire was already tightening his loins—and *that* with just the sight of her. He didn't understand why she had such a volatile effect on him, but he understood that he wanted her—he wanted her warm and willing in his arms, in his bed.

Two

Lisette stared at Colonel Montague, her heart doing a somersault. 'It is?' His smile sent a flood of warmth through her body to settle in a hot flush upon her cheeks and other, less exposed places.

'Most certainly.'

Without relinquishing his hold on her arm, his touch igniting fires inside her, fires that flared to a startling intensity when he led her to a private place at the back of the shop. She found herself standing so close to him that she could almost hear the beating of his heart. He looked down at her so intently that he might have been trying to commit every detail of her features to memory.

As before, when he had met her on the dock, Ross felt a faint stirring of recognition, like the ghost of a memory long submerged, but it drifted away when he saw the warmth in her eyes.

He didn't waste time on unnecessary words of politeness. 'This is a trace of luck our meeting like this. Are you alone?'

She shook her head. 'No, I'm with Miss Arbuthnot. She wandered off. I suppose I must go and find her before I lose her altogether,' Lisette said, although she was most reluctant to do so on finding herself in the presence of Colonel Montague once more. She could not rightly say what it was about him that held her attention. She felt utterly fascinated, like a child beholding a favourite toy. He was quite unlike anything or anyone she had ever known.

Ross stared at her profile, tracing with his gaze the classically beautiful lines of her face, the unexpected brush of lustrous ebony eyelashes. He had never seen the like of her. She was quite extraordinarily lovely. She had an untamed quality running in dangerous undercurrents just below the surface, a wild freedom of spirit that found its counterpart in his own hot-blooded nature.

Something in his stare made Lisette's fingertips tingle. The tingle crept up her arms with sweet warmth, into her chest, and straight into her breast. She did her best to ignore the sensation.

'Tell me, Miss Napier, how are you finding London? Is it to your liking?'

'I have seen little of it. This is the first time I've been away from the house, but I must confess that I am finding it all so strange—and exciting, of course, and so different from what I am used to.'

'I imagine you are missing India.'

Lisette was spared answering his question when a pretty, fashionable young woman dressed in a beautiful blue gown with a matching hat perched atop a riot of gleaming brown curls appeared at his side.

'Ah—so this is where you've got to, Ross. Little wonder I

couldn't find you when you were lurking at the back of the shop.' Her eyes looked Lisette up and down, in an appraising way. A little smile formed on her lips. 'And I can see why. Will you do me the honour of introducing your companion?'

'Of course. Allow me to present to you Miss Lisette Napier. Miss Napier—my sister, Miss Araminta Montague. This is the young lady I spoke to you about, Araminta.'

Lisette bobbed a respectful curtsey, looking from one to the other. 'For what reason did you have to discuss me, Colonel?' she enquired, surprised and deeply touched to know he had spared her a passing thought.

'I recall you telling me you were looking for another position. When my sister mentioned that she was in desperate need of a maid, I thought of you.'

'And now we've met it will save us the trouble of writing to you,' Araminta said.

'Would the position be to your liking?' Ross asked, cocking a quizzical, amused eyebrow. 'Although, when I recall you telling me that you are wilful, stubborn and headstrong, perhaps I should question your suitability!'

His wry tone made Lisette burst out laughing, and Ross found himself captivated by the infectious joy, the beauty, of it. He'd never heard the music of her laughter before, nor seen it glowing in her magnificent eyes.

'I also recall telling you that I am not proud, Colonel—although I would be honoured to be offered the post of your sister's maid,' Lisette said, fighting down a sudden absurd surge of happiness.

Standing against a backdrop of ribbons and lace, laughing up at him, Lisette Napier was unforgettable. Ross realised it as clearly as he realised that if he became her employer, there was every chance he was going to find her irresistible as well.

'My brother tells me your present position is shortly to be terminated. Is this correct, Miss Napier?'

'Yes. My employer will have no need of me when the family moves to Brighton.'

'Why don't you ask Miss Napier to come to the house, Araminta? It's highly irregular to carry out an interview in such a place as this and for you to be doing it. Shouldn't Aunt Grace—or is it the housekeeper who usually sees to the hiring of servants?'

Araminta gave him a cross look. 'Usually it is but since I am the one requiring a maid I shall have a say in who is employed to see to my needs. I am in London for the Season and will shortly be leaving for our home in Derbyshire,' she said, addressing Lisette. 'Would you mind?'

Lisette stared at her. Mind? Of course she wouldn't mind. From what she could recall of the English geography lessons her father had taught her, Derbyshire was miles away from London—somewhere in the north. That would suit her perfectly. Colonel Montague had thought of her when he knew his sister was requiring a maid of her own and put her name forward—like a friend would. She looked at him. Her heart was beating hard in her chest. She wanted beyond anything to accept the post since it represented decency, security, respectability and a release from the gnawing fear and uncertainty of the past months, and going to Derbyshire would certainly solve her current predicament.

'No,' she said. 'That would suit me very well.'

'Still,' Araminta said, suffering some discomfort when she was jostled from behind by an exuberant shopper, 'Ross is quite right. This is hardly the place, but I think you will do very well. Can you come to the house?'

Lisette shook her head. 'Unfortunately that's not possible. There is so much to be done before my employer leaves for Brighton. I shall be fully occupied.'

'Then come to the house when they have left. Ross will give you directions. Present yourself to the housekeeper and we will take it from there. I shall tell her to expect you.' Tilting her head to one side she looked at Lisette with renewed interest. 'Did you travel from India on the same ship as my brother, Miss Napier?'

'No. I sailed on the *Portland*. Colonel Montague was on the *Diligence*—the first vessel of the fleet to dock in London.'

Araminta's eyes opened wider, more and more intrigued by the second. 'Then how did you meet?'

'My horse panicked when he was taken off the ship and Miss Napier calmed him,' Ross explained shortly, 'which was immensely brave of her and for which I was truly grateful.'

'Oh, I see. You are not afraid of horses, Miss Napier?'

'Far from it,' Ross quipped before Lisette could open her mouth. 'Bengal's a peppery beast at the best of times. She handled him admirably. But I cannot see that this has anything to do with Miss Napier being your maid, Araminta.'

Araminta looked at her brother and laughed. He really did look put out by her questioning. 'Forgive my curiosity. You know what I'm like. Now are you ready, Ross, or is there something further you wish to say to Miss Napier before we leave?'

Ross turned his back on his sister to speak to Lisette, giving her directions to his aunt's house in Bloomsbury. Meeting her gaze he realised that when he had met her before and looked into her eyes, he had thought them strange. Now he could not understand how he had ever thought that. He now saw those astonishing eyes as the perfect expression of her unique self. Now she seemed absolutely perfect.

His voice was laced with concern when he said, 'Will you be all right? Would you like me to wait with you until Miss Arbuthnot appears?'

'That will not be necessary. I see Miss Arbuthnot is in the process of purchasing some ribbons. You have been most generous, Colonel, and to be sure I am grateful that you saw fit to speak of me to your sister. If she considers me suitable for the post, then I shall appreciate the shelter, protection and stability of the position and to be valued for the qualities I know I possess.'

For a moment Ross didn't move—he studied her with speculative blue eyes, pleasuring himself with the sight of her. 'Which I am certain you have in abundance. I'm happy to have been of help.' He reached out and took her right hand in his firm grip. 'I'm so glad to have met you again, Miss Napier,' he said, shaking her hand.

With her heart racing, Lisette sucked in a breath. For one definable instant she felt trapped. 'Yes,' she said, feeling utterly foolish. She was so aware of the touch of him, his skin against hers, the feel of her slim hand held in his broad grasp, and as she gazed into those penetrating blue eyes, she suddenly felt herself drawn to him as if by some overwhelming magnetic force.

She opened her mouth to tell him they had met before and to thank him for saving her life, then closed it again. As much as she wanted to she could not. A ribbon and lace shop was hardly the place for such an intimate revelation. And besides, to do so would bring about a change to their relationship. He would look upon her differently—he might regret the passion they had shared, feel ashamed, even, and decide against hiring her as his sister's maid. She desperately needed the security of this employment and would do nothing to jeopardise that. In any case, it seemed he did not recognise her as the girl he had rescued, and in the grey of London colourful, vibrant India seemed half a lifetime away.

'I shall look forward to seeing you if not in London, then in Derbyshire.'

Lisette could find no words to say, and merely bobbed a little curtsey and picked up her basket.

'Good day, Miss Napier.'

Leaving the shop, Ross's lips curved in a satisfied smile. He'd sensed the awareness that had flared at his touch, the quiver of consciousness she hadn't been able to hide. Known among his contemporaries to be single-minded in pursuit of what he wanted, he was supremely confident that in no time at all he would succeed in tempting the delectable Lisette Napier into his bed.

As Ross approached the modest lodging house in Cheapside, the only thing that occupied his mind was that even after the horrors of war were over, the Montague family was in trouble. Ross feared that the arrival of this woman, Alicia, and her child into their midst, a woman who apparently called herself the Marchioness of Hatherton, had the power to shake the foundations of Castonbury Park to the core.

On seeing her, his first impression was that she did not remotely resemble the conventional image of a noblewoman, not even a lady of fashion. Her hair was fair and neatly arranged, her gown simple and unadorned, and over her arm she carried the freshly laundered clothes of an infant. But not even her plain clothing or the fact that she had probably laundered the clothes herself could make this woman look common. Petite and slender, she held herself with a dignity, a calm intelligence and a self-assurance he had not expected. Her hair framed a face of striking beauty; her skin was creamy and glowing with health. Her eyes were light blue, with long curling lashes.

'I owe you an apology for turning up like this,' Ross said, having thought that by not giving notice of his visit he would put her at a disadvantage. She seemed surprised and a little agitated by his sudden arrival and her eyes darkened with anxiety, but her generous mouth curved in a smile of welcome.

'Not at all, Colonel Montague. You are most welcome. I thank you for coming to see me. I wrote to the duke informing him of the situation, explaining to him fully, in great detail, everything that happened before Jamie was killed.'

'My uncle had already been notified of my cousin's disappearance by the British authorities.'

'So I understand. I wrote telling the duke of Crispin, our son, who is the duke's heir now Jamie is dead. I made no claim to anything for myself in my letter, only that Jamie's son is taken care of.'

Which showed great delicacy on her part, Ross thought with cynicism. But could the family reconcile themselves to the fact that the Jamie they knew, admired and loved would marry without their blessing?

'I—I expected someone to contact me,' Alicia went on hesitantly, 'but…I did not know when or who it would be. Would you like some refreshment—tea, perhaps, or coffee?'

'No, thank you. I do not wish to put you to any trouble.'

Moving towards the fire she sat rather nervously on the edge of a chair and motioned Ross to the chair opposite. He did so, trying to read her.

'Is there anything more I can tell you?' she asked, trying to ease the tension in her voice.

'What was your reason for being in Spain?'

'I was employed as companion to a lady whose husband was out there. Sadly he was killed in action and she returned to England. Having already met Jamie by that time I remained behind and we were married. If—if you're wondering about my suitability, I was born into a respectable family. I was an only child—my mother died when I was quite young. My father was a clergyman in the village of Shafton in Wiltshire. Unfortunately when he died I was quite impoverished and had no choice other than to seek employment, which was how I came to be a lady's companion.'

For the next few minutes, with tactful consideration, Ross tried to test her on little things he recalled about Jamie—his appearance, things about his past he might have told her. His questioning seemed to unsettle her and he noticed how she clasped her hands in her lap to keep them from trembling.

'You—you must forgive me, Colonel Montague, if I appear a trifle vague,' she said. 'You must understand that Jamie and I were not together very long. I confess that most of his background is still unknown to me. I know he has three brothers— Giles, Harry and Edward—and that they are all military men.'

'Forgive me. My questions were impertinent.'

She seemed to relax. 'It all happened so quickly. Jamie had no time to write to his family to inform them of our marriage. Sadly he never saw his son.' She lifted her head and looked at her visitor, her gaze long and searching. This time there were tears in her eyes, and it seemed to Ross he read in them a profound sadness, tinged with reserve and pride.

She rose then and crossed over to a bureau, extracting some papers from a drawer. 'Forgive me. I am not entirely myself these days. Emotion lies too near the surface. I expect you would like to see these.' She handed the papers to Ross. 'You will see that one is a letter from an army chaplain confirming our marriage.'

'And the chaplain? Where is he now?'

'He was killed during the battle at Toulouse.'

So, Ross thought as he scanned the document, thinking it looked authentic enough, the marriage could not be confirmed or denied in person. How plausible it all sounded. But was she telling him the truth?

The other document was a birth certificate.

'Your son has been baptised, I see.'

'Yes, here in London.'

The birth certificate only reflected what the chaplain had been told.

'I…also have Jamie's ring.'

Ross took it from her. It was old, gold and engraved with the crest of the Marquis of Hatherton, one of Jamie's titles, proof that it was his.

'May I ask how you come to have it in your possession?' he enquired, handing it back to her. 'Jamie's body has not been found and I find it difficult to imagine he would have removed it from his finger. It holds great significance and meant a good deal to him. He would not have left it lying around.'

'You are quite right to question me about it—and to be suspicious about how I come to have it,' she said, seemingly not in the least offended by what his words implied, but the worried look Ross had seen in her eyes earlier was still there and he suspected she would be relieved when his visit was over. 'But when Jamie and I married he was unable to obtain a wedding band so he gave me this until the time when he could give me a proper ring.' Looking down at it a wistful smile touched her lips. 'It was far too big for my finger,' she said softly, 'but he insisted that I should take it.'

'You will understand,' Ross said, 'that your letter informing my uncle of your marriage to Jamie came as a shock to him—as it did to the whole family.'

'I can understand that,' she replied, her voice quite calm, without surprise, as if she read his thoughts correctly. 'If they think I wrote the letter to stake my claim, they are mistaken. Jamie's death was a great shock to me also. Before I wrote to the duke I had already come to the conclusion that you would all be perfectly right to dislike me, and to consider me either a usurper or an imposter.' Taking the documents from him she placed them back in the bureau. 'I assure you I am neither of those things, Colonel Montague.' Her eyes held her visitor's for an instant before looking away.

Ross wished he could say making pre-conclusions were stupid, but found that he could not. Yet there was no shadow in her eye, no tone in her voice, that gave him reason to believe she was anything other than what she claimed to be. Jamie's wife.

'Jamie did tell me something of his home and his family. I am looking forward to meeting them.'

'Yes, the Montagues are a fine family.'

She bent her head, and Ross had a shrewd suspicion it was to hide a smile. 'I am sure they are, Colonel. Do you think I could pay them a courtesy visit? Would that be appropriate?'

For the first time since entering the house, Ross smiled. 'I am sure that could be arranged.' He got up to take his leave. 'I shall inform my cousins of our meeting. I am sure Giles will be contacting you.'

Ross had much to think about when he left the house. His mind was split in two conflicting directions. One direction made him wonder how much it had cost her to write to his uncle, the Duke of Rothermere—to make the swing from pride to humility.

For the first time since his cousin had gone missing, he found himself blaming Jamie for Alicia's situation. If she was indeed his wife, then considering the kind of work he was doing, surely he could have taken some thought for the future. In war sudden death could come at any time to anyone. He must have known that by making no provision, he left his wife to his family's mercy, to their charity. A letter home to his father would have spared all this.

The other direction reminded Ross that as a born sceptic, he wasn't entirely convinced about the validity of Alicia's claim. There were too many questions left to be answered for his comfort. It had been obvious from her manner and speech that her background was respectable, but was she clever enough and ambitious enough to raise herself from a lady's companion to a marchioness and ultimately a duchess? Or was she as she seemed to be—not ambitious, and innocent of any deviousness?

Another thought cast doubt. The Jamie he knew would have written to his family informing them of his intentions—could he really have been so blinded by his love for Alicia it had robbed him of all rational thought?

★ ★ ★

As soon as the Arbuthnots had left for Brighton, dressing simply and neatly in her most suitable gown and bonnet, Lisette presented herself at Mannering House in Bloomsbury. She was greeted at the door by a stiff-faced footman in dark green livery. On requesting to see the housekeeper he showed her into a glittering entry hall and told her to wait.

Feeling terribly nervous her gaze scanned the impressive hall. Never had she seen the like. This house surpassed her wildest imaginings. In magnificent splendour a marble staircase rose gracefully to the upper floors. A vase of sweet-smelling blooms beautifully matched and arranged had been placed on a side table beneath a huge gilt mirror. Folding her gloved hands at her waist, her body stiffened when, on looking up, she saw Colonel Montague.

She studied him as he slowly descended to the hall—his broad, muscular shoulders, deep chest and narrow waist—before lifting her eyes to his darkly handsome face. In a linen shirt, tight-fitting riding breeches and polished tan boots, every inch of Ross Montague's tall frame positively radiated raw power, tough, implacable authority and leashed sensuality.

For what seemed an eternity, she stood perfectly still, existing in a state of jarring tension, struggling to appear completely calm, clinging to her composure as if it were a blanket she could use to insulate herself against this man who disturbed her like no other. His gaze was steadily fixed on her and on reaching the bottom of the stairs he paused and they stared at each other for a second, with several yards of marble hallway still between them.

She watched him in fascination as he approached her at a

leisurely pace. Her heart skipped a beat. He was certainly the stuff of which young ladies' dreams were made.

Looking down at her, Ross noted how tense she looked. Her beauty caught him like an unexpected blow to the chest. 'Miss Lisette Napier. How very nice to see you again. You had no difficulty finding the house?'

Her eyes were alight with pleasure and she glanced around her. 'Not at all. It is a wondrous house,' she said softly. 'You might have warned me.'

'If you think this is grand, then wait until you see Castonbury Park. So you are here to take up your position as my sister's maid?'

The deep, velvet tones of his cultured voice made her stomach flutter. 'If I am considered suitable,' she replied, giving a slight curtsey.

He smiled slowly. His guarded stare travelled over her, noting the gentle flush mantling her cheeks. He didn't think he would have much persuading to do to make her succumb to his desire. The young beauty was not the expert that he was at hiding her feelings.

'Since I am to be the man who pays your wages, Miss Napier, your interview with Mrs Whitelaw is a mere formality. It is my considered opinion that you will be perfect for the post.' He lifted one eyebrow slightly after his words, as though challenging her to question them.

Lisette's knees knocked beneath her skirts, threatening to give out as she faced Ross Montague in all his male magnetism. 'I want to thank you again for thinking of me for the position,' she murmured. 'It was…generous of you.'

'Generous?' he echoed, both raven eyebrows arching high.

'Yes.' She nodded fervently. Something in his stare made

her fingertips tingle. The tingle crept up her arms with sweet warmth into her chest. She ignored the odd sensation with a will, lowering her gaze. 'I am extremely grateful. When Mrs Arbuthnot told me I would have to look for work elsewhere—and at such short notice—unaccustomed as I am to this huge metropolis, I confess I found the prospect of going from door to door seeking another situation extremely daunting.' Colonel Montague shocked her when he touched her gently under her chin. She caught her breath sharply as he tilted her face upward again and looked into his eyes.

Her gratitude appeared to entertain him—his chiselled face softened considerably as he held her gaze. 'I am happy to be of service, Miss Napier.'

Her heart pounded at the light but sure pressure of his warm fingertips against her skin.

He smiled and lowered his hand to his side. 'The Arbuthnots have left for Brighton?'

'Yes, this very day.'

'And you have brought your luggage with you?'

'Yes, sir, although I do not possess much, as you see,' she answered, indicating her one bag by the door.

'One of the footmen will see it is carried to your room.'

Lisette showed her surprise. 'But I have not yet met your housekeeper. I have my reference…'

'Which I have no doubt will give you an excellent character, but I prefer to judge for myself.' A woman seemed to appear from nowhere. 'Ah, here is Mrs Whitelaw. I'll leave you in her capable hands.'

Ross entered the hallowed rooms of White's, the gentleman's club in St James's, where he had arranged to meet his cousin, Lord Harry Montague. The rooms were cloaked in the quiet, restrained ambience, redolent of the masculine smells of sandalwood, leather and cigars.

He scanned the room, his gaze coming to rest on a tall, dramatically dark gentleman clothed in black. He stood watching the play at the hazard table. With no wish to join in, raising a brandy to his lips, the impression Harry gave off was of bored indifference. Lifting his head, the instant he saw his cousin, his handsome countenance lightened. The two strode towards each other and they met in the doorway to the card room, where they clasped arms, laughing.

'Good to have you home, Ross,' Harry said. 'Back for good, are you?'

'No—extended leave.' Ross took Harry's arm and led him to a table that offered privacy.

A worried shadow darkened Harry's eyes as he seated himself across from Ross and thought about the strangely vague note asking him to meet his cousin here. After politely enquiring about the health of Araminta and their maternal aunt, Lady Grace Mannering, he sat back and waited for Ross to enlighten him as to the purpose of this meeting.

'Glad to learn you made it back from Waterloo, Harry, but it was bad news about Edward,' Ross said, ordering a couple of brandies.

The emotions Harry suffered over the death of his younger brother at Waterloo and carefully concealed from others were evident now in the tautness of his clenched jaw as he glanced at his cousin. 'It is a tragedy felt by the whole family. It was one hell of a battle, but we finally got those bastards.' Drinking deep of his brandy he looked at Ross. 'Anything in particular you wanted to see me about? I got the feeling there was a sense of urgency about your note.'

Meeting Harry's arrested stare, Ross hesitated and then he said gravely, 'I've received a letter from Giles. He asked me to speak to you about Jamie.'

'Jamie's still listed as missing.'

'I believe he disappeared when the army made the push for Toulouse. He wasn't with the rest of them when they crossed the river. I understand he was swept away.'

'Jamie is…was a strong swimmer.'

'I imagine the current was too strong, Harry.'

'It looks like it. You know how I always looked up to Jamie.'

'I know. There is something else—a couple of things, in fact, that make it imperative that you go to Spain, to search for Jamie's body, or at least learn what happened to him as quickly as possible.' Harry gave him a questioning look when he hesitated, but waited patiently for him to go on. 'The first concerns the Montague finances. Shortly before Waterloo your father gambled on Napoleon winning the war. He sold his government bonds and lost a substantial amount of money. He took out a loan which has to be repaid.'

Harry stared at him with something like incredulity and amazement. 'Good Lord, I had no idea.'

'You've been in Spain. How could you?'

This was true, but Harry remembered the terrible rumours that had ignited London when word reached the city that Wellington had lost the battle at Waterloo, causing panic in the financial markets and the stock exchange to crash. In their desperation, London stockholders had wanted out of their investments immediately, believing they would need the money to survive. The market panic was halted when news of Wellington's victory at Waterloo arrived, but too late for the countless innocent people who had lost their life savings, and hundreds of reputable merchants and noble families had been ruined.

'There are many outstanding debts,' Ross went on. 'The creditors are being held off for now, but the deadline for repayment draws ever closer. As you know Castonbury costs a ransom to run. As things stand, its income doesn't match its expenses by a long way. The danger is that along with the contents of the house it will have to be mortgaged to pay off some of these debts.'

Harry's skin whitened. He was clearly shaken by this. 'Good Lord! As bad as that?'

'According to Giles, it is. Your father's grief at the loss of Edward and the situation with Jamie sent him into a decline, and the guilt he feels over his haste to sell off his shares is almost too painful for him to bear. As you know, when your mother died, as the firstborn and according to her marriage settlement, her immense fortune went to Jamie. Your father is banking on the money helping the family financially if proof can be found of Jamie's death.'

'Well, it will all go to Giles now. You said there were two things, Ross. You have told me the first. What is the second?'

'A short time ago a letter was delivered to your father from an unknown woman. It was sent from Spain. The woman is called Alicia Montague. She claims to be Jamie's widow.'

Ross waited through a long moment of awful suspense, knowing exactly where Harry's thoughts would turn next. Finally, when he spoke, his voice was rough with emotion, as if the words were being gouged out of him.

'What is known about her?'

'On Giles's request I have been to see her.'

'What did you make out?'

'She is an intelligent woman—she is also likeable and quite charming. She has a child she claims is Jamie's heir, and she also has a letter from the chaplain who performed the marriage ceremony—and Jamie's ring.'

'But…that is preposterous. As the heir, on a matter of such importance, it would be so unlike Jamie to commit himself to marriage without consulting with or at least informing his family first.'

'I agree. However, having met her she could very well be the type of woman Jamie would have fallen for.'

Harry felt a prickling along his nape. His instincts urged him to use extreme caution in making any judgement. 'What do you think, Ross? Could this woman be an imposter?'

Ross sighed and shook his head slowly. 'I don't know that. In fact, in all honesty I don't know what to think, which is why the truth concerning the marriage must be determined—along with the facts concerning Jamie's demise—before disaster strikes.'

'And if it is proven that Jamie is dead and the child is indeed his son, then as heir the estate will pass to him on father's death. And Mother's money too.'

'It looks like it. And should no body be found, then it will be seven years before an act of Parliament is passed officially declaring Jamie dead. In the meantime his finances will have to remain untouched. You've been to Spain, Harry. You have knowledge of the country, and being attached to the diplomatic service in London means you are ideally placed to go there and search out the truth. We need hard evidence that Jamie is dead.'

Leaning his head against the back of his chair, Harry closed his eyes and drew a long, deep breath. Spain! He didn't want to go back. Reminders of that time evoked painful, personal memories he preferred not to recall. And now Ross was asking him to go back.

'You are right, Ross. I must return. If this woman's claim cannot be disproved, then her son is heir. It could be devastating to the whole Montague dynasty. Dear Lord, Ross, how has it come to this? As youths we lived like princes, champagne was drunk as though it were water and guests invited to Castonbury Park to partake of the Montagues' hospitality were open-mouthed at the liberality and display. We hunted with the best of the county, the stables filled with expensive hunters, the kennels full of hounds—the hunt servants, the display of wealth. How is it possible that it's in danger of disappearing? It cannot happen. We cannot let it happen. We have to stop it.'

Ross knew that Harry would do everything within his power to seek out the truth. The Montagues' attitude to family was possessive and protective. They were a warrior clan defending what was theirs at all costs, their instinct being to hold on to what they had won. 'What are your chances, Harry?'

Harry's eyes narrowed into a slight frown and his features took on a pensive expression. 'The answer is that I don't know.' His tone implied the chances were not extremely good, but then he had contacts in Spain who might be able to help him so it was not entirely hopeless. 'But to find out what really happened to my brother is a mission I am duty-bound to undertake—and to find out what I can about this woman and if her claim is genuine. Leave it with me. I'll make arrangements to leave for Spain. Unfortunately I have commitments to fulfil regarding my work here in London so I am unable to leave right away. I'll write to Giles at Castonbury informing him when I can depart and again as soon as I have anything to report.'

Although Lisette had learned to contend with the varying moods and whims of Lottie Arbuthnot, this, she feared, was a different environment and a different mistress entirely. She had complete care of Miss Araminta's wardrobe and it was her duty to clean and repair any garment that needed it. She attended her toilet and arranged her hair—a task Lisette was taught by the maid who had attended Araminta before Lisette took up her position.

Her young mistress was a leading belle of the *ton*, and to Lisette's despair she was unpredictable and problematical. But she was also warm and open and there was something about her that Lisette liked.

She had completed her first week and was arranging Miss Araminta's hair when there was a knock on the door. Meeting Lisette's eyes in the mirror, Araminta gave her a knowing smile.

'That will be Ross—impatient as ever.' She bade him enter.

Contrary to Araminta's comment, Ross sauntered in and made himself comfortable in a chair facing his sister. He'd made it a practice to visit her in her room each day, and although he kept his visits brief, he found himself nevertheless looking forward to them because it gave him the opportunity to see Miss Napier. Out of uniform, Colonel Montague was the very epitome of an elegant gentleman. With his dark hair brushed back and shining, he was the image of relaxed elegance in his black and white evening clothes and one well-shod foot propped casually atop the opposite knee.

'I thought I'd come and see what's keeping you, Araminta. We're expected at the Bosworths' in half an hour.'

'I know, and I'm sorry, Ross. As soon as Lisette has finished arranging my hair I'll be ready.'

'I'm sure they'll understand if we're a bit late,' he said, content to sit and observe the delectable Miss Napier put the finishing touches to his sister's toilet. Even his expression was casual.

Looking at Lisette through the mirror Araminta eyed her in watchful curiosity, noticing her wandering attention and the soft flush that had risen to her cheeks when Ross had entered. She wondered what lay behind her maid's lovely face, for she really was exceptionally beautiful and in the right clothes she would be stunning.

'Tell me, Lisette, do you speak any other languages besides English?'

'I speak Urdu and Hindustani,' she answered, aware of Colonel Montague's eyes observing her every move and willing herself not to think of it. 'My parents taught me well and were quite insistent that I learn the language in order to understand the people and the culture of India.'

'That must have been difficult.'

'Not really. I was young so it came naturally.' Suddenly she felt like disappearing into the floor, for her announcement might have sounded like boasting and probably branded her a bluestocking in her mistress's eyes. But it had done no such thing. It had only increased her mistress's growing respect for this unusual maid of hers.

'Do you play the pianoforte and sing too?' Ross asked with a teasing smile.

Lisette returned his smile through the mirror and said, 'Oh, no. I can't do either. I gave up the piano in frustration, and when I opened my mouth to sing, to my immense relief my mother covered her ears and gave up on me.'

'And do you like working here, Lisette?' Araminta asked.

'Of course. I consider myself extremely fortunate to be working for such a fine family.'

'I am glad my brother brought you to my attention.'

'Our meeting on the docks was brief. I'm surprised he remembered me at all.'

'I'm not. You're very pretty, Lisette. Exceptionally so, and never have I seen hair so dark as to be almost black—in fact, I do believe it is. It's a beautiful shade—exotic, even, the perfect frame for your features and creamy skin. Do you not agree, Ross?'

Caught completely off guard, Ross said cautiously, 'Forgive me, Araminta, I'm not sure what you mean?'

'Either you're extremely unobservant or else your eyesight is afflicted. I was talking about Lisette's hair. It's quite extraordinary, don't you agree?'

'I am sure Colonel Montague has many things to think about other than my hair, Miss Araminta,' Lisette remarked. 'It is black and quite ordinary, which I do not find in the least exciting and is a common shade in India.'

'You don't like it,' Ross summarized.

'Not really,' she answered, touching Araminta's light brown tresses with something like envy in her eyes, 'but one must be satisfied with what one is born with. I would imagine that living in India and seeing nothing but dusky skins and black-haired natives day in and day out you would find monotonous, Colonel Montague.'

'Not at all—quite the opposite, in fact,' he replied, his gaze shifting to that exotic hair twisted and coiled neatly about Miss Napier's well-shaped head, with not a hair out of place. His fingers ached to release it from the pins and to let the heavy mass tumble in waves over her shoulders and down her back, to run his fingers through the tresses and to smell its fragrance.

It began to register on Lisette that the expression on his face wasn't dislike at all. In fact, he really did look almost admiring—and she saw something primitive flare in his eyes, which stirred her alarm and which she chose to ignore. Meeting his gaze she favoured him with an irrepressible sidewise smile. 'You mean you really do like it?'

Ross liked it. He liked every damn thing about her. In fact, he wanted nothing more than to thrust his sister out of the room and snatch Miss Napier into his arms, to kiss the smiling mischief from her lips until she was clinging to him, melting with desire. She'd indicated a feminine concern about her hair, then calmly accepted it. This gave him the distinct impression that pretence and pretension were completely foreign to her, and that she was refreshingly unique in those ways and probably many other delightful ways as well.

He leaned back in his chair and steepled his fingers beneath his chin, continuing to watch her from beneath hooded lids. 'That is what I said.'

'And my brother's opinion matters,' Araminta said smoothly, regarding Ross with fascinated disbelief. It was time for them to leave for their appointment, but there was something about the undercurrents flowing between her brother and her maid, something so very strange about everything, that she was reluctant to break the mood.

'I am glad you think so, Araminta, since it is my opinion that Miss Napier is in need of some new dresses as befits her position—although it would be more pleasing to the eye to see her decked out in satin and lace.' He studied Miss Napier surreptitiously. Beauty was moulded into every flawlessly sculpted feature of her face, but her allure went much deeper than that. It was in her voice and her graceful movements. There was something inside her that made her sparkle and glow, and she only needed the proper background and situation and elegant clothes to complement her alluring figure and exquisite features.

'Really, Ross,' Araminta chided lightly, 'it's very ungentlemanly of you to remark on that.'

A lazy smile transformed his harsh features. 'Surely I haven't done anything to give you the impression that I'm a gentleman!'

It was the exaggerated dismay in his voice that brought a smile to Araminta's lips. 'Nothing at all, and if you must know a trip to the modistes to purchase Lisette some new clothes is imminent—but ball gowns are quite out of the question.'

'Of course they are,' Lisette said quietly. 'It's quite ridiculous to contemplate such a thing—although Colonel Montague has my gratitude.'

He gave her a puzzled look. 'For what?'

Those candid eyes lifted to his in the mirror, searching, delving, and Ross had the fleeting impression that with time she might see straight into his devious soul. She obviously hadn't gotten his true measure, however, because a warm smile touched those soft lips of hers.

'Why, for providing me with this opportunity.'

Her gratitude only made him feel guilty about everything, more of a disgusting fraud, for letting her think of him as some gallant white knight, instead of the black-hearted villain who had every intention of luring her into his bed.

Having watched the byplay between Ross and her maid and quite enthralled by this teasingly flirtatious side of her brother, Araminta's eyes twinkled mischievously. 'Ross never forgets a pretty face, Lisette. I'm quite certain that if I hadn't mentioned that I was in need of a maid, he would have concocted some other means of renewing your acquaintance.'

Lisette flushed with embarrassment. 'Oh, I—I never meant...' She saw Miss Araminta's pitying look and knew she was being seen as completely besotted.

'No, of course you didn't. But be wary,' she said, meeting her brother's eyes with something akin to cynicism. 'Don't let my brother's charm sway you. Many a villain has been god-like in appearance, and such an attribute can be to the dire cost of the poor victims.'

And there speaks the voice of experience, Lisette thought, beginning to realise that her young mistress might not have come out of her broken betrothal as unscathed as some might think, after all.

She was proved right a moment later when Araminta pulled herself up straight and smiled, her eyes meeting Lisette's in the mirror. 'As clever as you are, Lisette, and looking as you do, you no doubt will want to find a husband eventually.'

Lisette stiffened at those words and tried to ignore the fact that Colonel Montague was listening most intently. She could not detect any hint of ridicule in Miss Araminta's voice, but she must be laughing at the very idea that someone might want to marry her.

'As a matter of fact there is nothing further from my mind, but if I were, I see nothing wrong with that.'

'Well, if marriage is your goal, pray let me dissuade you from it. You may think me something of a radical, but I have come to think that womankind is rendered helpless by her dependency upon men. At their mercy we are no better than rabbits in a trap. It is far better in life to remain unencumbered, if possible.'

'Thank you for your cynical view on the subject, Miss Araminta, but it is not a view I share. I would like to think that marriage is a partnership based on mutual love and respect, and companionship, not an encumbrance.'

'You are quite right, Miss Napier,' Ross remarked. 'I can see that when I single out the object of my matrimonial intentions, I would be wise to seek your advice.'

Over her shoulder, Araminta threw him a glare of mock offence. 'Ladies are not objects, Ross. Little wonder you have failed to secure yourself a wife. And if you did I can only assume that you would toss her over your shoulder, carry her off and beat her into submission.'

'You mean,' Ross said straight-faced, 'that *isn't* the way to handle the matter?' His gaze shifted to Lisette's in the mirror. 'What say you, Miss Napier?' He awaited her reply with more interest than Lisette realised.

Lisette saw the humour lurking in his eyes; she burst out laughing, and to Ross it seemed as if the room were filled with music. 'Ladies—that is *all* ladies, be they well-born or otherwise,' she clarified a moment later with a look that clearly implied his past experience had probably been with females of quite another sort, 'have very definite ideas of the way they wish to be treated by the man who wins their heart.'

'Please enlarge on that,' Ross said as she stuck another pin through a curl on Araminta's head. 'Just how do ladies like to be treated?'

'With respect, loyalty and devotion—and she wants to think that he has eyes for no one but her, that he's blind to everything but her beauty.'

'In which case, he's in imminent danger of tripping over his own feet,' Ross pointed out, grinning broadly.

Araminta shot him an admonishing look. *'And,'* she said emphatically, 'she likes to think he's a romantic, which you obviously are not, dear brother.'

'Not if I have to grope my way about like a blind idiot,' he teased. 'What else do ladies like, Miss Napier? I am all ears.'

Having said more than she had intended and spoken more sharply to Miss Araminta than was seemly in a maid, under her mistress's penetrating gaze some of Lisette's confidence slid away. Apart from Messalina she had never known how to converse with people her own age, and for the first time since leaving India, she felt gauche and ill at ease.

'I will leave you to work that out for yourself, Colonel. I am sorry, Miss Araminta. I was impertinent. I should not have been so outspoken when you voiced your opinion on marriage.'

'Why on earth not? I like people who speak their mind and you were quite right. I was very rude and there was no call for it.'

Standing up and smoothing her satin skirts, Araminta felt a new respect for her maid. Lisette knew her role but to be sure she was no dullard. Her impish smile and darting golden eyes betrayed the quick wit of an urchin. No doubt she had already knitted together the strands of Araminta's own tragic story from below stairs gossip. Still, she was aware of Lisette's capabilities and had already come to value her honesty and discretion. In just one week she had assumed far more than her intended measure of responsibilities and in doing so had made herself indispensable.

Three

Seated beside the window to catch the light for her sewing, Lisette was surprised when, following a brief knock on the door, it suddenly opened and Colonel Montague strolled in. Her heart missed a beat. His grey coat of Bath superfine hugged his broad shoulders, its excellent cut emphasising his broad chest and much narrower hips. His dark hair glowed softly in the sunlight slanting through the windows. With rigid calm she placed her work on the table in front of her and, rising, she bobbed a small curtsey.

He stopped just in front of her, and stood gazing into her eyes with a thoughtful expression. He seemed to peer down into her very soul.

'Miss Napier,' he greeted her, his blue eyes aglow, a beguiling little smile on his lips, 'how pleasant to see you and how well you look. Please, do sit down. I have no wish to interrupt your work. I'm here to see Araminta.'

Lisette did as he bade and sat back down, taking up her sewing. 'Miss Araminta is taking a bath. She shouldn't be too long—although sometimes she does like to wallow among the suds. Perhaps you would prefer to come back later.'

'I'm on my way out and would like to see her before I go. I'll wait,' he said, unable to think of anything better than spending a few minutes with this exotic young woman. It was the first time since she had taken up her position that he had found the opportunity to speak to her alone.

Lisette was aware of his aroused interest. From beneath dark brows he observed her with close attention, and then seated himself in a chair facing her, and with quiet patience he waited, like a cat before a mouse hole. He was watching her steadily, and she sensed the unbidden, unspoken communication between them.

Ross was thinking how lovely she was. Her hair drawn back from her face and coiled in her nape was very neat and tidy, and her cheeks were smooth and slightly golden. She wore a grey woollen dress and a starched and frilled white apron tied at the back of her small waist in a large and perfect bow, hugging her slender contours and emphasising their softness, leaving him with an urgent longing to fill his arms with their warmth.

'I have to confess that in the beginning I wasn't convinced you'd turn up here,' he said softly.

In disregard of the doubt she had felt during the time she had seen him at the Exchange, she said, 'I had no choice. When the Arbuthnots left for Brighton, I had nowhere else to go. Besides, I am not all that enamoured of London and the thought of Derbyshire appealed to me.' She could feel his gaze on her bent face. With a stirring of irritation and something else she could not put a name to, resolutely she lifted her head and met his eyes. 'Have you had an edifying look at me yet, Colonel?'

Quite unexpectedly he smiled, a white, buccaneer smile, and his eyes danced with devilish humour. 'You don't have to look so irate to find yourself the object of my attention. As a matter of fact I was admiring you.'

Unaccustomed as she was to any kind of compliment, the warmth in his tone brought heat creeping into her cheeks. 'You must excuse me if I seem a little embarrassed, Colonel. I'm not used to flattery.'

'I was merely thinking how lovely you are, Miss Napier.'

She shot him an amused look. 'And how many women have you said that to?' she asked, a smile trembling on her lips.

'Several. And it's always the truth.'

'I dare say you'll be eager to see Castonbury Park again.' Lisette looked down and did another stitch, eager to divert the conversation away from herself and relieved that she had something to occupy her hands.

His fascinating lips lifted fractionally. 'Eager enough, Miss Napier. I am concerned with family matters just now and my uncle's health is not what it was.'

Lisette wished his voice was not so very deep; it made her nerves vibrate.

A moment passed before he said, 'I wanted to have a word with you, Miss Napier.' She raised her head and waited for him to continue. 'You don't need me to remind you how unusual it is for a girl of your age to be working as a lady's maid. I know my sister has great confidence in you—indeed you will find as time goes on that she will confide in you in a way that is perhaps not entirely fitting, but because we have given you so much, because we chose you over a more experienced lady's maid, I know you will always be discreet. I know you will soon pick up your duties, but the habit of loyalty cannot be bought. Do you understand me?'

Lisette nodded. 'Yes. Be assured, Colonel, that whatever Miss Araminta confides in me, will go no further.'

Holding her gaze he nodded and smiled. 'Thank you. I know I can trust you. Have you no family, Miss Napier?'

She shook her head. 'No. My parents died of the cholera in India. As far as I am aware there is no one else.' As she said this she thought of the letter she had dispatched just yesterday to her father's lawyer in Oxford informing him of her parents' demise, and then her thoughts turned to Princess Messalina. Though not related, she was the closest she had to family.

'You must miss your parents.'

'Yes, I do. Very much.'

'What was your father doing out in India?'

She smiled. 'My father was something of an eccentric as well as being an academic. Not only was he a linguist he was also a botanist. He was working out there for the University of Oxford.'

'And your mother? Did she like India?'

'Yes, although she would have gone anywhere my father asked her to go. They were very close. They met in Italy—she was half Italian on her mother's side.'

'Then that explains your hair colouring. The only other women I've seen with hair as black as yours are Indian women. It must have been a difficult time for you when you lost your parents.'

She nodded. Remembering that time, she thanked God that was over and she was here. 'Yes, it was. Ever since, I've felt like a pawn on a chessboard, with no choice but to move forward, one step at a time.'

When she resumed her work he began to speak of his life in India, recalling his travels and battles and life with his regiment. Soothed by the deep warmth of his voice, Lisette was fascinated by his recollections, and glad of them too, for it brought India closer.

'My parents are dead too,' he said. 'My mother died when Araminta was born and my father was killed in France. He was the Duke of Rothermere's younger brother. My aunt and uncle took pity on us and installed us at Castonbury. We've lived there nearly all our lives.'

'Does the duke have a large family?'

'Six offspring. There is Jamie—the eldest, but he's currently listed as missing presumed dead. It's been very hard for the whole family. Then there is Kate. I haven't seen her in five years but I believe she devotes her life to worthy causes. You are sure to come into contact with her at Castonbury. She has her own ideas on equality between the sexes and is of the opinion that women should try and rise above their servitude.'

'It's easy for someone with means to be so forceful and outspoken in their opinions, but if she were to suddenly find herself without means, then she would come down to earth with a bump.'

He gave her a wry smile. 'Maybe so, but being the kind of person she is, she'd have a damned good try anyway.'

'I understand what you mean,' Lisette said, lowering her head over her work. 'But one could also look upon so privileged a life as a great comfort.'

'I do not take my position for granted, I assure you. I fully understand and appreciate how fortune of birth has given me all the opportunities and physical comforts of life—and I think I can speak for my cousin Kate too.'

'It is far more than that,' Lisette replied, sudden passion in her voice. 'You have a place in the world. You know what it is and where you belong. That is a very comforting thing.'

Her sudden intensity startled Ross. She was clearly a person of deep feeling, and there was a great deal of passion there. It all lay beneath the surface.

'You can have no comprehension how it feels not to belong anywhere,' she went on with an odd little catch in her voice. 'To have no roots that tie you to a place and give you purpose. I envy you that.'

'You no longer have a home of your own so it is understandable that you feel rootless. But you shall find your place one day. Everyone does, eventually.'

She smiled. 'I do hope so, Colonel. Now, you were telling me about your cousins at Castonbury Park. Who else is there?'

'Giles, Harry and Phaedra. She is horse mad. She would have come to London with Araminta for the Season, but she was still in mourning for her brother Edward. He was killed in the battle at Waterloo.'

'I'm so sorry. And you? Do you have many siblings?'

'There is just Araminta and me.'

'Where did you live before you went to Castonbury Park?'

'Here in London. My father, of course, grew up at Castonbury Park—the ducal seat. When he married my mother, who hated the country, they decided to make their home in London.'

'Did you like living in London all of the time?'

Looking through the window at the busy square, Ross shook his head. 'Not really. I like the country better. Fortunately my father had settled a sizable sum on both Araminta and me. My inheritance was quite substantial.'

'You didn't think to buy a house of your own?'

'Not then. I had my mind set on a military career and I always knew Araminta would be taken care of and marry eventually. Perhaps one day, when I am no longer a soldier, I will give the matter some thought.'

'When you take a wife, you mean—as most men do when they realise they need an heir.'

Ross's disinterested shrug and brief smile dismissed all the usual reasons for marriage as trivial. 'I have no intention of adhering to custom, now or in the future, by shackling myself to a wife for the sole purpose of begetting an heir. For a man such as I,' he said with mild amusement that failed to disguise his genuine disregard for wedded bliss, 'there does not seem to be a single compelling reason to commit to matrimony.'

Lisette studied him intently, her eyes alight with curiosity and caution, and the dawning of understanding. 'In other words you are married to the army.'

He grinned. 'You might say that. Since going to India I've been expanding my own assets there.'

Observing the glint in his eyes, she dared to enquire, 'And what is your enterprise of choice?'

'I invest in anything from tea to marble.'

Lisette stared at him. 'But you are a soldier.'

One dark brow rose. 'Among other things.' Finding conversing with her extremely pleasant, he shifted in his chair, making himself more comfortable. 'What would you like to do with the rest of your life, Miss Napier?'

'What can a woman do with her life? Men can do whatever they want, but if women are not wives, if they are without means, then what are their hopes? Domestic service is the only thing open to them.'

'You're quite wrong there, Miss Napier. A clever woman can do almost anything she likes if she would go about it as a woman should. Women as well as men can be as free as they choose to be.'

'In your world, perhaps, Colonel. Not in mine—as I have already pointed out.'

'In an ideal world they could be.'

'That is possible, but this is not an ideal world.'

'Just now you likened yourself to a pawn on a chessboard. If you are familiar with the game you will know that eight paces brings the pawn to the other side and she becomes a queen.'

'So if I just keep on going, I can be a queen,' she said. 'Even if there's already a queen—or more, on the board.'

He nodded. 'There can be as many queens as there are pawns—as long as the pawns are ambitious enough or lucky enough to go the full distance.'

She slanted him a curious look, understanding perfectly what he was saying—that if she was ambitious enough she could become anything she wanted to be in life. 'Are you by any chance a radical, Colonel?'

He grinned, his mouth wide over his excellent teeth. 'I would not go as far as to say that.' He became thoughtful. 'But I do have notions which do not always agree with those of my associates—especially here in England. Perhaps I have lived too long in India.'

'Or not long enough,' Lisette said on a wistful note. She was quite fascinated by this extraordinary conversation and by the strangeness of having it and her eyes glowed with their interest in his startling opinions. 'When I was in India I used to help my father collect his plants and sort out his specimens and send them back to the university. I hoped to carry on helping him with his work—it all seemed so probable then.'

'So, Miss Napier, will you continue being a lady's maid?'

She laughed lightly. 'Someone has to be. Someone has to look after the aristocrats and the gentry.'

'Quite right,' he replied with mock pomposity. 'I never do a thing myself if I can get the servants to do it for me.'

'But everyone should be capable of being self-sufficient. What would you do if you suddenly found yourself without anyone? Why,' she said, noticing his boots, 'look at your boots. Who cleans them?'

'Blackstock—my valet. I suppose you're going to tell me I should clean them myself.'

'No. You'd probably make a mess of them.'

He laughed at her pointed remark. 'As a matter of fact you're wrong. When I was a very small boy my father would make me clean my own boots religiously—riding boots, walking boots, everyday boots. I had to rub them until I could see my face in them. But you didn't answer my question. Do you intend being a lady's maid forever?'

Lisette put her work down in her lap and contemplated his question. 'Oh, I don't know. I haven't had much time to think about it since coming to England. But no, I don't think so.'

'Araminta speaks highly of you, says you're a real asset. She'd be sorry to lose you.'

'She won't. Not yet anyway.' She sighed. 'I would like to go back to India one day. I shall always hope something will turn up, but in my case—well, I'm not so sure. Maybe I could go as a companion to a rich old lady and travel the world.'

She laughed. 'But listen to me. I sound like a dreamer. I'm sure it will pass.'

Ross did not laugh. 'What's wrong with having dreams and longings? We'd be nowhere without them.'

'But in the end I have to be realistic. I can't see my situation changing dramatically in the foreseeable future. This is the real world. No one's going to wave some magic wand.'

'If one believes in magic, it could come true.'

He fell silent and beneath his gaze Lisette could feel his eyes on her as she sorted out a tangle of vividly coloured ribbons, painstakingly unravelling them and rolling each bright satin strand into a neat coil. His manner was all consideration and regard as he made a study of her person with a strange sort of intensity she could not define. She looked as she always did, so she had no illusions that he had cause to deem her worth staring at.

It was with some amusement that she raised her head and looked across at him. 'Colonel Montague, you study me most intently—as if I were an artefact. Or maybe I have a smut on my nose? Is that it?'

Ross leaned back in his chair. His eyelids lowered as his gaze raked over her with the leisure of a well-fed wolf. 'Your nose is perfect,' he replied, his voice husky. If ever he had discounted the possibilities that a woman's features could be flawless, then he was swiftly coming to the conclusion that Lisette Napier would set the standard by which all other women would have to be judged, at least in his mind. If her face wasn't at the very least perfect, it came as close to being so as he was able to bear. Several feathery curls had escaped their confines at her temples and in front of her ears, lending a charming softness to the hairstyle. In contrast to her dark tresses, her golden skin seemed more fetching by far than other ladies. A faint rosy hue adorned her cheeks and her soft, winsomely curved lips. As for her large, silkily lashed warm amber eyes, their appeal was so strong that he had to mentally shake himself free of their spell.

'I'm trying to read your expression,' he remarked, giving no indication of where his thoughts had wandered. 'And as for studying you as if you were an artefact, do not be offended. Artefacts are rare and mysterious things, intriguing and often difficult to interpret. It is not unusual that incorrect conclusions are made about them.'

Lisette's hands tightened on the ribbons in her lap. What was he saying? she thought wildly. That he did not see her as a servant? 'Are you saying that I am a mystery, Colonel? Because if so I assure you I have never thought of myself as either secretive or mysterious. I am no great mystery at all.'

Ross leaned forward in his chair, and looked at her as if she were of the utmost importance. 'I know very well what you are—but I also know you are a good person. I've never thought otherwise, not for one single moment.' He paused. 'I hope my sister is not driving you too hard. Accustomed to socialising with only the best in society, she tends to treat other humans as subjects. She is only happy if she is the centre of attention, being unreasonably demanding and imperious, and she takes violently against anyone who criticises or disagrees with her.'

Lisette smiled. 'You judge her too harshly. I have no complaints.'

He grinned. 'And you wouldn't tell me if you had. Your loyalty does you credit. However, I am hoping your calming influence will help keep her in line.'

'It's not my place to do that.'

'Nevertheless I live in hope.'

Suddenly remembering her mistress when she heard her call from the bathing chamber, putting her work down Lisette stood up and smoothed her apron. 'Excuse me. I must get on. I'll tell Miss Araminta you are waiting.'

Lady Mannering's two well-sprung travelling chaises travelled north to the splendid Castonbury Park that was the principal Montague residence. The first was occupied by Araminta and Lisette, the second filled to capacity with Ross's baggage and all of the trunks of clothes and accessories Araminta had deemed absolutely essential for any extended visit.

Lisette enjoyed the journey through the English countryside. Watching Colonel Montague riding on ahead with Will Blackstock, she longed to be able to join him on horseback. There were times when he tethered his horse to the back of the coach and joined them inside, his long legs stretched out in the luxurious conveyance. She was conscious and more than a little uncomfortable beneath his watchful gaze.

The weather had turned pleasantly warm and he often discarded his coat. His pristine white shirt and neck cloth contrasted sharply with his black hair and dark countenance. His body, a perfect harmony of form and strength, was like a work of Grecian art and most unsettling to Lisette's virgin heart. Each time their eyes met her heart tripped in her chest. Araminta's artless chatter filled any silence that could have been constrained.

It was the second day of their journey. Strolling away from the inn where, after consuming her dinner, Araminta was making use of the facilities in the ladies' room, observing Lisette stroll towards a stream that bubbled over its rocky bed to the rear of the inn, Ross smiled slowly and with a wicked glint in his eyes sauntered after her.

Ross was beginning to discover the whole tenor of his life was changing with Miss Lisette Napier in it. Constant awareness of her presence kept him in a perpetual state of delighted confusion. The stream ran through a sunlit glade. Having removed her shoes and stockings, Lisette was dangling her feet in the cool stream. Gazing at her, he was struck afresh by her loveliness. It was easy to forget she was his sister's maid. What was difficult was controlling his physical reaction to her nearness. An exercise in fortitude, he thought grimly. His body was achingly aware of her, even though she occasionally favoured him with a distant glance from those cool amber eyes of hers.

His throat went dry as he stared at the exposed skin along the back of her neck. Her hair was fashioned into intricate twists at the nape of her neck. Tiny combs somehow held it in place, and it gleamed in the sunlight like jet. He wanted to go to her and take it down, slide his fingers through the heavy mass of it.

Becoming aware of his presence, Lisette turned and looked up at him. 'Oh—Colonel Montague! How long have you been standing there?'

A slow, appraising smile touched his lips. 'Long enough.'

'Long enough for what?'

His smouldering gaze passed over her. 'Long enough to come to the conclusion that you are worthy of a higher position than that of a servant, Miss Napier.'

Lisette's mouth parted slightly, and she stared up at him in surprise, unconscious of the lovely vision she presented. 'Colonel Montague, it would be most improper for you to think of me as anything else.'

'Oh, yes, I can—and I do,' he asserted. 'Am I intruding?'

'Why, no. Did you follow me?' Lisette enquired, unsettled yet strangely thrilled by his words.

'Do you mind?'

'Who am I to mind? As my employer you are at liberty to seek me out whenever you please.'

He cocked a sleek questioning brow. 'For whatever reason?'

'No,' she stated firmly, her beautiful eyes sparkling with mischief, '*within* reason.'

His mouth curved in a devilish grin and the slight breeze teased a strand of his dark hair. 'Methinks you bait me, Miss Napier. If that is your game, then lead on. I will welcome your attention and the challenge.'

Lisette considered his words. She really did desire this man, that she could not deny, but having listened to the gossip of the other maids and being made aware of the serious repercussions should any one of them overstep the mark by forming any kind of relationship with gentlemen outside their sphere, she was afraid of the repercussions should she be found out.

'And where do you think it would get me if I were to give you my attention? It would create difficulties I can well do without.'

He grinned roguishly. 'It could be fun while it lasts.'

'Fun? Your arrogance really is quite amazing, Colonel Montague.'

In what was meant to be a display of mock disdain, her eyes skimmed his powerful frame. In the warmth of the day he'd removed his jacket. His white shirt was open at the throat. But her gaze faltered as the realisation flashed through her mind that there was nothing she could see she could poke fun at. He was hard and all lean, firm muscles.

It was clear he did not recall their meeting in India, that he had dismissed it entirely. She couldn't. When he looked at her as he was looking at her now, it made her recall aspects of that time in vivid detail—his warm, hard mouth and the feel of his hands and his body pressed against hers. It was wholly unnerving the way memories of lying alongside this magnificent man haunted her. Discomfited, she chastised herself for allowing her thoughts to suggest what her body wanted to experience again.

Unable to bear the weight of his heated regard, she withdrew her feet from the water and dabbed them dry with the hem of her skirt. Much fascinated, Ross sat on the ground, his broad shoulders propped against a tree trunk, his knee drawn up, where he rested his arms to enjoy more leisurely what had become his favourite pastime since leaving London: watching Miss Napier. She surely could not guess the depth of torture she put him through, for beneath his cool facade he burned with a consuming desire for her.

He was ever conscious of her, and whenever he saw her seated in the carriage with Araminta, she appeared trim and fragile, like a budding rose. But when he was close to her, Ross was painfully aware that though indeed she was neither very tall nor heavily rounded, she was very much a woman, and he wanted her.

Standing up, Lisette slipped her feet into her shoes, shoving her stockings into the pocket of her dress, denying him the pleasure of the sight of her slender legs by pulling them on. She watched him get to his feet. Her mouth curved into a tantalising smile as she came towards him with almost sensuous grace.

When he took her hand her heart accelerated inside her

chest. What charged it more, her horror of being seen alone in his presence, or the sensation of his strong fingers holding her hand, she could not say. He drew her to him, and she let him put his arms around her. It was nice.

She felt him shudder. Anxiously she said, 'What is it?'

He looked at her. 'Do you realise how lovely you are, Miss Napier?'

'Oh, no. I am quite ordinary. I have never pretended otherwise.'

'You hide behind your modesty—although modesty is an adoring quality and you wear it well.'

He was looking at her with such intensity she became still. Her cheeks were hot. She should have looked away, but she didn't. She went on staring back, with the wondering start of a smile, knowing she was lost, but not caring. He raised a dark brow and considered her flushed cheeks and the soft, trembling mouth. His gaze moved even lower and surveyed her bosom, until Lisette wondered wildly if he could see right through her dress. Beneath his steady regard, her breasts burned. This was not what she had expected. Everything seemed to spin— the light from the sun intensified, the trees seemed to close in. She waited for what was to happen next, and then she found herself held close in his embrace.

Her heart was racing now. The next moment he bent his head and she felt the warmth of his mouth. He pulled away a little, then kissed her again. The touch of his lips on hers was soft. Feeling a tumult of feelings well up inside her, she relaxed her lips in a faint echo of his kiss.

Unbidden, into Ross's mind came a memory, a memory that he had once kissed a girl like this before, and that her lips had been just as sweet—but he did not dwell on the thought and it drifted away.

Encouraged, he moved his lips against hers. Lisette could feel his breath warm on her face. He opened his mouth a little. She pulled away.

He looked puzzled. 'Don't you like it?'

In truth, his kiss evoked so many memories of the time when he had kissed her before, and all the times she had wanted it to happen again, that she tilted her head and allowed him to kiss her once more. There was nothing threatening, nothing violently uncontrollable, no force or dominance—just the reverse. This kiss was a shared pleasure and she gave herself up to the magic of it.

His lips parted and she felt the tip of his tongue. He teased her lips apart. She relaxed. He sucked gently at her lower lip. She felt dizzy.

'Open your mouth,' he urged softly.

She did as he asked and felt his tongue again, touching her lips, passing between her parted teeth, and probing into her mouth. She was filled with the need to hold him, to touch his skin and his hair, to feel his muscles and his bones. Her tongue met his and she was thrilled by the intimacy of it. He held her for what seemed an eternity. There were no minutes, no measures, only sensations and heartbeats. Although her head was spinning with a sickening mix of forbidden love, desire, guilt and unworthiness, she knew she must steady her thoughts. He was the first to break the kiss. His breathing was uneven, his eyes burning with intensity.

Touching her face he looked down at her. 'You see how much power you have when you choose to wield it, Miss Napier.'

She did see. It awed her and excited her that she, who had travelled halfway across the world, who had convinced herself she had no influence over anything in her life, who had placed herself in the position of desiring a man who didn't remember who she was, had the power over the very man she so desired. Suddenly, ordinary Lisette Napier felt as captivating and alluring as any woman, and a joy she had never felt blossomed inside her.

'Was that your first kiss?' he asked.

'No,' she whispered, saddened because he didn't remember. 'My second.'

'And how do I compare?'

'It is not a competition, Colonel, but I will say that you compare equally as well.'

He looked at her in mock dismay. 'That is high praise indeed—but not high enough. Is that all my kiss was worth? I am insulted. I believe my kiss should be valued more highly than that. I am a lord and a military colonel, after all.'

'So was he.'

'Really? I must remember to ask you about him one day,' he murmured. 'Then we are equal in more than just kissing. However, I know you enjoyed the kiss as much as I, Miss Napier.'

He saw a hint of blush come into her cheeks, and he thought her the most enticing thing he had ever seen. Kissing her could be the prelude to all the delicious imaginings in his mind, imaginings that would compromise his honour and her innocence. He was a soldier and a gentleman, he reminded himself, something that had never been hard to remember. Over a lifetime of fulfilling the obligations and duties of his military position, of obeying the strictures of an upbringing of discipline, no matter what his rank and title, a true gentleman did not corrupt an innocent young woman, especially one in his employ, and he should step back. But by God he knew he wanted her.

He raised the stakes higher.

'There is nothing wrong in sharing a kiss,' he stated, now in a more assured tone. 'A mere kiss,' he said, his voice sounding low and husky, 'can be far more tempting than you realise. In fact, I think we might get to know each other better, Miss Napier. So long as we resolve to be discreet,' he said, having no wish to create a scandal by forming a relationship with his sister's maid. 'I don't think either of us would enjoy all the attention we would receive at Castonbury Park.'

Lisette stared at him in disbelief at what he was suggesting. Though her stomach clenched with fear she slowly smiled, for she could not deny to herself that she liked the way he touched her. But to become closer would be a dangerous game to play, one that she would not willingly choose to become involved in, not because it would be distasteful—for she found Ross Montague desirable in every way—but because she could never be anything to him other than his mistress, and she had too much self-respect for that.

'I think that what you are suggesting is an illicit attachment, sir—in which I shall be judged to be a scheming hoyden. I would despise myself—and you. I have done nothing to invite your attentions or encourage the feelings that have taken root.' She stepped away and turned from him. 'Excuse me. I must go back.'

Ross's burst of laughter halted the flow of words abruptly and Lisette spun round, her eyes flashing with indignant sparks.

'How quickly you rebuke me, as if you're sorely in the wrong. And there you are, all soft and tempting. And then you chasten me for looking at you and kissing you. Fickle woman,' he teased.

'You deserve to be rebuked,' she was quick to add.

'You think so?' Ross took her in his arms once more. He knew he was playing with fire, but it was the risk that made a game exciting. He did not want to give up the torment-ing delight of being alone with her. It was like an addiction, an addiction to the game of testing his desire for her against his resolve.

And so he kissed her again—her hair, her cheek, caressing her lips with his own. He pressed her back against a tree, and his mouth travelled downward to where her neck disappeared into the collar of her dress. Lisette held her breath, and the fires of passion and wild, wanton sensations again began to flare within. A touch, a kiss, a look, and he could rouse her. What madness.

'Your heart beats much too quickly for you to claim disin-terest, Miss Lisette Napier.'

Her lips trembled as he claimed them fiercely with his own. For a long moment his hungering mouth searched the sweetness of hers. Then she pulled back. 'Please let me go,' she said, her soft lips still throbbing from the demand of his. 'I have been away long enough. I must go back. Miss Ara-minta might have need of me,' she announced abruptly, em-barrassed by her own musings.

Gleaming whiteness flashed as Ross grinned down at her. He took her hand in his and looked deep into her eyes. His skin was warm to the touch and somehow reassuring. But he seemed too much of a man, too knowing and strong, too able to bend her to his will. She was dizzy with conflicting emotions and the turmoil made her momentarily speechless. She wanted to tell him to go away, and at the same time wanted him to lean closer and kiss her again.

Ross smiled and for a moment looked wickedly mischievous. 'I believe there is a danger of you stealing my heart, Miss Napier. If you do I pray you will be gentle with it.' He kissed both her hands and then released them.

Something in their exchange pulled Lisette back from the brink of dangerous recklessness, and she remembered the deference due to the man before her. No matter how much he desired her, she was his servant. She depended on him for almost everything, and he had indeed been generous to her.

'Colonel Montague, I—I beg you not to do this. You have been good to me. I…am in your debt. But I am maid to your sister. I can never be more to you than that.'

Her speech was halting. His eyes held hers as he said, 'We shall see. I find what is called fate often has the workings of most worldly hands. Sometimes a whim or a fancy, a base desire, can deny the best-laid plans.'

Ross did not try to detain her further. When she turned away he followed along in her wake, appreciatively watching her hips as they swayed with a natural graceful provocativeness. She turned languidly and looked back, smiling to herself when she saw how he strode after her with that slowly deliberate saunter that reminded her so much of a hunting animal.

It wasn't until she got back to the inn and went to the ladies' room to put on her stockings that she realised she had lost herself and all sense of propriety. She was quite horrified by her behaviour. Colonel Montague would think her forward and impertinent. Shame swept over her like a fever, washing her face in colour. He was her employer and she must see that nothing like that happened again.

After that, whenever she saw him ride by or join them in the coach she could hardly bring herself to look at him, knowing that if she did she would begin to tremble. He had a particular gift. He possessed a unique ability to compel and captivate with his words, and this, combined with his handsome features, meant there was no woman he could not persuade.

Over the following days that episode would stay with her. She did what was expected of her and tried to smother those feelings to which her heart had succumbed. But her pulse would leap at the sight of him or the mention of his name, and she could not quench the forbidden spark that smouldered in her heart.

Accompanied by Blackstock, Ross felt an odd sensation of unreality as he rode through the wrought iron gates of Castonbury Park.

The drive wound through the neatly tended deer park to the upper lake. Here a beautiful cascade spanned by a three-arched bridge separated the upper and middle lakes, the bridge providing a splendid view of the grand and impressive sprawling mansion with its Palladian central facade embellished with Georgian lavishness, the immense stone steps rising on either side to the marble hall behind the portico. Linked by curved corridors, at each end of this splendid building were the family apartments on the left, and to the right the usual range of domestic buildings—kitchen, stables and workshops, and at the back, almost hugging the house, stood the old chapel.

Being home again made Ross feel uncharacteristically nostalgic. It was five years since he had been to Castonbury but of his welcome he had not a doubt. His uncle, Crispin Montague, the Duke of Rothermere, was well-bred and well set up, and he presided over the gargantuan Castonbury Park.

Drawing Bengal to a halt in front of the house, before he'd had time to dismount at the basement door, which was the everyday entrance to the central block, it was already being opened by Lumsden, clad in his usual black. Lumsden had been the butler at Castonbury Park from time immemorial and had always possessed uncanny timing. Leaving Blackstock to attend to the horses, Ross looked at this old retainer and smiled. It was Lumsden who'd found him sampling a bottle of his uncle's French brandy when he'd been nine years old. It was also Lumsden—who was not averse to sampling a drop of His Lordship's liquor himself—who took the blame for the missing bottle, explaining that he'd accidentally dropped it.

At the moment Lumsden's eyes were passing fondly over Ross's face. 'Good afternoon, my lord,' he intoned formally. 'And may I say how good it is to have you home at Castonbury.'

'Good afternoon, Lumsden. It's good to be back. It's been a long time and sadly much has changed in my absence.'

'Indeed it has, my lord,' Lumsden replied gravely. 'Everyone is deeply saddened by the deaths of Lord Jamie and Lord Edward.'

'Yes, I am sure they are. My sister will be here shortly. I rode on ahead in order to get a clear view of the place.'

'You will see the fabric of Castonbury is as it was before you left—although in this present financial climate, you will observe unavoidable signs of wear and tear here and there.'

'I think we have the wars to blame for that, Lumsden.' Ross entered the large hall. It was an impressive room with sixteen columns supporting the weight of those in the magnificent marble hall immediately above. A small army of footmen and housemaids seemed to be lurking about, ostensibly going about their work. As Ross looked around him they stole long, lingering looks at him, then turned to exchange swift, gratified smiles. With his mind on getting cleaned up before his meeting with his uncle, Ross was oblivious to the searching scrutiny he was receiving, but he was dimly aware as he walked through the hall that a few servants were hastily dabbing at their eyes and noses with handkerchiefs.

Seeing a tall man with dark hair coming towards him he quickened his stride. It was his cousin Giles. They were the same age and of a similar height. Smiling, he held out his hand and the two hugged each other warmly. So much had happened to them both and the family as a whole since their parting five years earlier.

'Giles! It's good to see you.'

'You too, Ross. Damn good, in fact.'

Ross stood back, anxiously studying the deeply etched lines of strain at his cousin's eyes and mouth, but he looked better than he'd expected. 'You look like hell.'

'Thank you, Cousin,' Giles said drily. 'I'm delighted to see you too.'

Ross laughed and slapped his back good-humouredly. 'And I you. You have no idea how much—but I would like to see you looking better.'

'You can put it down to hard work. It's backbreaking work running an estate the size of Castonbury—and don't think that now you're back you're going to be allowed to escape,' Giles threatened light-heartedly. 'I'll have you hard at it first thing.'

'I'll be glad to be of help in any way I can.' Ross laughed.

Dismissing the subject with a casual wave of his hand, he drew him towards the stairs off to the right. 'Let's go up to the library. You can pour me a drink before I go and change. Five years is a long time and we have a lot of catching up to do.'

Entering the library on the first floor of the house, that was the moment when Ross really did feel that he had come home. He had spent many industrious yet happy hours in this room poring over books. His gaze was drawn to the painted plaster busts of Greek and Roman worthies and he smiled when he recalled his uncle Crispin telling him they were intended to encourage studiousness.

The cousins sat in companionable silence on opposite sides of a log fire, its light shining on the steel fender. They each held a glass of brandy from which they sipped appreciatively. There was a slight similarity of features between the two, and like Ross, Giles was not very good at showing his emotions.

'How is my uncle?' Ross enquired. 'I understand he isn't well.'

Giles grimaced. 'No, he is far from it. He has good days and bad days and there is an inconsistency in his behaviour. His mind wanders and he sits staring at nothing for long periods. It came as a blow to him when Jamie was listed as missing during the push for Toulouse, and when young Edward was killed he seemed to retreat inside himself.'

'Is there still no news about Jamie?'

Giles shook his head, a shadow passing over his grey eyes. 'Nothing. You know I resigned my commission after Waterloo.'

'I was sorry to hear it. Did you have to do that? I know how much your career meant to you.'

'Duty demanded it. When Edward was killed and with

Jamie missing, Father summoned me back home. I was in London at the time. He pointed out most forcibly that now, as his heir, my place is at Castonbury. I never envied Jamie being the heir—the responsibilities. When I got back here, knowing that in all probability it would one day be mine, they became like jewels too heavy to carry, too valuable to neglect and too enormous to ignore. I believed it had all come down to me—or so I thought until we got Alicia's letter. If it turns out that she *is* Jamie's wife and her child his son, then if Harry can discover irrefutably that Jamie is dead, the child, Crispin, is the heir. It's all such a mess. You saw her in London?'

'Yes, I did.'

'What did you make of her? Is she genuine do you think? Is she telling the truth?'

'I honestly don't know the answer to that, Giles. She was convincing—though nervous, I thought. She has all the necessary papers.'

'Then we'll just have to see what turns up.' He took a long drink of his brandy. 'Coming home kept me sane enough to deal with the broken man who is my father, to deal with those who came to pay their respects and to hold together the frayed strings of the household. Although Aunt Wilhelmina does a sterling job of keeping things shipshape and the household in order. She is out at present visiting Lady Hesketh in Hatherton. She is expected back before dinner.'

'And cousin Kate?'

'My sister is off on one of her travels—the Lake District, I believe, but Phaedra is here. She will be glad Araminta is back from London. She spends most of her time with her precious horses but I think she's missing Kate. I cannot guarantee what kind of reception you'll get from father. As I said, you'll find him much changed.' He grinned suddenly. 'And you'll have to get past Smithins first.'

'Smithins!' Ross exclaimed, recalling that rigidly superior gentleman's gentleman, who rarely deigned to speak to anyone but his uncle, the duke. 'Good Lord, is he still here? I'd forgotten about him.'

'Come now, no one forgets Smithins. A legion of soldiers couldn't do a better job of guarding my father than he does. Even I have to get past Smithins to see him.' He laughed, beginning to sound more like his old self. 'Goodness, I'm glad you're home, Ross. There's a definite sense of the military about you. God, how I miss it. Your presence will bring back some normality to the house. And how is the adorable Araminta?'

'Still adorable and very well, considering her broken engagement. She'll be here any time. I rode on ahead. She is in transports over coming back to Castonbury. When the time is appropriate, she has planned parties and goodness knows what so I doubt you'll have a moment's peace and quiet.'

'I shall welcome it,' Giles said, getting up and walking over to the side table and pouring himself another liberal glass of brandy. 'It's just what this house needs to shake it out of the doldrums. Although be warned. Whatever activities she is planning, she will have to gain Aunt Wilhelmina's approval first. She hasn't changed.'

For the next half-hour they sat in congenial companionship as Giles gave him a detailed account of what needed to be done on the estate, which through lack of money had been neglected. He went on to tell him of myriad business ventures and family holdings the Montagues had managed to hold on to, but it was clear Giles was concerned about the state of the finances.

'I would like to help,' Ross offered. 'Not only have I come home to offer my support but also to offer financial help to tide you over until the family debts can be settled.'

'Thank you, Ross. That's extremely generous of you. I appreciate your offer but I cannot accept it—not yet anyway. I have money of my own and I'm managing to keep things afloat just now. We're banking on Harry coming up with firm evidence of Jamie's death. Although if it is proved that Alicia's son is indeed the heir, then Jamie's wealth will pass to him.'

'Think about it. I owe your family a great deal—especially your parents, who gave me and my sister a home when we needed one, and extended as much affection to us as they did to their own children. The offer remains if you should change your mind.'

Four

Nothing could have prepared Lisette for the exquisite splendour that was Castonbury Park in the heart of the Derbyshire countryside. She saw it from a distance sitting like a grand old lady surrounded by beautiful parkland, timeless, gracious and brooding, its elegant beauty expressing power and pride.

When the carriage drew to a halt in front of the house, scarlet and gold-liveried footmen appeared and descended to strip them of the mountain of baggage. Lisette stepped into the bustling, alien environment that was to be her world from now on, acutely aware of the rich trappings of the interior.

The house was awe inspiring, the atmosphere of comfort and luxury, of elegance and a style of living she could never have imagined. The butler, Lumsden, stood aside as they entered, keeping a keen eye on the footmen to remind them of their duties as their eyes kept straying with frank approval to the young maid who stood beside Miss Araminta.

Unaware of their admiring looks, with her eyes opened wide with wonder and awe, Lisette followed her mistress along an assortment of corridors to the west block, where Araminta and other family members had their rooms. Lisette attended her mistress's toilet and helped her change into fresh clothes in which to meet the family, before seeking her own chamber. She was pleasantly surprised to find she had been allotted an adequately furnished room overlooking the park at the south-facing front of the house.

Having washed her face and tidied herself, Lisette found her way to the domestic quarters to introduce herself to Mrs Stratton, the housekeeper.

'Wait here,' a young housemaid by the name of Daisy said when she asked if she might see Mrs Stratton. 'She's in her parlour with Mr Everett, the steward. I'll tell her you're here.'

Lisette did as she was told, standing just inside the kitchen door and glad of it, for it gave her a chance to look at this splendid room which was a hive of activity. Every surface was so highly polished it reflected the light. There were two enormous tables bearing bowls filled with all manner of ingredients and chopping boards. There was much stirring and chopping and whisking at this table, a tumultuous frenzy, as dinner was prepared for the family. Covering a whole wall was a huge dresser that reached from floor to ceiling with what seemed to be hundreds of pieces of crockery of every sort, along with copper utensils, silver-covered dishes and much more. A massive range took over the whole of another wall, with an iron contraption with hooks on which to hang kettles and such like for roasting meat.

A young male cook in a pristine white apron and white hat was leaning over the range, the wooden spoon with which he had just stirred a sauce at his lips. He tasted the mixture speculatively, his darkly handsome face set in lines of deep concentration, then he turned to a kitchen maid and, with an air of one who makes a momentous decision upon which the lives of hundreds might depend, he said with a strong foreign accent, 'A half-teaspoon more of pepper, if you please, Nancy, and not a spec more.'

Lisette turned when a neatly dressed woman with a rustle of stiff black silk and a jangle of the keys secured to her waist appeared.

'I'm Mrs Stratton and you must be Miss Napier, Miss Araminta's maid.'

'Yes. I'm pleased to meet you, Mrs Stratton.'

'How is Miss Araminta? Well, I hope?'

'Yes, she is very well and meeting her family just now. The footmen are sorting out the baggage at present so I thought I'd come and familiarise myself with the routine in the domestic quarters.'

Mrs Stratton looked her over and what she saw evidently satisfied her. A woman with greying blond hair, she was of a gentle and quiet nature and treated the maids fairly and with kindness. Over the coming days as Lisette got to know her better, she would find that she was one of those rare women blessed with a temperament that was constant and reliable, and that her loyalty to the Montagues exceeded that which was normally expected of a servant for her employers.

On seeing Miss Napier's interest in the male cook, she smiled.

'That is Monsieur André. He has the entire superintendence of the kitchen, while several maids are employed in roasting, boiling and all the ordinary manual operations of the kitchen. I'll get Faith Henshaw to show you the ropes—

she's Lady Phaedra's maid and extremely competent. I'm sure
you'll be glad of her help.'

Lisette was immensely grateful. Faith—or Henny as she
was addressed—was a few years older than she was. Very
slim and with dark brown hair and always on the go, she was
an experienced lady's maid, kind and thoughtful. She was to
marry Sandy, one of the footmen. It was from Faith that Lisette learned of the household duties and the routine of the
household.

The day of Ross's return was one of high spirits at Castonbury. The housemaids gathered in corners and whispered between themselves. Mrs Stratton instructed Monsieur André
to make up his favourite chocolate sponge cake, and the following morning Giles took him on a tour of the estate lest he
had forgotten where he lived.

It was late afternoon when Ross made his way to his uncle's
suite of rooms. Smithins, small, with thick white hair and his
habitual poker face and keen eyes, met him in the anteroom
to the duke's bedchamber.

'Welcome home, my lord,' he said haughtily.

'Thank you, Smithins. I've come to see my uncle.' When
the valet made no reply, he looked at him enquiringly, raising his eyebrows. 'Is he awake?'

Smithins considered the colonel, inclining his head and
pursing his lips in an effeminate manner. 'On the doctor's orders I gave him a draught earlier. It has relaxed him. In fact,
I was about to get him into bed. I am reluctant to allow any
new stress foisted on him.'

'I am not here to cause him stress,' Ross stated, struggling to hold on to his temper, somewhat put out at being kept waiting as though he were a casual caller.

'I'm sure you're not, Colonel, but—'

'I would like to see my uncle,' Ross interrupted in a glacial voice, feeling impatience grow in him as the valet bristled waspishly. 'I will stay just a moment.'

Smithins sniffed and with his nose in the air turned towards the door. 'Very well, if you insist.'

Ross was admitted into the bedchamber. It was dominated by a huge bed decorated with palms and ostrich feathers and hung with blue silk damask. It was a comfortable, spacious room, but there was an air of tension about it which manifested itself in the old man seated in a chair by the window, and the slow metronome ticking of the clock which seemed to herald the coming of something the duke might not care for. The room was warm, for Smithins was of the opinion that warm air helped fragile lungs to breath more easily.

Ross went to his uncle. 'Uncle?'

The duke lifted his head then and saw him. Ross was taken aback at the sight. Even Giles's words had not prepared him for his appearance. All his life he had been a tall, well-built man, his face full, firm and strong looking. Now it was much altered, the life gone from it, drained and empty, the flesh already sunken into the shape of his skull. His eyes were a dead, flat grey. They had lost all their bright intelligence that he had always associated with his uncle. He coughed, gasping to take his next breath. Ross waited while Smithins gave him some water. Gradually some colour came to his face and his breathing became easier. His eyes lost their blankness and filled with an expression of recognition as they settled on Ross. But Ross could see that his uncle was half the man he once was, shrunken, bent, slower and bereft without Edward and Jamie.

When he spoke he was coherent, his voice low and threadlike. 'Ross, my boy, Giles told me you were back. You look well. India must agree with you. You are on leave? How long have you got?'

'A few weeks—longer if I am needed here.'

He nodded, his gaze drawn to the window which offered an extensive view of the park, staring with an air of fixed absorption of some secret worry. 'That's good. Giles will be glad to have you around. You know about Edward—and Jamie…'

'Yes.'

'Sometimes I forget…I think they are still here—and then I remember. I can't take it. Why don't they come home?' He could not go on for a moment and his hand fell away to his lap where it clutched desperately at the wool of the rug which covered his legs. His gaze remained on the window and the yellow gold wash of the sun on the curtains. After a moment, speaking slowly, almost to himself, he said, 'I cannot believe they are both gone from here—that all that life and vigour, that passionate conviction, that vital, hot-headed emotion that sent them to war is…'

With those words trailing off into silence, Ross looked down into the face of the man who stared somewhere into the far-off distance into a nightmare world in which no one existed but himself. He knew everyone who came to see him, to stand beside his chair and express hope and belief that some miracle would bring his sons back to Castonbury.

Drawing himself up, Ross laid a gentle hand on his uncle's shoulder and nodded to Smithins to show him out.

★ ★ ★

It was chance that brought Lisette into contact with Ross following his meeting with his uncle. Upon climbing the stairs on her route to Miss Araminta's room, she found him at the top of the landing. They were not entirely alone, as two footmen were lighting the candles along the corridor where they met. She stopped awkwardly and looked directly at him. He seemed perfectly self-possessed. The shadows were resting softly along his cheek and chin. He brought his gaze down upon hers heavily and with a slight smile, reaching out his hand, he gently touched her cheek with the tip of his finger.

Lisette looked away, not on account of shame, but because his gaze was loaded with desire. He stepped back, dipped his head to her graciously before proceeding down the stairs.

After a moment she turned. Mrs Stratton was watching her from the shadows, and in that instant Lisette felt as if all her vices had been unmasked. She shrank back, ashamed of her conduct, and resolved once more to dispel all her absurd longings, however impossible this task seemed. After all, what right had she to entertain even for a moment, a desire for anything more than what she had now?

But— Oh, dear sweet Lord! To be embraced by him, kissed by him! She had never known such a feeling. It was as if every particle of her might come apart in his arms. Until that moment she had never known the true force of her emotions. It was like nothing else on earth. It contained in it all the fierceness, all the violence, of a hurricane. It was the very essence of the sublime.

Whenever they met, she did her best to avoid meeting his gaze, but he did not endeavour to avoid hers; in fact, he occupied himself with nothing else.

★ ★ ★

Despite Ross's homecoming, which should have been cause for celebration, dinner that night was a subdued affair in the grand dining room. The long table shone with silver and crystal ware. Up above the ceiling was richly decorated with a series of paintings of the four seasons and continents. Gilt-framed paintings of hunting scenes adorned the stone-coloured walls, and the white marble mantelpiece was supported by Roman figures.

Looking particularly regal yet wraithlike in a gown of saffron silk shot with green, her grey hair immaculately coiffed beneath an elaborate arrangement of feathers, the Honourable Mrs Wilhelmina Landes-Fraser presided over all of it. Diamonds and emeralds sparkled at her neck, earlobes and wrists. Seated at the opposite end of the table to Giles, she regarded the family with a stern eye and an attentive expression in her eyes as they settled on Phaedra and Araminta before nodding to the servants to begin serving.

As sister-in-law to the Duke of Rothermere she cared a great deal for the fads and fashions of the day, although she, unlike the majority of her contemporaries, refused to allow her tall, slender figure to run to fat. A stickler for protocol and doing the right thing, she had the aloof, unshakable confidence and poise that came from living a thoroughly privileged life. In this world of hidden meanings and unspoken rules, there was no mistaking her value.

Ross inwardly gritted his teeth. Aunt Wilhelmina was effectively the matriarch of the family. Acknowledging the power she wielded was something the Montague men had to do.

The meal progressed with Phaedra complimenting Ross on his magnificent horse, who had lost no time in making himself at home in the stables, and Giles sang the praises of his betrothed, the lovely Lily Seagrove.

'You'll be meeting her shortly, Ross—and her father, the Reverend Seagrove. He often calls to spend some time with Father and frequently joins us for dinner.'

'I remember Miss Seagrove, Giles. Not having seen her since she was a girl, I'm sure I shall find her much changed. This is excellent soup, by the way,' Ross commented, spooning the rather unusual but mouthwatering soup up. 'I compliment the cook on her culinary art.'

'We have a chef in the Castonbury kitchen—a Frenchman, Monsieur André,' Giles informed him. 'French chefs are in demand in London—in the hotels in particular. When Father was ailing, we lured Monsieur André to Castonbury with promise of future advancement if he could tempt Father to eat in order to maintain his health.'

'I'm impressed,' Ross said, having finished the soup and looking forward to the next course, which he had no doubt would be a culinary delight.

'Giles tells me you have been to see this woman who claims to have married Jamie?' Wilhelmina said, settling her sharp eyes on Ross. 'What did you think of her? Is she genuine?'

'I can't say. I found her likeable and quite convincing, but...'

Wilhelmina lifted her aristocratic brows. 'But *you* were not convinced.'

'Not entirely.'

'Did you see the child?'

'No, I did not.'

'I see. I would appreciate it if we kept this within the family,' she said, lowering her tone a notch with Lumsden and his minions close within earshot. 'Hopefully we shall hear from Harry very soon and it will put an end to this nonsense.'

'It may not be nonsense,' Ross remarked. 'I greatly fear that, like it or not, there is every chance that Jamie married the woman in Spain and that the child is his.'

'I believe the woman to be an impostor—an opportunist, out for all she can get,' Wilhelmina remarked sternly.

'Not necessarily, Aunt,' Giles dared to argue, draining his glass and nodding to Lumsden.

Lumsden went to an alcove where a huge trough of Sicilian jasper was filled with iced water and bottles of wine. Taking out a bottle of white wine he replenished the glasses.

'I read the letter,' Giles went on, 'and I have to say she came over as pretty genuine to me.'

'I think if you had troubled to read it properly—between the lines as I did—you would have realised that she is not what she seems,' Wilhelmina retorted. 'But if her claim is proven, then how could Jamie have let this happen—and for a child to have been born of their union is just too dreadful to contemplate and will set in motion all manner of inheritance issues. It is bound to cause bad feeling within the family.'

'It doesn't have to be like that,' Giles said.

'But it will happen,' she exclaimed sternly, having been brought up to understand that good breeding mattered more than wealth. 'For generations the bloodlines of this family have been unsullied. The Montagues are descendants of the nobility. Yet Jamie may have married an utter nobody, a person without bloodlines or breeding or ancestry to produce the next heir. We know absolutely nothing about this woman. Little wonder your father's mind is unhinged with all this going on.' In supreme frustration, she turned her ire on her nephew. 'You must see my point, Giles.'

Giles leaned back in his chair, his expression wry. 'Very well,' he said amiably. 'It is certainly desirable and fortunate to be well descended, but until it is proven otherwise we must give her the benefit of the doubt.'

Wilhelmina cast him a killing glance, but she said nothing more on the subject and the rest of the meal passed in silence.

Three weeks after coming to Castonbury, while her mistress was dancing her feet off at the Assembly Rooms in the nearby town of Hatherton and entrancing more beaux, Lisette sat in Mrs Stratton's comfortable parlour sharing a cup of tea and mending some fine Brussels lace on one of Araminta's petticoats.

When Mrs Stratton was called away to attend to a crisis in the kitchen, feeling strangely restless and in need of some fresh air, Lisette put down her work and, wrapping a shawl about her shoulders and begging a couple of apples from Monsieur André, she left the quiet buzz of conversation in the servants' hall and went outside.

It had been raining all that day and at last it had stopped. It was a clear night, the sky littered with stars. Walking away from the house and trying to avoid the puddles, she followed the path to the stables, a path she often took when she found she had time to herself. Walking into the shadowy dimness of the yard where an occasional lantern attached to the walls cast an orange glow and filled the yard with shadows, the familiar fecund smells of straw and grain and warm animals and manure assailed her nostrils. There were several grooms who had their quarters over the stables which were quite extensive, for besides housing horses to ride, there was also space for carriages.

Going inside she smiled when she saw Bengal. His head reached out to her over the door of his stall where he was quartered. He whickered in welcome, pleased to see her.

'You can wait,' she said laughingly, bypassing him and stopping by another horse. This was Merlin, a magnificent chestnut stallion. He belonged to Lord Jamie, the Montague heir who had disappeared in Spain. Stretching out his long neck, he took the proffered apple with obvious delight.

'Do you need help, Miss Napier?'

She turned and smiled when she saw Tom Anderson, the elderly head groom, coming towards her, a pitchfork in his hand. 'No, thank you, Mr Anderson. I just wanted some air so I thought I'd come and see the horses. I've brought Merlin an apple and Bengal too. See, Bengal is reaching for his.'

Having told him of her love of horses and her experience with them in India, Anderson gave her a conspiratorial smile. 'No doubt you'd rather be on his back than feeding him apples.'

'I most certainly would, Mr Anderson, but think of the shock and horror should the household—both upstairs and down—see Miss Araminta's maid riding hell for leather through the park.'

Anderson chuckled. 'They'd be no more shocked and horrified than they were when Lady Phaedra took to wearing breeches when she started working the horses. She's a firm believer that they must have regular exercise and she does know good horseflesh when she sees it. Aye, well, fed and watered they're all settled for the night so I'll bid you goodnight, miss.'

Lisette watched him go. He was going badly. With his arthritis he was not as able as he was. Holding her shawl with one hand Lisette offered Bengal the apple, smiling broadly when he greedily snatched it from her hand and began to munch. Reaching out with the other she stroked his nose, laughing softly when he tried to nibble her fingers, too wrapped up in her enjoyment to notice Ross's approach.

Returning from his club in Hatherton and reluctant to enter the house just yet, Ross was drawn to the stables and his horse. Being close to his precious mount never failed to soothe him. However, he was surprised to find Miss Napier stroking Bengal's nose. Ross's cool gaze took in the fetching scene. Standing in an orange glow highlighting her gleaming dark hair held in place by a black net, her profile was serene. With long black lashes shadowing her cheeks and a faint suggestion of a smile playing about her generous lips, she had a look of complete absorption on her face as she spoke softly to Bengal.

'And what brings you out here at this time?'

Lisette spun round and looked at him. She had not heard him approach and in that moment he might have been a figment of her imagination for he did not seem real. He had stepped, silently, from the dark shadows of the yard and as her eyes sharpened with the return of her senses she saw him clearly.

'Oh, Colonel Montague! You—you startled me.'

'Miss Napier! We seem destined to meet in the oddest places, do we not? But I'm sorry if I surprised you.'

'I came out to see the horses,' she replied simply. 'Miss Araminta is attending a dance at the Assembly Rooms in Hatherton. I felt like some air and I couldn't resist coming to take a look at the horses. Is something wrong?' she asked when she saw him staring down at her feet.

He felt compelled to point out the obvious. 'You are standing in a puddle.'

'Oh,' she said, following his gaze and seeing that she was and that the hem of her skirts was wet. 'So I am.'

'You appear to have a fondness for getting your feet wet.'

Knowing he was referring to the time he'd caught her dangling her feet in a stream, she laughed. It was a joyous sound, happy and full of the magic of youth and moonlight. It took Ross completely by surprise, and for a long moment he stared down at her incredulously, conscious of a swift flash of admiration.

'When I was in India there were times during the dry seasons that I would have given anything to see a puddle,' she confessed. 'Indeed, when it rained I often went outside to dance in them. You more than anyone should understand that—how it felt with the never-ending heat and drought all year round, except for the times when the monsoons came.'

He smiled, leaning against the stable door, which Bengal took as a cue to push his nose against his shoulder. 'I shall never forget,' he said softly. 'The summers are so hot that the air shimmers over the land in waves—it's often so hot it's difficult to breathe.'

'And the heat makes your flesh feel stretched so tight over your bones it hurts,' she murmured, closing her eyes and rubbing her cheeks with the tips of her fingers as if in remembrance of the hot Indian sun.

Ross lowered his gaze to her face, watching her fingers brush her skin. Though it may have been stretched tight in the tropical heat, there was nothing but softness to it now. Lust hit him with such unexpected force that he could not move.

Opening her eyes Lisette met his gaze. 'I never did mind the rain. I loved it.'

'As much as you love horses?'

She laughed again. 'Perhaps not as much as that. The rain here in England is especially nice. It's so gentle and the gardens look beautiful afterwards. The fragrance of wet grass and damp leaves is lovely.' She let out a breath in a deep sigh and he could almost hear her regret.

'But?'

'But it's not India. In India I would love the feel of the rain on my face. I would often become soaked to the skin—which always roused my mother's wrath and she would scold me unmercifully.'

For the moment Ross could not form a coherent reply, for in some dim part of his consciousness, he could appreciate what she meant. But after what she had said he could not do much in the way of thinking. Standing close to him was a woman whose body he was certain was a hidden treasure, a woman whose hair was as black as jet, a woman whose eyes were the exact shade of warm amber, a woman who loved the fragrance of damp grass and leaves—and a woman whose innocent pleasure of getting soaked in the rain was proving as erotic to him as any aphrodisiac could be.

Recalling their kiss and her rejection of his suggestion that they take matters further, with all the discipline he could muster, he set his jaw and reminded himself of his position and hers. She worked for him, she was a servant, and there were rules about men of his stature getting too close to servants. But as his gaze remained focused on her face, he found it virtually impossible to think of her as a servant. To know her better, to spend time with her, was well worth the risk of being caught out.

'I get the impression that you are homesick,' he murmured.

Lisette met his gaze. His voice had deepened to a husky timbre that plucked at her senses like clever fingers unlacing her stays. 'Yes,' she replied, 'I think I am.'

'Since you and I have much in common—'

'Only our shared love of India,' she was quick to point out.

'Which is a great deal considering the size of the country.'

'You will go back to your regiment?'

He frowned and shook his head, his expression hardening. 'I shall return in some capacity. No doubt I shall resume the rank in the service to which my seniority and my talents entitle me. I only hope that as a result of my promotion to colonel I will not be removed from regimental duty and set to work in an administrative capacity which often happens. Why do you smile?' he asked when he saw the corners of her lips twitch.

'Because I cannot imagine you sitting at a desk.'

Ross's vivid blue eyes, which had darkened to almost black in the dim light, captured hers. 'No? Then in what capacity do you imagine me?'

'Governing and controlling vast expanses of lawless territories, and with a lust for conquest without tainting your love and understanding of the country and its peoples. I imagine you leading your regiment into battle and claiming victory.'

What she said made him laugh. 'You are too generous, Miss Napier—you also have a fertile imagination. I wish I could share it, but I suspect I shall not be permitted to return to my regiment.'

Her expression became serious. 'Then for your sake I hope you are mistaken.'

'Thank you. So do I. And talking about my love of India and your own, I would like to show you some of the art that I've collected on my travels and brought back with me. It's still packed in crates, but when I've unpacked it I would like to show it to you.'

Lisette quivered. She knew what Colonel Montague was doing, casting that spell of his again, with his dark-velvet voice and beguiling little smile. As simple and innocent as she was, she knew what game he played, and yet she could not understand why a person of quality would wish to tarnish their reputation by publicly associating with a maid.

She looked at him lounging against the stable door, two hunting hounds sniffing about his feet. In the dim light his face had a melancholy cast and he seemed to be totally indifferent to his inherited position. It was something Lisette rarely saw, but she recognised it instantly. It was something that could not be acquired or reproduced. It had to have time to develop, like a patina that told everyone you had no doubts about your place in the world or that you were concerned about others' perceptions of you.

The noise of the horses moving about in the stalls brought her back to the present and she rubbed Bengal's nose to soothe him when he whickered loudly, tossed his head and banged his hoof against the door. 'The horses seem restless tonight.'

'The reason for that is there's a mare on heat. All the stallions start kicking their stalls and nipping the grooms—even the geldings start to misbehave.' Looking at her soft features, with tendrils of her black hair brushing her cheeks, desire still stirring his loins, Ross was tempted to say that men were like geldings when physical passion was denied them.

His explicit talk embarrassed Lisette and she looked away

to hide her flaming cheeks. When he chuckled softly, clearly amused by her embarrassment, she turned and met his gaze. Shoving himself away from the door, he reached out and pushed a strand of hair away from her face, finding himself unable to pull his hand away. The skin of her cheek felt warm and soft beneath his fingers, and he wondered how a woman who had lived in the heat of India for most of her life could have skin as soft and fine as this. He touched his fingers to her lips, remembering their kiss. How could her lips feel as velvety as this? If anything, the feel of her flesh beneath his fingertips added to the awareness of sensuality he felt emanating between them.

'When I first saw you,' Ross said quietly, 'I had this strange feeling that we had met before. It was as if a moment out of time burned between us. But how could that be? I asked myself. Surely I would have remembered. How could I forget?'

Unable to move, Lisette was looking at him, her eyes wide with surprise, but in their depths, there was also something else, something that reflected what he was feeling. Remembering how it had felt to be held by him, to be kissed by him, desire was in her eyes and in the rapid wisp of her breath against his fingers. It was in the way she stood so still, tense and poised like a young deer about to flee. If he lowered his hand to her chest he would feel her heart beating as hard as his own. It moved a little in that direction before he drew it back.

In matters of the heart Lisette's judgement had always been clouded, but in those moments when all her senses seemed to be heightened nearly beyond all endurance, this feeling that she had only ever come across twice before—with this man in a raging river and again on the journey to Castonbury Park— robbed her of all judgement. Mentally, she was experiencing all of a woman's physical needs and longings and desires that could only be matched by one man—this man.

'It's time I returned to the house,' she said, backing away from him. 'Lady Araminta will be back soon and I have things to do.'

'My sister seems much taken with you, Miss Napier,' he said, reluctant to let her go. 'Indeed, she cannot stop singing your praises. But I feel that her broken betrothal—which I am sure you know all about since it is in her nature to confide in those close to her—has affected her and I'm not convinced she has recovered from it, though she denies it emphatically. She cannot remain at Castonbury forever and it's high time she had a suitable husband and a home of her own. I cannot return to India until I have seen that she is settled.'

Lisette glanced up at him obliquely, a little smile playing on her lips. 'Why, what is this? Are you to play matchmaker, Colonel?'

He grinned down at her. 'If that's what you would like to call it, then yes—providing she approves of the outcome and that she is happy.'

'Then it might be a very long time before you find you can return to India. At this present time your sister has her head firmly set against marriage to anyone.'

'We shall see. I work fast, Miss Napier,' he said, his gaze holding hers before lowering to her lips. 'But I am not concerned. There are a number of distractions I've already noted which will, I am convinced, make my stay worthwhile.'

The warmly mellow tones of his voice were imbued with a rich quality that seemed to vibrate through Lisette's womanly being. The implication of his words evoked a strangely pleasurable disturbance in areas far too private for an untried virgin even to consider, much less invite. As evocative as the sensations were, she didn't know what to make of them. They seemed almost...wanton. But then, the image of her meeting with him in India had been scored into her brain and had undoubtedly heightened her sensitivity to wayward imaginings. But she was not going to be intimidated. And yet, with her heart filled with gratitude and her desire for him overflowing, he seemed completely wonderful and omnipotent—a mighty defender who had charged to her rescue and saved her from drowning.

She looked at him obliquely, a smile curving her lips. 'I am intrigued, Colonel. I would not have thought there was anything at Castonbury of sufficient note to claim the attention of a gentleman of your...' She stopped herself, biting her lip, suddenly realising she was about to overstep her position. But he was not about to let her off the hook.

A well-defined eyebrow jutted sharply upward. 'Of my what? Inclination?' The rush of colour that flooded her cheeks answered his question. He smiled knowingly. 'Why, Miss Napier, what can you mean? Do pray enlighten me.'

Lisette met his challenging look and considered doing just that, but she said, 'If you don't mind, Colonel, I would prefer not to answer that. This conversation is not to my liking. It—it is not proper.'

Ross appeared to consider her words carefully, then he stepped closer so they stood shoulder to shoulder. He looked down at her sideways, a wicked gleam lighting his eyes. His lips widened leisurely into a rakish grin as his gaze ranged over her. Though she had been leered at any number of times while strolling along the streets of London, this was an entirely different matter. Those warmly glowing blue orbs gave her cause to wonder if his expression would have changed even remotely had she been standing before him entirely naked. Indeed, she could almost swear from the way he was looking at her that he did have designs upon her person.

'Not proper? Very well, we shall speak of something else,' he said, while his eyes gave their message of seduction and his expression told her that this was only the beginning. 'I could be an avid pupil if you wish to teach me about plants and things in your spare time. After spending your time assisting your father with his work I expect you must have become knowledgeable about such matters.'

Despite her perfectly rigid resolve, Lisette's lips twitched. 'And pigs might fly, Colonel,' she returned. 'Not for one minute do I believe such trivia would be of interest to you. And besides, I am as ignorant of English botany as you are. I am here to take care of your sister. I have no time for anything else.'

'For which you have me to thank.'

Lisette looked into his eyes, into his face, and felt a most peculiar shiver slither down her spine. 'You are not, by any chance, attempting to make me feel grateful—so that I'll imagine myself in your debt?'

His brows quirked, his mesmerising lips curved. His eyes—blue, intent and oddly challenging—held hers. 'It seemed the natural place to start to undermine your defences.'

Lisette felt her nerves vibrate to the velvety softness of his voice, felt her senses quiver as she registered his words. Her eyes locked on his as she struggled to think of some sharp retort, but none came.

Ross's features relaxed and he shook his head slowly. The last thing he wanted was for her to feel indebted to him in any way. From the very beginning he had been concerned by her situation and he had seen that there was more to her than met the eye. The undercurrents that surrounded her were considerable, running inexplicably deep. He had wanted to aid her, without letting on he was doing so. Pride was something he understood—he was sensitive to hers.

'I like you, Lisette. I desire you—which you already know.' His tone was softly earnest. 'And you know I mean that seriously.'

His words put her thoughts in turmoil. They looked at each other, neither of them speaking, their glances locked, speaking words which could not be heard but which both understood. Lisette's mouth was dry and immodest sensations were beginning to fill her body. She felt the heat in her face, and then the heat spread, filling every part of her at that nakedly desirous look. It was a look that was at once an invitation, a need and a certainty. He was as sure of her as that. But it could not be so. The feelings that assaulted her frightened her. She wanted him, desired him, but she also feared him—but more than that she feared herself.

For a while she had been carried away by the sheer pleasure of his company and by the soft aura of the night and the stables, and for that time she had allowed herself to forget the reality of her situation, but it was over. She was painfully aware of the gulf between her status and his—a maid was a servant, noble blood was noble blood. She did not belong there. Men of Colonel Montague's ilk were not for the likes of her.

She hesitated, searching for words, then she said, 'I know what you are saying but I have got to be sensible. We both have to be. I may be a maid, a domestic servant, but I am the daughter of a gentleman. You are a nobleman, successful, a man of wealth and position. With all that entails in time you will make a good marriage. It would be most unwise for us to form any kind of alliance. I could never be anything to you but your mistress. I am not looking for a protector. I may not have much, Colonel Montague, but the little I have I value. I have strong feelings for you—you know that—but I have too much self-respect to be any man's mistress.'

He considered her apace, then nodded slowly. 'I could promise you ease and comfort.' He paused and tipped his head without releasing her gaze. 'Would that be a kindness or a curse?'

'Kindness or curse?' Lisette scoffed. 'Your wisdom escapes me. What you are asking of me is a sin. My upbringing, meaning the teachings of my parents, taught me the difference between right and wrong and I will not go against that. I will not be your mistress, nor anything else you think is appropriate for a servant girl. I'm worth more than that.'

'Along with everything else that draws me to you, I applaud your sincerity, Miss Napier.'

'I mean what I say. I don't like being made sport of, Colonel, but you obviously enjoy causing me discomfort. I am employed by you to take care of your sister's needs. My duties end there. It has to be that way.'

He nodded slowly, his blue eyes sparkling with humour. 'I can see you are a highly intelligent female, Miss Napier.'

'I'm glad you think so,' she answered, wondering where this unusual conversation was going to take her next.

'That was not a compliment,' he corrected.

Lisette looked at him with curious displeasure that silently demanded an explanation for his remark. He answered as he reached out and touched her cheek with his forefinger, tracing its smooth, delicate texture.

'Were you less intelligent, you would not spend so much time considering all the possible consequences of belonging to me, and you would simply accept our situation along with the benefits attached to it.'

'Benefits? What benefits might they be?'

'Think of all the things I could give you. I would take good care of you.' Her eyes widened with indignation, but Ross continued with imperturbable masculine logic. 'Were you a woman of ordinary intelligence, you would be concerned with matters of normal interest to a woman, not torturing yourself about such subjects as the differences between us. Accept the situation now. It is inevitable.'

Lisette stared at him in disbelief. '*Situation?* Accept my *situation?*' she repeated. 'I am not in a "situation," as you so nicely phrased it.'

His eyes softened. 'I would never hurt you, Lisette. I promise.'

'Don't,' she said quickly, liking the sound of her name on his lips but she must not let it be. 'My name is Miss Napier and please don't make promises.'

Aware of her discomfiture Ross smiled, amused by it. One brow lifted arrogantly. He stood very close, totally commanding her vision.

'Why *there* you are!'

They both turned and beheld Nancy Cooper descending on them like a galleon in full sail. Ross frowned. The entire East India fleet wouldn't have been more unwelcome, but to Lisette, the maid's interruption was a godsend and saved her from replying to Colonel Montague's question.

'You are looking for Miss Napier?'

Despite his politeness, Lisette sensed his irritation, his annoyance, that Nancy's appearance had caused.

Nancy, a red-haired, white-faced kitchen maid, bobbed a curtsey, a rather sly, knowing smile on her thin lips. 'Indeed I am, sir. I'm sorry to drag you away,' she said to Lisette, 'but Miss Araminta has returned from the Assembly Rooms early and is asking for you.'

At that moment the carriage that had deposited Araminta and Phaedra and Aunt Wilhelmina at the door to the house swung into the stable yard.

'Then I shall come at once.' Bobbing a little curtsey, she uttered, 'Goodnight, Colonel Montague.'

Ross met her eyes. His smile still in place, he inclined his head. 'Miss Napier.'

Walking swiftly back to the house, Lisette sighed. Having left his presence the night seemed quieter, less colourful, less alive.

Nancy had to run to keep up with her. 'The colonel seems to have an eye for you, Miss Napier. It's not gone amiss.'

Her words and what they implied brought Lisette to an immediate halt. 'What on earth are you talking about, Nancy?' she asked crossly, not liking one bit what the maid was implying.

'I expect the colonel's like most men in that he's just as susceptible to a pretty face as the next man. I know this is your first position in a big house and I'm only saying this for your own good, but a handsome man like the colonel can pose a hazard to an innocent girl. They know the right words to entangle a gullible female mind, and I feel I should warn you about the risks you could encounter if you go on meeting His Lordship as you have tonight.'

Lisette almost staggered back, shocked by what Nancy had said. 'But I didn't arrange to meet him. We met purely by chance.' She put her hands to her burning cheeks, astounded by Nancy's insinuation. 'Oh, Nancy, I hope you don't think— but that's dreadful. I—I didn't think…'

Having worked in service since she was a girl and knowing what was what in a 'big house,' as she called Castonbury Park, Nancy scoffed at her naivety. ''Course you didn't. I know you like to see the horses, but be careful. With a face like you've got it's hardly surprising that you've caught the colonel's eye. But if you become entangled with a titled gentleman, you may well come to regret it. You could easily be sullied and then tossed aside, leaving you in a delicate condition with little hope of attracting a respectable husband. Affairs like that have a way of ruining lives. No man wants spoiled goods.'

As Lisette continued on her way, Nancy's words had made one thing clear. To protect herself from Colonel Montague's corrupting influence she would endeavour to stay out of his way. There was no chance she'd succumb to a handsome face and a devilish smile.

And yet if she had been in the privileged position of Miss Araminta, the sparring and fencing humour he deployed would have been most enjoyable. What fun that would be. But as she entered the house her frown deepened at the road down which her thoughts travelled.

Oh, yes, Colonel Montague was definitely corrupting.

As soon as Lisette entered Araminta's room she heard the wrenching sound of grief being poured into a pillow. Her young mistress lay in a crumpled heap of chiffon and silk on the bed sobbing her heart out. Alarmed by the distraught girl, immediately she went to her, sitting on the bed beside her.

'Miss Araminta! What's this all about? What on earth is the matter? What has happened to make you cry like this? Oh, you poor girl.'

'Oh, Lisette,' she wailed, turning her tear-washed face up to hers. 'You can have no idea. Antony was there—at the assembly. I couldn't stay. I couldn't bear it. I just wanted to come home. I told Aunt Wilhelmina I wasn't feeling well.'

'You still love him, don't you?'

Araminta confessed that she did and that she had made a terrible mistake when she had broken off their betrothal, that it had all been a horrid misunderstanding. Lisette pointed out that the fact that Lord Bennington hadn't married anyone else might well mean that he still loved Araminta. Her eyes filled with renewed hope, Araminta said she would write to Antony and ask him to meet her.

'But he mustn't come here. Ross mustn't know. I'm sure he blames Antony for what happened—and he's right, it was Antony's fault. But I know Ross. If he knew how much I have suffered because of Antony's betrayal, he'd probably call him out. You can't imagine how awesome he is when he's angry.'

'Then perhaps you should think again before you write to Lord Bennington. Although, if you don't, he might think you don't care for him, after all, and return to Cambridgeshire.'

With that motivation, Araminta allowed Lisette to coax her out of her finery and into her nightdress and brush her hair, as she did every night, looking compassionately now and then into the pensive face in the mirror. She talked to her soothingly, saying anything that came into her head. Her voice was dreamlike to Araminta, giving the impression that she was in some vague, slightly unreal world of hopeless and despairing resignation and yet behind her blank face her mind was slithering like a duck on a frozen pond as she tried to formulate a plan to get Antony back.

Five

When Lisette finally left Araminta tucked up in bed mentally wording a note to Antony Bennington, she felt restless and confused following her encounter with Colonel Montague, so she went down to the kitchen for a cup of hot milk before seeking her own bed. It was relatively quiet with just the odd footman and maid passing in and out as they finished their duties for the night. They all had an early start.

Will Blackstock was in the servants' hall in conversation with Smithins, who sniffed and left when Lisette entered. After warming some milk on the stove she sat at the table with Will. She got on with Will—mainly because they had both spent time in India and always had plenty to talk about. He talked as he worked, rubbing the brass buttons on one of the colonel's military coats.

Fair-haired and cheekily attractive, he was a firm favourite with everybody. With his ready smile, sharp wit and the tales he told of his travels in India he had everyone enthralled. His devotion and loyalty to Colonel Montague was never in doubt, and he had a definite twinkle in his brown eyes whenever they lighted on Daisy, a pretty young housemaid.

Will and Lisette chatted amiably as she drank her milk, discussing the menus for the following day and the chickens which the kitchen staff had dressed earlier and were now residing in the larder awaiting Monsieur André's expertise to turn them into something quite delicious.

'Do you recall the markets in India,' Will said, 'when the livestock were brought in from the countryside—how the chickens were kept in cages and weren't killed until they were sold?'

'I do—very well—and the ducks and geese. Mother was always very good at bartering and invariably got them at a knock-down price.'

'How very primitive,' Nancy interrupted. There was a note of scorn in her voice. She saw Lisette as something of an upstart and was jealous of the attention Will paid to her.

Lisette looked at her. 'It's just a different way of life, Nancy.'

'A way of life that would not appeal to me. Nor could I understand it.'

'A person is always better off for understanding something,' Lisette pointed out calmly. 'In my imagination life as it is in India will go on indefinitely.'

'In your imagination, water could go uphill and cats speak French,' Nancy retorted, and with a toss of her head she flounced away in a huff.

Lisette shot Will an amused, conspiratorial glance. 'Oh, dear,' she murmured. 'I don't think I'm one of Nancy's favourite people.'

'You're not the only one,' Will remarked. 'Mrs Stratton set her on after Christmas but she's too haughty for her own good that one—and lazy. If she doesn't start pulling her weight, you mark my words—she'll be out on her ear before much longer.'

Mrs Stratton walked in followed by Lumsden.

'Good evening, Blackstock—Miss Napier,' Lumsden said, his manner precise as always. Taking out his watch attached by a fob to his waistcoat he checked on the time. 'Mrs Stratton and I are to share a nightcap before I check to make sure that everything is locked up.'

'I'll just get some hot water from the kettle,' Mrs Stratton said, disappearing into the kitchen where André, always considerate to her needs, had left provisions for her late-night beverage. 'Have your usual tipple by all means, Mr Lumsden, but I'll settle for a cup of tea tonight.'

Having witnessed the brief show of intimacy between Lisette and Colonel Montague on the day following their arrival at Castonbury, Lisette was relieved that Mrs Stratton had made no comment on the incident. However, she was under no illusion that it had been forgotten and that from that moment her behaviour would be under the closest scrutiny.

Lisette liked Mrs Stratton. Her voice did not hold the superior tone one would expect of the housekeeper of such a large and noble establishment. She was a widow with one son, Adam. The last time he'd come home to Castonbury to see his mother it was to tell her that he'd left the navy and was to try his hand at business. Mrs Stratton had been horrified to learn that he'd given up a promising career. Disappointed by his mother's reaction, Adam had stormed off, vowing he would not return until he had made his fortune. Mrs Stratton was saddened that he had not been in contact since then, but she concealed it beneath her quiet demeanour.

'I trust you haven't forgotten that in the morning we are to make an inspection of the guest rooms, Mrs Stratton,' Lumsden said when she reappeared carrying a small teapot. 'It's so long since they were in use that we must make an inventory of things to be done to make them suitable for occupation.'

'Of course not. I made a note of it earlier—ten o'clock, I believe we said. And we must remember that should a certain lady arrive sometime in the future, there is a child to consider, so I think we should take a look at the nurseries.'

It was a topic much discussed with all parties taking sides. Only Lisette said nothing, which was not unusual. No one asked her opinion directly but as Miss Araminta's personal maid they believed she was privy to all the information they craved. Lisette knew no more than they did about this mysterious woman Lord Jamie was supposed to have married, but if she did she would remain silent out of loyalty to her mistress.

'If the rumour about the woman is true,' Nancy said, suddenly flouncing into the kitchen and almost bumping into Mrs Stratton, 'then what can he have been thinking of to marry a woman no one has seen? The duke's heir at that.'

'Well, I am inclined to sympathise with the young woman,' Mrs Stratton said, 'since I, too, was widowed and left with a child to care for. If she is indeed Lord Jamie's wife, then the child will be the duke's heir and it is only right that he is treated as such and comes to Castonbury. She must be given the shelter of this house. Now come along, Mr Lumsden. My tea is getting cold.'

Bidding goodnight to Will and Nancy, Lisette sought her bed but she couldn't sleep. She couldn't stop thinking about her meeting with Colonel Montague. He commanded her attention, filled her thoughts, almost to the exclusion of all else.

His attitude, his appearance, his movements, that dangerous velvety voice—all reeked of seduction.

She told herself it meant nothing, that she shouldn't make too much of it, that it could simply be that he'd found nothing more scintillating at Castonbury, no lady more enticing, with whom to spend his time. Yet her heart leapt one notch, one rung higher up the ladder of irrational hope, every time he appeared in Araminta's room. When she finally succumbed to sleep he even followed her into her dreams.

Entering her mistress's room the following morning Lisette wasn't really surprised to see her seated at her escritoire penning a note to Lord Bennington. The housemaid whose business it was to make the fire was on her way out. On seeing Lisette, Araminta got up, having folded and sealed the note.

'I want you to do something for me, Lisette,' she said, handing her the note. 'I've written to Antony and would like you to take this letter and give it to one of the grooms. Ask him to ride to Glebe Hall which is outside Hatherton. He is to deliver it in person to Lord Bennington and wait for a reply.'

Against her better judgement, Lisette did as her mistress asked, but she could not quell the apprehension that gripped her or the feeling that she was colluding in something that would come to no good.

Returning to her mistress's rooms to inform her that she had done as she had instructed, her heart did a somersault when Colonel Montague strolled in every bit as handsome and imposing in his dark, brooding way as she remembered.

Lisette was putting away the brushes, the comb, the curl papers and ribbons which littered the surface of the vanity. The smile on Colonel Montague's face, curving those firm, fascinating lips, was more than enough to make her drop the comb. A blush came quickly to her cheeks, mounting high as she experienced the sensation of being stripped naked by his bright blue gaze. Picking up the comb she inwardly swore that she would not give him the pleasure of knowing how flustered she felt.

His broad shoulders were encased in a brown hacking jacket and his calves in shiny black boots. Taking an arrogant stance against the hearth, one hand resting on the mantel, in daylight his features were as hard edged as they had been last night. He watched her go about her chores with lazy interest, his predator's smile still in place.

But no matter how many distractions Lisette heaped on Ross, he was not immune to the change in Araminta this morning. Her cheeks were flushed and her eyes overbright, and as he listened to her extol the equestrian merits of the locality, she seemed jumpy and apprehensive and avoided meeting his eyes. He frowned with a mixture of curiosity and concern.

'You do not seem yourself this morning, Araminta. Are you feeling unwell?'

Araminta glanced almost nervously across the room at Lisette and then back to her brother. She laughed a little nervously. 'I confess I have a headache—probably too much wine at the assembly. A good gallop is just what I need to take it away. I'll go and see if Phaedra would like to accompany us,' she said, crossing quickly to the door. 'She'll be most put out if she knows we've gone riding without her.'

When she'd gone Ross looked at Lisette, a concerned frown etched on his brow. She bustled about, dropping objects onto the dressing table and floor—a sure sign the nervous maid was in a taking over something.

'What is wrong with Araminta? It is clear that she is not herself this morning. Has something happened that I should know about?'

'As she said—too much wine at the assembly,' Lisette replied. His eyes were probing hers, looking for answers. She bent her head over her task lest he saw the anxiety in her eyes.

'As I recall she came home early from the Assembly Rooms. You would tell me if there was something wrong, wouldn't you, Miss Napier? My sister is wilful, her conduct sometimes borders on inappropriate. It seems a weakness of hers to get into scrapes. If she is up to something you can be certain it will be something foolish and outrageous, so I would like to know about it before it happens.'

'It is not my place. I am here to see to the needs of Miss Araminta, not to divulge her confidences—if she had any, that is.'

'Is she up to something?'

Lisette looked at him direct. 'Colonel Montague, when you employed me you asked for my discretion and my loyalty. I will not talk to you about Miss Araminta.'

'Even though it is my wish?'

'Even so.'

'That is a shame. I have the greatest reliance on your judgement.'

'Then you are to be disappointed. You must forgive me if I tell you I have nothing to say to you on this matter.'

'And you are the most wilful woman I have ever met, Miss Napier.'

Ross relinquished his stance and moved to the vanity where Lisette was placing things tidily in the drawers. He stood behind her, his silence more eloquent, more powerful, more successful in impinging on her senses than Araminta's garrulous chatter. She didn't know why she felt apprehensive at his attention, for after his sister's warning not to take men's admiration too seriously, she would like to simply smile and accept any compliments they paid her. But Colonel Montague was a man who could not be ignored.

'Be assured that if there is anything wrong with my sister, I shall find out.' She looked at him before turning her head and lowering her eyes so she would not have to look at his penetrating eyes. His firm lips curved in a slight smile. 'I enjoyed our conversation last night, Miss Napier,' he said on a softer note, raising a hand and gently tucking a loose strand of her hair behind her ear, 'and I can't tell you what a pleasure it would give me to invite you to ride with us this morning.'

Lisette stilled, shocked, then raised her head. 'Don't do that!' A warm glow suffused the area he'd touched.

'You're frowning—you look cross.'

Drawing herself up and taking a step back, she turned and fixed him with a censorious look. 'That's because I am cross. I must insist that you refrain from speaking to me unless it concerns Miss Araminta.'

Inwardly Ross stilled. He looked down into her disapproving eyes, distracted by myriad emotions playing in her expressive eyes. 'Why? Do you not feel comfortable when you are with me?'

'Something like that.'

'Are we talking about the feelings that I arouse in you, Miss Napier? Come, tell me. I am all eager attention.'

'If you must know, then yes, that is exactly what I mean.'

Suppressing his urge to smile, Ross smoothed his expression

into an admirable imitation of earnest gravity. 'Oh, dear—that bad.'

Her eyes searched his, then her lips compressed. 'Last night I should have left the stables when you arrived. There must be no more conversations between us like that. I have no desire to bring censure down on myself. People will gossip and, should it reach Mrs Landes-Fraser, I will be dismissed.'

'Heaven forbid it would go that far. I apologise if my attention offended you, but I did not force you to yield to me when I kissed you.'

No, Lisette thought. In all fairness he hadn't. It was as if some spell had been cast over her and she had wantonly, willingly joined in her own seduction.

'Let us assume I am not your employer,' Ross said, his voice soft and provocative, his eyes preoccupied with her rosy lips. 'How would you react to my advances then, Miss Napier? Would you fall into my arms and allow me to kiss you to distraction?'

Her delicate brows drew together and amusement teased the corners of her generous mouth as she surveyed him, considering her answer. 'Based on what I already know of you, I might very well be tempted,' she confessed, unable to deny the truth since he seemed to know her thoughts so well. 'But the fact remains that you *are* my employer and that is the trouble.'

'And I feel compelled to point out that an employee should never contradict her employer.'

'Whenever I find myself in your company you forget yourself. Is your lofty rank supposed to intimidate me, Colonel?' she asked in her quiet voice, a surprising hint of anger in it that Ross had never heard before. 'Because if so, then you are mistaken. I am the daughter of a gentleman, and my parents brought me up decently.'

His eyes narrowed on hers. 'Your parents brought you up in India, where the climate is hot and allied to a different culture. That makes you inescapably different to other English girls. You can't change what you are.'

'And what am I?' she asked bitterly. 'Do you presume that because I am a servant, I'm fair game to be seduced?'

'I do not, and nor do I wish to seduce you—at least, not this minute. If I had wished it, it would already have happened.'

Lisette gasped at his arrogance. But the potency of his desire could not be denied. 'I will not let it happen. You presume too much where I am concerned, Colonel.'

The words were low, laced with contempt, bitter with an emotion Ross could not place. 'Do not doubt my needs, Lisette,' he chided softly with a lusty stare, as if he could read all that was in her mind. 'Or my intention of having you.'

'You rate yourself too highly, sir. I belong to no man. Please don't speak to me like this.'

His chuckles sounded low and deep. Her face gave no sign of softening. Even so, its beauty fed his gaze and created in his being a sweet, hungering ache that could neither be easily put aside nor sated with anything less than what he desired.

'We don't have to speak at all if that is what you want, Lisette. For myself I would prefer not to.' His gaze settled on her lips. His eyes darkened and his hands came up to frame her face. 'Forgive me but I have to do this.' Then, tilting her face up, his descended. When his lips touched hers, Lisette couldn't have quelled the shudder that passed through her had her life depended on it. Stunned, poised to resist, she mentally paused. Soft but sure, bringing sweetness and pleasure, they covered hers, moving slowly, languorously, as if savouring her taste, her texture.

His kiss was slow and deliberate, yet there was nothing threatening or hurried in his lips' caress. Indeed, it was beguiling, luring Lisette's senses. Her lips were soft and hot, and he pressed his mouth to hers as if drinking in her heat. As her lips began to respond, in some part of her mind a warning bell began to ring, but she was long past listening. His lips felt and tasted just as they had before. Unable to resist the temptation to return the pressure, she parted her lips, slowly exploring the sensations of delight that infused her as his lips played against hers. Growing lightheaded, she rested her hands on his chest to steady herself.

She was sweet and pliant, her body pressing willingly to his. Taking advantage of her weakening, untutored response, Ross slid his tongue between her lips, slowly, with his customary assured arrogance, quite certain of his expertise and his welcome. But he held the reins of his desire in a grip of iron and refused to let the demons loose. Primal instincts urged him on—experience held him back.

She was giving a little more of herself every time they met; he knew it, but in her heart, deep in her heart, where no one could hear it or know of its existence, a small wordless whisper was beginning to woo her. His male body yearned to go on, to satisfy itself as it had always done. He was thinking like a man who is intent on seduction, and he supposed he was— but in the back of his mind was the thought that she was not the kind of woman to be rushed.

Her desire, her passion, answered his call and he knew she would be his after a little tender persuasion. But there was no need for hurry. She was innocent, naive, untouched, unused to the demands of a man's hands. He would not go too fast, otherwise she would turn skittish and balk and then he would have to work harder to win her back. Passion lay heavy, languid, between them. He let it sink into her senses so she would not forget, and next time he would savour her slowly and it would be sweeter, for the end was never in doubt.

Raising his head he looked down into her flushed face. Her eyes slowly opened, then she blinked, and stared straight at him. He couldn't stop his rakish grin.

'What are you doing?' she whispered as his head bent to hers once more. 'It would take some explaining if your sister should come in and see us.' At this thought a hand seemed to grip her heart and panic streaked through her. Neatly she slipped away from him. To her relief he straightened and drew back, but his confident smile didn't waver.

'A man can speak to the woman he wants any way he chooses,' Ross said, his male arrogance edging his voice again, his lips quirking in a mirthless smile. 'This will happen. I promise you.'

A cold shiver went down her spine. The idea that he was amusing himself, without any real intent, died, slain by the look in his eyes. It was intense. It couldn't have been clearer had he put it into words. She knew it was wrong, and yet what he promised was so wickedly exciting, like nothing she had ever experienced before. That she was deeply attracted to this man was undeniably true, but she must not go blindly, emotionally rushing into what might have many pitfalls and would end in tears.

'I am not regretful about our kiss,' he went on, 'nor will I regret having you when the time comes.' She glared at the arrogance of this statement, but Ross forged ahead with what he'd intended to say in a calm, philosophical tone. 'I could say that you are blameless in all this, that what happens is not your will—but mine. But that wouldn't be true, would it?' He knew that as soon as he asked the question he wanted her to assure him that he spoke the truth, that he didn't want her to deny that she'd felt all the things he had in their kiss, or that she wanted him almost as much as he wanted her. As if he suddenly needed to test her honesty and his instincts, he persisted, 'Isn't that right?'

Lisette didn't want to make it easy for him, nor to let him think she was so dazzled by his masculinity that she was almost drowning in her own pleasure as the wanton sensations ran through her body at his every touch, but she was unable to tell a lie.

'Yes!' The word burst out of her, without shame but filled with a thousand other feelings Ross couldn't identify.

'Yes?' he repeated, while a heady sensation of relief burst within him. 'Then I am not wrong.'

It was not the tone of relief in his voice that made her answer. It was, instead, her sudden memories of the way he had kissed her, memories of his incredible combined gentleness and passion. Added to that was the memory of her own urgent desire to experience more than his kiss, to become a part of him, at one with him, to expand on the exquisite sensations he was making her feel. She opened her mouth to utter a denial to his statement, but her conscience strangled the words in her throat. She had found glory, not shame, in their kiss, and she could not make herself lie to him and say otherwise.

'It was not my will for this to happen between us,' she answered in a muffled whisper. Dragging her mortified gaze from his blue gaze, she turned her head away and added, 'but once I was in your arms, it was not my will to leave them either.'

She had looked away, so she didn't see the new tenderness in his slow smile.

Forbidding herself to linger for fear of getting caught up in him again, she picked up one of her mistress's gowns that needed ironing and, draping it over her arm, she left the room.

Still smiling, Ross watched her go. Beneath her plain servant's garb, Lisette Napier was a natural temptress, alluring and provocative, with the slender body of a goddess, the smile of an angel and an unspoiled charm that made him smile whenever he thought of her. She was warm and lovely and as elusive as a butterfly. He couldn't get her out of his mind—the taste of her, the feel of her, the heady scent of her, wreathed his senses. He had given up trying to understand the reasons why he wanted her.

He did, and that was reason enough.

The following morning, pleased with a diversion from her duties, accompanied by Faith and Daisy, Lisette set off to walk into Castonbury village to purchase some yarns. It was a happy trio that sauntered along the High Street, pausing now and then to gaze into the shop windows and to watch a stagecoach deposit its passengers at the Rothermere Arms.

Unfortunately Mrs Hall's shop from which Lisette was to make her purchases was closed. In the bow window where an array of colourful ribbons and yarns were on display, there was a notice saying Mrs Hall had been called away and that she would be back within the hour. Faith and Daisy had to hurry back but Lisette said she would wait. Her companions left her sitting on a bench near St Mary's Church to await the shop's opening.

By the time she had made her purchases and started on the mile journey back to Castonbury Park, rain clouds were gathering. Heavy spots soon became a downpour. Finding shelter under a large oak tree she settled down to wait for the rain to abate.

In the distance a horse and rider appeared from the direction of the house. The rider's tall figure was outlined against the sky, a liver-and-white hound in his wake. It was Colonel Montague. Lisette was conscious of the sudden tension and nervousness in her as he drew closer. There was nowhere to hide. After their encounter the previous day, she didn't know how to behave towards him.

Holding her basket containing her small purchases in front of her, she drew herself up straight as he came closer, dismounted and strode towards her. He tossed his tall hat on the horn of his saddle, water dripping from his long riding cape. For one wild, unreasoning moment Lisette's life flared into vivid, lively colour. All the drab routine that had become her life faded away.

'Well, this is a pleasant surprise, Miss Napier,' he said, and there was a touch of irony in his tone. He bowed, smiling at her from deep blue eyes. A dimple in his cheek was deeply and wickedly cleft as he stood before her. The memory of their last encounter rose between them, intangible but strong. Taking a deep breath she tried to stifle her rising emotions. Colonel Montague somehow always caught her at her most vulnerable.

With an effort she said in a voice that she hoped sounded matter-of-fact, 'Good day, Colonel Montague.'

He raised one well-defined eyebrow, watching her. A faint

half-smile now played on his lips as if he knew exactly what was going on in her mind. 'I never expected to see you here. What are you doing?'

'Exactly what it looks like. I am sheltering from the rain under this tree,' she replied primly, resenting his effect on her, the masculine assurance of his bearing. But she was conscious of an unwilling excitement, seeing him arrogantly mocking, and recklessly attractive. Here they were, just the two of them, together sheltering from the rain under a tree, in an atmosphere bristling with tension and subdued emotions.

Ross's eyes did a quick sweep of her lightweight dark grey dress and summer bonnet. 'I would advise you to wear something more substantial the next time you decide to walk into the village when rain is threatening.'

'There was no sign of rain when I set out. Unfortunately the proprietor of the shop from which I wanted to purchase some items was gone on an errand and I had to wait for it to open. Daisy and Faith had duties at the house and were unable to wait, so as you see, Colonel, I am quite alone.'

Ross gazed down into those brilliant amber eyes and that entrancing face. His decision to have her no matter how much trouble she put him to had now become an unshakable resolution. A slow, admiring smile drifted across his face as he said, 'Then you must forgive me if I take advantage of the situation and use the time to enjoy your company and to savour the anticipation of what is to come—although I am becoming heartily tired of the wait.'

'Then you will have to learn to curb your impatience, Colonel, for the weather is hardly conducive for a romantic tryst. If you do not agree with me, perhaps you should cool your ardour and step back out into the rain.'

Ross bit back a laugh, trying to keep his eyes off the alluring display of her breasts rising and falling beneath her gown. 'I observed you were not alone when you left the house. I saw the other two return without you.'

Lisette was not unaware of the possessive gleam in his blue eyes as they roved over her, or that he was bent on charming her again today. 'How observant you are, Colonel. Were you looking for me?'

'I was concerned.'

'Oh, I see. I suppose I should be honoured,' she said coolly, 'but as you see I am quite all right. I'm sure you have better things to do with your time than to come looking for me.'

'On the contrary. Your failure to show up with the other two gave me the perfect excuse to come looking for you.'

'And do you need an excuse, sir?'

'No, I don't.'

His devilish gaze that gleamed into hers touched a quickness within her, and she quickly averted her gaze. 'Had I known you were about, I would have sought a different tree—one with a trunk stout enough to hide behind.'

Ross grinned and stretched out a hand to smooth a strand of hair from her face. 'Ah, Miss Napier, do you fear me?'

Lisette straightened indignantly and pushed his hand away. 'It is only that I prefer not to be mauled and ogled as you seem to have a penchant for doing. Your eyes betray the path of your mind,' she accused him brusquely. 'It is rude to stare so openly.'

'I was admiring you.' The blue eyes glowed, and his grin was almost taunting. 'You are an extremely beautiful young woman, and like most men I always admire beauty.'

'You are bold, sir,' she scolded. 'I feel ravished every time you look at me.'

Ross's grin grew almost into a leer. 'You read my thoughts well, Miss Napier. Frequently I have fantasies of you naked in my arms.'

Lisette blushed scarlet. There was still so much of the girl in her at war with the young woman, and this man had the knack of bringing it quickly to the surface. 'It would seem that the kisses you stole from me have hardly cooled your lusts.'

'Not at all,' he confided lightly. 'Indeed, it has done much to stir them.'

When he would have come closer, Lisette placed her hand pointedly on his chest, stopping him in his tracks. 'Try to restrain yourself, sir,' she cautioned. 'I am returning from an errand to the village, not seeking a secret rendezvous with you. Now I wonder if it is safe to stay until the rain has stopped. You seem never satisfied.'

Ross's eyes burned behind his dark lashes. 'Aye, you tempt me sorely, Miss Napier. But I would not wish you to get a drenching on account of my *lusts*.'

Lisette faced him squarely, meeting his gaze, even now feeling prey to that hawkish stare. 'Then will you behave?'

'Although your nearness tests me sorely, I promise I will try.'

'Thank you. That is kind of you.'

'Contrary to what you may think of me, I have been known to be kind on occasion.' Laugh lines appeared at the corners of his eyes, though he did not smile. 'But I confess I am not being kind just now.'

'Yes, I know, and it is not going to work.'

He tried to look innocent. 'What isn't going to work?'

'This blatant attempt to charm me into yielding another kiss—and other such tactics.'

'I know you are far too intelligent to be fooled by charm and trickery, Miss Napier. I use the only weapon I have.'

'Persuasion?'

'Temptation—if I can.'

For all her annoyance with him, Lisette knew it wouldn't be too difficult for him to tempt her into his arms. She was very much aware of everything about him, of the long, strong lines of his body, of the skin of his exposed neck, tanned and healthy. She tried to change her thoughts, finding her emotions unsettling. The dog that accompanied him bounded up and whimpered and sniffed about her feet. 'What a lovely animal,' she said, bending down. There was a note of affection in her voice as she patted the dog's head, fondling its ears.

Carelessly her hand brushed his when he grasped the dog's collar to drag him back. She felt a sudden stillness envelop them. Vividly aware of the damp scent of the wet grass, she was still overwhelmingly conscious of the man facing her. Confused, she straightened and looked away. She was irritated by the way in which he had skilfully cut through her superior attitude, the artificial posturing she had assumed to save herself from him. But the magnetic attraction still remained beneath all the irritation.

He cocked an eye at her; a sudden burst of light through the clouds flickered over his thick black hair outlining his devilishly attractive face. Then a full smile touched his lips. 'I imagine you are cross with me, Miss Napier—for taking advantage of you yesterday.'

'And the time before that,' she said with sudden impudent defiance as she tried to fight the power of his charm. He seemed amused as he studied her. She saw the twinkle in his eye, the twist of humour about his beautiful mouth.

'I don't recall you raising any objections to my kissing you at the time. There are more discomforting and less civilised experiences than kissing, Miss Napier.'

'And you would know that, would you, Colonel Montague?'

'I know that in a smart gathering of civilised beings, there run many dangerous and treacherous undercurrents, like dark, bottomless pools. The women, with their little jealousies and intrigues, have much warmongering amongst them, weaving webs of deceit.'

'And what are the gentlemen doing while the ladies are warmongering, Colonel?'

'Trying to better the next man, with their pious, self-righteous condemnation.'

Lisette was surprised at his speech, at the cynicism of its content, then, seeing the teasing expression in his startling blue eyes, allowed the rich peals of laughter to escape from her throat.

'I do believe you jest with me, Colonel—quite an unexpected pleasure from one of such rank as yourself.'

He stared at her, liking the sound of her laughter. 'I am glad you see it as a pleasure, Miss Napier. You see I am not an ogre. You should know that by now.'

'I never thought you were.'

'And good manners would prevent you from saying so.'

'No, sir. The fact that you are my employer,' she replied candidly. 'Should I verbally abuse you in such a manner, I would find myself without a job, which is why, where you are concerned, I must tread with caution—even if you are unmannerly at times,' she added, the little smile playing about her lips mischievous.

Quite undaunted, a dazzling smile broke the determined line of his mouth and he stepped closer to her, looking down into her lovely, upturned face and capturing her eyes. 'Why? Because I stole a kiss or two? I never pretend to be anything other than what I am, but you, Miss Napier, are indeed a most attractive woman.'

Vividly conscious of her proximity to him, Lisette again placed a hand on his chest to hold him back before he could realise just how much he affected her. 'You're not going to kiss me again, are you, Colonel?'

Ross glanced down at the small, delicate hand laid upon his chest—heat was seeping through his clothes, desire already tightening his loins—and that with only her hand upon his chest. 'Reluctantly no—not unless you want me to. If so, I would willingly oblige.'

She sent him an admonishing look and dropped her hand. 'I have no doubt that you would, but no. It is not appropriate. Besides, it has almost stopped raining. I really should be getting back. Your sister will wonder where I have got to.'

'I will walk with you.'

'No—I would prefer it if you didn't.' She was quick to reply. 'Should we be seen together by any one of the servants, they would assume that I have caught your eye and that I dally where I should not.' She straightened her bonnet and stepped into the open. 'Now, I must be on my way so I will bid you good day, sir.'

Araminta was in a frenzied state of excitement as she paced her room waiting for the reply to her letter to Antony Bennington. It was just before luncheon when the reply was delivered directly to her. Tearing it open she held her breath as she read her beloved's words.

'Well?' Lisette asked, unable to bear the suspense a moment longer. 'What does he say?'

'Oh, Lisette, he wants to meet me tomorrow.'

'Where? Is he to come here?'

'Oh, no, that would never do. He asks me to meet him at the Dog and Partridge Inn on the Manchester Road.'

Lisette was more than a little scandalised to think that Lord Bennington should have suggested such a thing. 'And how far is that?'

'About five miles.'

'But you can't possibly. And anyway, it's out of the question that you go alone.'

'Of course I must. I refuse to have a groom tagging along watching everything I do and reporting back to Ross.' Araminta held the note to her breast and closed her eyes, whirling and twirling around the room. 'Oh, Lisette, just think. This time tomorrow Antony and I will be together. I can't wait to see him.' On seeing Lisette's frown of disapproval she scowled. 'I'm going, Lisette, and nothing you can say will put me off.'

Seeing the stubborn set of Araminta's chin, Lisette switched her tactics. 'Miss Araminta, please—think of your brother. What will he say if he finds out?'

Araminta hesitated, feeling the force of her brother's unwaveringly cold stare as if it were this minute focused upon her. She drew a long breath, then expelled it slowly. 'I am going, Lisette, and that is that. Not a word to anyone. I shall be back long before dinner. This morning's ride has given me an appetite. After luncheon I want you to get your bonnet and we will take a walk. I'm far too excited to remain cooped up in the house all day.'

Often when Araminta was on edge, irritable over nothing, bored and inclined to sigh with tedious regularity, Lisette would get their coats and bonnets and together they would walk into nearby Castonbury village to browse in the shops or climb the hills to take in the breathtaking views.

The terrain on the hillsides was often difficult, hostile to those unused to it, but Lisette loved it and felt the weight of her spirits lighten. She loved the freedom, the wind blowing off the moors and the scattered sheep and the rain that came from the west, the clouds breaking above the peaks that separated Derbyshire from Yorkshire.

The morning's rain had blown away, so it was windy but warm and sunny when they set out for their walk that afternoon. It had been Lisette's turn to choose the direction they would take today and she had chosen to walk round the lake. Araminta was in blue, the colour of speedwell, her bonnet perched on the back of her head, allowing the arrangement of her ringlets to be seen.

While they remained in full view of the house they walked as sedately as possible, but with the precincts of the house behind them, the decorum was thrown off. Picking up their skirts, they ran along the path before leaving it and winding their way through the trees. At one point, quite breathless, they stopped with their backs leaning against a tree and looked up through the branches that showed a spattering of blue.

'How lovely,' Araminta remarked, her eyes shining and her face flushed from her exertions.

'Why is it that running is considered most unladylike?' Lisette said. 'Men run, so why not women?'

'I don't know, but it's fun. Come along, Lisette, I'll race you to the bridge.'

It was their girlish laughter ringing out from across the lake that drew the attention of the two riders. They were completely unaware that they were being watched by two gentleman on horseback who had been checking on the work being done in the park and paused on their way back to the stables to observe the two girls.

'That girl with Araminta, Ross. Who is she?' Giles enquired with a curious frown.

'Lisette Napier. Araminta's maid.'

'The girl from India?'

Ross glanced at him. 'You know?'

Giles gave him a wry look. 'This is Castonbury, Ross. Nothing is secret, as you know. Araminta tells me you both arrived at the same time in London.'

'True. We sailed from India with the East India fleet. She was on the *Portland*. Miss Napier's parents died of the cholera out there. Without means she was forced to seek employment.'

'She's an attractive girl. I expect there isn't a male servant either indoors or out who wouldn't like to get to know her better. By the way, I think you should know that Father received a letter from Alicia.'

Ross turned and looked at him. 'I see. Have you communicated with her since I saw her?'

'No. I meant to, but with Father being like he is, he forbade it until he has given the matter more thought. I've told him that we can't go on avoiding the issue forever. She isn't going to go away and something has to be done about the child.'

'What does she want?'

Giles gave him a wry look. 'Money. What else? She states

that she is quite destitute and she will soon have to move out of her lodgings unless her situation changes for the better. Of course, she put great emphasis on the child, stressing that it isn't right that Jamie's son is being kept in abject poverty when he is heir to such a vast estate as Castonbury Park.'

'If she is indeed Jamie's widow, then she does have a point. On the other hand, until we hear from Harry you might be wise to stall her a while longer.'

'I know. And until Father agrees to it, I cannot give her a penny piece.'

They fell silent and continued to watch as Araminta and Miss Napier headed for the bridge that spanned the narrow part of the upper and lower lakes. Suddenly the wind gusted strongly, loosening the bow that kept Miss Napier's purple bonnet in place and whipping it from her head.

'Oh, my goodness,' Lisette shrieked, decorum forgotten as she watched it soar into the air and be carried by the wind towards the lake. Indeed, even if decorum had been remembered it would have been ignored, for the sheer joy of running had her in its grip as she sprinted like a whippet towards the bridge with Araminta in pursuit of her bonnet.

The two girls paused in the middle of the bridge to look down with variable degrees of interest at the cascade of water that flowed from one lake to the next. The bonnet was bobbing about on the swirling water. Without thought, and certainly with no concern for what she was about to do, with the agility of a mountain goat, Lisette ran off the bridge to the water's edge. Kicking off her shoes and bunching up her skirts, she waded into the water towards the bonnet. Araminta followed, her face split into a huge grin of enjoyment, shouting her encouragement in a most unladylike way, wishing it were she who had the pluck to kick off her shoes to forge into the lake.

Ross and Giles stared in astonishment. Giles's face was a study of mixed emotions—incredulity and amusement, indicating that he'd never seen the like before. But as Ross watched Lisette wade towards the swirling water beneath the fast-flowing cascade, his expression turned rock hard as a suspended memory broke free and he recalled another time, another place and a raging river.

'Oh, my God! The little fool!'

His breath left his body and immediately he vaulted out of the saddle, already stripping off his jacket as he broke into a run, racing towards the bridge, more frightened than he had ever been in his life. In the space of one second, rage replaced his fear—rage that she had terrified him with her stupid recklessness.

Reaching out for her precious bonnet, the water from the cascade sprayed up in a shimmer into Lisette's face. As her fingers made contact with it, the wind was loosening the pins that held her hair in place, and she stumbled. Regaining her balance she turned to laugh in dismay as her skirts slipped from her clutching fingers, trailing in the water, her plait snaking loose and falling down her back.

'Goodness, it's cold,' she gasped. Reaching the bank she stumbled and slithered on the smooth mossy stones beneath the water. From nowhere a shadow appeared or so it seemed. She looked up, her eyes like stars in her face flushed with joyful laughter.

'What the hell do you think you're doing?' Ross demanded. With long, powerful strides he swooped down on her like Satan in his entire frightening wrath. The sound of her voice broke his angry reasoning, and with it went the terrible speculation, which for several moments had filled him with panic. It was as though something infinitely precious had been restored to him.

'You little fool! You stupid girl! You could have drowned.' Lisette lifted her head and blithely looked at him with that long, unblinking stare of hers, seeing the concern in his eyes. A smile was on her soft mouth, her colour gloriously high. But what Ross noticed, as he gazed at her, was the look in those liquid amber eyes. They were imploring him to soften, to smile at her. His mindless terror gave way and his expression softened.

Lisette stepped from the water, letting her skirts fall and slipping her wet stocking feet into her shoes. 'I'm sorry if I frightened you. I only went in to retrieve my bonnet. I wasn't in any danger.'

'With the amount and force of the water pouring into the lake from above, didn't you realise the current could have dragged you under?'

'It didn't occur to me,' she confessed, 'but I'm an excellent swimmer. I was perfectly safe and I don't think I did anything wrong.'

'Neither did the keeper's dog that drowned here some years back!' he said quietly.

'I'm so sorry about that,' she said, aware that Araminta had frozen into stillness, her face a picture of bewilderment and alarm as she stared at her brother. Never had she seen him so affected by anything. 'I really am sorry if I frightened you. Truly I am.'

In silence, Ross gazed down at her smiling, upturned face. 'You're not afraid of anything, are you?'

'I'm not afraid of the water—or you,' she announced blithely. She was deeply touched by how alarmed he'd seemed. His voice had been hoarse with concern when he'd appeared in front of her, his face ravaged with worry as he had called her a little fool.

'I'm glad,' he said. 'I wouldn't want you to be.' He looked down at her dripping skirts, trying to ignore how delectable she looked with damp tendrils of hair clinging to her face. 'Go and change your clothes.'

Six

When Ross had finally regained some of his composure, retrieving his jacket from where he'd tossed it, shrugging himself back into it he turned to his horse and swung himself up into the saddle.

Stupefied, Giles stared at him, thoroughly amused. It was unbelievable that Ross, who always had absolute control over his emotions, who treated women with a combination of indifference, amused tolerance and indulgence, could have been driven to such an uncharacteristic outburst of feelings by a mere maid. It was clear that Miss Napier's behaviour and imminent drowning had both alarmed and terrified him.

In stark contrast, instead of the haughty disdain one would expect to see on Giles's face, he had regarded Miss Napier from atop his horse with laughing admiration. In his opinion Ross's reaction had been a bit over the top. The water beneath the cascade wasn't deep and Giles didn't believe Miss Napier had been in any danger of drowning. Noting that Ross's eyes were still fixed on the young maid, rather than wait for an explanation he plunged right in.

'At the risk of intruding into your thoughts, Cousin, might I ask why you came down so hard on Miss Napier? As you tore yourself away from your horse, your thoughts appeared to be damnably unpleasant—in fact, the look on your face told me you were going for blood, no less.'

'I was,' he ground out in an attempt to conceal the terror that had almost consumed him when he feared she was in danger of being swept away. 'What a damned reckless and irresponsible thing to do—to go wading into the lake like that—after a bonnet!'

Giles gave him a laughing, sidelong look. 'Come now, Ross. When we were boys, did we not throw ourselves from that very bridge—times too numerous to count—into the cascade? We came to no harm—and I have to say that Miss Napier looked more than capable of taking care of herself.'

Ross threw him a black look. 'It can be hazardous. Even when the water looks calm there are eddies there. But I didn't realise you were being so observant, Giles,' he growled with a hint of mockery.

Giles's chuckling merriment could not be restrained and he laughed out loud. 'No more than you, Coz. After all, Araminta tells me that when she mentioned she was seeking a maid of her own, you were the one to recommend Miss Napier. I have to say that she has been blessed with the most incredible looks. With your reputation for the ladies—the dark and dusky maidens of India in particular, Ross—I can see perfectly well why you are attracted to her.'

Ross's frown was formidable. 'It depends on one's taste—which is something we never did agree upon—although,' he said with a reluctant smile, his mood returning to normal, 'I do agree that your Lily is quite perfect.'

Giles's features softened, as they never failed to do when his beloved Lily was mentioned. 'I agree with you absolutely.'

They rode on in companionable silence, following Araminta and Miss Napier at a steady pace. Ross turned his thoughts to what had just happened. It proved that Miss Napier's courage, her sense of adventure and of rebellion against the satin chain which bound her set her apart from her contemporaries. How many of the housemaids would have had the nerve to kick off their shoes and wade into the lake to retrieve their bonnet?

In fascination he watched the sway of the thick, shining black pigtail which hung down Miss Napier's back, and the movement of her hips as she walked over the grass with lithe, liquid movements—like a dancer, he thought.… In some far corner of his thoroughly distracted brain memories stirred and his pulse gave a wild leap of recognition.

And then, in that brief flash of time, like an arrow thudding into his heart, he stilled as troubled memories flooded back. An image drifted into his mind, of a girl in a star-spangled sari, a veil drawn over her hair—a shining black pigtail exposed to the sun.

Ross continued to follow her, his mind in turmoil, convinced there must be some mistake. There had to be.

'Wait,' he called. Both Miss Napier and Araminta stopped and turned to look back at him. Ross addressed his cousin but without taking his eyes off Lisette. 'There is something I have to say to Miss Napier, Giles. Take Araminta back to the house. I'll be along shortly.'

With a puzzled frown and no questions asked, Giles dismounted. Looking at Lisette, Araminta was about to protest when Giles took her arm, but after taking one look at her brother's formidable features, she allowed Giles to lead her away.

Alone now, Ross rode closer to Lisette, pulling Bengal to a halt just a few feet away. His eyes became fixed on her up-turned face. She said nothing, nor did she move. She stood quite still, looking at him with wide, startled eyes.

'Tell me something. When your parents died I recall you telling me that you were living near Delhi.'

'Yes, Colonel, that is correct,' she replied, feeling slightly uncomfortable beneath his penetrating blue gaze. 'But I cannot see what that has to do with me wading into the lake just now.'

'Can you not, Miss Napier?' he said tightly. 'I can. Tell me, what did you do? How did you travel to Bombay—an English girl alone?'

'I travelled with others who were going south. Sometimes I walked and sometimes I was offered a lift in a bullock cart.'

'As an English girl?'

She looked at him, nervous now, clutching her wet bonnet to her chest. He remembered her. Suddenly her whole existence had shrunk, narrowed, until there was nothing but this moment—bright sunshine, the man looking down at her. 'No. For my own protection and to be less conspicuous I passed myself off as a native girl. In a land of many tongues and races, it was easier than I had feared to conceal my identity—and I speak both Hindi and Urdu.'

'How fortunate for you, and because of your colouring you resembled a native girl.'

'Yes.'

He was watching her now, his gaze intense. 'Did you travel south in a bridal party—in the retinue of the Rajah Jahana

Sumana of the state of Rhuna, who had a daughter by the name of Messalina?'

'Yes,' she replied quietly.

'And when you left the bridal party, did you have to cross swollen rivers on your journey to Bombay?'

'All rivers in India become swollen during the monsoon. You should know that, Colonel.'

'But did you ever fall into a swollen river?'

With some consternation she looked away. 'Yes.'

'And how did you get out?'

'Someone—someone saved me.'

'A British officer?'

'Yes.'

'How did he save you?'

Lisette felt the net draw tight, felt paralysis set in as his predator's senses focused on her. It was as if the world stopped spinning, as if some impenetrable shield closed about them, so that there was nothing but her and him—and whatever it was that held them.

'He—he—'

Ross sprang from his horse and went to her, and taking her upper arms he stared hard into her face. 'He?'

She nodded. 'Yes.'

'And did the two of you by any chance spend the entire night marooned on a sandbank?'

She looked at him and searched his eyes, but couldn't read his thoughts beyond the fact that he was considering her. 'Yes,' she whispered.

'And in the morning you left your rescuer?'

'Yes,' she answered, her voiced strained. 'Yes, I did. It was unforgivable of me.'

'Why?' he demanded. 'Because you didn't thank him for saving your life?'

'Yes.'

He just stared at her. 'Well, well,' he said at length. 'So, it was you. I cannot believe that after all this time… I would not have believed it possible. Did it not occur to you how worried I might be, that I thought you might have been swept away by the river while I slept?'

Lisette's heart almost broke as she stared at him. It had never occurred to her that what had happened to her would affect him so deeply.

'Why did you go? Tell me that?' Taking her chin between his fingers, he forced her to look at him, the expression in his eyes suddenly grave. 'And do not play games with me. It is not kind, Lisette. Tell me.'

'I don't want to go over it. I can't.'

'I *need* to know,' he insisted forcefully. 'Can't you understand that? Not knowing what happened to you tortured me. I thought you were dead. It was not until I reached the bank and saw your footprints in the mud that I realised you were alive.'

'I'm sorry,' she cried. 'I didn't know. I left because I wanted to avoid any awkwardness—any questions—and…and you had made your intentions quite clear what you would demand of me later.'

'And what was that?' he asked softly. 'Remind me.'

'I recall you telling me you intended "bedding" me. I believe that was the term you used.'

'And you left me stranded because I said that?'

'You weren't exactly stranded. The river had fallen during the night and it was a simple matter to reach the bank.'

'As an English girl alone, I can understand why you disguised yourself as a native girl—easier that way, fewer questions asked—but did it not occur to you that as a British officer I was in a position to help you reach Bombay safely?'

'No—no, it didn't.' Tears filled her eyes. It was the one reaction Ross was not prepared for and it not only disconcerted him but left him feeling helpless. 'I was alone. I did not wish to draw attention to myself. When I left Delhi I was desperate. My parents were dead. I thought I would die of grief and loneliness. Messalina—she was my friend and was to journey to Bhopal to marry a prince. She suggested I travel with her part of the way. Her father was always kind to me and he agreed.' Gazing up at him a sorrowful look entered her eyes. 'On the dock—in London—you didn't know me.' A tear trailed down her cheek. Ross was ashamed because he hadn't recognised her, but he had never forgotten the Indian girl whose life he had saved—and thank goodness he had. 'I didn't expect you to.'

'No, I didn't, but I knew as soon as I laid eyes on you that there was something familiar about you—I just couldn't remember. How could I? The night we spent in the middle of the river was pitch-black, and when I'd seen you previous to that, I truly thought you were a native girl. My abiding picture of you was from the first time I saw you with the bridal party. I thought you were the Princess Messalina's sister.'

'She doesn't have a sister.'

'I didn't know that. Only seeing you from a distance I never saw your face. You talked to those in your own party and I did not have reason to address you. I just looked at you, sitting with the princess, wearing costly silks over your dark hair, the lower half of your face veiled. And then I moved on. I did not see you again until the river.'

'Then—just now when you called me back? How did you know?'

'You have a way of walking that is distinctive—like a dancer. It suddenly came to me who you were. Why in heaven's name didn't you tell me who you were, Lisette?'

'When we met in London I almost did, but something held me back. Later, when you suggested that I work for your sister, I considered it prudent not to remind you. I wanted the work rather badly, you see. Knowing who I was could only complicate matters between us.'

Ross was suddenly aware of a disturbing mixture of emotions that he did not wish to analyse just then. 'Go and change, Lisette. We'll talk about this later.'

Backing away from him she gave him one last look. 'Yes. If you will excuse me, Colonel, I have duties to attend to. Your sister will be wondering what has happened to me.'

'As I did on the night you left me.' His eyes darkened with memory. Lisette saw the warm glow within their depths and was suddenly afraid that because of that night his attempts to seduce her might become more intense.

'Nothing happened between us, Colonel. Let us just say we became caught up in the moment. You saved my life. I am grateful to you and that is all,' she said, pressing home her point with calm reason. 'It was nothing.'

'Obviously.'

'We both survived, didn't we?'

'Yes.'

'Well, then, there is no reason why we have to mention it again, is there?' she demanded with a soft, beguiling smile.

She had neatly managed to put him in a position of either agreeing with her or else, by disagreeing, admitting that she had been more to him than a flirtation in the middle of a raging river.

Ross let her go, trying to come to terms with what he now knew—that she was the woman he had risked his life for. Co-incidence or fate, the knowledge put a whole new slant on his relationship with Lisette Napier.

The following morning Lisette rose to the sound of howling wind. Heavy rain clouds raced across the sky and a yellow-ish light seemed to shroud the land. She begged and pleaded with Araminta to cancel her assignation with Lord Benning-ton, but the girl remained deaf to her entreaties.

And so Lisette watched her go and waited in a state of acute apprehension for her to return. The day wore on and the rain played havoc with her nerves. Lightning streaked across the sky, illuminating the entire room, and thunder boomed until the windows shook. Lisette closed her eyes and prayed Araminta would come back soon.

When the gong sounded for dinner she jumped. Araminta still hadn't come home. That was the moment she was no longer able to sit and wait passively. Worried for her safety—fearing she might have been thrown from her horse in the storm and be lying in a ditch somewhere, Lisette did the only thing she could. She made her way to Colonel Montague's room feeling as if she were going to her execution.

Ross was about to go down to dinner when there was a small tap on the door.

'Who is it, Blackstock?'

'It's me,' Lisette murmured, moving towards him, a worried look on her face.

Lisette was the last person he'd expected to see and he

sensed quite rightly that she had come on behalf of his sister and that it had nothing to do with what had transpired between them the day before.

Looking from one to the other, Will hesitated. When Ross gestured with his head that he should make himself scarce, he nodded and went out with a knowing smile. Will had sharp eyes. Nothing much escaped him, and he knew the colonel had taken a bit of a shine to Miss Napier. Not that there was anything wrong with that, and not that anything could come of it mind—with their difference in status—but there was no harm in a little dalliance to pass the time, if the lady was willing like.

When Blackstock had left, Lisette hesitantly broke the news to Ross of Araminta's assignation with Lord Bennington. As he listened she observed his reaction, saw his jaw clench so tightly that a muscle began to throb in his cheek. Gradually his face became so outraged that fearing he might lash out at her she took a step back.

'And you say she went alone—without even a groom in attendance?'

'Yes,' Lisette whispered.

Ross stared at her, his eyes boring into her. In frigid silence he accused her of complicity and treachery. He swallowed the oath that sprang to his lips, swallowed the wave of anger at the thought that Lisette had allowed Araminta to go galloping off alone to who knew where for a liaison with Antony Bennington.

His temper, a true Montague temper, was never a wise thing to stir. Right now it was prowling, a hungry wolf seeking blood. If anyone had harmed his sister, that equated to an act of aggression against him, and the experienced soldier concealed beneath the veneer of an elegant gentleman reacted and responded appropriately.

His eyes narrowed to dark blue shards. Lisette lowered her head. 'Look at me, damn it! Where did they arrange to meet?'

'At the Dog and Partridge Inn on the Manchester Road.'

Unable to quell the cauldron of emotions that were seething inside him, his fury escaped him—it vibrated around her. 'This is insane!' His anger scorched her. 'You knew what she intended and yet you let her go?'

'No,' she cried as he began tearing off his jacket. 'I tried to stop her—I begged her not to go, truly, but her head was set. She refused to listen to reason.'

'You do not have the slightest concept of the importance of appropriate behaviour. If you had you would have tried harder to dissuade her or come to me. *I* would have talked her out of it,' he flared, stalking to his dressing room and returning with the first riding jacket he could lay his hands on. Thrusting his arms in the sleeves he dragged on his boots over his evening trousers. 'I *knew* she was up to something yesterday. That girl hasn't a grain of sense or propriety, jaunting all over the countryside in this weather. I swear I'll strangle young Bennington with my bare hands if any harm has come to her.'

Lisette went with him to the door. 'Is there anything I can do, anything…?'

'I think you've done enough,' he snapped. Suddenly he turned and faced her. 'Does anyone else know about this?'

'Just the young groom who rode to Glebe Hall to deliver the note to Lord Bennington.'

'What was his name?'

'Jacob.'

'I'll speak to him.' He walked on. 'Instruct Lumsden to offer my apologies to Aunt Wilhelmina for our absence at dinner and say that we have made other arrangements.'

'What will you do?'

Turning to look at her, his expression became more forbidding than before. 'Find her, and when I do she will feel the full force of my displeasure. That I promise you. My compliments to you, Miss Napier,' he reprimanded contemptuously, 'on your duplicity, your deceit and your disloyalty.'

Lisette's heart wrenched with pain at the unfairness of the accusations he flung at her. 'Colonel, please,' she implored, taking a few hesitant steps towards him. 'Your sister deeply regrets separating herself from Lord Bennington and desperately wants to make amends.'

Ross started towards her, his expression threatening. 'If Araminta wanted to see him, then she should have approached me. I would have dealt with the matter myself and paid young Bennington a visit, which would have been the appropriate action to take. What she has done goes way beyond the bounds of propriety,' he uttered scathingly.

Lisette began talking faster as she automatically backed away. 'But you must try to see it from her perspective—'

'Must?' he interrupted scathingly, his eyes hard and contemptuous. 'I think you are getting above yourself, Miss Napier. If you are wise,' he said in a soft, blood-chilling voice, 'in the future you will avoid me very carefully, and if you collude with my sister in anything as outrageous as this again, then you will find yourself looking for another position. Is that clear?'

In stunned silence Lisette watched him stride swiftly along the landing and bound down the stairs. She felt frozen inside, her mind blank. Upon her soul, she had never been spoken to in such a harsh and brutal way. Unable to form any coherent thought she left the colonel's room, too dazed, too numb to think or feel, but she could hear over and over again, the words Colonel Montague had so cruelly flung at her—*duplicity, deceit and disloyalty*…and dismissal.

Like a moth blundering in the lamplight, she stumbled her way through the maze of the house's many corridors, her only instinct guiding her to the refuge of her own bedchamber. Once inside the privacy of her room, she closed the door behind her and clamped her hands over her ears, but it was a futile gesture. She could still hear the colonel's words ringing in her ears, muted only by her own sobs as her heart fractured into tiny pieces.

Thunder clouds, dark grey and menacing, raced across the sky and a leaden curtain of drenching rain descended on Ross. Shrouded in his greatcoat and gritting his teeth, by the time the family sat down to dinner at Castonbury Park, he was heading in the direction of the Manchester Road, his horse's hooves pounding the muddied ground.

It was dark when he returned with a remorseful Araminta. Waiting in the basement hall, her back against one of the columns, having pulled herself together but with a vestige of pain still lingering, Lisette watched them enter. Colonel Montague was wearing a caped greatcoat and the wind had ruffled his hair. With the light behind him he was a dark silhouette made even larger by the capes of his coat spread wide by his broad shoulders. Shrugging it off he handed it to a footman.

Not until she moved did Ross notice Lisette. His voice was as cold as his eyes. 'Take my sister to her room. She is to stay there until further notice.'

Without a word Lisette turned from him and accompanied

her distraught mistress down the length of the hall. Colonel Montague's voice suddenly halted her.

'Miss Napier, wait.' Araminta went on ahead. Lisette turned back to face him. He came close and stood looking down at her. 'I trust you are aware of the seriousness of this and that you will not utter one word to anyone about Araminta's transgression.'

Deeply offended and angered that he thought she would, Lisette stiffened. 'I will not.'

'In the meantime,' Ross said, with cold practicality, 'Araminta must socialise and act as usual—as if nothing untoward has happened. It is my hope that everyone will be blessedly unaware of this day's debacle and that lurid versions of her activities are not already spreading like wildfire from Derbyshire to London. If the story of the episode at the Dog and Partridge is circulated, she will be ruined.'

'All that sounds rather harsh and unfair to me—that society can be so judgmental,' Lisette uttered tightly.

Her ignorance of English protocol and the behaviour of society brought a mocking smile to Ross's lips. 'You have lived too long in India, Miss Napier. If a scandal ensues, in the eyes of the *ton* Araminta will be seen as a shameless wanton, soiled and used and unfit company for unsullied young ladies, gullible young heirs and polite society in general. But as things stand, love him or hate him, Araminta will marry Antony Bennington. I insist on it. Do I make myself clear?'

'Perfectly, Colonel.' Lisette was too tired to argue or protest further. Colonel Montague's actions were what one would expect if a man had compromised his sister. 'Now if you will excuse me I will go and attend to her.' Dipping a stiff curtsey and lowering her eyes lest he saw the anger there, she turned and left him.

Lisette chafed at his harsh reprimand. She could hardly believe he was the same man she had met in India, the same relentless, predatory seducer who had taken advantage of her, who had held her clasped to him while his hungry mouth devoured hers. It was as if he were two people, one she could like and one she feared and mistrusted—with excellent reason since he had threatened to dismiss her.

On reaching the landing Lisette met Phaedra coming from the drawing room where she had been taking coffee with her aunt Wilhelmina.

'Good heavens,' she said, 'was that Araminta who just scooted past me? She's extremely wet,' she remarked in sympathy. 'We wondered why she wasn't at dinner. One of the grooms said she'd been gone all afternoon. Don't say she was lost in the rain all that time.'

'No, she—she came upon a shelter in the woods and stayed there until the rain let up a little while ago.' It seemed the wisest thing to say. Since no one knew of Araminta's assignation with Lord Bennington, Lisette had every wish to avoid a scandal, which would surely ensue should anyone find out. 'Excuse me, Lady Phaedra. I must go and prepare Miss Araminta a bath.'

On entering her mistress's rooms, Lisette searched her strained face. 'Are you all right?' she asked concernedly, proceeding to help her out of her damp clothes.

Araminta nodded, pulling her arms out of her sleeves. 'Yes, Lisette. Although Ross was extremely angry.'

'I expect he was.'

'You told him where to find me.' Her words were more of

a statement than a question. Lisette was relieved there was no hint of accusation.

'When you didn't come home I feared you might have had an accident. I had to do something.'

'It's all right. I really should have listened to you. Still, it's done now. The most important thing is that Antony still loves me and assures me that everything will be all right. Ross insists we marry as soon as it can be arranged. I think he's afraid my indiscretion will get out and create a scandal.'

'Which I imagine would be most unwelcome for the Montagues after everything that has happened.'

Lisette did not see Colonel Montague again for two weeks—whether it was by chance or his own choosing she had no idea, but she strongly suspected it to be the latter.

Alone, she was carefully laying out the dress Araminta would change into for the afternoon when she came in. Colonel Montague was behind her, carrying some small packages. They'd taken the carriage into Castonbury to do some shopping. With a bottle of lotion in her hands, Lisette stopped what she was doing, watching as Colonel Montague placed the packages on the bed. When he turned to face her he studied her with the casual interest a man might assume when he meets for the first time a woman he does not consider particularly attractive and therefore hardly worthy of his attention.

Lisette wanted to leave, but she knew she was trapped. His tall, powerful frame barred her way to the door, and his expression was like granite and as forbidding as it had been since that fateful day of Araminta's fall from grace. She had no choice but to remain. Her pulse pounded as she looked at him. Their gazes locked—a tremble ran the entire length of her body.

'Miss Napier! I trust you have not been colluding with my sister in any more undesirable escapades.' His voice was sharp, without any hint that his attitude had softened towards her.

'Ross,' Araminta chided, coming quickly to her maid's defence. 'Lisette had nothing to do with what happened between me and Antony, so will you please refrain from being horrid to her. I will have nothing said against her, do you hear? None of it was her fault.'

Ross cocked a mocking, amused brow at Lisette. 'You are asking me to be nice to someone who not only colluded in what you did but also encouraged it.'

The unfairness of his accusation brought Lisette's head up and, on meeting his, her eyes flared. 'I most certainly did not. I tried extremely hard to dissuade her. Miss Araminta will testify to that,' she said, keeping the anger and hurt boiling inside her tightly shut down. If he expected her to squirm beneath his anger and contempt he would be disappointed. She was not going to weep or run begging for forgiveness—not that she had done anything that warranted forgiveness. She would not let herself be bullied. She was learning not to let her face show her feelings.

'Lisette is quite right,' Araminta retorted. 'You are being unkind to me and discourteous to Lisette. What I did was wrong. But I do love Antony and that cannot be wrong—and what do you think, Lisette?' Araminta said, almost bubbling over with excitement. 'Ross has given his permission for Antony and me to marry as soon as it can be arranged—here at Castonbury, in the chapel. Isn't that wonderful?'

Lisette smiled at her. 'I'm so pleased for you—truly. I hope you and Lord Bennington will be very happy together.'

'We will be. How could we not? Since our betrothal was of many months' standing before I foolishly broke it off, Ross sees no reason for us to wait—and then he can go back to India. Is that not so, Ross?'

'It is, but not until there's word from Harry,' her brother replied. 'Hopefully when he contacts Giles he will have news about Jamie.'

'Good news, I hope,' his sister said, beginning to tear open the packages to inspect the items she had bought in Castonbury village. 'Poor Uncle Crispin. It must truly be awful not knowing if your son is dead or alive. And then there's the woman who claims to be Jamie's wife... What a muddle it all is.'

'And nothing for you to worry your head about, Araminta. You have quite enough to occupy your mind with your forthcoming betrothal party. You might like to go into Buxton for a new ball gown or wedding gown or something.'

Araminta's eyes lit up and she reached up and kissed his cheek affectionately. 'You are so good to me, Ross—the best brother in the whole world. Oh, how I shall miss you when you go back to India. Now, Lisette. I have not forgotten that it's your afternoon off so run along now. If I need help to dress I'll get one of the other maids to help me.'

'If you're sure.' Placing the bottle of lotion on the dresser, Lisette went towards the door. Colonel Montague was standing in her way. 'Excuse me, sir,' she said tightly.

He raised enigmatic eyebrows as his eyes met hers and he stepped aside, polite, incurious, totally indifferent to her as a female, he would have her believe, but in his eyes there was a shadow that did not quite conceal his innermost thoughts and his secret emotions.

His total lack of concern gave him away, for a man who had held a woman in his arms cannot but help retain the memory of that moment. Something remains and the studied blankness of his expression showed how hard he was trying to hide it. It was still there, that bond between them, pulling at them, tormenting them, no matter how Ross Montague tried to hide it.

'After a year of mourning, I think the time is right to invite people in again, Ross,' Giles agreed when Ross approached him about a wedding party for Araminta.

'Your father must be consulted, of course. Will he allow it—or even consider it?'

'I think he will. Until we know what has happened to Jamie we cannot mourn him, and the official period of mourning for Edward is over. I can see nothing wrong with putting on a party for Araminta, and I'm delighted she's going to marry young Bennington, after all. As the eldest son of the Earl of Cawood his credentials are impeccable and she would be a fool to allow him to slip through her fingers a second time. Go for it, Ross. A few new faces about the place will be a pleasant change. Will his parents be travelling up from Cambridgeshire for the event—and his delightful sister, Caroline? She's quite a beauty as I recall—just had her first Season.'

'As to that, I wouldn't know. I imagine they will all come— although because they are close friends of the Lathams, I expect they will stay at Glebe Hall.'

'I'll speak to Father about it—although he's so out of it at times I doubt he'll object, or even notice for that matter.'

'Thanks, Giles. I'll see it won't be a crowded, animated affair but it will do for Araminta. As long as she marries Antony Bennington she will be perfectly happy about it.'

Having finally received a reply from her father's lawyer, Mr Sowerby, in Oxford, Lisette had much to think about and consider. So it was on her afternoon off that she climbed halfway up to the high peaks where she could be alone with her thoughts. As she walked past the stables, although she kept her eyes averted, she was aware of Colonel Montague in conversation with his cousin, Lord Giles. She felt his eyes on her, following her, but she did not look back. His attitude, his cruel, angry words, his threat to have her dismissed, had reminded her of her humble position—that she was a servant and therefore dispensable.

Her initial reaction had been violent hurt and she could not, even now, truly suppress it. After her efforts that had sent her fleeing from India, she'd thought she'd conquered hurt. She'd been wrong on that score.

Climbing upwards through the park, she noticed three bored gamekeepers with dogs. They watched her pass with an admiring interest that she was in no mood for. Walking on she left the woods behind, emerging onto an open hillside. Climbing higher and walking round the sheep that looked at her with curious stares, she eventually found a suitable place to sit in the shade of a stone barn and read her letter once more.

Mr Sowerby had written to offer his condolences over the demise of her parents and went on to inform her that her father, who had been well rewarded for the work he had carried out in India for the university, had left her a substantial legacy of five thousand pounds. Lisette was astounded. She didn't know anything about any money. Her father had never spoken of such things to her. But to suddenly find that she was a wealthy young woman in her own right and that she need not fear for her future again, was such a wonderful feeling she could not believe it at first.

Fixing her gaze on the horizon, she made her first decision about her future. She would leave Castonbury Park. She could not stay here. To be near Colonel Montague, to continue being his sister's maid, knowing the disdain with which he regarded her, was an intolerable prospect.

But where else could she go? What could she do? She had done nothing but help her father with his work and for a few short months she had been a maid. For the first time she began to wonder if there were other possibilities for her future. She decided it was time to stop believing she had no choices in her life. It was time to begin deciding her own destiny. Perhaps it was even time to have a bit of fun. She would remain until Araminta married Lord Bennington. Araminta would then leave Castonbury Park—and maybe she could fulfil her dream and return to India.

Having watched her walk away from the house, Ross had been unable to resist the temptation to follow her. For the first time he saw her with her hair unbound. It was black and shining and moved like waves on a beach as she walked. He had not been alone with her since that day she had come to his room to tell him about Araminta's assignation with young Bennington. He had treated her badly, said harsh things he did not mean, things he knew must have hurt her, and he wanted nothing more than to make amends. Hopefully the gift he would present her with would go some way to aiding his cause.

Silently he approached. He paused and studied her, seated

on the grass with her arms clasped around her drawn-up knees watching a scatter of magpies scuttling about the remains of a dead rabbit in the tussocky grass down the slope. Her gaze shifted to a shallow, slow-moving stream which, when it reached the valley bottom, would wind along the valley floor. The sun was warm on her face, the air sweet, and she breathed deep of it into her lungs, leaning back against the stone wall.

She wore a light floral printed dress with a demure white fichu tucked into her neckline, her slender arms concealed in three-quarter-length sleeves. Staring at her delicate wrists and long fingers made him long to know her touch on his bare skin. For long uncounted moments, Ross simply looked, let his eyes drink their fill of her soft curves, of the shining gloss of her unbound hair, of her intrinsically feminine expression, the simplicity of her pose. He felt the surge of emotions that gripped him. He didn't know why he'd been so furious with her when she had told him of Araminta's assignation with young Bennington. After all, it wasn't her fault, but for some reason he had been incensed.

But he had come to regret his condemnation of her, for Araminta's disgraceful behaviour was her affair and had nothing to do with her maid.

Lisette could feel his presence all around her. She did not look round since she had known he would come. He was dressed in breeches, an open-necked shirt beneath his jacket and knee-high riding boots. Without a word he moved to lean beside her, crossing his arms over his broad chest, and they stared out over the splendour of the wide, wild open hills and bracken-clad moorland together.

'How did you know I would be up here?' she said at last,

carefully folding Mr Sowerby's letter and putting it in the pocket of her dress.

'Because I followed you. Araminta mentioned it was your afternoon off—remember? And when I saw you walk past the stables and head for the woods, I thought you might like some company. I was about to ride into Hatherton.'

'Then why didn't you? Why did you follow me?' She did not look at him but continued to gaze at the broad expanse of moor that had entered her heart the first time she had seen it, like a child settling in its mother's lap. 'What is it that you want from me?'

'You.' That was the moment Ross realised how true this was. His attitude to love had always been of the easygoing, take-it-or-leave-it variety, and now he found himself stunned by the force of his desire. Never had he wanted a woman so much, and never had he felt less sure of his ability to get what he wanted.

'I will be no man's plaything, Colonel.'

'If I wanted a toy I would buy one, Lisette. I wanted to talk to you and to apologise for my behaviour when you came to tell me about Araminta—and again when I saw you earlier. I was boorish, I know.'

'Boorish? You were downright rude. But then, you are my employer and entitled to speak to me how you see fit if you consider I have done wrong,' she said with more than a hint of sarcasm, 'even to go so far as to dismiss me should my *duplicity*, my *deceit* and *disloyalty* not meet with your approval.'

'You are wrong, Lisette,' he said softly. 'I should not have spoken to you like I did and I'm sorry if I hurt you. Not one of those words applies to you. It was unforgivable of me. My temper got the better of me.' He smiled grimly. 'I should try singing from Aunt Grace's hymn sheet.'

'What do you mean?'

'That I should be firm to the servants without being severe, kind without being familiar, to converse with reserve and distance of manner and be particularly careful to maintain respect for their feelings.'

'Goodness, I have much to learn about my superiors as well as my own kind.'

'Why did you come up here and why did you seem unsurprised to see me? Did you expect me to follow you?'

She ignored his question and asked one of her own. 'Why did you want to talk to me? What have you and I to say to each other?'

'I told you. I wanted to apologise.'

'You could have done that at the house without following me all the way up here.' She pushed her hair back from her face and looked at something in the distance, as though it didn't really matter what he said.

'I want to talk about us, Lisette. About you and me.' His words were spoken quietly and did not take her by surprise.

'There is no us. There never can be.' She sighed deeply and turned for the first time to look at him, having to tilt her head to look up into his face. 'You are a titled gentleman, a man of some importance and wealth, and I'm just a maid employed to look after your sister. If Mrs Landes-Fraser was to see me up here with you she'd have me out of Castonbury Park in a snap.'

'My aunt is not your employer.'

'No, and you are not my master. No one owns me,' she told him, getting up and brushing down her skirts.

'I do not play the game according to society's rules, Lisette.

I write my own. That is something you will have to come to terms with.'

'And why should I do that? We can never mean more to each other than what we are now. You are Colonel Lord Ross Montague while I am a mere maid, a domestic—the lowliest of the low. You belong to a place like Castonbury Park and I belong in your sister's boudoir as her maid. You are soon to return to India. We are too different—worlds apart, in fact.'

'Why?' he demanded.

'Because we are.'

'Defend your argument.'

She inhaled sharply, feeling as though she was getting nowhere. 'I've told you why,' she said on a weaker note. 'I cannot be more explicit—and we are different in our values.'

'How? How are we different?' he persisted.

Her eyes snapped and she almost shouted, 'Because you are who you are and you are too eager to judge. I have just suffered your outrage at first hand…and your indifference—'

'I am never indifferent to you, Lisette.'

'Don't interrupt. I suffered your indifference for some unwitting transgression.'

'For which I have apologised.'

Emboldened by his attentive, angry stare, she forged on. 'Perhaps you can be satisfied with a clandestine relationship but I need more than that—and I do not mean riches or rank. I fail to be dazzled by all that.'

'Because you feel that may only make me want you more,' he uttered quietly. 'What is it going to take for you to let me hold you—kiss you?'

'I don't have a price, if that is what you mean. I have no interest in money or jewels. I am not for sale.'

Ross smiled and moved closer. 'Well, well, Lisette. It seems you have a temper. I knew there was more to you than meets the eye.'

'Why are you so interested in me?' she cried. 'There are plenty of other girls you could have—who are far prettier than I.'

'Your question is simple to answer. It is because I don't want anyone else. I want *you*.'

'For what purpose?' Lisette exclaimed. 'Oh, but of course— to warm your bed. That's it, isn't it?'

'More than that.'

'Why?' She just wanted to hear him say, *Because I love you*— to say those words—but not if it wasn't true.

'Because I do,' he answered, refusing to say it.

'This is not about what *you* want. Is that all you care about?'

He studied her irate face for a second, then he began to laugh softly. 'You are so adorable when you're angry—do you know that?'

'What?' She was bemused and growing flustered as he drew closer.

'I have just one question for you,' he murmured, staring into her glorious amber eyes, 'and I want you to answer honestly.'

'What?'

'Do you want me?'

She stared at him, and when he reached out and brushed her cheek with the backs of his fingers, she quivered. 'I—I… Oh, don't do that. Please don't…'

Ross realised the effect his caressing fingers were having on her senses, but he responded with a questioning lift to his brows. 'Why not?' he asked, running his fingers down her neck. 'You like me to touch you.'

'I—' she began, uncomfortably aware of the knowing look in his eyes.

'Yes?' he prompted.

Lisette swallowed hard and turned her head away, telling herself she must be strong. 'I don't know—exactly,' she admitted. All she knew for certain was that, for just a moment, she would have liked to be in his arms.

Suddenly he laughed and took hold of her hand. His mood had changed. 'Come, Lisette—we will continue this conversation later. But first I have a present for you.'

Totally bemused, Lisette followed him to the other side of the barn where two horses were tethered side by side. One was Bengal, the other a beautiful white mare she had often favoured with an apple. Puzzled, she looked up at Colonel Montague.

'You did not come alone?'

'Oh, yes.'

'But…I don't understand.'

He grinned roguishly. 'Knowing of your passion for horses—and that you have not had the opportunity to ride since you left India, which must be torture in itself, I thought you might appreciate a gallop.'

Lisette stared at him, unable to believe the marvel of what he was offering. 'But…how can I? If I am seen atop a horse out of the Montague stable—have you any idea how I will be made to suffer?'

'Don't think of it, otherwise it will spoil our ride.'

'But…the risk if we are caught…'

He grinned. 'I'm prepared to risk it if you are. It will be well worth it.'

She returned his smile, too excited with anticipation of the ride to care.

'Let's get you into the saddle and we'll be away. To have ordered the groom to fit a side-saddle onto the horse's back would have raised eyebrows, so you will have to ride astride.'

She laughed, thrilled by the prospect of being back on a horse. 'I ride no other way.'

Seven

· ·

Lisette sat tall and straight-backed in the saddle; her shoulders were slim and square, her head erect instead of submissively bent as becomes a gently nurtured woman. But to Ross riding beside her as they rode among the green-clad hills, her plain servant's garb seemed to emphasize her femininity far more than the graceful folds of a lady's velvet habit. The straight lines of her body showed the swell of her breasts and her slender waist and rounded hips.

The mare was galloping at full stretch, and it was doubtful anyone could have turned her—but Lisette made no effort to do so, as she crouched over the saddlehorn with her weight thrown forward and without any idea where they were going.

At first she worried Ross with her recklessness, bent so low over her horse's neck with her face almost buried in the dancing mane, riding as no lady should and astride. But his fears were soon dispelled. She was one of the most skilled riders he'd ever seen—man or woman—light and lovely in the saddle. He gave a shout of laughter as Bengal thundered over the hard green turf alongside her. Riding at breakneck pace, Lisette took each jump with an effortless, breezy unconcern for style that Ross had never seen before. He grinned approvingly. There was jubilant simplicity as she soared over each jump, at one with her mount—confident, trusting and elated—its tail floating behind like a bright defiant banner.

They had been too occupied to pay much attention to how far they had ridden. Dreading the moment when she would have to dismount, they slowed their horses to a walk.

'I never knew a woman could ride like that,' Ross exclaimed with an admiring laugh. She was smiling broadly, her generous lips drawn back over perfect white teeth, and her colour was gloriously high. 'I think it's time we turned back.'

The horses wandered forward unchecked, pausing occasionally to crop a mouthful of grass and moving on again while their riders were content to go with them. Coming to the brow of a hill they paused and looked down the slope at parkland which rolled away into the distance. Lisette's eye was caught by some sort of encampment with an assortment of brightly painted caravans and carts. Some of them had a shabby appearance. Dogs roamed and several piebald and skewbald ponies grazed nearby. While children played, men and women stood about talking and others sat around a fire where ribbons of smoke spiralled upwards out of the embers. Swarthy skinned and with shiny black hair, they had a foreign look about them. Gold earrings glinted in some of the men's ears and brightly coloured scarves were tied loosely around their necks.

'Who are those people?' Lisette asked curiously.

'Gypsies.'

'Are they trespassing?'

'No. They have permission to set up camp in the park. They always come at this time of year to help with the harvest.'

'Are they harmful?'

'As a rule, no. They're hardworking people and always behave themselves. They abide by the law of the land while they are here. Their help is invaluable.'

They rode on. On reaching the barn where they had started from, Ross swung himself out of the saddle and went to assist Lisette, who was most reluctant to get down.

'Thank you so much,' she said, taking a moment to rub the spirited mare's wet muzzle against her palm. 'It was wonderful to be back on a horse again. I can't tell you what it means to me. I had a horse—she was called Silva. She was so beautiful.'

Ross moved to stand behind her. 'What happened to her?'

'I left her with Messalina.'

Placing his hands on her waist and drawing her hair aside, Ross kissed her nape. 'Well,' he murmured, his breath warm on her flesh, 'since you don't want money or fancy jewels from me—and to present you with a horse would raise more than a few scandalised eyebrows—I shall have to give you a present you will approve of.'

She trembled, casting about feebly for her ability to resist him. 'Please—please don't do this. I really must be getting back....'

'Why?' he breathed, his whisper fraught with wicked seduction, taking her earlobe gently between his teeth. 'It's your day off, remember. You have all the time in the world—and so have I.' He turned her to face him and drew her into his arms.

'This is how we held on to each other that night, isn't it?'

'Yes,' she whispered.

'I have a confession to make.'

'What is it?'

'I knew that night that if the river had risen, neither of us would have seen the dawn. We would have been washed away like so much flotsam.'

'I know. I was so afraid. If I hadn't had you to hold me…'

'We shared a moment in our lives known only to us—binding us together like nothing else can.'

Keeping one arm securely around her waist, with his free hand he lightly traced his finger down her cheek to her chin. He gazed at her lips, at the soft rose-tinted curves he was beginning to know so well. Their shape was etched on his mind, their taste imprinted on his senses. 'I came up here because I wanted to be alone with you, Lisette.'

Lisette's entire body began to vibrate with a mixture of shock, desire and fear. It was one thing to be kissed by him in the middle of a raging river, but here, with absolute privacy and nothing to prevent him from taking all sorts of liberties, it was another matter entirely. Struggling desperately to ignore the sensual pull he was exerting on her, she drew a long, shaky breath.

'Why should you think I wanted to be alone with you?'

His relentless gaze locked on hers. 'Because I remember how it felt to hold you in my arms that night in the river.'

'It was both dangerous and foolish.'

'Foolish or not,' he murmured, 'I wanted you. We wanted each other. I want you now.' Lisette made the mistake of looking at him, and his deep blue eyes captured hers against her will, holding them imprisoned. 'Neither of us has anything to gain by continuing this pretence that what happened in India is over and forgotten. When I kissed you in Araminta's room it proved that it wasn't over. I've remembered you all this time, Lisette—and I know damn well you remembered me.'

Lisette wanted to deny it but couldn't. 'Yes—all right,' she said shakily, 'I never did forget you. How could I?' she added defensively. 'I would have drowned if it had not been for you.'

He smiled and his voice gentled to the timbre of rough velvet. 'Yes, you would. Now, come here.'

'Why?' she whispered.

'So that we can finish what we began that night.'

Lisette stared at him, fear mixed with violent excitement. 'How?'

Lowering his head Ross lightly touched her lips with his own, feeling the heat, the compulsion, that surged in each of them. He held from pressing down on her lips, content for one timeless moment simply to touch and be touched, but not denying it. The beauty of the fragile moment stretched, their heightened awareness washing over them.

Curiously breathless, Lisette quivered. A small, insidious voice in her mind urged her to enjoy this time they were together, that she was entitled to some stolen passionate kisses if she wanted them. Another voice warned her not to break the rules of convention and leave him. But it was too late. She was already losing the battle to resist the desire that engulfed her whenever they were close. It was an effort to raise her heavy lids. At that moment her mind emptied itself of all thought. She was proud, but she was also young and sensual.

A blankness took over and with a soft sigh she relaxed against him, warm and trusting as he began to kiss her neck, teasing her senses into glorious awakening for him, her power to push him away fading fast. When he raised his head she offered him her mouth and he claimed her lips immediately, his arms going round her, and she revelled in his embrace despite her earlier determination not to let this happen. She closed her eyes tight to concentrate on the sensation. His mouth moved against hers, and it seemed natural to part her lips. Her mouth and body had suddenly become extra sensitive, so that she could feel the slightest touch.

At length he ended the kiss and held her fevered stare. At that moment they smiled into each other's eyes like equals. When he took her hand she did not resist as he led her inside the barn where he removed his jacket and dragged her into his arms once more. His lips found hers, finding them eager, warm, parted and moist. She clung to him, her arms about his neck. His shirt was fine lawn. Through it she could feel the heat of him.

Their bodies fitted together, and her very softness tensed his muscles, her curves fit against him, their mouths fused, moving, caressing, their tongues touching. He put his hand to her head, entwining his fingers in her hair which fell in a shining black mane of living silk down her spine. She lifted her chin and his lips slipped beneath it and along her jaw. He was murmuring her name as he kissed her breasts through her gown, and then, eager to view her beautiful body unfettered, his hands went to the tiny buttons of her bodice which slipped open and the ribbons of her chemise needed no more than a tug to release them. The bounty he'd captured, their softness filled his hand, and lowering his head he took the hardness of her rosy nipples in his mouth.

His lips burned and Lisette gasped with sheer pleasure. He pushed away her dress and slipped it from her shoulders. Her chemise soon followed, bearing her aching breast fully to the soft light, the warm air and his attentions. His hands moved with infinite care as he began to remove her clothes, pausing now and then to caress and to fondle, roaming above her stockings and venturing above her garters, meeting bare skin. When there was nothing else to remove, swinging her up into his arms he carried her across the barn and laid her down on a pile of hay, a lovely bed, soft and ready for them.

Lisette watched as he stripped himself of the covering of civilisation to reveal his beautiful male body, brown and hard and eager. That was the moment she was made to realise that there was no going back, no escaping what was to happen and at last she accepted it.

Joining her in the hay he gathered her to him, her breath feathering his cheek as her fingers lightly touched him, sliding, gliding over his flesh, cindering his will.

'Show me,' she breathed. He was all heat and shockingly hot hardness. 'Show me what to do.' She wanted to know all of it.

Her words vanquished the last of Ross's resistance, the last remnant of caution. She was exuding something else besides the fragrance of flowers. It was as if some part of her, hitherto hidden or held back from others, was being offered to him. He wanted her with every fibre of his being, and she wanted him. Those demons that drove him urged him on, lending their talents to achieving victory in the most satisfying way. Reaching down he caressed her legs, his hand slowly moving up her inner thigh. Lisette gasped. All thoughts beyond this place, this moment, this man, fled. Forbidden pleasure turned to bliss as his lips kissed every part of her and his knowledgeable fingers explored those secret places known only to her.

They beguiled her until a delicious tension coiled so tightly inside her it broke loose with a vengeance. His face was a mass of concentration etched with passion as he intimately learned all about her, filling his male senses with her feminine se-crets, driving her to a sensual excitement with practised ease. She melted, sinking into the soft hay, moaning, arching. In that moment, totally aroused, he could have taken her. She was his to do with as he willed. She was his instrument. Her body and, more alarmingly, her soul were fully open to him.

Ross felt her surrender and inwardly smiled, satisfied that she was taking all he lavished on her. He held her for one ach-ing moment, and then he covered her and thrust powerfully, deep into her body, breaching her maidenhead. She cried out and he held still for just a moment, before his demons claimed him and drove him on, far beyond thought and reason.

Lisette clung to him, holding tight as their passion took flight, every sensation new, battering her overloaded senses. She thrilled to each new intimacy, determined to feel it all, to know the sheer hard delight of his body anchoring her, to glory in the hardness that filled her, claiming her, to sense her vulnerability in her nakedness, to revel in the shameless excitement that swelled and grew, then flooded her—more powerful than desire, deeper, more enduring than anything she had experienced in her life. She gave herself up to it, shar-ing it through her hungry kisses, through the worship of his body. And then he let go, allowing his body to do what came naturally and driving them both over the edge as the explo-sion broke over them.

Breathing heavily, their bodies damp with sweat, Ross felt the shudders rack him. Lisette felt, deep inside her, the strong ripples of his release, and then he became still. It was only then that he came to his senses, reminding himself of the inevitable consequences of what he had just done.

'Lisette?' he whispered, bracing himself on his arms and

looking down at her. 'Open your eyes and look at me,' he commanded quietly.

Her lashes fluttered and he stared down into the warm amber of her eyes. 'Did I hurt you?'

She swallowed and shook her head, fighting down the wanton urge to plead with him to take her again, to beg him to love her not just with his body but his heart also, which was what she wanted more than anything in the world. In a few short minutes he had broken down every barrier she had erected against him, battered down her defences and left her weak and eager for him as if she'd been a naive girl.

'Then why the sad face?' he murmured. 'You do…want me, Lisette?'

'Yes,' she admitted in a fierce, suffocated little voice. 'But…I don't *want* to want you.'

A sound part groan, part laughter escaped him as he shoved his fingers through her lustrous hair, imprisoning her face between his hands. 'And I want you,' he told her, kissing her flushed cheek, 'more than you will ever know.'

'You shouldn't.'

Placing his finger beneath her chin, he tilted her face to his. 'I told you that I do not play the game according to society's rules, that I write my own. In bed or out of it, I consider you my equal in every way, Lisette. Never forget that.'

Moments later, Ross swept his hand along her thigh as she pressed alongside him and nestled her head within the crook of his arm. 'You are very lovely,' he murmured, dragging his gaze away from her shapely legs long enough to give her a smile. 'Truly, my love, I've never seen the equal of your perfection.'

Returning his smile, Lisette ran her fingers through the

fascinating feathering of dark hair covering his chest. 'You are far from imperfect yourself, Colonel.'

Frowning, Ross tipped her face up to his. 'Ross. My name is Ross, Lisette. Considering our long acquaintance—not to mention what has just transpired between us—I find it ridiculous that you call me "Colonel."'

'Very well. Ross it is—but only when we are alone.'

His gaze did a slow admiring sweep of her body stretched out alongside his. 'I want to see you again. When I can—when you can. No one need know. It could be here—or somewhere else.'

'But people would talk. It wouldn't be good, for me or you.'

'Who has to know?' he replied, and Lisette could see gentle laughter in his eyes. 'It will be good to fade into the background from time to time. You didn't mean this to happen,' he went on, and his voice was stronger, deeper, more persuasive with every word. 'But we couldn't help it. We're two of a kind. We recognised it in each other. I'm glad.' He took a deep breath. 'Has anyone ever told you how utterly beautiful you are without your clothes?'

With her hair streaming loose and a shamefaced smile, she pressed her brow against his lean cheek, saying, in a breathless pretence at reproach that was nothing of the kind, 'Only you. You really are the most sinful man I can imagine.'

As he kissed the top of her head, he answered, 'And you the wildest woman I know—so, a good match.'

With a deep sigh of contentment Lisette settled against him. 'I suppose we should be getting back.'

Ross's arm tightened about her. 'We will—but not just yet.'

At the insistent urging of his knee, she lifted a slender limb and laid it over his hip, allowing his thigh to encroach between hers. Somewhat in awe of her handsome lover, she admired the steely bulges of his shoulders and the taut ribs, the manly nipples. She began to brush kisses over the ridges and hollows. Ross watched her, amazed by her gentle passion.

When she curled into his side, he tried to come to grips with reality. With his arm holding her close, he couldn't explain what had happened to him. All he knew was that no other woman had ever been like this. He was the first man she had known and he knew it and triumphed in it. It therefore came as no surprise to discover, as his sated senses cleared, that he was once again possessed of an urgent desire.

His need evident to Lisette, she sighed and stretched, lifting her arms above her head, deliberately displaying her proud breasts for his hands to cup, and it began again, this time slowly, lingeringly, exploring each other's bodies, kissing and smiling until he lay over her, plunging into her again and again until she wept with rapture and great joy of what he did to her and he groaned as though he were in agony.

Clearly, with his skill as a lover, he could take her to the heights of desire. He devoured her and she knew that nothing would ever be the same again. She felt beautiful, feminine and absurdly happy at this moment. How delightful that coupling with a man could do that to a woman. It was an extraordinary thing, she thought as she went falling into a white-hot haven of pure sensation, until he pushed her over the edge of oblivion.

As they began to replace their clothes, the late-afternoon sun had moved round in the sky and the light in the barn was dusky but they were reluctant to leave this moment, this time, this wonderful thing they had discovered together.

Ross had made love to many women but had loved none of them. He knew the difference now and the ecstasy he had just experienced with Lisette was an awakening for him. He'd thought he knew it all and he hadn't—until now.

He wanted her—in his bed and in his life. There was no doubt of that fact, no room for manoeuvre or negotiation. Her loveliness had flowered and blossomed in his arms, and his masculine desire for her was intense. He had the kind of feelings for her that a man can only feel for one special woman, though what the hell he was to do about it he didn't know and at this precise moment he didn't give a damn. She was his, she belonged to him—he could tell it by the expression in her eyes, by her lack of surprise when he'd appeared.

Lisette was well aware of the startled looks they drew as the group of keepers and one red-haired female on the other side of the lake took note of them together, Ross leading the two horses by the reins.

'I anticipated this. It is exactly what I hoped to avoid,' she told him. 'I had reservations about agreeing to walk back with you and shouldn't have agreed to it—and to make matters worse I believe that is Nancy Cooper, one of the kitchen maids, talking to them.'

Ross was not unaware of the curiosity that rippled among the keepers as they walked side by side, and he could only imagine how the rumour mill would soon churn. He was an old hand at dabbling in scandal and as a rule he always ignored it, but if their affair was made known it would be too distressing, too upsetting, for her to withstand.

'Forgive me, Lisette. I should have paused to consider the possible repercussions that would occur if we were seen. I should have let you walk back alone.'

'It's too late now. Nancy Cooper has ears as big as a rabbit and through practice she can move from a keyhole with the lightning speed of a weasel. Be assured, before the day is over the whole of Castonbury Park will know we have been together.'

'I sincerely hope that will not be the case. I prefer to keep what is between us private for the time being.'

There was something in his voice that bemused and unsettled Lisette. In the time it took them to reach a place hidden from prying eyes, she had time to think about it, to dwell on the consequences of what she had done, to the realisation that a man who has marriage on his mind will speak of it. Ross Montague had not and she marvelled at her own naivety in believing that he would. She flushed hotly when she recalled how she had sighed and melted and moaned in his arms, and though she did not deny that she loved him and always would, she should not have allowed him so much liberty.

Slowing her steps until she had stopped altogether, she turned and looked at him. '"For the time being," Ross? And what then? You are soon to leave Castonbury. Until that time what are we to do? Do you intend taking me whenever you fancy—expect me to lie down for you for an hour's pleasure? Is that why you followed me—trapped me up there on the hill?'

'Trapped you!' A wicked gleam appeared in his eyes. 'You were as willing as I was and don't deny it. What is it you want, Lisette?'

Shaking her head she turned away. 'Nothing, Ross. I don't want anything from you that you are not prepared to give willingly.' It was a bitter pill to know that though he was able to marry her, for nothing but his family stood in his way at this present time, he would not. He had decided that this was how it would be. Had she really thought he would marry her?

Had she really been that naive and stupid in thinking that he loved her enough to make her his wife?

Ross stared at her, trying to comprehend her thoughts. Did she expect him to marry her, was that it? It was a measure of the deep feelings he carried in his heart for her that he had already begun to consider the idea of making her his wife. She had become a necessity in his life, like food and water, but at this time it would be socially impractical to bring it about.

She was lovely and gracious, and in fashionable gowns she would hold her own in any society, but until Araminta's wedding was over and because the Montagues were on tenterhooks awaiting communication from Harry with news of Jamie, he would prefer not to add to the family's worries by announcing his affair with his sister's maid.

Reaching out he cupped her chin with his hand which moved on and gently caressed her warm cheek. 'Be patient, Lisette. I am trying to avert scandal—goodness knows the Montagues have had their fair share in the past and this is not the time to create another.' He thought he saw a sheen of disappointed tears in her wide amber eyes. She was badly hurt, he knew it, but at present there was nothing else to be done.

Feeling the tide of pain rise in her, Lisette stood for a moment. If he was indeed the man of courage she believed him to be, he would have been prepared to fly in the face of prejudice and hypocrisy his family and his social equals would have turned on him. But he was not prepared to do that and the realisation was overwhelming and hurt her deeply. Her heart was in shreds as the battle for common sense and her love for him fought tooth and nail for dominance. Managing to claw back some of the self-esteem he had stolen from her, she knew what she had to do. She would not beg him to marry her and it was some measure of her strength that her pride came to the fore.

'You are quite right not to want a scandal at this time,' she said, drawing herself up straight and calmly meeting his piercingly blue gaze. 'If our affair—or whatever you care to call it—should become known, it would certainly create one. It would alter my relationship with my employers and they will look at me with different eyes. I will be considered to be getting above my station, which, after all, is the lowest it could be.'

His eyes passed lovingly over her face and a smile curved his lips. 'An adorable servant, Lisette.'

She smiled a bitter smile. Not adorable enough, it would seem, she thought. 'It is in my best interests that it is kept between ourselves—as well as your own,' she added as if it were an afterthought and his concern for his own well-being not on the same level of importance as her own.

'I'm glad you understand. For the time being I believe it is the most sensible course to take. Get used to the idea, to the knowledge that you are very special to me, that I will make a decent life for us both, that I will take care of you and that you have nothing to fear. What we feel for each other is quite unique, that is evident, and all it needs is time—and we have plenty of that.' Lisette looked at him, wanting to sink against him, to be held to his chest in strong arms which would tell her he loved her. To sigh and melt and feel again that languorous magic drift through her...

'Yes, you're right, of course.'

When they parted, walking back to the house she gave herself up to her thoughts. Had she been seduced, beyond recall, not by Ross but by *her* desire for him? She knew in the depths of her heart that it was a most pertinent distinction. This desire was of the kind that had trapped women since time began into loveless unions. She had every reason to distrust the emotion, to avoid it, to reject it.

But she could not—perhaps before today, but now this rogue emotion was too strong, too compulsively within her, for her ever to be free of it. But this in itself brought no sadness, no pain, and indeed if the act itself could illicit such power and joy, such boundless excitement, such pleasure that she was addicted to it, then given the choice she would have the experience rather than live the rest of her life without it.

Having made her decision she was aware of a kind of peace stealing over her. But like a dark cloud coming over the sun, she knew this small sense of peace and happiness she had felt so briefly in Ross's arms could not continue—not in the face of what was real.

Ross began visiting Araminta's room more often. He began to waylay Lisette whenever he could. Sometimes when she was going to and from the kitchen he would stop her for no reason at all other than to hear her voice. Having stressed his desire for secrecy, Lisette could not believe how he flirted with danger and ran the risk of being caught dallying with a servant girl in a house that bred scandal.

He came up behind her and wrapped his arms wordlessly about her. On turning, her heart almost stopped when she saw his lazy, dazzling white smile that swept slowly across his handsome face, and the way his vivid blue eyes crinkled at the corners. He kissed her softly, gently, his lips travelling across her face to the corners of her eyes, smoothing her cheek, before releasing her and allowing her to go on her way.

But this happy state of affairs could not last. With sly hints and insinuations from Nancy Cooper, gradually the other servants began to take notice of the attention Ross paid her, and not only to notice but to disapprove. Some accepted the situation they suspected existed between the colonel and one of their own—after all, there was nothing new in one of their lordships having an eye for a pretty maid as long as they were discreet about the liaison. But some of the more strait-laced were horrified that a servant should be guilty of such an atrocious error of judgement, a wicked deviation from the accepted code of conduct, and to be allowed to get away with it.

Her fears that Nancy Cooper had done her worst were realised when Mrs Stratton summoned her into her sitting room early one evening before dinner. Mrs Stratton's sitting room was a comfortable room with a good fire in the grate. There were deep, comfortable armchairs on either side and a table on which stood a white china teapot with cups and saucers to match. Lisette liked this room. It was so warm and welcoming as a rule, but not today. Mrs Stratton, who always treated her kindly, was seated at the table, and by her blank expression and cool manner, it was clear she had something to say. She did not invite Lisette to sit down.

'Is anything wrong, Mrs Stratton?'

'It depends how you define the word *wrong*, Miss Napier. I felt I had to speak to you. It has been brought to my attention that you and Colonel Montague share a…relationship.'

Lisette suppressed a bitter smile. 'I see Nancy has already given you her version.'

'I abhor gossip and I will not have it in the servants' hall.'

'It is a rumour, Mrs Stratton, no more,' Lisette said, hating the falsehood but she could hardly tell the housekeeper the truth. But how could she look Mrs Stratton in the eye after this lie?

'In my experience all rumours have a ring of truth about them. Two days ago you were seen walking down from the hills together.'

'That is correct, Mrs Stratton. There was nothing furtive about our meeting. It was my afternoon off and I went for a walk. I encountered Lord Montague. We walked back to the house together, that is all. Having come from India, we share a common interest.'

'I am sure that is true, but it has been noted that it was not the first time he has sought your company. Indeed, I recall seeing the two of you together myself on your arrival at Castonbury, which I chose to overlook at the time. Your position as Miss Araminta's maid requires a certain code of behaviour which I am not at all convinced you share.'

'I do understand the need for such a code.'

'I am relieved to hear it. It is a part of my duty to protect and encourage virtue, especially in the unmarried girls of the house. I am in a position to establish rules, Miss Napier—those rules apply to everyone.'

'I know that, Mrs Stratton.'

'A word of advice, Miss Napier. One must carefully avoid all reproachful, familiar terms when speaking or ministering to the family. This is one rumour I would prefer to keep below stairs. Should it reach the ears of Mrs Landes-Fraser I doubt she would be as lenient as I. Many a servant has lost a comfortable home, and a mistress a useful assistant, by forming unsuitable relationships—that goes for upstairs as well as below stairs. You will do well to remember that a maid is more interested in retaining a good position than her employer is in retaining her, and that no matter how the maid might strive to achieve it, she can never be her employer's equal. Do you understand what I am saying, Miss Napier?'

Lisette took a deep breath and lifted her head. 'Oh, yes, Mrs Stratton.' And Lisette did understand. She understood perfectly well.

'Miss Araminta speaks very highly of you. It is important that you guard your good name. Whatever the truth of it, there is nothing more detestable than defamation, so if you wish to remain as her maid, then you must avoid it.'

'I will bear that in mind.'

'I understand you had little experience when Lord Montague employed you as Miss Araminta's maid.'

'That is true, Mrs Stratton.'

'Well, then, I hope you understand you were very fortunate to be given this position.'

'I do.'

'Very well, Miss Napier.' Standing up she smiled and her expression softened. 'Colonel Montague is an attractive man— indeed all the Montague men are very handsome—there's little wonder some of the maids have their heads turned. But I must remind you that it is fitting for every servant to maintain a good character—they have nothing to depend on but their good name. But you are a sensible girl. I think you know what happens when a servant behaves improperly with their master.'

A wave of colour mounted Lisette's face. She bit her lip and lowered her eyes. There was a constriction in her throat and there was a feeling inside her of…what? Shame? Regret? She didn't know, but she didn't like it. Her voice sounded very small as she answered. 'I take your meaning, Mrs Stratton.'

'What Colonel Montague does in his spare time,' Mrs Stratton went on, 'which is private and not for us to comment on or wonder at, is his own business. But when one of the servants becomes involved it is my duty to speak out.'

Lisette smiled. 'I do understand, and I will give you no reason to have to speak to me again.'

'That's all I ask. Attend to your duties.'

As Lisette closed the door to Mrs Stratton's sitting room she asked herself what she had done. The enormity of her transgression hit her. The housekeeper had implied that a maid who crossed the line was in danger of finding herself in a delicate situation. Please God it hadn't happened to her.

The days passed and the smooth flow of life at Castonbury Park was to be temporarily disrupted by the arrival of a small party of guests to celebrate the marriage between Araminta and Lord Antony Bennington. Such an occasion would be a useful tool in their avowed endeavour to convince the world that the Montagues were not on their uppers as some people thought.

It was an exciting time for the servants, especially for the maids. With the guests would be coachmen, grooms and perhaps the odd footman. There was speculation, too, among the menservants about the numbers of ladies' maids who would accompany their mistresses, to ensure they looked their best at all times.

As preparations got under way, beneath the frenetic rush ran a sense of gathering excitement. Mrs Stratton gathered the household staff to warn them about forming hasty liaisons with the servants of the guests. It was one thing for a maid to fall pregnant to one of the Castonbury menservants—many marriages had started that way—but it was quite another to bring a man to the altar who lived many miles away and would probably deny all responsibility.

The servants were also reminded that the esteem in which the Montague family was held would suffer if they did not work hard to ensure that this party was deemed a great success.

With her marriage to Lord Bennington only three weeks away, eager to get started on her bridal trousseau, Araminta gave herself over to the seamstresses who travelled from Buxton. Amid swirling bolts of fabric bringing a riot of colour of every imaginable shade to the room, not only was she to be fitted for a new wardrobe for her new position, they were to make her wedding gown. With Araminta standing for what seemed an eternity on a raised platform, smiling and expressing her pleasure and stating her preference, she was measured and pinned and tucked and turned.

Never had Lisette seen the like. She looked around at the dizzying array of chiffon and gossamer, sumptuous silks and soft batistes, embellished with gold and silver.

Not until Araminta had left with Ross to visit Antony Bennington at Glebe Hall was Lisette able to restore order to the room. She was in the dressing room repairing a seam on one of Araminta's gowns when they returned. Wanting to get it done she carried on sewing.

She lifted her head when she heard Ross saying, 'Will you mind going to live in Cambridgeshire, Araminta? It's important for me to know you will be happy there.'

Then came Araminta's voice answering, 'When I am married to Antony I will be content to be wherever he is. His parents are perfectly happy about the marriage and relieved we have put that unpleasant business behind us.'

'You mean the broken betrothal.'

'Yes. They are hoping very much that Antony's sister, Caroline, will make a good match too.'

'They must know someone who'd be right for her.'

'As a matter of fact they don't, but I do. I was thinking that over in the carriage on the way home.'

'And?'

'I realised I do know someone—a man who will meet her father's lofty criteria. I am in no doubt that he is the right man for her.'

'I am sure her father will thank you for that. Who is he?'

'You.'

The word hung on the air while Ross almost choked on a hearty laugh. 'Araminta, I am *not* a candidate!'

'Why not? You would be perfect.'

Lisette froze, her heartbeat suddenly too rapid and loud in her ears. It wasn't admirable, eavesdropping on anyone's conversation, but she couldn't force herself to move.

'You know, Ross,' Araminta went on, 'Caroline is exceedingly pretty, irresistible and charming and would do very well for you. The family also have connections with India which should appeal to you—I believe her uncle invested heavily in the East India Company. Now you are a colonel and you may be given more sedentary duties, you really ought to be thinking of settling down.'

'I have been thinking along those lines myself so cease your worrying.'

'What? A wife and children?' she asked, her voice excitable at the prospect.

'Precisely. I have thought about my responsibilities. To marry well, to ensure that I have at least one son, to make the future as secure as possible for my descendants, have become the primary duties of my life. I have postponed them in favour of my regiment for too long.'

'Oh, Ross, I'm so glad. Caroline is exactly the sort of wife you should have. I do so worry about you. I can't wait for you to meet her and to introduce you to the Earl and Countess of Cawood. Now go and get ready for dinner while I seek out Phaedra. I promised I would give her a full account of our visit to Glebe Hall.'

The door opened and closed again. Stunned by what she had heard, her cheeks burning and drowning in humiliation, with trembling hands Lisette dropped the work into her lap. All the fears that had engulfed her following her interview with Mrs Stratton returned with a vengeance. She sat there for a long time as the quiet of the house settled about her, feeling the burden of her lowly state more than she ever had before.

To marry well, Ross had said, for was that not expected of him, how he had been raised to think?

She had believed that when Ross took her into his arms, he had been mastered by the same attraction, and suffered the same irresistible revelation, as she had herself. She had been foolish to confuse physical desire with love. Just because a man made love to a woman with such fierce intensity didn't mean his heart was engaged. She had merely served to distract a man who, for the sake of relieving his boredom, had seduced her—and because she had known no different she had given herself gladly.

What had she done? How could she have allowed such a thing to happen? She had let herself be borne away on a tidal wave of passion. She, Lisette Napier, had succumbed like some overheated village girl, to the coercive, compelling force of Ross Montague's masculinity. For a brief eternity nothing had existed for her but him. He had drowned her reason with his kisses, playing upon her virgin senses as a master musician plucks the strings of a familiar violin, arousing her body with such skilful tenderness and breaking down every barrier of her reserve. He had made her a willing, hungry accomplice to his lusts, and for that she despised him.

It made her sick with grief and horror to think that she had been simply a toy for him. Had she snatched up the reins of her own life only to hand them over to the first man capable of putting heat in her belly? The memory of their kisses and caresses which, not so very long ago, had been so sweet, now burned her like a red-hot iron. Utterly overcome with shame and jealousy of a woman she had not even seen, a woman who would tempt him if she had the irresistible charm Araminta had spoken of, with a sick yearning in her heart she covered her face with her hands and began to cry as though her heart would break.

At some point she made it to her room to be alone with her wretched thoughts. With her back pressed against the hard wood of the door she was no longer crying, nor was there present in her that dreadful feeling of humiliation. In its stead there was a white flame of anger. It was a new emotion and was burning her up inside. It had a strength all its own, a separate mind of its own, and it was telling her what to do. She couldn't face him—not yet, not until she managed to collect herself and her battered emotions.

Eight

· ·

During the following days Lisette went out of her way to avoid Ross. When he visited his sister she would disappear into the dressing room and wait until he had left before emerging.

Putting the finishing touches to Araminta's toilet, Lisette glanced at her mistress in the looking glass, thinking how pretty she looked in a gown of lavender silk, with dozens of small buttons fastened up the back. Araminta was excited because Lord Bennington and his good friend Roland Latham were to dine with them this evening, along with his parents, Lord and Lady Latham from Glebe Hall. Mr Seagrove and his daughter, Lily, were also invited.

'What an exciting time this is,' she enthused. 'I really can't wait to marry Antony. After the wedding breakfast, Aunt Wilhelmina has decided that something must be done to entertain the guests. There will be dancing afterwards in the salon. The salon was always used as a ballroom in the past and is not used nearly enough nowadays. Aunt Wilhelmina thought that several people who do not live very far away and will not have to be accommodated should be invited.'

'That will be nice,' Lisette replied quietly, preoccupied with her thoughts and not really listening. 'What jewellery were you thinking for tonight?'

'The diamond necklace, I think, Lisette. Here, I have it already.'

Lisette draped it round Araminta's neck and fastened it securely, saying quietly, 'There is something I wish to say, Miss Araminta. It's only right that I tell you now.'

'Why, what is it, Lisette?' Araminta asked, admiring the necklace in the mirror. 'You do look serious.'

'I—I have heard from my father's lawyer. It would appear that he has left me a small legacy.'

Araminta met her eyes in the glass and smiled broadly, genuinely pleased for her. 'Why, that's wonderful.'

'Yes, it is—only I've decided that when you marry Lord Bennington, I won't be going with you to Cambridgeshire. I intend to resign my post.'

Araminta swung round on the dressing stool and looked straight up at her, disappointment clouding her eyes. 'But— Oh, Lisette! I will be so sorry to lose you.' She stiffened and gave her a sharp look. 'Has something untoward happened to you?'

'No, not at all,' Lisette hastened to assure her, hoping she sounded convincing. She could not bear it if Araminta learned she had overheard their conversation and Ross's eagerness to become acquainted with Caroline Bennington.

'Must you leave?'

'Yes. My mind is made up.'

'But…what will you do? Where will you go? You told me you have no family of your own.'

'That is true. I've decided to go back to India. I don't know yet what I will do. I'll decide when I get there.'

'I see—well, what can I say? You have clearly made up your mind.'

'Yes, yes, I have. But, for the present, I prefer no one else to know.'

'Not even Ross? I should tell him what you intend.'

'No—please. I would rather he didn't know—at least, not yet—not until I've made my plans. I will tell him myself when I am ready.'

'You know, Lisette, I did think that you might have feelings for Ross—not that anything could have come of it.'

Lisette straightened up, once more reminded of her lowly station. 'No, Miss Araminta,' she uttered stiffly. 'Colonel Montague is your brother—my employer. That is all he is and all he will ever be. We may have a shared interest in India, but nothing more than that.'

'Of course not. I—I'm sorry, I didn't mean to imply anything or give offence—but I shall be sorry to lose you, truly.'

Lisette's expression softened and she smiled. 'Yes. I shall be sorry to leave.'

Lisette was leaving Araminta's rooms when she saw Ross's imposing figure walking towards her. He was elegantly attired in evening clothes, the dark fabric of his coat moulding his powerful shoulders.

Ross smiled when his eyes lit on her, thinking she looked so fresh and lovely, it almost took his breath away. He found her slender body more than capable of arousing him. The sudden tautness of his own body whenever he came near her proclaimed louder than words how much he was attracted to Lisette, and how difficult he was finding it to control his physical reactions to her. Their lovemaking had been unique in his experience, satisfying him totally yet leaving him longing for more.

When she was close that tender spot at the curve of her neck looked so appealing that when she was within reach, throwing caution to the winds, he gave in to the urge to taste it. Lightly grasping her arms, he planted a swift butterfly kiss on her silken skin.

When she gave a start and pulled away, he grinned with quick, boyish warmth. 'Where have you been hiding yourself? I've missed you, Lisette.'

He thought she had simply been startled by his intimate gesture, but Lisette visibly stiffened at his words. She didn't seem at all pleased to see him. When she quickly averted her gaze, his grin faded.

Lisette had been startled by Ross's brief caress. Casting a nervous glance around her to be sure no one else had seen his kiss, she turned away from him. The words she had so unfortunately overheard were still spinning in her mind. Ross wanted only what she could give him—the means to slake his physical lust. He had done that. She wouldn't humiliate herself further by letting him know how much she craved his kisses, his touch.

'I have not been hiding,' she replied stiffly, forcing the words past the tightness in her throat, trying not to be intimidated by his towering masculine presence. 'I've been kept extremely busy of late—as I am sure you will understand.'

Her tone, her very posture, was cool and aloof. Ross peered

down at her, trying to read her expression. He was puzzled and frankly astonished that after all the exquisite passion she had shown him, she had suddenly turned cold. Her response disturbed him, as had the way she'd flinched at his touch. He wasn't sure what had happened, but he didn't like to consider the possibilities.

The corner of his mouth twisted wryly in a gesture that was not quite a smile. 'You do not look pleased to see me. I presume our relationship gives me the right to speak to you privately.'

'This is not the time.'

He regarded her darkly, his gaze narrowed and assessing. 'Then do you mind telling me when it is the right time?'

'There isn't one. It is best if we do not meet again like this while the house is full of guests.'

'Lisette, would you mind telling me what is going on?' She wasn't merely objecting to seeing him, she didn't appear to want to at all. 'Is there some problem I don't know about?'

Lisette managed to return his gaze briefly. 'Problem?' she asked quietly. 'I don't know what you mean.'

A muscle flexed in his jaw. 'The way you're behaving—so stiff and formal. I thought after...'

'Am I being stiff? I didn't realise.' If she sounded cool, perhaps even haughty, then she was glad. Glad that Ross couldn't see what an effort it was to be so close to him.

'I think you do. I am glad to find you haven't lost your tongue,' he commented, a wry note in his voice.

'Of course I haven't. It's where it's always been.'

'You are angry. I can see it in your eyes.'

Lisette's heart slammed against her breastbone and all her new-found confidence was in danger of deserting her. There was something in his eyes, something in his voice, that hurt, that made her remember the woman she had been before she had met him, a woman blissfully unaware of how heartbreak felt. She drew a deep, steadying breath. That woman was gone, and the woman who had taken her place was not going to feel any pain because of him.

'Surely you did not seek me out to comment on my eyes.'

He searched her face, hesitating a long moment before he replied. 'Would you like to meet me later? Somewhere private where we can talk.'

'No,' she replied.

'No? What do you mean, no?'

'I won't meet you. I fear I have so much to do that I shall be quite weary later. I shall retire as soon as Miss Araminta is in bed.'

'I see.' His eyes began to flash quietly and his face hardened. 'Please excuse me.'

She walked on, thinking that she'd managed to cover her hurt well—until she reached her room and couldn't stop her tears.

Ross watched her back as she walked away, tempted to go after her. Instead he went to find Giles. Together they would greet the guests due to arrive shortly.

The evening was a pleasant one for everyone except Ross, who was quietly seething following his encounter with Lisette. Sherry was served in the drawing room as the guests arrived, though most of the gentlemen preferred to take a glass of brandy to crisp the stomach before dinner. Antony Bennington, Lord and Lady Latham and their son, Roland, a handsome brown-haired young gentleman who had been at school with Antony, were the first to arrive. In their early sixties, Lord Latham was a tall angular man, his wife small and on the plump side.

Antony's parents, the Earl and Countess of Cawood, due to arrive in the next few days, were to stay with the Lathams at Glebe Hall.

Ross was both proud and delighted with the way Araminta greeted their visitors with charm and self-assurance. It was almost as if she had suddenly matured, as if tonight marked the end of her life as a girl and the beginning of her life as a wife. He noted how Antony watched her, too, with adoring eyes. With the incident at the Dog and Partridge Inn behind them, Ross had no qualms about Araminta marrying this tall, fair-haired young man.

The conversation was merry, with Ross, seated next to Araminta, and Giles at the end of the table outdoing each other in telling tales of their experiences in India and Spain. Araminta, too, was in high spirits as she quipped across the table with her adored Antony and Mr Seagrove and Lily on Giles's right, who wanted to know how preparations were progressing for the wedding.

'You will officiate, Mr Seagrove?' Wilhelmina said. 'Araminta has a notion to be married in the chapel here at Castonbury Park.'

'I shall be happy to, Mrs Landes-Fraser. Here or at St Mary's in the village—it will be an honour. It is only fitting that Araminta should be married in the family chapel. I hope it won't be too long before I can officiate at my own daughter's wedding.' He twinkled a smile at Lily.

'It won't,' Giles said, giving his betrothed an adoring look.

Ross had fallen silent, content to listen to what was being

said. Becoming distracted, he reached for the glass of wine Lumsden had placed before him, looking at Lily. He imagined another young woman seated at the table, with hair as black as Lily's, though her eyes were amber and her skin golden. Despite her lowly rank Lisette was undoubtedly a lady, regal in her bearing and possessing the unconscious grace of a true thoroughbred. For Ross she represented everything most desirable in a woman. The thought was pleasing to him, but he knew his family would think differently and refuse to countenance even the idea of such an association with a girl they would consider lowlier than a vicar's foundling daughter.

He was deeply troubled by Lisette's cold attitude towards him earlier. What the hell had gotten into her? Whatever it was he intended to find out.

Ross was leaving his rooms the next day when he saw Lisette carrying some clean linen to his sister's room. Ross was unable to resist a moment in which to question her about her behaviour the previous day and to recapture that enchantment they had known in the barn.

'Lisette!'

The blood drained from Lisette's face when she saw Ross bearing down on her with a look of wrath. Letting out a small cry she turned to retrace her steps, but before she could do so, his hand was planted on her elbow.

'Don't you dare,' he warned. 'Come with me. We are going to go somewhere private where we can discuss what the hell this is all about.'

She twisted free, scorched by his touch. 'Don't,' she exploded, her body shaking with wrath. 'Why guard my sensibilities now when you've made a laughingstock of me since the day we met. Why stop now?'

He caught her elbow and none too gently drew her into his bedroom and closed the door behind them. Relieving her of the pile of linen he deposited it on a chair.

'What do you think you are doing?' Lisette tried to push past him but taking her arm he pressed her back against the hard wood of the door. 'Let go of me, damn you,' she cried, trying to prise his arm out of the way. Being so close to him caused her heart to pound with wild confusion and her foolish body to react much as it had when they had made love. In fact, her burning reaction to him was even worse now. His smell was that of pure, potent masculinity, and when she planted her hand on his chest to try to push him away once more, she felt the heat of his body through his clothes.

'Such language,' he drawled, his eyes glittering with reproach as he refused to release his hold. 'This is no way to greet your lover, Lisette.'

He looked much too large and darkly threatening to Lisette. 'You are not my lover,' she retorted, her magnificent eyes shining with tears of humiliation and wrath.

'Lisette,' he chided softly. 'You are mine. Do not doubt it.'

'The devil I am! I belong to no man—and you should not have dragged me in here. I have things to do.'

'They can wait.' A glint of wicked intentions passed behind his eyes. Staring down at her in chilly, fierce reproach, he lowered his head, his lips hovering close to hers.

But Lisette wouldn't allow it. While she still had some small vestige of sanity she had to end this madness. Though her treacherous female body was ready to arch itself to accommodate his, gathering all her emotions into a tight, hard knot of pride, she struggled free.

Ross eyed her warily, unable to understand what had got into her, so sure had he been in his belief that her need must be as great as his and she would soon respond to his warm, moist mouth and searching hands.

'Please don't do this,' she said, her voice trembling with fury. 'How dare you think you can drag me down whenever the fancy takes you. I'm not some—some loose woman who'll lie down for you as you seem to think.'

Her words pulled Ross up sharp and he just stared at her. 'Well. Well,' he said at length, unable to believe all his romantic plans were being demolished. 'It seems I've found myself a little spitfire. The perfect servant, eh? I knew there was more to you than meets the eye.' His brows creased. 'My desire for you is hard driven, Lisette. Do not push me away. What is this about, and why have you been avoiding me?'

It was his voice that made her want to lay her head against his chest and weep, that beautiful deep voice, and his face— that harsh, handsome face she adored. It was as though she had been living all these weeks in a fantasy world, a world where dreams would come to fruition if she was only patient, a world where his loving had lulled her into a false belief. How could she have been such a credulous fool? To give in to him now would be to sacrifice her independence, which, she realised now, she had fought for and won, even if it was only as a servant, and little by little would be completely possessed by him, completely absorbed, and it terrified her.

'Please don't ask me—don't question me. Let it be enough when I tell you it is over.' Lisette meant it. She couldn't let him see how desperately she was in love with him, how her heart yearned for a reciprocated love, not this one-sided affair where all the emotion seemed to be on her side, and where all his tenderness was simply borne out of a man's natural lust for a woman. 'What we did should never have happened.'

His brows snapped together in an ominous frown. 'Are you saying you regret what we did?'

Lisette swallowed painfully and nodded, averting her eyes. 'Yes,' she lied. 'Yes, I do. Now let go of me.'

'Did I displease you? Is that what all this is about?'

In a voice fraught with emotion, she said, 'How can any woman be displeased with you? Looking as you do and with such impeccable credentials, I have no doubt you are the dream of every woman living in Derbyshire.'

'Is that the way you feel about me?'

Lisette groaned within herself. If only he knew how her heart ached for him, he wouldn't even consider asking that question.

'Let me look at you, Lisette,' he cajoled gently, but when she complied by lifting her head, his brows gathered in perplexity. The tears glistening in the long silken lashes were difficult to ignore. Laying a lean hand alongside her cheek, he gently wiped away a droplet with his thumb. 'What is troubling you so much you feel the need to cry?'

Embarrassed because she couldn't contain her emotions, she responded with a frantic shake of her head. 'I'm not.'

His hand moved to the tender column of her throat, and he came to marvel at the rapid pulse he felt beneath his palm. She was far more upset than she wanted to admit. 'Then why are your lashes wet? If they aren't tears, then what would you have me believe they are?'

Lisette recognised the threat of her emotions welling forth

in greater volume and tried to turn her head aside, but his hand, gentle yet unyielding, remained on her throat, refusing to allow her to escape his close inspection. She could do nothing but submit to his probing gaze.

'Please, Ross, let me go.'

'I will when you tell me the cause for your dejection,' he bargained gently.

Forcing his hand away she walked to the centre of the room and whirled on him, her hands clenched into fists at her sides. 'Why can't you let it be? Why do you have to keep chipping away at me? I've said all I want to say on the subject. I really don't want to talk about this now. My tears have nothing to do with what happened between us.'

'On the contrary, Lisette. I think what we did is at the very heart of your despondency, and if you'd care to enlighten me, I'd be most grateful.'

'No,' she uttered sharply. 'The fact is that I have changed since...' She cast her gaze downward to avoid his eyes. 'I dislike the situation and I have decided that it would be for the best if we put it behind us. Henceforth you may go your way without giving me a thought. I want no more of it. *Indeed*, I can bear no more of it.'

'You're not being rational,' Ross argued striding towards her. Reaching out a hand, he rested it gently upon her forearm as he sought to calm her. 'I must get to the bottom of this. I have no intention of ending our relationship unless I have reason to believe that your contempt for me—if that is indeed what it is—is beyond the measure I can bear. Come, my love. You'll feel different if you just let me hold you.'

'No, I won't! I'll feel exactly the way I do now!' she cried, throwing off his hand. 'Except that I will hate myself a little bit more.' Her voice broke with emotion as she demanded, 'Please! And don't call me your love. I'm not your love—nor have I ever been.'

'Lisette, for pity's sake—be reasonable,' Ross pleaded, and tried to draw her towards him.

'I'm freeing you from any commitment you may feel towards me,' she declared resolutely, shrugging free. 'As far as I am concerned there is no more to be said. You have to understand that it is finished between us!'

Elevating a dark brow and folding his arms to restrain his hands from touching her, he continued to gaze down at her. His eyes narrowed, because he could not link the figure standing before him with the lovely young woman who had loved him with such passion—a transition had taken place.

'Do you think that making love to you meant nothing to me, you foolish girl?' he said abruptly, his lips curling in slight mockery. 'Do I look like a man who is playing games? The hell I am! How dare you dismiss me without any sort of explanation? Exactly whom, Miss Lisette Napier, do you think you're dealing with?'

Lisette fought the urge to shrink from his show of bluster and forced herself to sound as calm as possible. 'I know precisely who I'm dealing with. That's the trouble. We do not suit, Ross. We have been fooling ourselves.'

'Why?' he demanded.

'Because we are too different. We have been through this before. I don't want to have to go through it again.'

'And neither do I.'

'Why do you want me?' she cried. 'There are plenty of women prettier than me in your world.'

'I don't care about them any more than you care for my status. I want *you*,' he added, even more decisively as he began prowling towards her.

'For what purpose?' she exclaimed. 'Wouldn't it be best to find a woman who doesn't work in your household?'

He shrugged, dismissing her question. 'I don't care about any of that. It is you I want. You are the most delightful lover any man could be fortunate enough to take to his bed.'

Lisette clamped her jaw and glared at him, his casual remark raising her ire to the fore. 'And that is precisely what I am—your lover, Ross, and I will be your lover no longer.'

'Lover? Good God, woman! You make it sound as though I chose you as I would a decent hunter—because you had a beautiful face and figure and the kind of nature that would suit my purposes admirably. I didn't *choose* you, Lisette. What man in his right mind would choose a woman whose acquisition creates nothing but problems? The truth of it is that I was attracted to you from the first. I couldn't help myself.'

'So you admit that by association I will bring you nothing but grief, which is what I have been saying. This is why it cannot go on. I cannot believe I let you do what you did to me, but all I can do is pray for forgiveness for my lapse from grace. Now will you allow me to take my leave or do I have to shout for help?'

She threw back her head and Ross was alarmed to see not only rage but what looked like a mixture of contempt and... was it anguish? His jaw hardened. He unfolded his arms and his long, lean, handsome body rose to its full height.

'Very well, but may I ask what has brought about this temper you are in?'

'*Temper*? I wasn't in a temper until you dragged me into your bedroom.'

'How else was I to speak to you?' They wanted each other, they both admitted that with brutal honesty, so why the hell were they glaring at each other with what seemed to be hatred? They were both free and could do as they pleased so why was she making it so complicated?

'Why are you going over this again?' he asked, and even as he spoke his mind his senses were bemused by the way the light from the window shone in the blackness of her hair neatly coiled into a chignon in her nape. The heat of her anger had also put a flush beneath the creamy smoothness of her skin and her amber eyes blazed at him from beneath the fine arch of her brows. 'I thought we'd had all this out. I have told you it is not important.'

'It is to me.' Lisette felt her heart contract with pain, and tremors seemed to flow into every part of her body. She loved him so, she knew that now, more than her own life, and yet it would soon be over and she would never see him again.

'Don't struggle like this, Lisette. Don't fight me. I am not your enemy. I want nothing more than to help you—to love you.'

'That's the trouble, Ross. That's how I got into this—this dilemma.'

He looked at her sharply as a thought struck him. 'Are you with child? Is that what this is all about?'

She almost laughed as she stared at him. After the talking to Mrs Stratton had given her, she was amazed at having escaped the consequences of her transgression. 'There will be no child, Ross.' What she would have done faced with such a predicament she had no idea. At least now she could move on. 'I can't afford you! Your *help*, as you like to call it, has cost me my reputation and my good name.'

'And for that you blame me?' His eyes were colder than an icy winter sky and there was a thin, white line about his mouth. He watched her, his anger fierce and knife-edged, hating her, loving her, wanting her. His voice softened for a moment, since he adored the very ground she walked on, but when he put out a hand to restrain her she shook him off and backed away.

'I am not blaming you. All I am saying is that it should not have happened—*I* should not have let it happen. Whatever you have to say to me I don't want to hear it. I don't want you to come near me again. Ever. Get on with your life and I will get on with mine.'

His nostrils flared, and he responded with a violence to match her own. 'You dare to speak to me like that! You forget, Lisette—'

'Forget! Can I ever forget that this is pretence? Can I ever forget your noble birth or your military rank? Yet I do dare to say that what we had is over. I am no lady, but I have been your equal in love, and for this I dare to tell you how I feel.'

He stalked towards her, tall, formidably muscular. He stared at her, intensely, the hard lines of his jaw and cheekbones starkly etched. 'Don't do this, Lisette. A word of warning. If you send me away I won't come back. I'm not a man to beg.'

'Don't threaten me. I will not be threatened. There is a saying, Ross—we live and learn—and I have been very slow to learn, lacking in experience you understand. But if I have learned anything at all, it is never to make the same mistake twice.'

'Damn you, Lisette.' He thrust his face, which had become hard and uncompromising, into hers, his rage growing, his frustration at her unwillingness to listen boiling inside him.

'Since you are clearly not as enamoured of me as I so foolishly thought, I trust you will not object if I find someone more amenable.'

'Do that, and I wish you joy in her.'

'Oh, I assure you I shall.' His voice was mocking and his eyes gleamed sardonically, though he was still white-lipped with anger. 'And you can go about your business carrying that pride and bloody determination on your shoulders for all I care.'

'Leave me alone,' she said, turning away. She did not want to hear any more for she could feel her weak woman's body straining towards him, yearning to give in, to lean against his strong male body, to have him enfold her in his strong arms. 'I have nothing more to say to you.' Picking up the linen she strode out of the room.

To Ross she looked like a young queen, with her head held high and proud, her body moving with unconscious grace. He watched her in silence, feeling the familiar, hot need for her rising in his loins, the longing he'd felt for days to seek her out and gather her into his arms and lose himself in her. He went back into his room, but he was unable to shake off the image of a tempestuous beauty with blazing amber eyes and a face alive with fury and disdain. The picture became etched on his mind along with a voice that trembled with emotion. She'd actually looked and sounded as if she meant everything she'd said to him, and he was still puzzled as to the reason why.

As Lisette walked away from him, it was strange, but all the anger had gone from her. There was a coldness in her, an empty coldness. All the strength seemed to be draining out of her. She did not feel the need to cry, but a great need to sleep, to shun this life and dream that she was back in India with her parents, with her days filled with simple happiness and pleasures—before she had ever come across the man called Ross Montague.

There was great excitement and rushing about as more guests began to arrive. The housemaids were given the lowly task of ensuring the fires in the guest bedrooms were kept alight, coal scuttles replenished and hearths kept clean. They were also to ensure that washbasins were emptied and cleaned, water jugs kept filled and hot water carried upstairs for baths. The footmen who weren't employed doing other duties did the heavy carrying.

It was a particularly busy time for Lisette. Not only had she Araminta to take care of, she was called on to stand in and wait on some of the other ladies who had come without their maids. Once they left their rooms to partake in the celebrations, her duties became far less onerous.

Everything was planned and when the first of the guests arrived, a happy feeling of excitement pervaded the house—an unusual feeling nowadays because of the time spent in mourning two of its sons.

In the domestic quarters the air was heavy with the smells of cooking and there was a din of clattering pans and shouted orders. Monsieur André, his darkly handsome face flushed with heat and hurry and wearing a pristine white apron, was preparing dinner at a huge table with the aid of half a dozen young kitchen maids.

He was hailed as a genius by everyone upstairs and downstairs. He could cook an egg in fifty different ways. He was considered economical because he could produce an inexhaustible variety of dishes without any waste of ingredients, and the elegance and piquancy of flavours which are necessary to stimulate the appetites of all. His attention was chiefly directed to the stew pan, in the manufacture of stews, fricassées, fricandeaus and the like.

Overseeing this apparent chaos from a gallery, which was reached by a servants' corridor from the main part of the house, was Mrs Stratton. She stood watching the frenetic activity with an unperturbed expression, satisfied that everything was in order and perfectly organised to her experienced eye, and that the guests' meal would be ready on time.

In the servants' hall Lisette accepted a glass of Madeira from Mrs Stratton. She was seated at the table from which the servants' evening meal had been cleared away, with her workbox beside her and her sewing in her lap.

Suddenly the door swung open with a clatter as a couple of young footmen carrying a tray loaded with plates and cutlery marched in. They looked very handsome in livery of knee breeches and silk stockings. Becca, a young scullery maid, took one of the trays and carried it to the sink.

'Are they a pleasant lot?' she asked, not really interested, for being a scullery maid she never got to see any of the guests.

'They're all the same to me,' Sandy, one of the footmen replied. 'Lady Kate's just turned up,' he said, placing an untouched pyramid of grapes on the table and giving Faith a teasing wink. 'I see she's still got Miss Fisher in tow. Smithins will be delighted, I don't think! She breezed in and strode after her mistress as if she owns the place.'

A pained look crossed Mrs Stratton's face. 'Oh, dear! No change there, then.'

'Fat chance,' Sandy said, popping a succulent green grape

into his mouth, which earned him a frown of disapproval from the housekeeper.

'Lady Kate was expected back today or tomorrow so I've had a fire lit to warm the room. I'll go up and see her when she's settled. I doubt she'll want to join the guests so I'll prepare her a tray and have Daisy take it up—unless Miss Fisher comes down for one.' Getting to her feet she fingered the keys on her belt. 'Are the ladies in the drawing room?'

'They'll soon be coming out, Mrs Stratton.'

She looked at Lisette and Faith. 'In that case, you two will be needed upstairs by your mistresses.'

Picking up her workbox, going ahead of Faith, who stopped to have a word with Sandy the footman, who was her beau, Lisette left the kitchen and began the long walk to her mistress's room. It had been another long day and it wasn't over yet. The servants were all very tired, but they still had the task to finish clearing up after the guests and the family, and it would be a long time before some of them went to bed.

She climbed the narrow flight of carpetless stairs used only by the servants. It came out on the top of the main staircase. Closing the door behind her she paused and looked over the banister to the bottom of the grand staircase. Some of the ladies were taking coffee in the conservatory to the right of the stairs.

She was about to move on but paused when Ross appeared. She knew she should go about her business but she had never seen such fashionable, glittering ladies and gentleman. Her gaze remained fixed on Ross. As she looked down at his lean, undeniably elegant form, her feet remained glued to the top of the stairs.

He was talking to Caroline Bennington, who beamed up at him. This young woman Araminta would so like to become romantically involved with her brother was incredibly lovely. Golden haired and with sparkling green eyes, her small and slender form attired in a cream silk gown, any man would have to be blind and insensible not to be drawn to her.

Ross was holding a glass of champagne in his hand—the same hand that not so long ago had caressed every inch of her body, and his lazy white smile was as devastatingly attractive as ever. Attired in formal black evening clothes with a white waistcoat and frilled white shirt, he looked quite splendid.

Suddenly, as if he could feel her gaze, he looked up and checked at the sight of her looking down. His eyes looked straight into Lisette's and she felt a tremor of alarm as he contemplated her. Unaware of the storm that was raging in the young maid's breast, he inclined his head ever so slightly before placing his hand beneath Lady Caroline's elbow and steering her into the conservatory.

Recollecting herself, Lisette melted into the shadows.

Staring fixedly ahead, concentrating on what Caroline was saying proved difficult, because Ross couldn't stop thinking about Lisette. Whenever she was in a room with him, he had trouble keeping his eyes off her. When she was absent, he couldn't seem to keep his mind off her. He'd wanted her from the moment she'd jumped in front of his out of control horse.

No, he thought, he'd felt something for her even before that—from their meeting in India, when he'd thought she was an Indian girl, wearing a star-spangled sari. He loved her intelligence and her unaffected warmth. He loved the way she felt in his arms, and the way her mouth tasted. He loved her spirit and her fire and her sweetness, and her honesty. My God, that he should feel this way about her, that he should love her!

After a succession of meaningless affairs, he had finally found a woman he wanted, a woman who wanted only him. He'd known that from the very first and his instinct told him she hadn't changed, no matter how much she proclaimed otherwise. He was so stricken with the innocence of her, that he could not rouse himself to seek relief in someone else's bed.

In the days before the wedding, the house party rode and hunted and jaunted off to nearby Castonbury village and further afield to explore the delights and drink the waters at the spa in Buxton. The evenings were filled with sumptuous feasts cooked by Monsieur André, brilliant conversation, cards and for some of the gentlemen a game of billiards.

It was a beautiful sunny morning for the wedding. The ceremony was conducted in the thirteenth century church which stood in its own grounds at the back of the house. It contained monuments and effigies which reflected the ancient lineage of the Montague family.

Since it had been impossible to invite some of their friends and omit others, and because the family was only recently out of mourning, the decision had been made to limit the wedding guests to immediate family only, which avoided offending the sensibilities of friends and made it a quiet, intimate affair. But the villagers had conspired amongst themselves to gather together and waited in the grounds of the church to see the bride and groom as they emerged as man and wife.

Araminta had insisted that Lisette be among the privileged servants to occupy the back of the church to watch the ceremony. Having straightened the bride's train and handed her her bouquet of pale pink roses, trying hard not to look at Ross, whose presence was like a tangible force, powerful and magnetic, Lisette hurriedly took her place between Lumsden and Faith, who was craning her neck so she wouldn't miss the moment when Miss Araminta entered the church beneath the chevron-moulded arch.

The duke and Mrs Landes-Fraser, Lily Seagrove and the bride's cousins, Lady Phaedra and Lady Kate, occupied the box pews in the chancel to watch the proceedings. The groom and his best man faced Reverend Seagrove, waiting patiently for the bride to appear.

'Here comes the bride,' Faith whispered when the music soared.

Like everyone else, Lisette was caught up in the moment. Every head turned to look at Araminta as she walked slowly down the knave, her hand tucked into her brother's arm.

'Oh, isn't she simply beautiful?' A woman sighed.

'Exquisite. And did you ever see such a gown?' whispered another as the bride passed the south transept which housed an alabaster tomb chest with lifesize figures of a knight and his lady. 'All ivory gauze and silver lace… Oh, and just look at her bouquet.'

Lisette paid little attention to the comments of those around her—had she not dressed the bride in her finery? She was staring at Ross as he walked his sister slowly down the aisle, his tall, muscular frame moving with that easy, natural elegance already so familiar to her. His attire was simple but beautifully cut—light grey trousers, a plum-coloured cut-away coat, black satin waistcoat and crisp white neck linen. As he walked, smiling and bowing his dark head to those he passed, for one unwelcome instant Lisette felt the barbs of envy pricking her heart when his eyes seemed to linger for an exceedingly long moment on Lady Caroline Bennington.

But for the whims of fate, Lisette thought bitterly, she might have been the one to receive his admiring gaze. It was almost as if she had suddenly and cruelly been made aware that the prize to which her own soul had secretly aspired had just been handed over to someone else.

The ceremony went smoothly, and when Reverend Seagrove announced Araminta and Antony were now man and wife, a collective sigh went through those present, joyous smiles dawned brightly and eyes misted with tears.

When the wedding breakfast had been cleared away, the company rested and readied themselves for the evening's festivities, a steady stream of luxurious conveyances, mostly containing local gentry, began to arrive at the house, waiting to pull up before the brightly lit facade to unload their passengers.

'It looks like a Grecian temple,' one female guest was heard to remark as she was led by her escort up the immense stone steps and entered the house through the great north portico to be confronted by the marble hall designed to be no less impressive than the exterior. Pinks and greens had been chosen for the ceiling, with panels of military trophies and arabesques.

The gown of duck-egg blue trimmed with lace slithered over Araminta's head. The neckline was extremely low, showing off the tops of her small white breasts. Lisette stood back to cast a critical eye over her handiwork. Then she smiled and stood back to admire her mistress.

'You look a picture, my lady. Your husband will be quite dazzled by the sight of you. I doubt he'll allow anyone else a dance.'

'Oh, I do hope so, Lisette. I'm so excited,' she said, dancing to the door but hurrying back when she remembered her reticule. 'Wish me luck,' she breathed before whirling about and rushing off to find her new husband.

Watching her go, a pang of envy wrenched Lisette's heart. Lisette was just twenty years old—her birthday had come and gone. She was young. How she wished she could go to the ball, to laugh and have fun—to dance in Ross's arms.

But it was not for her.

When the dancing was under way, several of the servants found their way to the salon to take a peek at the gentry enjoying themselves. It was a beautiful room, a high-domed rotunda, contained behind the triumphal arch of the south front. Like the marble hall it rose to the full height of the house with rosettes carved on the dome. Lisette stood on her tiptoes among the jostling press in riveted curiosity, trying to peer over Daisy's head to see through the crack in the door to the brilliantly lit salon. What she saw took her breath.

'Heavens,' she breathed, never having seen the like.

Splendidly dressed couples were dancing the waltz on the wooden sprung floor, and urns and plinths were placed in alcoves. Red silk damask chairs and settees were designed to echo the curves of the walls, ringed just now by a colourful array of local belles and beaux.

Catching sight of Ross dancing with Lady Caroline Bennington, Lisette's heart sank. His dark head was bent close to the lady's beautiful face—whispering pretty compliments, no doubt—and she was simpering and pouting and fluttering her eyelashes with all the vivacity of a born flirt. Lisette felt the pain in her chest where her heart lay—the bitter pain caused by the malevolent pangs of jealousy. *He doesn't even know I'm here*, she thought. Abruptly she closed the door and gave her attention to finding her way back to the kitchen and ignoring her sinking heart.

Nine

The servants had their own special celebration. Several bottles of sherry had been brought up from the cellar to toast the happy couple. When Lord Giles and Colonel Ross Montague strode into the kitchen, they could see that already several glasses had been drunk. Normally the household staff conformed to a rigid, centuries-old hierarchy, with the head butler and the housekeeper at the pinnacle of it, but it was obvious to the two gentlemen that the consummation of liquor had been something of an equaliser.

Their appearance in the servants' hall caused quite a stir. Lisette's gaze riveted on Ross the instant he came into view, and the sight of him had the devastating impact of a boulder crashing into her chest. She had not expected him to appear among them and wondered what all this was about. Of late she had made sure he only saw her from a distance—she had learned the art of disappearing when he was about and in a house the size of Castonbury with its hidden corridors used by the servants to remain invisible, it wasn't difficult.

Standing across the room between a chambermaid and a laundress, with servants in their various household uniforms in front of her, gave her a chance to study him. The overall expression of his masculine face was one of intensity and precision. Looking at him now—and she could see she was not the only one—with his thick black hair, deep blue eyes and tall, athletic physique, Ross Montague was magnificent. Lisette seemed to forget all about telling him to leave her alone, and she found herself falling under his unfathomable spell much as she had experienced before.

'We are not here to disrupt your festivities,' Ross intoned, 'in fact, quite the opposite.' As his gaze swept the room, as though his brooding eyes and deep velvety voice could mesmerise any unsuspecting victim, he was like a snake charmer Lisette had once seen in the bazaar in Delhi. 'We hope you are all enjoying yourselves.' He turned to Lumsden. 'Have some champagne opened for everyone to toast the happy couple, will you, Lumsden? Carry on.'

When the fiddler began scraping a sprightly tune, becoming caught up in the moment, Giles laughingly gathered a surprised Mrs Stratton in his arms and began waltzing her around the floor to the amused delight of everyone present. Joining in the spirit of the occasion, footmen and maids alike grabbed a partner and joined them.

The company neatly under his control, Ross glanced oh-so-casually at Lisette, a discreet glimmer of devilry in his eyes. Lisette shook her head at him in bewilderment, wishing she could melt into the background and slip through the door into the passage beyond, but he was not going to let her escape. His wicked smile in answer to her thoughts and his slight, private nod merely seemed to say to her, *Oh, no, Lisette, you're not going to escape me now.*

Obviously he'd decided that both he and she were wasting their time on differences, and he was playing an amusing game designed to either divert her or discomfit her entirely, she wasn't certain which. He deftly steered his way towards her. Watching him, Lisette could not help admiring his bold, confident walk, as if he could march through fire and not get burned.

When he finally stood in front of her, the subtle scent of his tangy cologne wafting over her, her nerves had wound taut, coiled tight in her stomach. She was deeply and embarrassingly conscious of every eye in the room focused on her. She wanted to say something but she now found herself tongue-tied.

'Miss Napier. My sister would like to share her happiness with everyone at Castonbury, which is why we came down. She also insisted that I dance with you.'

He stood very still. Lisette lowered her eyes. Had she not done so she might have seen the flicker of victory in his eyes and then the sly satisfaction that curved his lips. Knowing she could not possibly refuse, she allowed him to lead her into the dance, where he swept her up into his arms.

'You should not have done this,' she whispered.

'No?' he murmured, both raven eyebrows arching high now. 'And why not, pray? I could think of no other way of getting you to come to me.'

'But…you sought me out?'

'And you could not refuse to dance with me.'

'Yes, I could.'

He smiled with mild amusement. 'And regretted doing so.

You should have gauged by now that I am capable of removing obstacles in my way.'

'You shouldn't have singled me out. As if things aren't difficult enough for me. Already I am the subject of gossip. My life will be impossible now.' He gazed down into her eyes with that same thoughtful expression she'd noticed before. He seemed to peer down into her very soul.

'I'm sorry our affair has had adverse effects on your standing, Lisette, but what is life without a little danger?' he countered, flashing her a dangerous smile. 'We have both had our share.'

'Yes, indeed. And you expected me to dance with you as a reward for rescuing me from a raging river?'

'My dear, Lisette. If I had done it for the reward,' he murmured, his warm breath caressing her face and his hand tightening about her waist, 'I promise you, I would be asking for more than a dance.'

The sheer wickedness of the slow lazy smile he gave her made her catch her breath against the tightness of her buttoned bodice. All of a sudden she longed to be rid of it, rid of all her clothing, when he looked at her that way. Her strong determination to distance herself from him, which she thought had worked when they had last spoken days ago, was completely overwhelmed by his palpable expertise, and she thought again of what it was like to have him make love to her, to caress and kiss her body into insensibility—and she was tempted.

Looking down at her, all soft, entreating woman in his arms, drugging his senses with the sudden familiar scent and feel of her, he remembered the one time he had made love to her—how could he forget, for it had been the most wildly erotic, satisfying sexual encounter of his life? He had marvelled at the heady, primitive sensuality of her, real and uncontrived.

'Come to me later, Lisette.' His voice was low and husky, his eyes compelling with his need.

Until this moment Lisette had felt strong in her determination to abide by her decision to steer well clear of him, but she was so happy to see him, so achingly thrilled to have him this close, and so much in love with him, that nothing else seemed to matter. Yet the words he used sent a chill coursing along her spine. She struggled to free herself from the trance-like state induced by the intoxicating closeness of this strangely irresistible man and the touch of his hand holding hers, filling her with conflicting emotions.

'But I said…'

'I know what you said and why you said it, and now I want you to forget it,' he murmured in the lazy, sensual drawl that always made her heart melt.

'But I don't want—'

'Yes, you do,' he said, wanting to give her a shake to make his full meaning sink in. She met his gaze and he smiled, content in his belief that he had measured the weakness of her character in the strength of her passion. 'There is no gulf between us that cannot be bridged. What we feel for each other cannot be denied. You *will* be mine tonight. We both know it, so do not fight me, Lisette,' he said softly, his voice a caress. 'I know you too well. I know how you feel.'

'Please leave me alone,' she whispered, her cheeks hot, her pulse racing as she tried to control her emotions.

'I'll *never* leave you alone.'

He spoke softly, holding her with his gaze, knowing that she, too, was a victim of the overwhelming forces at work between them. She stared back at him, and he was sure he heard a soft moan escape her.

Lisette wished she were alone with him, away from all these people with their knowing eyes and judgemental looks. She wanted to fling herself into his arms and kiss his mouth, his face, his neck, as if nothing in the world existed for her but him. Shocked by the unladylike drift of her imaginings, she warded off the wayward thoughts before she could complete them. She studied his lips for a second, then shook off the shiver of awareness that ran through her body. And then the dance ended. Releasing her, taking her hand, he lifted it to his mouth and pressed the palm against his lips.

'Later, Lisette. I *will* see you later.'

Then he turned and with Giles left the hall, satisfied that Lisette would do as he asked.

In the beginning he had deeply resented her decision to avoid him. He had seethed with frustration each time she disappeared as he approached, simmered with inept rage whenever she left a room rather than remain in his company for a moment. But tonight she would come to him in his rooms—and if not he would go to hers.

Leaving an excited yet apprehensive Araminta to await her bridegroom, Lisette went to her room without any conscious effort or awareness of doing so. How long she sat beside her bed she didn't know, but when at last she got to her feet, she felt strangely calm. She would go to Ross. In two days she would leave Castonbury. She would leave Ross. Would it be so wrong of her to want just this one night?

Stepping quietly from her room she negotiated her way to the west block. Arriving at the room she sought, she stood looking at the door when suddenly she froze. She couldn't go in. Would the joy of being together for just a short while be worth the agony of parting? Had she not been lucky to avoid the consequences of their last tryst—surely this would be tempting fate to try it again? Would it not be better if they stayed apart, not to see him at all? Blindly she turned on her heel and retraced her steps.

Ross heard a sound outside his door. As a soldier trained for war, he'd developed the faculty of detecting the slightest out of the ordinary sound and coming instantly alert. Immediately he crossed to the door and looked out, just in time to see the figure of a woman disappear round a corner. His instinct told him it was Lisette. Without hesitation he hurried after her.

Knowing she was being followed, Lisette found herself in the massive Marble Hall she had first seen on her arrival to Castonbury Park—a room meant to overawe and to establish a sense of Roman grandeur, rising to the full height of the house and recalling the open atrium at the centre of a Roman villa. But now, in the dim silvery light, eerie shadows draped the walls. She paused, looking around.

About her the great house lay slumberous, the cloak of night temporarily disturbed before settling back like a muffling shroud. And then she heard the soft footsteps of someone who walked quietly towards the hall. Silently she slipped behind one of the twenty alabaster fluted Corinthian columns that dominated the room, holding her breath and standing as still as the cold, blank-eyed statues that occupied the niches about the hall. The footsteps came to a stop just a few feet from where she hid. She shrank back, flattening herself against the cold column, thinking he might hear her heart beat. But then he moved away, the sound of his footsteps tapping on the inlaid Italian marble floor, leaving her in silent darkness.

Or so she thought, for she was unprepared when she slipped from her hiding place to find herself face to face with Ross. A silent moment passed as his eyes settled on hers. They seemed to draw her towards him.

'Come to me, Lisette.'

Closing the distance, placing her hand into his palm, suddenly became the easiest, most natural thing she had ever been asked to do. He looked down at her and stared into her eyes before allowing his gaze to travel, slowly and lovingly, over every inch of her face. Without relinquishing his hold on her hand he led her back to his room. Lisette crossed the threshold and he shut the door. She walked into his arms, wrapping her own around his waist and placing her cheek on his broad chest.

The curtains were drawn against the night, and the room, so spacious and elegant, was warm and secure against the things that lurked outside. There was a silver moon but it did not intrude into the golden glowing room. A mother-of-pearl-and-gold clock ticked on the mantelshelf. Everywhere was rich comfort, even the hound lying in front of the fire was accustomed to sleeping on a thick pile of Turkish rugs.

The logs crackled in the fireplace, carried up by one of the footmen from the stack behind the stables. One spat as the sap within it dripped into the flames, eliciting nothing more than a lift of the dog's ears.

Ross tilted her face up to his. His eyes were a dark sapphire blue in a tanned face and his eyebrows were raised in quizzical enquiry. 'Why did you run away?'

'I suddenly got cold feet,' she answered, looking up at him.

Ross couldn't blame her. If he was honest, from the very

first he'd set himself up with his attempts at masterful manipulation. 'I want you, Lisette, you know I do, and I know you want me.'

As he studied her, words rang in her head. The prize wasn't the same as what he habitually lusted after. This time he wanted a great deal more and he knew why. It was because Lisette was different, because in her heart she carried the same things he did. They were like two halves of a broken coin waiting to be mended.

He'd known the first time he'd laid eyes on her, the instant he'd held her in his arms and kissed her. They fitted together, and he'd known instinctively, immediately, on a level deeper than his bones. He wanted all of her, not just the physical her, but her love and devotion and her heart. He wanted it all. He would settle for nothing less than that.

'Why did you make me come to you?' he breathed.

Leaning back, Lisette tipped her head to one side. 'It has not escaped my notice that you have been otherwise occupied.'

'My darling,' he chuckled tenderly, 'you are the only female alive who would bring up Caroline Bennington at a time like this.' Sighing quietly he cupped her face in his hands as if it were a precious thing, kissing her mouth in such a way that the sweetness, the tender honesty of it, swelled her heart. 'Caroline means nothing to me. Believe it, Lisette, for it is true.'

Lisette closed her eyes and no longer wondered what had drawn her to this man. Initially she thought it might be his compelling good looks and his powerful animal magnetism. She had convinced herself that it was so, that the strange hold he had over her was merely his ability to awaken those intense sexual hungers within her. Now she realised this was just the tip of an iceberg, that the truth lay in its hidden, unfathomable depths. What she felt for Ross Montague went far beyond either physical or romantic love.

'Ross.' Her mouth murmured the word against his.

Without taking his mouth from hers he lifted her in his arms and carried her across the room. Placing her on the bed he knelt beside her and with slow, deliberate hands he undressed her, loving every inch of her naked body before gathering her up and nestling her against him with what seemed to be perfect content.

She knew it was wrong, and yet she felt it couldn't be. Did she care? Did it matter that she was a servant when his mouth and his hands and his powerful body were demanding of her what she knew only she could give him? No, she thought. She loved this man. She wanted him and it was enough.

Ross shrugged out of his clothes and lay beside her, in no hurry. His manner implied this would be as good as it had been before, the firm flat muscles of his body pressing against hers, the exploration of his hands on her skin, the sweeping caresses that set her purring and glowing, but when he entered her she felt the heated frenzy come upon her which demanded that she be possessed by him. She cried out and so did he, while all about them the great house and the servants slept and the lovers were unheard.

And then she slept, her head resting on his chest, his arms about her, his lips against her hair. But Ross did not sleep, for his thoughts were occupied with how he was to keep this beloved woman in his life. Before he closed his eyes he knew there was only one way and having reached his decision he was content.

Before dawn Lisette sat up and her loveliness struck him. Her raven-black hair tumbled about her round, peaked breasts and her graceful shoulders and back. Without a word she slipped out of bed and fumbled into her clothes, smoothing back her flowing hair and securing it in a knot in her nape. Then she leant over and kissed him.

'I must go before anyone is about.'

'Yes, you should. We will talk later,' he murmured, his body sated, his spirit quietly joyous, caressing her cheek.

Lisette left him then, his kisses still warm on her lips. With the house slowly stirring to life, she moved swiftly back to her own room with a heavy heart, for it was as though he had taken the spring of life within her. The thought that she would not be with him again tormented her, and she could not bear a day, a month, let alone an eternity beyond that, without him. The weight of it, her love, was almost more than she could bear. Her heart ached with the desolation of it and with the loss that must come next.

When Smithins appeared in the breakfast room and issued a summons to Giles and Ross for them to attend His Grace in his rooms, they were surprised. He had become such a solitary person of late he seldom disturbed the males and females of the household or saw them except when it suited him—avoiding everyone except Smithins and the Reverend Seagrove when he came to call.

Ten minutes later they stood before him seated in his chair. It soon became clear that he wished to speak to them on a matter of grave importance, for not even the dedicated Smithins was allowed to remain.

His Grace fixed his rheumy eyes on his son and nephew. The death of two of his sons had left him feeling tired, old, ineffectual and useless, but Jamie's son had given him something to think about, something to fight for, injecting new life into him. He sat straight in his chair, and when he spoke his voice was more controlled than it had been in a long time.

'There is something that you should know right away—something I have decided concerning Jamie's wife and the child.' He said it quietly, but the room was hushed and waiting for something which would not be pleasant when it came. 'Young Crispin is my heir so he is my responsibility. I am trustee to the estate and therefore his guardian, so it is for me to make some sort of provision.'

'There is still an element of doubt that Alicia is telling the truth,' Giles said, sitting opposite his father and indicating for Ross to do the same. 'We have no proof that Jamie married her. Until we hear from Harry I suggest we do not commit ourselves to anything.'

'And what happens to the child in the meantime? He cannot be ignored—and nor would I wish to.' His voice was high, every word stressing his indignation. He cast Giles a stern look. 'Since Jamie was taken from us, on my request you have assumed the position of heir apparent well, Giles.'

'Of course, but you know it is a position I have never coveted.'

'I know that and Jamie's son will relieve you of the responsibility. The inheritance issue can no longer be ignored. We cannot disclaim that young Crispin is Jamie's child and we must recognise him legally, not only to give him his name but to have papers drawn up with the utmost speed. We have the same blood running in our veins. No class or legality can wipe out that fact. I am thinking of taking certain steps with regard to the child and having him brought to Castonbury.'

'And the mother?' Ross asked, conscious of a sudden feeling

of unease creeping over him. His uncle Crispin believed in his right to ride through the heritage of the Montague family, and when he had his mind made up about something, he would not allow any obstacle to stand in his way.

'Some provision will be made for her.' The duke stared at his nephew for a moment, then he said, 'You have met the woman, Ross. Tell me, how did you find her?'

'Likeable and civil—given the circumstances.'

The duke's face twitched. 'The circumstances?'

'She is a poor widow with a child to raise alone. It cannot be easy for her.'

'Did you see the child?'

'No, I did not. But I believe she is a good mother and she spoke fondly of her son.'

The duke made a sound in his throat and after a moment he muttered thickly, 'I wish to see him. The child is my grandson, my heir, and I want him to be brought up as such. If what you say is correct and the mother has no means of supporting him, then I'm sure she could be persuaded to let him go.'

Unable to believe he was serious, Ross studied him in cool silence, noticing for the first time that there was an infuriating arrogance about his uncle, his thin smile, and even the way he was sitting in the chair. 'Let him go? What are you saying?'

'It is my will that the child should be removed from her.'

Giles was staggered by his father's words and deeply shocked by what he intended. 'We cannot do that. She will not part with him.'

'Why not? She will be amply compensated. Arrangements will be made for her and an offer to place her in some comfort elsewhere.' His voice was impatient. 'The child is being brought up in poverty and I will not allow it to go on. I could

take her son away from her by the simple matter of going to
the law.'

'Are you saying that you would remove the child by force?'

'If necessary. Possession is nine-tenths of the law, don't
forget. If the child was out of her reach for a time, then she
might be brought to her senses through argument and discussion. Of course, she could take the matter to court under the
heading of abduction—'

'Or kidnapping,' Ross interrupted, absolutely astonished at
what his uncle was planning to do.

'She couldn't afford to do that. The law has ways and means,
and if I decide to make it a legal matter she wouldn't have a
leg to stand on.'

'I know what you are saying, Father, but it is not right. It
is not right to separate a child from its mother.'

He came back at Giles sharply. 'Right? Of course it's right.
The child will have everything he could wish for and nursemaids to look after him.'

'Nursemaids are no substitute for a mother,' Ross pointed
out.

'I second that,' Giles said. As children he and his siblings had
been kept in deferential awe of their parents. Indeed, they'd
seen little of them. As babies they had been given over to the
care of wet nurses and later cared for by nursemaids and nan-
nies, with just the occasional duty visit from their parents. If
what Ross said was true, then young Crispin's closeness to his
mother was surely better than that.

Banging his hand on the arm of his chair, the old man's
eyes swung to Ross, madness and desperation in their milky
depths. 'Who is this woman anyway? A nobody by all ac-
counts. A woman who had to work for a living before she

married Jamie. She is not fit to call herself the Dowager Marchioness of Hatherton. I will not acknowledge her. I am still a powerful man. I have ways and means to get what I want, and a position such as hers offers me numerous ways and means.... You understand me?'

Both Giles and Ross understood him—and with the understanding their fear grew. He was right; he had the power to take the child from Alicia. Of late he had become possessed of only one idea, and that was to have Jamie's child under his care. He had even gone to the extraordinary lengths of ordering Mrs Stratton to have all the nursery floor redecorated, setting the whole household agog. It was plain to both his son and his nephew that His Grace would have his grandson by fair means or foul.

'The courts don't always do what is expected of them,' Giles pointed out.

There was a slight constriction in His Grace's throat. He moved his thin blue lips, one over the other, then looking at Giles with hard eyes, he said, 'Which is why it would be wise to have this matter settled once and for all—quietly and without fuss. I want you to send a letter to this woman, informing her that I wish to see her—and her son. I expect you to respect my feelings.'

Giles nodded. 'I will write directly.' His father was still very much the master of the house and the family and his wishes must be obeyed.

It was a deliriously happy, shiny-eyed Araminta who greeted Lisette on her first morning as a wife. In fact, she was so caught up in her own happiness she failed to notice her maid's unusually quiet manner. It was when Araminta went to join her husband in the breakfast room to bid farewell to the guests who would be departing after breakfast that Mrs Stratton appeared to inform Lisette that Mrs Landes-Fraser wished to see her.

Lisette knew why she was being summoned into the presence of the great lady. She expected the worst.

Mrs Landes-Fraser gave Lisette a cold stare. Normally she never interfered with the hiring or dismissal or discipline of the household staff. She usually left that sort of thing to Lumsden and Mrs Stratton, but her loyalty to the Montagues was never in doubt, and if anyone threatened any one of them her stoic nature turned to steel and she became a lioness defending her cubs.

Her instinct told her that this extremely beautiful girl was such a threat. However, she grudgingly admitted that she was certainly presentable. She had the colouring, the carriage and the neck most young women of class would envy. She drew herself up, looking down her long patrician nose, making no bones over her disapproval. In her day all young ladies had known the rules, had been inducted from birth in the rituals of their world. But this young woman was from a different world entirely.

'I understand you wish to see me, ma'am.'

'Most certainly. You can be at no loss to understand the reason. Your own conscience must tell you. A report of a decidedly vulgar nature has reached me.'

She went on to berate Lisette on her unacceptable conduct, leaving Lisette in no doubt that her employment as Miss Araminta's maid was indeed at an end.

'The Montagues are descended from a noble line, Miss Napier—respectable, honourable and ancient. It is clear you have a clever head on your shoulders so you will know what I am saying.'

Standing straight and proud, Lisette raised her head and looked the superior lady in the eye. If she'd had any hopes at all of forming some kind of life with Ross, then Mrs Landes-Fraser's voice now attacked them with the cutting knife of reality.

'Perfectly.'

'Then if you have any sense of propriety and delicacy you will walk away.'

'I am aware of the embarrassment I must have caused and I would like you to understand that I am not aiming to claim anything more than an acquaintance with Colonel Montague. You need not trouble yourself that I will take advantage of our encounter. Colonel Montague has done nothing wrong. I assure you his sterling reputation is constituted by a keen observation of all the proprieties and a more than ordinary measure of honour. I hold him in the highest regard. I understand your concern, ma'am. I will leave at once.'

Without another word, with her head held high, Lisette turned and walked away. After packing her few things together she went to say goodbye to Araminta.

Araminta was astounded by Lisette's disclosure. 'You and Ross?' A smile curved her lips. 'I have to say that it comes as no great surprise to me. I knew from the very beginning that my brother showed an unusual interest in you. Why else would he have suggested that you be my maid?'

'You...don't disapprove?' Lisette asked tentatively.

'As a bride I feel so happy today that I would like everyone else to feel the same as I do, and if you make Ross happy, then why should I mind? It certainly explains why he was reluctant to encourage my sister-in-law into forming any kind of relationship. But must you go so soon? Please, Lisette, wait for Ross to get back from Hatherton.'

'I cannot. I am doing this for Ross. It is because I love him that I have to leave.'

'But—but if you love each other, he surely will ask you to marry him.'

'He has made no indication that he will. He must think of his future. One day he will meet someone he will be proud to introduce as his wife and to bear his children.'

'No, Lisette. If you loved him you would not put him through this torment.'

Lisette turned to go. 'Just ask him to forgive me.'

She next went to say goodbye to members of the staff who had become her friends—others slanted their eyes in her direction, all judging her, all condemning her.

Faith was genuinely upset by her dismissal and hugged her close. 'I'm sorry you're leaving, Lisette. I, for one, will miss your friendship sorely.'

'And I yours, Faith.'

'Whatever the truth of it, if it makes you feel better, Nancy with that treacherous tongue of hers has also been dismissed. She was idle and lazy to boot.'

'It doesn't make me feel better, Faith. But it doesn't matter now.'

'I am sorry for your situation, Lisette.'

Lisette smiled and embraced her friend. 'You are very kind. Be happy, Faith, and don't wait too long before you marry your Sandy.'

'I won't. Now you'd better go. John is waiting to take you to Buxton in the carriage.'

On arriving in Buxton, Lisette boarded the coach for the first stage of her journey. She intended travelling to Oxford to see Mr Sowerby and then on to London where she would book a passage on the first available ship bound for India. Clinging to a lifeline, she felt her life, which had slipped precariously since she had left Ross's bed, right itself for a moment in the emptiness of her heart which held all her love for Ross Montague.

Ross arrived back hardly half an hour before sunset. His happiness shattered the moment Araminta told him what had transpired. Entirely unprepared for the announcement, incapable of any kind of rational thought, what he felt at that moment was raw, red-hot anger. The possibility that Lisette might leave at once had never occurred to him. Araminta saw the colour drain from his face and a white line show about his mouth.

'What time did she leave?'

'Midmorning. I'm sorry, Ross. There was nothing I could do. You know what Aunt Wilhelmina's like. She draws blood. Why must she be so savage?'

'That's Aunt Wilhelmina. She's never more righteous than when she's in the wrong.'

'But she isn't, is she? At least not to her way of thinking. She saw Lisette as an obstacle that had to be removed and was adamant that she should go immediately.'

'It wasn't Aunt Wilhelmina's business to take Lisette to task.'

'She likes to hold all the reins. But Lisette had already decided to leave before that.'

Ross stared at his sister with eyes that were almost black

with anger. 'Leave? Why in God's name did no one think to tell me?'

'I wanted to, but Lisette was adamant that you should not be told.'

'How did she seem when she left?'

'Upset—although she tried not to show it,' Araminta said quietly, remembering how she had wanted to go to Lisette and clasp her hands and bring comfort to her in some way, for her eyes had looked so deeply sad, entirely lost.

'You say she intends to return to India?'

'That's what she told me.'

'She cannot afford it. She does not have the means.'

'Apparently her father left her a legacy—his lawyer wrote to her informing her of the fact. She no longer has any need to work for a living. Ross, what do you propose to do?'

'Go after her,' he said tersely. 'It's too late to do anything today.'

Araminta looked at him steadily. 'It's true, isn't it? You and Lisette... You've fallen in love with her, haven't you?'

Ross smiled bitterly. 'Is that such a bad thing, Araminta? Or are you of the same opinion as Aunt Wilhelmina and consider her too far down the scale of things to marry the nephew of the Duke of Rothermere?'

'I'm not sure that sort of thing matters much to me. I have your happiness at heart, you know that, and if you and Lisette love each other, then I am content.'

'I would love her however, whatever, whenever, dear sister.'

'As much as that.'

'More than that.'

'Then find her. Antony and I are to leave for Cambridgeshire the day after tomorrow. You no longer have to worry about me. Go after Lisette, find her and marry her and take her back to India. It's what you both want.'

With the knowledge that Ross was to leave Castonbury the following morning, it was a subdued family that met in the drawing room before dinner, with only the duke absent. Seated next to her husband on one of the four huge blue damask sofas that matched the walls, Araminta, who was already missing Lisette and dreading the moment when she would have to bid farewell to her beloved brother, was noticeably quiet. It was inevitable that the dismissal of her maid was raised, and by Ross, who was furious that his aunt had taken it upon herself to dismiss a member of his household's staff.

'I'm sorry I did not get to speak to Miss Napier, Ross,' Kate said, seated next to Phaedra. 'I would have liked to meet her.'

'I'm sure you would, Katherine,' Mrs Landes-Fraser remarked, 'and no doubt you would have made her your bosom friend, which would have been ridiculous—laughingly so—and given her ideas way above her station.'

'In other words, Kate,' Phaedra chipped in, 'Aunt Wilhelmina is reminding you that ladies of our social position are allowed to visit the deserving poor, to take broth and blankets to the old and infirm who would be obligingly grateful, but not become friends with them.'

'Precisely,' her aunt uttered coldly, taking a sip of her dry sherry.

'There's more to charity work than feeding them broth, Aunt Wilhelmina,' Kate said. She gave Ross a conspiratorial glance, noting that his jaw was clenched tight, his chin jutting and ominous as he struggled to remain calm. He bore little resemblance to the laughing, gentle man she remembered before he'd become a soldier and gone to India. Today, he was an aloof, icy stranger who was regarding Aunt Wilhelmina with glacial eyes and every word he spoke had a bite to it. 'Did you meet Miss Napier before she became Araminta's maid, Ross?'

'We met in India. I saved her from drowning in a flooded river.'

'How very romantic,' Phaedra commented.

Ross omitted to mention that at the time he'd believed her to be a native girl and that he'd failed to recognise her when he'd encountered her in England.

Mrs Landes-Fraser sniffed disdainfully and tossed her head, the feathers in her purple turban swaying precariously. 'An encounter she has clearly taken advantage of—a schemer if ever there was one.'

Fury ignited in Ross's eyes and he had to struggle to subdue his temper. 'A schemer—' he retorted, then he bit back the rest of his words, clenching his jaw so tightly a muscle jerked in the side of his cheek. 'You're wrong about her. She's not hard enough or brittle enough or ambitious enough to be accused of scheming. Lisette is without guile or greed. She is a rare jewel and I am going to marry her.'

'Then you will be making a grave mistake,' Mrs Landes-Fraser said in glacial tones. 'In suitability she will be on a par with the maids in the kitchen.'

Ross's eyes darkened with anger. 'Say no more. Lisette will never be on a par in any way with the kitchen maids. She is the daughter of an academic, a highly intelligent man and a gentleman. My decision to marry her does not stem from a flash in the pan.'

'Your ideas are quite unorthodox and I can see it's no use arguing.'

'No, it is not.'

'Then I am most disappointed in you and I cannot pretend otherwise. I cannot imagine what Crispin will have to say.'

'I don't think Father will have much to say on the matter,' Giles remarked, his expression grave. 'At this present time his mind is taken up with other things—namely Alicia and his grandson. Having the child brought to Castonbury is his one thought and concern.'

Kate gave him a sharp look. 'And is it true that Father intends to offer Alicia money in the hope that she will go away so he can raise the young boy himself?' she asked.

'So it would seem.'

'That is quite atrocious and I, for one, will not stand for it. I cannot understand this irrational hostility he has for a woman he has never met—a woman whom I hope will speak for herself.'

'Having met her I am sure she will,' Ross remarked. 'If my opinion of her is correct, she will not be parted from her child.'

'I sincerely hope not and Father is quite mad to suggest such a thing.'

'He has shown irrational tendencies of late, which, when all is considered, is understandable. I assure you I shall do all in my power to dissuade him from this action. I have written to Alicia inviting her here,' Giles informed them. 'You will be able to judge for yourselves when she arrives.'

'Then I suppose all we can do is wait for her to turn up,' Mrs Landes-Fraser said stiffly. 'I don't expect you will be here to welcome her, Ross.'

'I shall be leaving tomorrow. I am content that Araminta is in good hands and that you, Giles, have things at Castonbury under control. As for Alicia—I shall write to you. I shall be most interested to hear how things turn out. As far as Lisette is concerned, I think I have made my intentions clear, Aunt Wilhelmina,' Ross said. 'I have thought deeply on it and I will not welcome any interference in my personal life. If anyone feels the need to try to dissuade me from forming any kind of alliance with her, then I will not listen. The matter should be left to me and Lisette—and fate.'

'And Miss Napier...what does she say?' she enquired.

'I have yet to find that out.'

'But the girl will be halfway to London by now.'

'She is returning to India. If I fail to meet up with her on the road, then I shall do so in London.'

Epilogue

· ·

With money of her own Lisette had purchased some dresses that made her look less like a servant and more like a young lady of substance.

She stood at the rails as the ship got under way and she watched London slip away. She did not come up on deck again until they had reached the English Channel. It was much the same as the ship she had sailed on from India with a mixture of ordinary citizens and soldiers, but now the soldiers on board were returning from leave to take up their duties with their regiments.

The swaying deck beneath the creaking and flapping of canvas was a patchwork of shadows and vivid orange-coloured light from the oil lamps. A burst of laughter added itself to the noises of the night and Lisette turned to see a group of men who had imbibed too much liquor over dinner and were in high spirits. Smiling softly she turned away, drawing the shawl tighter about her shoulders when the cool wind blew off the water. The sun had set and the moon had risen, hanging pale and large above the shining levels of the Channel like some enchanted Chinese lantern.

There were footsteps and someone stopped behind her. She turned. It was Ross.

Lisette stared at him, feeling her heart give a joyful leap. Her mouth was dry and her eyes were burning. She couldn't believe that he was standing there—handsome, dark and authoritative in his scarlet and gold regimentals. His face was inscrutable, and after a long moment, with a groan he pulled her roughly towards him, wrapping his arms around her, and with a raw ache in his voice, he said, 'You little fool. You adorable, beautiful little fool. Did you really think you could escape me—that I would let you go?'

Lisette was startled. She had expected cold rage, for him to chastise her for leaving him, not this. Never had she known a man so perplexing. 'Ross! I think I must be dreaming and any minute I will wake up and find you aren't here.'

'I assure you I am flesh and blood. If you love me, Lisette, at least say you are glad to see me.'

The dryness was going out of her eyes, the moisture was filling them. On a whisper she said, 'I am glad to see you.'

'Just glad?'

She swallowed before she could utter the words, *More than glad.*

When the tears welled in her eyes, his arms went about her once more, and with his mouth on hers he kissed her with heart-rending tenderness, all the love that had been accumulating over the months he had known her contained in that kiss.

Lisette swayed a little, for she felt the dizzying, heady aura of his masculinity, his vigour, the strong pull which she now knew quite positively was his love for her, wrap itself about her. While she had vainly set herself against the carnal forces Ross inspired in her, something deeper, something dangerously enduring, had been weaving its spell to bind them inexorably together.

Raising his head Ross looked down at her upturned face. 'I love you, Lisette. I think I loved you the first time I saw you—I remember you were wearing a pink, star-spangled sari.'

Catching her breath, Lisette raised her brows in amazement, silently questioning, hoping.

'When Araminta told me you had left Castonbury I went dead inside. You see, I had come to realise just how much you mean to me. I have never had any real feeling of love for anyone. I've had the experience of many women, but that wasn't love. Since I first set eyes on you, you had an effect on me and I wanted you and needed you more than I imagined I would ever want or need anyone in my life. You have caught me in the tenderest trap of all.' On a sigh with a whimsical smile tugging at the corners of his mouth, he admitted the truth of it. 'What we have transcends all else. You are a rare being, Lisette Napier. We'll never be separated again, my love. Do you hear me? Never.'

'Thank you for saying that,' Lisette whispered, an aching lump beginning to swell in her throat. Lowering her eyes she raised his hand and solemnly placed her lips against his fingers. 'I love you, Ross. I love you as much as it is possible for a woman to love a man. I have loved you for so long, ever since you jumped into the river and saved my life, and when you kissed me as I held on to you, it sealed what I felt for you in my heart.' Raising her eyes, she looked at him, and the gentle yielding and the love in their melting amber depths defeated him. 'Does that make you happy, Ross, to know I loved you from the start?'

'Happy? Bless you, my darling,' he murmured hoarsely. 'I don't deserve you.'

'Yes, you do. How did you know...?'

'Where to find you?' She nodded. 'I heard what happened and that you'd had to face the wrath of Aunt Wilhelmina, for which I am deeply sorry. Araminta told me you had left for London.'

'I didn't go to London. I went to Oxford to see my father's lawyer. My father left me a legacy—more than I could ever have expected, which was why I decided to go back to India. I—I haven't decided what I will do when I get there....'

'That's not for you to worry about. Marry me, Lisette. Marry me today—now. Be my wife.' As she made to pull away from him, he held her tight. 'What is it?'

From within the circle of his arms, she stared up at him in wonder. 'Marry you?'

Ross probed for an answer. 'Do you understand, Lisette?'

'Of course,' she breathed. 'You want to marry me, you said.'

'Isn't that in the order of things when two people love each other?'

'And...you do love me?'

'More than anything. I'm sorry, Lisette. I should have made my intentions clear. If I had, perhaps you wouldn't have left Castonbury without seeing me.'

'Yes, you should. But it wouldn't have made any difference. Your family would never accept me and I wouldn't expect them to.'

'I have told you before, Lisette, that I make my own rules. Do you really think the difference in our backgrounds would make any difference to the way I feel about you? That sort of thing is not important to me. Come, my love, why are we playing this game? The past is past for both of us. There is only the future.'

The thought of being his wife filled Lisette with many contradictory emotions—shock, fear and a burgeoning excitement she didn't dare consider at the present moment.

'I've had a lot of time to think on the journey down here and then waiting to see which ship you'd book your passage on. Araminta told me what you intended doing. I was disappointed that you didn't tell me about your legacy and that you meant to go back to India.'

'I'm sorry, I knew you could never commit… Your family, Ross? How do you think they'll respond if I become your wife?'

'I can't let them govern my life. My life is my own and I must live it how I wish. But if it makes you feel better, we have the blessing of Araminta, Giles, Phaedra and Kate. Aunt Wilhelmina will no doubt never speak to me again—but it can be borne, since she is not really a blood relation of mine. You know she is my cousins' aunt, not my own. My uncle, the duke, has his head filled with dastardly plans of receiving his grandson at Castonbury, of separating the mother from the child. There is no room in his life for anything else at this present time.'

Lisette stared at him in disbelief, unable to understand the duke's cruelty. 'He intends to remove the child from his mother?' Ross nodded. 'But…that is a wicked, cruel thing to do. He must be completely heartless. I hope your cousin's widow refuses to comply with his wishes.'

'My uncle is a powerful man, Lisette. He will have his way,

although he has let the whole thing go to his head before it's even been settled.'

'Then I pray your family will make him see how wrong it would be. I have so much to learn about you, Ross. I'll never be able to live up to your position.'

He took her face tenderly between his hands and looked into her eyes, as if the only peace he could know would come from locking gazes with her. 'That's a trivial thing, of no importance to me. I'd like to gamble all I've got on the fact that I'll be the envy of every man who meets you. Now, ours is going to be the shortest courtship on record so I want your answer now. Lisette, will you marry me—now, here on the ship? The captain is prepared to officiate this very minute and Blackstock to bear witness if you accept. Yes or no?'

Looking at him now she no longer had any doubts. This man would always see her and know her, whatever she was doing, whatever she was wearing—his look had nothing to do with status or the concerns of the world. It was as simple as that.

'Yes,' she whispered, and the ship and the world seemed to tilt beneath her as he caught her up in his arms.

Ross led Lisette to the captain's cabin where the captain, Will Blackstock, his face split from ear to ear by a wide grin, and a first mate were assembled. Lisette was astounded that Ross had already planned this. The time had come upon her in such a rush that she wasn't at all sure she was mentally prepared for the nuptials.

Ross smiled into her eyes and, reaching out to take her hand, pulled her against him. The unease that Lisette had felt a moment before dissipated as her husband-to-be slid an arm around her waist and pressed his lips against the hair above her temples. Her eyes were as brilliant as the champagne they would drink afterwards. They glowed with some emotion which seemed to be a mixture of satisfaction, hope, excitement and something else known only to them.

'Are we really going to be married?' she asked wistfully.

'Don't you doubt it.' Ross smiled gently.

The captain, a grey-haired, middle-aged man with kindly eyes, stepped near.

'You are Miss Lisette Napier?' he queried with a friendly smile.

'I am, sir.'

'And you are entering into this marriage of your own free will, without coercion of any sort?'

The question was unexpected, and she glanced up at Ross in some surprise. He squeezed her hand reassuringly. 'Did you agree of your own free will to marry me?'

Though Ross asked the question, it was to Captain Cookson that she looked and answered in soft tones. 'Yes, sir. Yes, I did.'

With a satisfied smile, Ross took her hand and held it tightly, and facing Captain Cookson, they spoke the words that bound them together, the words reverberating through Lisette's heart. Lisette could feel her eyes misting as she repeated her own vows, and she lowered her gaze to the strong, lean hands that held hers in a gentle grasp.

After celebratory toasts and much ribald banter, Ross took Lisette off to their cabin. Inside there was peace and semi-darkness. Only one candle was lit on this nuptial night.

Lisette came to her husband in pale beauty, her face pale and ethereal, her luminous eyes penetrating the very depths of his being. She paused to stand before him, wide-eyed, trembling. Her breath was fragrant from champagne and the freshness of her youth.

A great tenderness welled up in Ross and caught his throat. His hand moved out and gently touched her cheek. She reached up and grasped his hand. Moved by an impulse, he half turned her and lifted her in his arms. Her arms went around his neck. She shook visibly, laying her head on his shoulder.

'We are both going home,' Ross said. 'Whatever happens when I rejoin my regiment, I shall see that we are together always. Are you happy, my love?'

Looking up at him her trembling ceased. 'I have never been happier in my life.'

He undressed her and caressed her and laid her down. His gaze moved over her body, taking in its beauty. The soft breasts, the small waist and slender hips and thighs did not move him to lust as it had before, but to a kind of awed ecstasy. Instead of the urge to take her quickly, he felt the need to be gentle and tender, to caress with body, mind and spirit. Every part of them drew the other as if filling a vacuum, thrilling, vibrating. He loved her until they were both sated and she closed her eyes and snuggled into his arms and slept.

She was his wife, to have and to hold as long as they both would live.

When Lisette awoke during the night with her husband's arms about her, she knew a sense of protectiveness and belonging such as she had never dreamed possible. She seemed to be merging with him into the womb of timelessness, in which there seemed to be no bodies but a single entity.

For Lisette the most surprising thing about sighting India at last was how familiar everything seemed. The gently waving palms against the lines of white sand and the splendid vivid blue sea—it was exactly as she remembered. On the shore she saw the native porters and coolies, naked except for a brief loincloth, baskets of spices and salt fish and wicker panniers full of oranges and limes, and the familiar smells of garlic, coriander and hot oil were wafted on the breeze. It was like finding herself back in a well-loved, well-remembered dream.

Standing by the ship's rails she looked at the beautiful clipper ships, the sturdy merchantmen anchored alongside. The water rippled deep gold in the sun, turning slowly with the sky to a lovely blue. She sighed and there was no sadness in that sigh, only sheer pleasure and satisfaction. When someone came to stand beside her she turned expectantly, her eyes gleaming in anticipation.

Ross smiled lovingly down at her. She wore a gown of apple green and silver grey. She looked lovely and elegant, her thick black hair neatly netted beneath her bonnet.

'Ready?' he asked.

Tucking her hand through the crook of his arm, she smiled up at him. 'I am now.'

They both took a deep breath and prepared to leave the ship.

Lisette knew she had come home.

★ ★ ★ ★ ★

Two timeless stories of love and intrigue
from *New York Times* bestselling author

Catherine Anderson

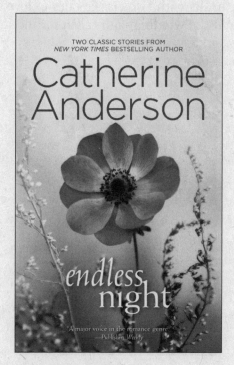

endless
night

Available now!

www.Harlequin.com

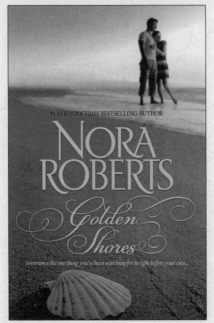

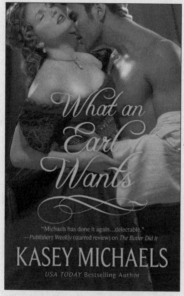

Join *New York Times* bestselling authors

FERN MICHAELS

and Jill Marie Landis, with Dorsey Kelley
and Chelley Kitzmiller,
for four timeless love stories set on one
very special California ranch.

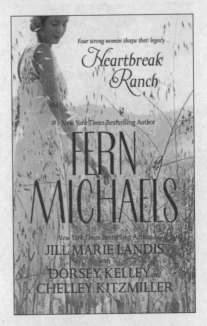

*Heartbreak
Ranch*

Available now!

PHIHR730TR

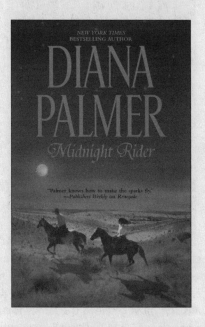

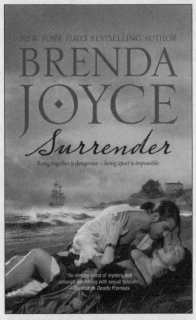